"If you want to hold my hand, Ellie, then all you hav

Max stopped and turne
simmering heat in his
formulate some respon
mute.

"But, Ellie?" There was a roughness to his voice, as if he was trying very hard to sound calm.

She held his gaze despite the weakness in her knees, the tremors shivering through her. Despite the fear she was making a mistake, the urge to retreat was almost as strong as the urge to surge forward. "Yes?"

"If you do, then I *will* kiss you. Maybe not here, in front of all these people, maybe not as we walk, but sometime, at some point, I will kiss you. And you—" his eyes dropped to her mouth, an almost physical caress "—you'll kiss me back. Are you ready for that, Ellie?"

e to do is take it."

d to face her. There was a
eyes. She gaped, trying to
se, to deny it. But she was

A WILL, A WISH… A PROPOSAL

BY

JESSICA GILMORE

MILLS & BOON

Published in Great Britain 2015
by Mills & Boon, an imprint of Harlequin (UK) Limited,
Eton House, 18-24 Paradise Road, Richmond, Surrey, TW9 1SR

ISBN: 978-0-263-25159-3

23-0815

Harlequin (UK) Limited's policy is to use papers that are natural, renewable and recyclable products and made from wood grown in sustainable forests. The logging and manufacturing processes conform to the legal environmental regulations of the country of origin.

Printed and bound in Spain
by CPI, Barcelona

A former au pair, bookseller, marketing manager and seafront trader, **Jessica Gilmore** now works for an environmental charity in York. Married with one daughter, one fluffy dog and two dog-loathing cats, she spends her time avoiding housework and can usually be found with her nose in a book. Jessica writes emotional romance with a hint of humor, a splash of sunshine and a great deal of delicious food—and equally delicious heroes.

To Jo, Rose and Sam—
the best godmothers any girl could ask for! Thank you for all the love and support you give my girl, she is very, very lucky to have you
(as am I!).
Love you all very much,
Jessica x

CHAPTER ONE

'WHAT ON EARTH were you thinking?' Max Loveday burst into the office and shook the printed out press release in his father's direction. True to form his father's chair was turned away from the desk, allowing the occupant to face the window. Apparently the view over the city 'inspired' him.

'What on earth is DL Media going to do with a dating app?'

More pertinently, where exactly were the millions of dollars his father had apparently paid out for the app going to come from? In the last year every budget had been squeezed and slashed to accommodate his father's spending spree; there was no more give in the entire company.

Steven Loveday swivelled the black leather chair around and looked at his son, his expression as guileless as that of a three-month-old baby. It was, Max reflected, the expression he always wore when he was up to something.

And he usually was.

'Max? What a lovely surprise.'

Steven's voice was as rich as molasses and just as smooth. The kind of voice that oozed authority and paternal benevolence, as did the warm brown eyes and wide smile. It was a shame he didn't have the business acumen to match the veneer.

'When did you get back from Sydney?'

As if Max hadn't dropped him an email the second he had landed. He tightened his grip on the press release.

'Two hours ago.'

'I'm touched that you rushed over to see me but there was no need, dear boy. Take the rest of the day off.'

His father beamed at him as if he was giving Max a great treat.

'Why don't you go and visit your mother? Have you heard from her at all?'

'I can't take the day off.' Max refused to be diverted. He held up the piece of paper his PA had pressed into his hand the second he had walked into DL Media's headquarters. 'What on earth is this? Why didn't you consult me?'

His father leaned back and stared at him, his chin propped on his steepled hands. It was a look he had probably seen in a film: the wise patriarch.

'Max.' There was steel in his voice. 'I know your grandfather gave you a lot of leeway, but can I remind you this is *my* company now?'

Just.

Max held a third outright, his father another third. But, crucially, the final third, the controlling share, was held in trust by his father until he retired. Then it would go to Max. If there was a company left by then. Or if Max didn't ask the board for a vote of no confidence first...

'Grandfather did *not* give me a lot of leeway.' He could feel the paper crumple, his grip tightening even more as he fought to control his temper. It was so typical of his father to reduce all his years of hard work and training to some sort of glorified work experience. 'He trusted me and trusted my judgement.'

As he never trusted you... The words were unsaid but hung in the air.

'Look, Dad, we have a five-year plan.' A plan his father seemed determine to ignore. 'A plan that kept us profitable through the financial crisis. We need to focus on the core business strengths, not get distracted by... by...' Max sought the right diplomatic words. *Shiny new toys* might be accurate, but they were unlikely to help the situation. 'By intriguing investments.'

Steven Loveday sighed, the deep breath resonating with regret. 'The problem with your grandfather was that he had no real vision. Oh, he was a media man through and through, and he knew publishing. But books are dead, Max. It's time for us to expand, to embrace the digital world.'

Max knew his mouth was hanging open, that he was gaping at his father with an incredulous look on his face, but his poker face was eluding him. His grandfather had had no vision? Was that truly what his father thought?

'He took DL global,' he managed after a long pause. 'Made us a household name.'

A name his father seemed determined to squander. What was it they said? One generation to found, another to expand and the third to squander? It looked as if Steven Loveday was going to prove the old adage right in record time.

Max's hands curled into fists. *Not if I have anything to do with it.*

'Everyone wanted this, Max. Have you seen the concept? It's brilliant! Bored and want to go out? Just log on and see who's free—make contact, get a reservation at a mutually convenient restaurant, book your taxi home.

And if the evening goes well you can even sort out a hotel room. It's going to revolutionise online dating.'

Possibly. But what did online dating have to do with publishing?

Max began to walk up and down the thickly carpeted office floor, unable to stay standing meekly in front of his father's desk like a schoolboy any longer.

'But we can't afford it. And, more crucially, it's not core business, Dad. It doesn't fit with the plan.'

'That was your grandfather's plan, not mine. We have to move with the times, Max.'

Max bit back a sigh. 'I know. Which is why we were the first to bring eBooks to the mainstream. Our interactive travel guides and language books are market leaders, and thanks to our subscription service our newspapers are actually in profit.'

He shouldn't need to be explaining this to his father. Max had always known that his father would inherit the controlling share of the company, even though Steven Loveday had only played at working over the last thirty years. He also knew how hard his grandfather had struggled with that decision, how close he had come to bypassing his son altogether for his grandson. But in the end even his hard-nosed grandfather hadn't been able to bring himself to humiliate his only child with a very public disinheriting.

And now the family business was paying the price.

The increasingly awkward silence was just beginning to stretch to excruciating when a loud and fast hip-hop tune blared out of the phone on his father's desk. It was the kind of ringtone Max would expect from a streetwise fifteen-year-old, not a fifty-eight-year-old man in a hand-made suit and silk tie, but his father's eyes lit up as he grabbed the telephone, his body swaying a little to the furious beat.

'Sweetie?'

Max could just make out a giggle from the caller. Not that he needed to hear the voice to know who it was. The inappropriate ringtone, the soppy expression on his father's face, the nauseating tone of his voice…

It had been six months. If his father was playing true to form he should be getting bored with his latest crush by now. But then none of this latest infatuation was running true to form. Not bringing it out in the open, not leaving Max's mother and setting up a love-nest in a Hartford penthouse… No, Steven Loveday's little affairs of the heart were usually as brief as they were intense, but they were always, *always* clandestine.

This…? This almost felt…well, *serious*.

His father looked over at Max. 'Mandy sends her love.'

Max muttered something inaudible even to himself. What was the etiquette here? Just what *did* you say to your father's mistress? Especially a mistress several years younger than yourself—and your own ex-PA. She'd giggled a lot less then.

To occupy himself while his father continued to croon sweet nothings down the phone, he pulled out his own phone and began to scroll through the long list of emails. As usual they were multiplying like the Hydra's head: ten springing forth for each one he deleted. His father's name might top the letterhead, but Max's workload seemed to have tripled in the last year no matter how many sixteen-hour days and seven-day weeks he pulled.

Delete, forward, mark for attention, delete, *definitely* delete… He paused. Another missive from Ellie Scott. What did Miss Prim and Proper want now?

Max had developed a picture of Ellie Scott over the last two months of mostly one-sided emails. She had to be of a similar age to his recently deceased great-aunt, probably wore tweed and had those horned reading glasses. In tortoiseshell. He bet that she played bridge, golfed in sturdy brogues and breakfasted on kippers and anaemic toast.

Okay, he had based her on all those old classic series featuring British spinsters of a certain age. But the bossy, imperative, clipped tone of her emails made him pretty certain he couldn't be that far off in his estimate.

And she lived to plague him. Her requests for information, agreement, input and, worst of all, his actual presence had upped from one a week to almost daily. Sure, the money his great-aunt had left to start a literary festival in a tiny village in the middle of nowhere might seem important to Miss Scott, but he had actual *real* work to do. At some point he was going to have to see if he could delegate or refuse the trustee post he had been bequeathed. *And* get somebody to sort out the house that was part of the same unwanted legacy.

There was just no time for anything that didn't involve clearing up after his father.

Max's finger didn't even pause as he pressed 'delete'. He moved on, reading another and another, and—hang on a minute. His eyes flicked back up the screen as he reread one, barely able to believe the words dancing in front of his eyes.

Irregularity...
Share of the company...
Your great-aunt...
Twenty-five per cent.

Max blinked, casting a quick glance over at his father. Did he know? Could it possibly be true that his recently deceased great-aunt had kept hold of her twenty-five per cent of DL Media even after she had walked away from her work and her family? The same great-aunt who had left her house and belongings to *him*? This could change everything.

Maybe Miss Scott's luck was in. A trip to Cornwall might be exactly what the lawyer ordered.

'Sorry about that.' His father's expression was a discomfiting mixture of slightly sheepish and sappy. 'Max, I would really appreciate it if you had a word with your mother.'

Here they went again. How many times had Max been asked to broker a rapprochement in the constant battlefield that was his parents' marriage? Every time he swore never to do it again. But someone had to be the responsible one in the family, and somehow, even when he could still measure his age in single digits, that person had had to be him.

But not this time.

'I'm sure she would rather hear from you.'

The sappy look on his dad's face faded. He was completely sheepish now, avoiding Max's eye and fiddling with the paperclips on his desk. 'My attorney has told me not to speak to her directly.'

Time stopped for one long second, the office freezing like a paused scene in a movie.

'Attorney? Dad, what on earth do you need an attorney for?'

'You're going to be a big brother.'

Max stopped in the middle of a breath. He was *what*?

'Mandy's pregnant and we're engaged. The second your mother stops being unreasonable about terms and we can get a divorce I'll be getting married. I'd like you to be my best man.'

His father beamed, as if he were conferring a huge honour on Max.

'Divorce?' Max shook his head as if he could magically *un*-hear the words, pushing the whole 'big brother' situation far away into a place where he didn't have to think about it or deal with it. 'Come on, Dad. How many times have you fallen in love, only to realise it's Mum you need?'

Max could think of at least eight occasions without trying—but his dad had never mentioned attorneys before.

'Max, she's demanding fifty per cent of my share of the company. And she wants it in cash if possible. DL can't afford that kind of settlement and *I* sure as hell can't. You have to talk her down. She'll listen to you.'

She wanted *what*? This was exactly what DL Media didn't need. An expensive and very public divorce. Max had two choices: help his dad, or involve the board and wrestle control of that crucial third of the company from his dad.

Either option meant public scrutiny, gossip, tearing the family apart. Everything his grandfather had trusted Max to prevent.

A pulse was throbbing in his temple, the blood thrumming in his veins. Talk to his mother, to the board, to his dad, go over the books yet again and try and work out how to put the company back on an even keel. There were no easy answers. Hell, right now he'd settle for *difficult* answers.

Steven Loveday was still looking at him, appeal in his eyes, but Max couldn't, *wouldn't* meet his gaze. Instead he found himself fixated on the large watercolour on the opposite wall: the only one of his grandfather's possessions to survive the recent office refurbishment. Blue skies smiled down on white-crested seas as green cliffs soared high above the curve of the harbour. Trengarth. The village his great-grandfather had left behind all those years ago. Max could almost smell the salt in the air, hear the waves crashing on the shore.

'I'm away for the next two weeks. The London office is shouting out for some guidance, and I need to sort out Great-Aunt Demelza's inheritance. You're on your own with this one, Dad. And for goodness' sake, don't throw everything away for an infatuation.'

He swivelled on his heel and walked towards the door, not flinching as his father called desperately after him. 'It's different this time, Max. I love her. I really do.'

How many times had he heard that one? His father's need to live up to their surname had caused more than enough problems in the Loveday family.

Love? No, thank you. Max had stopped believing in that long before his voice had broken, along with Father Christmas and life being fair. It was time his father grew up and accepted that family, position and the business came first. It was a lesson Max had learned years ago.

'Ellie, dear, I've been thinking about the literary festival.'

Ellie Scott turned around from the shelf she was rearranging, managing—*just*—not to roll her eyes.

It wasn't that she wanted to stifle independent thought in Trengarth. She didn't even want to stifle it in her shop—after all, part of the joy of running a bookshop was seeing people's worlds opening out, watching their horizons expanding. But every time her assistant—her hard-working, good-hearted and extremely able assistant, she reminded herself for the three billionth time—uttered those words she wanted to jump in a boat and sail as far out to sea as possible. Or possibly send Mrs Trelawney out in it, all the way across the ocean.

'That's great, Mrs Trelawney. Make sure you hold on to those thoughts. I'll need to start planning it very soon.'

Her assistant put down her duster and sniffed. 'So you say, Ellie...so you say. Oh, I've been defending you. "Yes, she's an incomer," I've said. "Yes, it's odd that old Miss Loveday left her money to Ellie and not to somebody born and bred here. But," I said, "she has the interests of Trengarth at heart."'

Ellie couldn't hold in her sigh any longer. 'Mrs Trelawney, you know as well as I do that I *can't* do anything. There are two trustees and we have to act together. My hands are tied until Miss Loveday's nephew deigns to honour us with his presence. And, *yes*,' she added as Mrs Trelawney's mouth opened. 'I have emailed, written and begged the solicitors to contact him. I am as keen to get started as you are.'

'Keen to give up a small fortune?' The older woman lifted her eyes up to the heavens, eloquently expressing just how implausible she thought that was.

Was there any point in explaining yet again that Miss Loveday hadn't actually left her fortune to Ellie personally, and that Ellie wasn't sitting on a big pile of cash, cackling from her high tower at the poverty stricken villagers below? The bequest's wording was very clear: the money had been left in trust to Ellie and the absent second trustee for the purposes of establishing an annual literary festival in the Cornish village.

Of course not every inhabitant of the small fishing village felt that a festival was the best thing to benefit the community, and most of them seemed to hold Ellie solely responsible for Demelza Loveday's edict. In vain had Ellie argued that she was powerless to spend the money elsewhere, sympathetic as she was to the competing claims of needing a new playground and refurbishing the village hall—but her hands were tied.

'Look, Mrs Trelawney. I know how keen you are to get started, and how many excellent ideas you have. I promise you that if Miss Loveday's nephew does not contact me in the next month then I will go to America myself and force him to co-operate.'

'Hmm.' The sound spoke volumes, as did the accompanying and very thorough dusting of already spotless shelves.

Ellie didn't blame Mrs Trelawney for being unconvinced. Truthfully, she had no idea how to get the elusive Max Loveday *to* co-operate. Tempting as it was to imagine herself striding into his New York penthouse and marching him over to an aeroplane, she knew full well that sending yet another strongly worded email was about as forceful as she was likely to get.

Not to mention that she didn't actually know where he lived. But if she was going to daydream she might as well make it as glamorous as possible.

Ellie stepped back and stared critically at the display shelf, temptingly filled with the perfect books to read on the wide, sandy Trengarth beach—or to curl up with if the weather was uncooperative. Just one week until the schools broke up and the season started in full. It was such a short season. Trengarth certainly needed something to keep the village on the tourism radar throughout the rest of the year. Maybe this festival was part of the answer.

If they could just get started.

Ellie stole a glance over at her assistant. Her heart was in the right place. Mrs Trelawney had lived in the village all her life. It must be heartbreaking for her to see it so empty in the winter months, with so many houses now second homes and closed from October through to Easter.

'If I can't get an answer in the next two weeks then I will look into getting him replaced. There must be *something* the solicitors can do if he simply won't take on his responsibilities. But the last thing I want to do is spend some of the bequest on legal fees. It's only been a few months. I think we just need to be a little patient a little longer.'

Besides, the elusive Max Loveday worked for DL Media, one of the big six publishing giants. Ellie had no idea if he was an editor, an accountant or the mail boy, but whatever he did he was bound to have some contacts. More than the sole proprietor of a small independent bookshop at the end of the earth.

The bell over the door jangled and Ellie turned around, grateful for the opportunity to break off the awkward conversation.

Not that the newcomer looked as if he was going to make her day any easier, judging by the firm line of his mouth and the expression of distaste as he looked around the book-lined room from his vantage position by the door.

It was a shame, because under the scowl he was really rather nice to look at. Ellie's usual clientele were families and the older villagers. It wasn't often that handsome, youngish men came her way, and he was both. Definitely under thirty, she decided, and tall, with close-cut dark hair, a roughly stubbled chin and eyes so lightly brown they were almost caramel.

But the expression in the eyes was hard and it was focussed right onto Mrs Trelawney.

What on earth had her assistant been up to now? Ellie

knew there was some kind of leadership battle on the Village in Bloom committee, but she wouldn't have expected the man at the door to be involved.

Although several young and trendy gardeners *had* recently set up in the vicinity. Maybe he was very passionate about native species and tasteful colour combinations?

'Miss Scott?'

Unease curdled Ellie's stomach at the curt tone, and she had to force herself not to take a step back. *This is your shop*, she told herself, folding her hands into tight fists. *Nobody can tell you what to do. Not any more.*

'I'm Ellie Scott.' She had to release her assistant from that gimlet glare. Not that Mrs Trelawney looked in need of help. Her own gaze was just as hard and cold. 'Can I help?'

'You?'

The faint tone of incredulity didn't endear him any further to Ellie, and nor did the quick glance that raked her up and down in one fast, judgemental dismissal.

'You can't be. You're just a girl.'

'Thank you, but at twenty-five I'm quite grown up.'

His voice was unmistakably American which meant, surely, that here at last was the other trustee. Tired and jetlagged, probably, which explained the attitude. Coffee and a slice of cake would soon set him to rights.

Ellie held out her hand. 'Please, call me Ellie. You must be Max. It's lovely to meet you.'

'*You're* the woman my great-aunt left half her fortune to?'

His face had whitened, all except his eyes, which were a dark, scorching gold.

'Tell me, Miss Scott…' He made no move to take her hand, just stood looking at her as if she had turned into a toad, ice frosting every syllable. 'Which do you think is worse? Seducing an older married man for his money or befriending an elderly lady for hers?'

He folded his arms and stared at her.

'Any thoughts?'

CHAPTER TWO

MAX HADN'T INTENDED to go in all guns blazing. In fact he had entered the bookshop with just two intentions: to pick up the keys to the house his great-aunt had left him and to make it very clear to the domineering Miss Scott that the next step in sorting out his great-aunt's quixotic will would be at *his* instigation and in *his* time frame.

Only he had been wrong-footed at the start. Where was the hearty spinster of his imagination? He certainly hadn't been expecting this thin, neatly dressed pale girl. She was almost mousy, although there *was* a delicate beauty in her huge brown eyes, in the neatly brushed sweep of her light brown hair that looked dull at first glance but, he noticed as the sunlight fell on it, was actually a mass of toffee and dark gold.

She didn't look like a con artist. She looked like the little match girl. Maybe that was the point. Maybe inspiring pity was her weapon. He had thought, assumed, that his co-trustee was an old friend of Great-Aunt Demelza. Not a girl younger than Max himself. Her youth was all too painfully reminiscent of his father's recent insanity, even if Ellie Scott seemed to be missing some of Mandy's more obvious attributes.

The silence stretched long, thin, almost unbearable before Ellie broke it. 'I beg your pardon?'

There was a shakiness in her voice but she stayed her ground, the large eyes fixed on him with painful intensity.

Max was shocked by a rush of guilt. It was like shooting Bambi.

'I think you heard.'

He was uneasily aware that they had an audience. The angular, tweed-clad old lady he had assumed was Ellie Scott was standing guard by the counter, a duster held threateningly in one hand, her sharp eyes darting expectantly from one to the other like a tennis umpire. He should give her some popcorn and a large soda to help her fully enjoy the show.

'I was giving you a chance to backtrack or apologise.'

Ellie Scott's voice had grown stronger, and for the first time he had a chance to notice her pointed chin and firm, straight eyebrows, both suggesting a subtle strength of character.

'But if you have no intention of doing either than I suggest you leave and come back when you find your manners.'

It was his turn to think he'd misheard. 'What?'

'You heard me. Leave. And unless you're willing to be polite don't come back.'

Max glared at her, but although there was a slight tremor in her lightly clenched hands Ellie Scott didn't move. Fine.

He walked back over to the door and wrenched it open. 'This isn't over, honey,' he warned her. 'I will find out exactly how you manoeuvred your way into my great-aunt's good graces and I will get back every penny you conned out of her.'

The jaunty bell jangled as he closed the door behind him. Firmly.

The calendar said it was July, but the Cornish weather had obviously decided to play unseasonal and Max, who had left a humid heatwave behind in Connecticut, was hit by a cold gust of wind, shooting straight through the thin cotton of his T-shirt, goose-pimpling his arms and shocking him straight to his bones.

And sweeping the anger clear out of his head.

What on earth had he been thinking? Or, as it turned out, *not* thinking. *Damn*. Somehow he had completely misfired.

Max took a deep breath, the salty tang of sea air filling his lungs. He shouldn't have gone straight into the shop after the long flight and even longer drive from Gatwick airport to this sleepy Cornish corner. Not with the adrenaline still pumping through his veins. Not with the scene with his father still playing through his head.

Who knew what folly his father would commit without Max keeping an eye on him? Where his mother's anger and sense of betrayal would drag them down to?

But that was their problem. DL Media was his sole concern now.

Max began to wander down the steep, narrow sidewalk. It felt as if he had reached the ends of the earth during the last three hours of his drive through the most western and southern parts of England. A drive that had brought him right here, to the place his great-grandfather had left behind, shaking off his family ties, the blood and memories of the Great War and England, when he had crossed the channel to start a whole new life.

And now Max had ended up back here. Funny how circular life could be…

Pivoting slowly, Max took a moment to see just where '*here*' was. The briny smell might take him back to holidays spent on the Cape, but Trengarth was as different from the flat dunes of Cape Cod as American football was from soccer.

The small bookshop was one of several higgledy-piggledy terraces on a steep narrow road winding up the cliff. At the top of the cliff, imperiously looking down onto the bay and dominating the smaller houses dotted around it, was a white circular house: his Great-Aunt Demelza's house. The house she had left to him. A house where hopefully there would be coffee, some food. A bed. A solution.

If he carried on heading down he would reach the sea-front and the narrow road running alongside the ocean. Turn left and the old harbour curved out to sea, still filled with fishing boats. All the cruisers and yachts were moored further out. Above the harbour the old fishermen's cottages were built up the cliff: a riotous mixture of colours and styles.

Turn right and several more shops faced on to the road before it stopped abruptly at the causeway leading to the wide beach where, despite or because of the weather, surfers were bobbing up and down in the waves, looking like small, sleek seals.

Give him an hour and he could join them. He could take a board out...hire a boat. Forget his cares in the cold tang of the ocean.

Max smiled wryly. If only he could. Pretend he was just another American tourist retracing his roots, shrugging off the responsibilities he carried. But, like Atlas, he was never going to be relieved of his heavy burden.

It *was* a pretty place. And weirdly familiar—although maybe not that weird. After all, his grandfather had had several watercolours of almost exactly this view hanging in his study. Yes, there were definitely worse places to work out a way forward.

Only to do that he needed to get into that large white house. And according to the solicitor he had emailed from the plane, Ellie Scott was holding the keys to that very house. Which meant he was going to have to eat some humble pie. Max was normally quite a fan of pie, but that was not a flavour he enjoyed.

'Suck it up, Max,' he muttered to a low-flying seagull, which was eyeing him hopefully. 'Suck it up.'

He was going to have to go back to the bookshop and start the whole acquaintance again.

Ellie was doing her best to damp down the dismaying swirl in her stomach and get on with her day.

She hadn't caved, had she? Hadn't trembled or wept or tried to pacify him? She had stayed calm and collected and in control. On the outside, at least. Only she knew that right now she wanted nothing more than to sink into the old rocking chair in the corner of the childcare section and indulge in a pathetic bout of tears.

The sneering tone, the cold, scornful expression had triggered far more feelings than she cared to admit. She had spent three years trying to pacify that exact tone, that exact look—and the next three years trying to forget. In just five minutes Max Loveday had brought it all vividly back.

Darn him—and darn her shaky knees and trembling hands, giving away her inner turmoil. She'd thought she was further on than this. Stronger than this.

Ellie had never thought she would be quite so glad for Mrs Trelawney's presence, but right now the woman was her safety net. While she sat there, busily typing away on her phone, no doubt ensuring that every single person in Trengarth was fully updated on the morning's events, Ellie had no option but to hold things together.

Instead she switched on the coffee machine and unpacked the cakes she had picked up earlier from the Boat House café on the harbour.

Ellie had always dreamed of a huge bookshop, packed with hidden corners, secret nooks, and supplemented by a welcoming café full of tasty treats. What she had was a shop which, like all the shops in Trengarth, was daintily proportioned. Fitting in all the books she wanted to stock in the snug space was enough of a challenge. A café would be a definite step too far. She had compromised with a long counter by the till heaped with a tempting array of locally made scones and cakes and a state-of-the-art coffee machine. Buying in the cakes meant she didn't have to sacrifice precious stock space for a kitchen.

It took just a few moments to arrange the flapjacks, Cornish fairing biscuits, brightly coloured cupcakes and scones onto vintage cake stands and cover them with the glass domes she used to keep them fresh.

'We have walnut, orange and cheese scones.' She deliberately spoke aloud as she began to chalk up the varieties onto the blackboard she kept propped on the table, hoping Mrs Trelawney would take the hint, stop texting and start working. 'The cupcakes are vanilla and the big cake is…let me see…yep, carrot and orange.'

'It's a bit early for cake…'

The drawling accent made her stop and stiffen.

'But I'll take a walnut scone and a coffee. Please.'

The last word was *so* evidently an afterthought.

Ellie smiled sweetly as she swivelled round. No way was she going to give him the satisfaction of seeing how uncomfortable he'd made her.

'It's self-service and pay at the till. You, however, are barred. You'll have to get your coffee somewhere else.'

'Look…' Max Loveday looked meaningfully over at Mrs Trelawney. 'Can we talk? In private?'

Ellie's heart began to pick up speed, her pulse hammering. No way was she going anywhere alone with this man. He might be smiling now, but she wasn't fooled.

'I don't think so. You had no problem insulting me in front of my assistant. I'm sure she can't wait to hear round two.'

He closed his eyes briefly. 'Fair point.'

'Oh, good.' She hadn't expected him to capitulate so easily. It was an unexpected and unwanted point in his favour. 'Go on, then. Say whatever it is you have to say.'

'I was out of line.'

Ellie folded her arms and raised her eyebrows. If Max Loveday thought he was getting away with anything short of a full-on grovel he could think again.

'Yes…?' she prompted.

'And I'm sorry. It's no excuse, but my family is going through some stuff right now and I'm a little het-up about it.'

'Tell me, Mr Loveday…' Ellie deliberately parroted his words back to him. 'Which is worse? Seducing a family man for his money or conning an old lady out of her cash? And which are you accusing *me* of?'

As if she didn't know. Well, if she'd conned the old lady he'd been right there with her; he was joint trustee after all.

'I think they're both pretty vile.' There was a bleakness in his voice, and when his eyes rested on Ellie the hardness in them unnerved her. He hadn't come back because he was stricken with remorse. He still thought her guilty.

'So do I.' The look of surprise on his face gave her courage. 'I also think making slanderous accusations against strangers and proffering fake apologies in order to get the keys to a house and a cup of coffee is pretty out of order. What do you say to *that*, Mr Loveday?'

'I'm prepared to pay for the coffee.'

It wasn't much of a retort but it was the best he could do when he was firmly in the wrong—as far as manners were concerned—and so tired that the wooden floor was beginning to look more than a little inviting. Flying Sydney to Boston to Hartford and then on to England in just a few days had left him in a grey smog that even first-class sleep pods hadn't quite been able to dispel.

'Look, you have to admit my great-aunt's will is pretty unusual. Leaving her entire fortune in the hands of a virtual stranger.'

The large brown eyes darkened with something that looked very much like scorn. It wasn't an expression Max was used to seeing in anybody's eyes and it stung more than he expected.

'Yes, she said more than once that she wished she knew her great-nephew more. I thought this was her way of trying to include you.'

Damn her, he hadn't meant *himself*—and he would bet a much needed good night's sleep she knew that full well.

'It was her money to leave as she liked. I didn't expect to inherit a penny. Nor do I need to. If she wanted to leave it all to charity that's one thing. But this...? This is craziness. Leaving it to you...to found a festival. I didn't ask to be involved.'

He just couldn't comprehend it. What on earth had his great-aunt been thinking? What did he know or care about a little village on the edge of the ocean?

'She didn't actually leave the money to me, to you or to *us*.'

Ellie sounded completely exasperated. Max got the feeling it wasn't the first time she'd had this conversation.

'I can't touch a penny without your say-so and vice versa—and we're both completely accountable to the executors. There is no fraud here, Mr Loveday, and no coercion. Nothing at all except a slightly odd request made by a whimsical elderly lady. Didn't you read the will?'

'I read enough to know that she left you this shop.'

No coercion, indeed. Ellie Scott wasn't just a trustee she was a beneficiary: inheriting the shop and the flat above it. The flat she already currently resided in, according to the will. It was all very neat.

'Yes…' The brightness dimmed from her eyes, and it was as if the sun had gone behind a cloud. 'She was always good to me. She was my godmother. Did you know that? My grandmother's best friend, and my own good, dear friend. I will always be grateful to her. For everything.'

'Your godmother?'

Damn, he had come into the whole situation blind and it was completely unlike him. It was sloppy, led to mistakes.

'Yes. But even more importantly she was your great-aunt. Which is why she wanted you involved in her legacy, why she left you the house. It was the house her father was born in, apparently. And *his* father was some kind of big deal sea captain. He would have been…what? Your great-great-grandfather?'

'Yes, although I don't know anything about him or about anything to do with the English side of the family. A sea captain?' A reluctant smile curved his lips. He had been in Cornwall all of an hour and had already discovered some unknown family history. 'My grandfather took me sailing all the time. He had a house on the

Cape. Said he always slept best when he could hear the sea. Must be in our blood.'

'You can hear the sea from every room in The Round House too. Maybe my godmother knew what she was doing when she left the house to you.'

'Maybe.'

It was a nice idea. But, *really*? A house? In Cornwall? A seven-hour flight and a tedious long drive from his home. It would have been far simpler if Great-Aunt Demelza had instructed her solicitors to liquefy the whole estate and endowed a wing at her favourite museum or hospital. *That* was how philanthropy worked. Not this messy, getting involved business.

Although it *was* kind of cool to find out about his distant Cornish heritage. A sea captain... Maybe there was a photo back at the house.

A voice broke in from the corner and Max jumped. He'd forgotten about their audience.

'This is all very entertaining. But what I want to know, Ellie, is are you planning to actually start this festival or not?'

Ellie looked at him, her face composed. 'I don't think that's up to me any more, Mrs Trelawney. Well, Mr Loveday? Are you willing to work with me? Or do we need to call the solicitors in and find a way around the trust?'

'I can't just drop everything, Miss Scott. I have a very busy job. A job in Connecticut. Across the ocean. I can't walk away to spend weeks playing benefactor by the sea.'

But even as he spoke the words a chill shivered through him. What did the next few months hold? Could he find a way to make his father toe the line—or was he going to have to force a vote at the board?

He would win. He knew many of the board members shared his misgivings. But then what?

His already fragile relationship with his father would be irrevocably shattered.

It was a price he was willing to pay. And if his great-aunt's house *did* hold the key to an easy win then the least he could do was help get her dream started while he was here. His mouth twisted. It wasn't as easy to walk away from family obligations as he'd thought, even when the family member was a stranger *and* deceased.

'I can give you two weeks. Although I'll be in London some of that time. Take it or leave it.'

Ellie's cool gaze was fixed on him. As if she could see straight into the heart of him—and see all that was missing.

'Fine.'

'So I can set up a meeting?' asked Mrs Trelawney. 'I have a lot of ideas and I know many other people do too.' Ellie's assistant had given up any pretence of working, her eyes bright as she leaned onto the counter. 'We could have a theme. Or base it on a genre? A murder mystery with actors? Or should we have it food-related. There could be baking competitions—make your favourite literary cake.'

Your favourite *what*? Max tried to avoid catching Ellie's eye but it was impossible to look away. The serious, slightly sad expression had disappeared, to be replaced by a mischievous smile lurking in the deep brown depths of her large eyes.

He could feel an answering gleam in his own eyes, and his mouth wanted to smile in response, to try and coax a grin out of her, but he kept his face as calm and sincere as he could, trying to keep all his focus on Mrs Trelawney.

But he couldn't stop his gaze sliding across to watch Ellie's reaction. She was leaning against a bookcase, her arms folded as her face sparkled in amusement.

'They are excellent ideas,' he managed, and was rewarded by the quick upturn of her full mouth and the intriguing hint of a dimple in one pale cheek. 'But we are at a very early stage. I think we need to talk to the solicitors and look at funds before we...ah...appoint a committee. I do hope you can manage to hold on to those ideas for just a little longer?'

'Well, yes.' Mrs Trelawney's cheeks were pink. 'Of course. I can make a list. I have a lot of ideas.'

'I for one can believe it.' Ellie pushed away from the shelves in one graceful movement. 'I'm expecting a delivery in an hour, Mrs Trelawney, so now would be a good time for you to take your break if that's convenient?'

'My break?' Mrs Trelawney's eyes moved from Max to Ellie and back again before she reluctantly nodded.

Ellie didn't speak again until her assistant had collected her bag and left the shop. 'Poor Mrs T. She's torn between being the first to spread the gossip and fear of missing out on any more. Still, the arrival of Demelza Loveday's mysterious American great-nephew should give her enough to be getting on with. And...' there was a tart note in her voice '...you certainly managed to stir things up when you walked into my shop.'

This was his chance to apologise. Max still wasn't entirely sure what to make of Ellie Scott, but what had his grandfather always said? It was much easier to judge from the inside rather than out in the cold. 'I had my reasons. But they didn't really have anything to do with you. I'm sorry.'

Ellie pushed back a piece of hair that had fallen out of the clip confining the long tresses. 'I can't say that's okay, because it isn't. But I'm willing to give you a second chance. It's going to be hard enough for two incomers to win the support of a place like Trengarth as it is, without being at war ourselves.'

'You're an incomer?' Max wasn't exactly an expert on British accents and Ellie sounded just as he'd expected her to: like the heroine of one of those awful films where girls wore bonnets and the men tights, all speaking with clipped vowels and clear enunciation.

'I spent most of my childhood summers here, and I've lived here for the last three years, but I'll still be an incomer in thirty.' She hesitated. 'Look, I'll be honest. I would be more than happy to see you off the premises and never have to deal with you again, but we have to work together for the next two weeks. You must be tired and jetlagged. Why don't you go and rest now and come back tomorrow? We'll start again.'

Her words were conciliatory, her voice confident, but there was a wariness in her posture. She was slightly turned away, the slim shoulders a little hunched, and her arms were protectively wrapped around her. She was afraid of something. Afraid of him? Of what he might discover? Maybe she wasn't as innocent as she appeared.

He'd been putting this off long enough, distracted by his father's extra-marital shenanigans and the all-consuming pressures of living up to the family legacy. It was time to talk to the solicitors, read the damn will properly and find out just what Ellie Scott was hiding.

'That is a very generous offer. Thank you.'

Ellie exhaled on a visible sigh of relief.

'Then I'll see you back here tomorrow. I'll telephone the solicitors and see if they can fit us in. Do you know how to get to the house?'

She walked around the counter, crouching down and disappearing from view before handing him a set of keys.

They were old-fashioned iron keys. Heavy and unwieldy. 'I'll find my way, thanks. See you later, honey.'

It was both a promise and a threat—and he was pretty sure she knew it.

CHAPTER THREE

THE SHOP HAD been busy. So busy Ellie hadn't had a moment to dwell on the morning's encounter. And even though she knew a fair few of her customers had come in to try and prise information about Max Loveday out of her—or out of the far more forthcoming Mrs Trelawney—they had all bought something, even if it was just a coffee.

Slowly Ellie began to tidy up, knowing that she was deliberately putting off the moment when she would head upstairs. She loved her flat, and normally she loved the silence, the space, the solitude. Knowing it was hers to do with as she pleased. But this evening she dreaded the time alone. She knew she would relive every cutting remark, every look, every moment of her bruising encounter with Max Loveday. And that inevitably her thoughts would turn to her ex-fiancé. It wasn't a place she wanted to go.

And tomorrow she would have to deal with Max all over again.

As always, the ritual of shutting up shop soothed her. From the day she had opened it the shop had been a sanctuary. *Her* sanctuary. She had planned and designed every feature, every reading nook and display, had painted the walls, hung the pictures, shelved each and every book. Had even chosen the temperamental diva of a coffee machine, which needed twenty minutes of cleaning and wiping before she could put it to bed, and sanded the wood she used for a counter.

She had been able to indulge her love of colour, of posters, of clutter. Nobody expected a bookshop to be tastefully minimalist.

By seven o'clock Ellie could put it off no longer. Every book was in its rightful place. Even the preschool picture books were neatly lined up in alphabetical order. A futile task—it needed just one three-year-old to return the entire rack to chaos.

The shelves were gleaming and dust-free, the cushions on sofas, chairs and benches were shaken out and plumped up, the floor was swept and the leftover cakes had been boxed away. She'd even counted the cash and reconciled the till.

There was literally nothing left to do.

Except leave.

Ellie switched the lights off and stood for a moment, admiring the neatness of the room in the evening light. 'Thank you,' she whispered. If Demelza Loveday hadn't encouraged her to follow her dreams, hadn't rented her the shop, where would Ellie be now?

And, like the fairy godmother she'd been, Miss Loveday had ensured that Ellie could always stay here, always be safe. The shop and the flat were hers. Nobody could ever take them away from her. And, no matter what Max Loveday thought, it hadn't been Ellie's idea. The legacy was a wonderful, thoughtful gift—and it had been a complete surprise. The one bright moment in the grey weeks following Miss Loveday's death and the unwelcome burden of the trust.

A rap at the closed door made her jump. The shop was evidently closed. The sign said so, the shutter was drawn, the lights dimmed right down in the two bay windows. But it wouldn't be the first time someone had needed an emergency gift. That was the thing about small towns: you were never really fully closed.

'Coming,' she called as she stepped over to the door, untwisting the lock and shooting back the two bolts before cautiously opening it…just a few centimetres. Not that there had ever been any robbery beyond the odd bit of shoplifting in Trengarth's small high street.

Ellie's hands tightened on the doorframe as she took in the lean, tall figure, the close-cut dark hair and stubbled chin.

She swallowed. Hard. 'I didn't think we were meeting until tomorrow.' She didn't open the door wider or invite him to come in.

'I wanted to apologise again.' Max held up a bottle of red wine. 'I found this in Great-Aunt Demelza's wine cellar. She had quite a collection.'

'It's your collection now.' Ellie didn't reach out and take the bottle, her hands still firmly clasping the door, keeping it just ajar.

Max pulled a face. 'I can't quite get my head around that. It seemed pretty intrusive, just walking in and showering in the guest en-suite bathroom, looking around at all her stuff. I mean, I didn't actually know her.'

Showering? Ellie immediately tried to push that particular image out of her mind but it lingered there. A fall of water, right onto a tanned, lean torso… Her fingers tightened as her stomach swooped. Her libido had been dead for years. Did it *have* to choose right this moment to resuscitate itself?

'I was planning on chocolates as well, but the shop is shut.' He gestured behind him to the small all-purpose supermarket. 'They were shut this morning as well. Do they *ever* open?'

Ellie looked over at the firmly drawn shutters, grateful for a chance to think about anything but long, steamy showers. 'They do open for longer in the school holidays, but otherwise the hours are a little limiting. It's okay if you know them, but it can be frustrating for tourists—and then Mr Whitehead complains that people drive to the next town and use the bigger supermarkets.'

There. That was a perfectly safe, inane and even dull comment. Libido back in check. She was most definitely *not* looking at the golden tan on his arms, nor noticing the muscle definition under his T-shirt. No, not at all.

'You really didn't have to,' she hurried on, forcing her eyes back up and focussing firmly on his ear. No one could have inappropriate thoughts about an ear, could they? 'Really.'

'I think I did.' His smile was rueful. 'I managed a few hours' sleep on the couch and when I woke up I felt just terrible. Not just because of the jetlag. My grandfather would have been horrified if he had heard me speak to a lady that way. He brought me up better than that.'

Grandfather? Not parents? Interesting...

'Anyway, I thought I'd make amends and get some air...have a look at this town my great-grandfather crossed an ocean to escape. I don't suppose you'd like to join me? Show me around?'

No, she most definitely would not. In fact she had a very important date with the new edition of *Anne of Green Gables* she had unpacked that very morning: hardback, illustrated and annotated. She also had a quarter-bottle of wine, a piece of salmon and some salad.

Another crazy evening in the Scott household of one.

Would anything change if she threw caution to the

wind and went out for a walk before dinner, book, bath and bed? In fact she often took an evening walk. The only real difference would be her companion.

He was her beloved godmother's nephew. Surely Demelza would have wanted her to make him welcome, no matter how bad his first impression? Hadn't she just been remembering just how much she owed her benefactress? She really should replay the debt. Besides, he was trying to make amends. She wasn't used to that.

A flutter started low down in her stomach. For so many years she had been told she was in the wrong, no matter what the reality. A man admitting his mistake was a novel experience.

Ellie swung the door open and stood back. 'Come in,' she invited him. 'I just need to change my shoes and grab my bag.'

It would have been nice to have some more notice. She was still in the grey velvet skinny jeans she had pulled on that morning, teamed with a purple flowered tunic. Her hair was neatly tucked back in a clip and she wasn't wearing any make-up. Not that she usually did for work, but she suddenly wished she had some armour…even if it was just a coat of mascara.

Ellie waited as Max stepped through the door, moving from one foot to the other in indecision. She needed to go upstairs, but she seldom invited other people into her flat. Would it be odd to leave him kicking his heels in the shop while she grabbed a cardigan and quickly brushed out her hair? At least there was plenty for him to read.

'You might as well come up.'

Not the most gracious invitation, but he didn't need asking twice, following her through the dark bookshop to the discreet wooden door at the back of the shop which marked the line between home and work.

Ellie was used to the narrow, low staircase, but she could sense Max taking it more slowly, his head brushing the ceiling as the staircase turned. He breathed an audible sigh of relief when he arrived at the top of the staircase with the top of his head still intact.

The narrow staircase curved and continued up to the third storey, where her bedroom, study and bathroom were situated, but she stepped out into the flat's main hallway. It was simply decorated in a light olive-green, with the colour picked up in the striped runner covering polished floorboards. At the far end a window overlooked the street. Next to it a row of pegs was covered with an assortment of her jackets, coats and scarves; boots and shoes were lined up beneath them.

On her right the kitchen door was slightly ajar. Her unwashed breakfast dishes were still piled on the side. Ellie fought the urge to shut the door, to hide them. In the years she had lived with her ex, Simon, she had learned quickly to tidy up all detritus straight away. Leaving dirty dishes out for a few hours was a small act of rebellion, but it made the flat hers, the kitchen hers. A sign that she was free of his control.

'Just go straight ahead.' She tried to keep her voice light, to hide what a big deal this was.

The living room ran the full length of the building, with a window at either end flooding the long room with evening light. A red velvet three-seater couch and matching loveseat were arranged at right angles at one end of the room; a small dining table with four chairs stood at the other. The walls were plain white, but she had injected colour with dozens of framed posters: her favourites from her last three years of bookselling.

Max stepped inside and looked around. 'No books?' He sounded surprised.

Ellie laughed, a little nervously. 'Oh, plenty of books. I keep them on the landing and in the study. I thought being surrounded by books all day and all night would probably turn me into a *real* hermit instead of practically being one.'

'Here.' He proffered the wine to her. 'Please, take it.'

Ellie looked at it. She needed to make her position clear before she accepted the wine…before she showed him round the village. Before she was distracted again by the evening sun on a bare arm or visions of showers. She had promised herself that she would always speak out, always be honest, never allow herself to be pushed back into being the quiet, submissive ghost she had been with Simon.

Only it wasn't quite so easy in practice.

She took a deep breath, her fingers linking, twisting as she did so. 'I'll be honest, Mr Loveday…'

His eyebrows flew up at her words but he didn't interrupt, just leaned back against the wall, arms folded as she spoke.

'You were very rude to me earlier. You don't know me, and you had no evidence for your words. If it was up to me you would be on your way back to New York right now but for one thing. Your great-aunt. It was her wish that we work together and I intend to honour that. But if you speak to me again the way you did earlier then I will be talking to the solicitors about resigning from the trust.'

She wanted to collapse as she said the words, but forced herself to remain standing and still. Although she couldn't stop her eyes searching his face for telltale signs. For narrowed eyes, a tightened mouth, flaring nostrils. Signs she knew all too well.

She clasped her hands, trying to still their slight

tremor. But Max Loveday's face didn't change—except for the dawning hint of respect in his eyes.

'Fair point—or should I say fair points? First of all, please, if we're going to work together, do call me Max. Secondly, I don't live in New York. I live in Connecticut, so if you do send me away please make sure I end up in the correct state. And third...' He paused. 'You're right. I was rude. There are reasons, and they have nothing to do with you. I can only apologise again.' He closed his eyes briefly. 'There are things going on at home that make it hard for me to believe in altruism, and my great-aunt *did* leave you this building.'

'I didn't ask her to.'

'No, but look at it from my point of view. I don't know you. I just see the cold, hard facts. She was on her own... possibly vulnerable. She left her fortune in your—in *our* hands—and bequeathed to *you* a home and livelihood. On paper, that's a little suspicious.'

Ellie hated to admit it, but he had a point—and she had been shocked by the will and her own prominent part in it. There was one thing he hadn't taken into consideration, though.

She laughed. 'You didn't know your great-aunt very well, did you? I can't see her being taken in by *anybody*. She didn't suffer fools gladly.'

'I didn't know her at all. She moved over here before I was born. I wish I'd made an effort to see her before it was too late.'

'You should have done. She was worth knowing. Right, I'm just going to...' She gestured upstairs. 'I won't be long. Make yourself at home.'

She slipped out of the room. She didn't care about impressing Max Loveday, but there was no way she was heading out without brushing her hair and powdering her face. Maybe a quick coat of mascara. To freshen up after a long day at work. That was all.

Trouble was, she wasn't even fooling herself.

So this was Ellie Scott's home. Bright, vibrant, and yet somehow bare. For all the posters on the walls, the cushions heaped on the inviting sofas, the view of the sea from the back window, there was something missing.

Photos. There were no photos. Not on the walls, not on the sideboard, nor on the mantelpiece over the cosy-looking wood-burning stove. He had never yet met a woman who didn't decorate her personal space with family portraits, pictures of friends, holidays, favourite pets, university formals. Max himself had a framed picture of his parents on his desk in his office, and a few childhood photos in his apartment. The picture of himself aged about ten on his grandfather's boat, proudly holding up a large fish, was one of his most prized possessions.

Maybe they were tucked away like her books, but somehow he doubted it. Where had she come from? What had made a young woman in her early twenties move to a tiny village miles from civilisation and stay there? Or had she walked out of the sea? A selkie doomed to spend her life in human form until she found her sealskin once more? With those huge brown eyes and long, long lashes Ellie certainly fitted the bill.

'Okay, ready when you are. I hope I didn't keep you waiting too long?'

When Ellie had said she would be a minute Max had been prepared for a twenty-minute wait. Minimum. Yet barely five minutes had passed since she had left. She had pulled a long light grey cardigan over her tunic, swapped her pumps for sneakers and brushed out her hair. That was it.

Yet she looked completely fresh, like a dryad in spring.

Anything less like the manicured, blow-dried, designer-clad women he worked with, dated and slept with was hard to imagine. But right now she was fresh iced water to their over-sugared and over-carbonated soda. Not that he was looking in any real way. It was the contrast, that was all. It wasn't that he was actually interested in wholesome girls with creamy skin. He just didn't know many. Or *any*.

'Yes. Ready.' He might be staring. He wasn't staring like some gauche teenage boy, was he? Reluctantly he pulled his gaze away. 'Come on, honey, let's go.'

The sharp breeze that had greeted him earlier in the day had died away, and despite the hour the sun still cast a warm glow over the village. The gentle warmth was a welcome contrast to the heat and humidity of home and the wet and cold of the Sydney winter—not that Sydney's worst could compare to the bone-chilling cold of a Connecticut winter, but it could still be unpleasant.

'There are more houses up there, the school and the children's playground.' Ellie pointed up the hill away from the coast. 'Useful things like the doctor's surgery and the bus stop that takes you to the nearest towns. But I don't suppose you're interested in those?'

'Not unless I was planning to move here.'

'What will you do with the house?' She turned and began to walk the other way, down the hill and towards the swell of the sea. He fell into step beside her.

'I don't know.'

The moment he had stepped into the wide hallway of The Round House, looked at the seascapes and compasses on the walls and heard the rumble of the sea through the windows he had felt a connection. But even the idea of keeping it was impractical.

'It's way too far away to be a holiday home, but now I know there's a real family link I'd hate to sell it on.'

'Trengarth has enough holiday homes. It needs young families to settle here, to put down roots. They're talking about closing down the primary school and bussing the kids over to the next town.' She paused and looked back up the hill. 'Once this was a proper high street: haberdashers, ironmongers, butchers, toy shop…the lot. Your great-aunt has some amazing photos, dating right back to Victorian times. Now it's all gift shops and art galleries, and the front is buckets and spades and surf hire.'

She sounded sad. Nostalgic for a Trengarth she couldn't ever have actually experienced.

'Is that why you moved here? To put down roots?' Was there a family in her future? A man she was hoping to settle down with? There had been no hint of anyone else in her flat. No hint of any family or partner.

'I moved here because it felt safe. Because there was someone here I loved and trusted.'

She didn't say any more, and he didn't push it as they carried on to the bottom of the hill. When they reached it she crossed over the road to a narrow sidewalk, taking the right-hand fork along the harbour wall.

On the other side of the road, houses faced out: brightly coloured terraced cottages in whites, blues, pinks and greens making a cheerful mosaic. Winding narrow streets twisted and turned behind them, with houses built higher and higher up the cliff.

'This is the old town. Most of these would have been fishermen's cottages once.'

'Once?'

'Some still are,' she admitted. 'Some are retirement

properties, and a few are owned by villagers. But probably half are holiday cottages. Which is fine when they're full. My business depends on tourists with money to spend and time to browse, and so do the cafés, the B&Bs, the art galleries and the bucket and spade shops. It's when they're empty, or they don't get rented out and are only visited two weeks a year, when it's a problem. That's why it's important that we really try and make this festival a success. It could bring so many more people here.'

She stopped and leaned on the iron railings, looking out over the curve of the old harbour.

'I love this view. The fishing boats safely moored inside the harbour, the powerboats and sailboats further out... Sometimes I wish I could sail, just set off and see where I end up.'

Her voice was unexpectedly wistful. Max stole a glance at her profile. She was in another world, almost oblivious to his presence as she stared out at the white-flecked waves.

'You don't sail? You live by the sea and don't sail? You must surf, then.'

He gave her an appraising look. She was very slim, almost to the point of thin, but there was a strength and a lithe grace in the way she moved. She would probably be a natural on a board.

She shook her head.

'Swim?'

'No.' A reluctant smile curved her mouth. 'I love the sea, but more as something to look at, listen to. I'm not so much one for venturing on to or into it.'

'Wow...' He shook his head. 'You live literally five minutes away and you just *look* at it? I was going to try and hire a boat while I'm here. I think I may have to offer to take you out for a sail. It'll change your life.'

'Maybe.'

It wasn't a refusal, and her smile didn't slip away as she resumed walking.

'Okay, if you take that road there it will lead you to the most important building in Trengarth: The Three Herrings. There *is* another pub further along, with a beer garden and a view of the harbour. It's lovely, but...' She lowered her voice. 'It's mostly used by tourists and incomers. The *real* Trengarthians frequent The Three Herrings, even though there is no view, the chimney smokes and the grub is very much of the plain and plentiful variety.'

'Got it.'

'Do you want to see the beach?'

'Sure.'

They turned around and walked back, past the high street and onto the wider promenade. No houses here. Just shops selling ice cream, sun cream and beach toys, a couple of board shops filled with body-boards, surfboards and wetsuits, which Max noted with keen interest, and a few cafés.

'The Boat House,' Ellie explained, when he stopped in front of a modern-looking glass and wood building on the ocean side of the road. 'Café by day, bistro by night, and a bit of a cool place to hang out. I used to have dinner with your Great-Aunt Demelza here on a Friday evening.' Her voice softened. 'I turned up as usual the Friday after she died...just automatically, you know? I didn't really take it in that she was gone until I was seated by myself.'

'I'm sorry. Sorry that you miss her and that I didn't know her. And that nobody came to the funeral—although we lost Grandfather just a few months before, and things were difficult.'

That was an understatement. His father had barely

finished the eulogy before he'd had started gathering up the reins at DL and turning the company upside down.

'It's okay. Really. I have some experience at arranging funerals.'

There was a bitter note to her voice that surprised him.

'Besides, she was very clear about what she wanted. I didn't have to do much.'

She turned away from The Boat House and headed towards the slipway that would take them on to the beach.

Max stood for one moment to take in the view. The slim figure all in grey was getting smaller as she walked along the wide golden sweep of beach. The cliffs were steeper on this side of the bay, green and yellow with gorse, and rocks and large pebbles were clustered at the bottom before the stony mass gave way to the softer sand.

The sea roared as the tide beat its inexorable way in, the swell significant enough to justify the presence of lifeguards' chairs and warning flags. Not that it seemed to deter the determined crowd of surfers bobbing about like small seals.

The breeze had risen a little. Enough for Max to feel a slight chill on his arms as he stepped on to the sand. He inhaled, enjoying the familiar tang of salt, and heard the cry of gulls overhead and the excited shrieks of a gaggle of small children who were racing a puppy along the tideline.

For the first time in a long time Max could feel the burden on his shoulders slip away, the tightness in his chest ease.

'Hey, Ellie!' he yelled. 'Wait for me.'

He took off after her, enjoying the burn in his calves as he sprinted along the resistant sand, enjoying the complete freedom of the here, the now.

'This is magnificent,' he panted as he skidded to a halt

beside her. 'What a beach. If I lived here I'd have two dogs, a boat, and I'd surf every day.'

She flushed. 'I do *walk* on the beach, even if I don't immerse myself in the sea. And I have thought about maybe getting a guinea pig.'

'A *guinea pig*? You can't walk a guinea pig.'

'Some people do. They have harnesses and everything.' But she caught his eye as she said it and a smile broke out on her face: a full-on, wide-mouthed grin.

It transformed her, lighting up the shadows of her face, bringing that elusive prettiness to the forefront. Max stood stock-still, stunned.

'Harnesses…right. I see.' He turned back as he said it, instinctively heading for the safety of the large white house just visible at the top of the cliffs.

He wasn't here to flirt, and Ellie wasn't giving off any signals that she might enjoy the kind of no-strings fun he'd be interested in. It was far better not to notice how her face lit up, not to notice the sparkle in the large eyes or the intriguing dimple in her cheek. Far, *far* better not to notice just how perfectly shaped her mouth was: not too large, not too small, but pretty damn near just right.

'Come on,' he said, bouncing on his heels. 'I'll race you back to the road. Loser buys the winner a pint. Ready? *Go!*'

CHAPTER FOUR

'THAT WASN'T FAIR. You had a head start.' Ellie pulled the long, tangled mass of hair out of her face, twisting it into a loose knot. Her heart was thumping from the unaccustomed exercise. She'd thought she was fitter than that, although she couldn't remember the last time she had run at full pelt, aware of nothing but her legs pumping, her heart beating fit to burst, the wind biting at her ears.

'If you're going to be a sore loser…'

Max looked annoyingly at ease, leaning on the railing and waiting for her, his cheeks unflushed, his chest not heaving for breath. Unlike hers.

'No, no, I concede. I'm not sure I'd have won even with a head start. Next time *I* pick the competition. Speed-reading, maybe.'

She stepped onto the causeway to join him, but as she did so she heard her name called from someone behind her and twisted round to see who it was. It wasn't often she found herself hailed in such a friendly way.

A group of wetsuit-clad surfers had left the sea and were making their way up the beach, boards tucked under their arms.

'Ellie, wait!'

She turned to meet them, all too aware of Max behind her. The surfers were all locals. Some were born and bred, and some were incomers like Ellie, lured to Trengarth by the sea, the scenery and the pace of life. Ellie often forgot just how many people her own age lived in the village, many working at The Boat House café or the hotel of the same name, others owning businesses they ran from their homes. The group in front of her included a talented chef, a website designer and an architect.

'Hi…' She wasn't sure why she was so self-conscious as she called back, but the heat in her cheeks wasn't completely down to her recent exercise.

'Are you coming to the quiz tonight?' asked Sam, the architect, as he jogged ahead of his friends to join her. 'We would never have won last week without you.'

It wasn't often she ventured out, but a week ago she had popped into the pub, completely unaware that it was the weekly hotly contested quiz night, and had been co-opted on to a team. She had felt unexpectedly welcome, and for the first time had been uneasily aware that her incomer status might be something she enforced on herself. Especially where the under-thirties in the village were concerned.

'Well, if you ever picked up a book you might have a chance. I sell quite a selection, you know. Come in and I'll make a personal recommendation.'

'Tempting…' Sam was standing a little closer, his blue eyes smiling down into hers in unmistakable invitation.

Ellie waited for that same jolt of libido she had experienced earlier. Sam was tall, handsome, he wore the tight-fitting wetsuit very well and was looking down at her with appreciation. But, no. Nothing. Not even a tiny electric shock.

Disappointing. He would be a much more suitable person to have a crush on. If only her body would agree.

She took a step back, breaking the connection. 'Besides, I was more than useless at the sports questions and I had no idea how terrible my geography was until last week. I've been paying extra attention when I shelve the travel guides to try and brush up a little.'

'So you'll come?'

The rest of the group had caught up with Sam and were waiting for her answer. She knew them all, but none of them was close enough to count as a friend.

She hadn't noticed the difference before.

'I…I might,' she said finally. 'I was about to pop down to the Herrings to introduce Max to the place so… Oh, this is Max Loveday. Miss Loveday's great-nephew. He's come over to sort out the house and help me make a start on the festival.'

She was aware of Sam's appraising gaze as she introduced the rest of the group to Max, and was glad when she could finally make her escape with the promise that she might see them later.

Max didn't speak for a few moments as they retraced their steps along the seafront, but the silence was tight, the easy camaraderie of the beach gone as if it had never been.

'Is he your boyfriend?'

Ellie felt her cheeks warm again. She didn't need to ask who he was referring to. 'No.' She was glad her voice didn't squeak. 'I'm not seeing anyone at the moment. Are you?'

What did they say? Attack was the best form of defence, and she really didn't want to be discussing her personal life with anyone. Especially not with Max Loveday.

'Me?' His voice was amused. 'Not at the moment. My last relationship ended a couple of months ago. I was always too busy to date, and it was apparent that our timetables didn't match, so I called it off.'

He sounded as detached as if he were discussing cancelling a dinner reservation, not ending an intimate relationship.

'Your *timetables*?' Had she misheard? Was that some kind of slang term for sexual compatibility? Or something really hip to do with auras?

'Stella wanted to get engaged this year, but I'm not going to get married before thirty. Ideally I would like to be around thirty-four, and I don't really want to think about kids until two years after that.' He shrugged as if that was the most natural reason to break up in the world.

'But…' She stared at his profile in fascination, looking for some hint that he was teasing her. 'Didn't you love her?'

'I liked her. We had a lot in common. She was from my world.' Max paused. 'That's what's important. That's what ensures a harmonious marriage. Love isn't enough of a bedrock to build a marriage, a family on. It's not solid enough, not real enough.'

'It isn't? Surely it's the most important thing?'

Despite her hideous three years with Simon and his warped idea of what love meant, in spite of her mother's inability to exist without it, love was still the goal. Wasn't it? Right now she might only find it in books and films, but one day, when her libido was behaving itself and she found herself attracted to the right man at the right time, she hoped she would fall in love. Properly this time. Not mistaking infatuation and fear for the real thing.

She hadn't even considered a timetable.

'My parents were madly in love.' His mouth twisted. '*Madly* being the operative word. Apart from the times when my father was in love with someone else. I don't know which was worse: the awful strained silences, the lies and the falsity when he was having an affair, or the making up afterwards. Once he bought my mother a Porsche. Red, of course. Filled it with one thousand red roses and heart-shaped balloons.'

'Oh, that sounds...' Ellie fought to find the right word and failed.

'Vulgar?' His voice was grim. 'It was. I don't want that kind of ridiculous drama in my life. Respect and mutual goals are a far tidier way to live. A lot less destructive.'

'My parents loved each other too.' The familiar lump rose in her throat at the memory. 'But there was no drama. They were just really happy.'

Max stared straight ahead. 'I spent most of my childhood either playing peacekeeper and go-between or being ignored as they went off on yet another honeymoon. Unless I was with my grandfather. It was all much more stable there.'

'Sounds like he wasn't so different from your Great-Aunt Demelza. She was one of the calmest people I knew.'

'Mmm...'

His mind was clearly elsewhere.

'Ellie, would you mind if I took a raincheck on the pint? I'm still pretty jetlagged and it's been a long few days. But tomorrow I'm going to start going through the house and I would really appreciate your help. You knew her best.'

'Of course.'

Ellie was relieved not to have to spend more time with him now. Especially not in the intimate setting of The Three Herrings, where the little cubicle-like snugs meant an easy drink could easily feel like a *tête-à-tête*. And it meant she could definitely get out of the pub quiz and curl up with her book, just as she had planned.

Yes, she was definitely relieved. She wasn't feeling a little flat at all...

* * *

For the longest time The Round House had been the place that Ellie loved best in all the world. It wasn't just its curious shape, like something out of a fairytale, with its high circular roof, the huge arched windows looking out to sea. Nor was it just the knowledge that in its rounded walls were rooms full of treasures. Whether your tastes ran to books, clothes, jewellery, home-baked food or collections of everything from stamps to fossils, somewhere in the various cupboards, cabinets and boxes there was bound to be something to catch your eye.

Once, at first, it had been her holiday home: the flagstone hallway liberally sprinkled with sand as she ran in straight from the beach, barely pausing to wrap a towel around her before heading to the kitchen for freshly baked scones and a glass of creamy Cornish milk. Later it had been a place for grief and contemplation, long hours huddled in the window seat on the first-floor landing, staring out to sea, wondering just where it was she belonged.

And then it had been a refuge. Literally. A place to regroup, to lick her wounds. Demelza Loveday had given her all the time, space and love in the world. It was a debt she could never repay. Making sure she helped her godmother's dream of a literary festival come true was the least she could do.

But today, watching Max open the arched front door and invite her in, a realisation hit her. One she hadn't allowed herself to articulate before.

The Round House would never be her home again. It belonged to Max Loveday. From now on it would be a second home, visited once a year, or sold on to strangers. Her last link to Demelza Loveday would be severed.

But for the moment at least nothing had changed. The

hallway was still furnished with the same aged elegance; the glass bowl on the sideboard was set in the same position. Only the hat stand was missing its usual mackintosh and scarf. Demelza's clothes had long since been gathered up and given away to charity.

'Is something wrong?'

Ellie started, aware that she had been standing immobile, staring around the hallway for far too long. 'No, sorry. It's just...' She hesitated, unsure how to articulate the strange sense of wrongness. Then it came to her. 'It smells all wrong.'

Max sniffed. 'It was a little musty when I got here, I've had all the windows open, though.'

'No, it's not that.' It wasn't what she could smell, more what she couldn't. That elusive sense that something important was missing. 'There's no smell of baking. No perfume in the air. Your great-aunt liked a very floral scent, quite heavy. It's gone now.'

Max leaned back against the wall, his casual stance and clothes incongruous against the daintily patterned wallpaper. 'The whole house was cleaned after her clothes were disposed of—she'd asked that they were given away or sold, and I guess the executors took care of that. But all her papers are here. Her books, pictures, ornaments. I have no idea what to do with it all.'

He didn't sound dismissive. Not exactly. But nor did he sound at all appreciative. He had no idea how special his gift was.

'Where do you want to start?' It wasn't his fault, Ellie reminded herself. He didn't have the links she did. What were treasured memories to her must just be so much clutter to him.

'In the library. The solicitor gave me the key to her desk. Apparently all the papers in there are mine now.

They sold off the stocks and other financial assets for the trust so it must all be family stuff.'

'More information about the sea captain?'

The pinched expression left his face. 'Maybe. That would be cool.'

In Ellie's admittedly not at all unbiased opinion, the library was the heart of the house. Demelza had turned what had been the morning room into a book-lined paradise filled with window seats and cosy nooks. In summer you could look out upon the ocean, basking in the sun through the open French windows; in winter a roaring fire warmed you as you read. The rounded walls held glassed-in bookshelves, reaching from floor to ceiling. Polished oak floorboards were covered with vibrant rugs in turquoises and emeralds. The same colours were reflected in the curtains and the geometric Art Deco wallpaper.

Would whoever bought this house keep the room this way? It was horribly unlikely.

Max had wandered over to the far side of the room, where he was examining a case of blue-bound hardbacks. 'She owned the entire catalogue…' His voice was reverential. 'That's incredible.'

'I was only allowed to touch those under strict supervision even when I was all grown up. She said they had too much sentimental value.'

Max raised an eyebrow. 'Not just sentimental; they're worth a *fortune* to collectors. These are all first edition Kerenza Press classics.' He opened the glass door and carefully slid one out. 'Just look at the quality…the illustrations. We stopped producing these years ago. I always wished we had carried on.'

'We?'

'DL Media. Kerenza was the very first imprint my

great-grandfather started. He named it after his wife, my great-grandmother.' His mouth twisted. 'It means "love" in Cornish.'

'It's a beautiful name.' No wonder Demelza had such an amazing collection of books, but why had she never mentioned that she was part of the DL Media empire? All those long talks about books, about the shop, about the festival, and she had never once let slip her literary heritage.

For the first time Ellie was conscious of a gap between her godmother and herself. Not of age, or privilege, but of secrets withheld, confidences untold.

'I knew that you worked for DL Media because of your email. I didn't know that you *were* DL.'

Ellie gave a little laugh, but it sounded false even to her own ears. Max was heir to one of the last big publishing and media companies in private hands. No wonder he wore an air of wealth and privilege like a worn-in sweatshirt: so comfortable it was almost part of him.

'She didn't mention it?'

Ellie shook her head. 'Never. She never really spoke about her life in America. Sometimes she would talk about her university days here in England. That's how she knew my grandmother. All she said about her working life was that she regretted never marrying but that in her day women could have jobs or they could have marriage, not both. She never mentioned her family or *where* she'd worked.'

'She worked for DL until my great-grandfather died. Then there was some kind of argument—about the will and the direction of the company, I think.' His face was set as he stared at the book in his hands. 'There's nothing to tear a family apart like money. Wills and family businesses must be responsible for more fractures than anything else.'

'Oh, I don't know…' That old bone-deep ache pulsed. 'Families fracture for many reasons. But sometimes we forge our own family ties. Blood doesn't always run deeper.'

'You're not close to your family?'

'I lost my father and brother in a car accident.' How could something so utterly destructive be explained in just a few words? How could the ripping apart of a family be distilled down to one sentence? 'My mother remarried.'

'I'm so sorry.' His eyes had darkened with sympathy, the expression in them touching somewhere buried deep inside her, warming, defrosting. But the barriers were there for a reason.

She stepped back, putting even more space between them. 'It was a long time ago.'

'Do you like your stepfather?'

'He makes my mother happy. She's not really the kind of person who copes well by herself. It's a relief to know that someone is taking care of her.'

It was the truth, so why did it feel as if she were lying?

'I'll definitely ship all this back, but nothing seems urgent.' Max stared at the floor of the library, now liberally covered in papers, paperclips and folders.

His great-aunt had definitely been a hoarder. And an avid family historian. There was enough here to write a biography of the entire Loveday clan—one with several volumes. But so far he hadn't found anything to indicate that she had still owned part of the company.

Ellie sat cross-legged close by, sorting through some of the newer-looking files, many of which were about village committees and his great-aunt's charitable commitments.

'This looks different. It's in a legal envelope and addressed to you, so I haven't opened it.' Ellie handed over a large manila envelope. His name was neatly typed on the label.

'Thanks...'

This could be it. His pulse began to speed as he reached for the envelope, and then accelerated as his hand brushed hers. His fingers wanted to latch on to hers, keep holding on. Her hair had fallen out of its clip while they worked and she had allowed it to flow free. Max could barely keep his eyes off the smooth flow of hair, constantly changing colour in the sunlit room, one moment dark chocolate, the next a rich bronze.

It had to be natural. He couldn't imagine Ellie sitting for hours in a hairdresser's chair. His mother had her hair cut and dyed monthly, at a salon that charged the equivalent of a month's rent for the privilege.

No wonder her alimony demands were so high.

'What is it? A treasure map for some ancient pirate Loveday's plunder?'

'Fingers crossed.' If it was what he was hoping for then it would be worth far more than any treasure chest.

Max slit the envelope open and pulled out a single sheet of paper.

'No X marks the spot.'

'Disappointing.' Ellie got to her feet in one graceful gesture. 'Shall I start tidying some of this lot up? I don't think there's any way you're going to get through this entire house in just two weeks.'

He could barely make out her words. All his attention was on the piece of paper he held. 'Read this. What does it say?'

She glanced at him, puzzled, before taking the paper. Max rocked back on his heels, his blood pumping so loudly he could barely make out her voice as she read the paper aloud.

'It says that Demelza remained a silent shareholder even after her severance from DL Media and that she's left her twenty-five per cent share of the company to you. Very nice.'

Yes! This was it. He quickly totted up the percentages in his mind.

'More than nice.' He was on his feet, his hand on hers where she held the precious paper. 'It means my grandfather only held seventy-five per cent of the company. And *that* means my father doesn't have a two-thirds majority. We're equal partners. Do you know what else, Ellie Scott? It means I can take him on and I can *win*. Thanks to my lovely Great-Aunt Demelza.'

'It does?' She was staring up at him, smiling in response, her eyes enormous, her cheeks flushed.

The breath whooshed from his chest as if he had been hit with a football at top speed. How did she do it? How did that elusive smile light her up, turn the pointed chin, big eyes and hollow cheeks into beauty?

And why didn't she smile more often?

Max took a deep breath, curling his fingers into his palms. All he wanted to do was touch her, trace the curve of her cheek, run a finger along the fullness of her bottom lip and tangle his hands in the thick length of hair. But he knew instinctively, with every bone in his body, that his touch would be unwelcome. There was a 'Keep Out' sign erected very firmly around Ellie. Trespassers were most certainly not tolerated.

She would have to invite him in. And he sensed that invitations were very rarely issued, if at all.

It was for the best. A girl like Ellie didn't know how

to play. She would need wooing and loving and protecting. All the things he had no interest in.

She stepped back, leaving the precious paper in his hands. 'You and your father are disagreeing?'

That was one way of putting it.

Max walked over to the window and stared out at the breathtaking view. The Round House was at the very top of the cliff. Just a few metres of garden seemed to separate the house from the sea stretching out to the horizon beyond.

'My grandfather was a visionary. He was an early adopter of technology, but managed to avoid the dotcom crisis, and we've weathered every financial crisis there's been. My father was always in his shadow, I guess. But since Grandfather died he's seemed determined to put his stamp on the company. He thinks anything new is worth investing in, and he's diversifying the brand into everything from jobs to dating. If there's an app for it he wants it.'

Ellie stepped forward and stood next to him, so close they were almost touching. *Almost.* 'Most media outlets have job sites and dating adverts...'

'Supported by their main publications, they can be useful income streams, yes.' He ran a hand through his hair. 'But he's not investing in the news sites at all. He's got rid of some of our most experienced journalists and is allowing bloggers and the commenting public to provide most of the content. There's a place for that, sure, but not at the expense of your main news. I came here to find a way to wrestle control of the company away from him. This—' he brandished the paper '—this means we either come to a consensus or every decision goes to the board. It's not ideal, but it's a helluva lot better than the current situation.'

'It sounds like your grandfather and your great-aunt all over again.'

He flinched at her gentle words. Was she right? Was another massive chasm about to open up in the family?

'It's not just work.' He was justifying his actions as much to himself as he was to Ellie. 'His personal life is a mess too. He's left my mother for my old PA, and just to twist the cliché has announced he wants a divorce.'

He couldn't talk about the pregnancy. Not yet.

'My mother is a mess, *he* is completely unrepentant, and DL Media is fragmenting. I have a lot of work to do.'

'Max, they're grown-ups. Isn't their marriage *their* problem? Getting sucked in too far never ends well.' There was a bitter certainty in her voice.

Max laughed, the anger in the sound startling him. 'Oh, their marriage *is* their problem. I'm not getting involved. Not any more. But I have to look after DL, whatever it takes. My mother is out for blood. She wants half the company. Can you imagine? The lawyers' fees alone could drag us down.'

'What would happen if you just walked away? They'd have to fix it then, wouldn't they?'

He shook his head. 'It's not so much them as the company. It's *my* responsibility, Ellie. I started in the distribution centre when I was fifteen. I was filing and photocopying at sixteen, writing up press releases at eighteen. I interned every year I was at Yale, and when I graduated I went straight into the New Media department. It's all I've ever known and I *won't* let them tear it apart.'

'I always wanted to work in publishing.' There was a longing in her voice. 'But I didn't go to university.'

'Why not?' It was a relief to change the subject, to focus on something else.

'My mother took a long time to get over my father's death. It was hard to leave her. And when she remarried I was...' She swallowed, her already pale cheeks whitening. 'I was engaged.'

'You were *engaged*?' He turned to look at her, shocked by her revelation. She was very pale. Even her lips were almost white.

'Yes. I was young and foolish and had no judgement.'

She smiled at him but he wasn't fooled. This smile didn't light up her face, didn't illuminate her beauty. It was only skin-deep, false.

The urge to protect her swept up, taking him completely by surprise. Somehow he knew, completely and utterly, that Ellie Scott had been badly hurt and that the scars were still not fully healed. Another reason to keep well away.

'It's not too late.'

'I'm doing a degree now, in the evenings. And at least I'm surrounded by books. It's not all bad. But what would you do if you weren't part of DL? If you weren't one of *those* Lovedays?'

But he *was* one of 'those' Lovedays. His identity was burnt into him like a brand. He couldn't escape his family history and nor did he want to.

'All I ever wanted was to make my grandfather proud and take DL to the next level.' It didn't sound like much, but it was everything. 'I can't let my father stop that.'

'Can't you work *with* him? Compromise?'

'He won't let me in, Ellie. I've tried, goodness knows. He wants me to knuckle down and accept him as head of the family. To tamely agree with every decision he makes, to meet the woman he's left my mother for and make her part of my family. We can't even be in the same room right now.'

'Then it's a good thing you're on the other side of the Atlantic.'

Max caught sight of his reflection in the mirror on the wall opposite, jaw set, eyes hard. He barely recognised himself.

'Maybe.' He made an effort to shake off the anger coiling around his soul like a malevolent snake. 'I need to get this faxed over to the company lawyers before I go to London. I can plan my next move from there. I'll get someone in to clear the rest of the house before I instruct the solicitors to sell.'

'You're not thinking of keeping the house?' Disappointment flickered over her face. 'Your Great-Aunt Demelza would have wanted you to.'

'My life's in Connecticut. When I'm in the UK I'm London-based. I have no use for it.'

Looking around, he felt a hint of regret. His family's history was soaked into the rounded walls. His eyes fell on a gilt-edged card as he spoke. It looked familiar and, curious, he picked it up.

'What's this?'

Ellie flushed and reached for it. Max held it a little longer, trying to read the curled writing, until with a pull she tugged it out of his fingers. 'Oh, that's mine. It must have fallen out of my bag. It's just some industry black tie thing. I've been nominated for Independent Bookseller of the Year. Nonsense, really, but quite sweet.'

'Are you going?'

'Oh, no. It's in London. The season starts this week. I couldn't leave the shop. Besides, I wouldn't know anyone.'

Max reached over and plucked the card out of her hand. Why was it striking a chord?

'DL have a table.'

That was it. The London office had asked him to attend and it would be the perfect opportunity for him to quell some of the rumours about the company's viability.

'You could come with me. That way you wouldn't be going alone.'

Her face turned even redder. 'That's very kind of you...'

'Not at all. I hate these things. It would be more bearable if I was with someone I knew. Especially if that someone was up for an award.'

'There's still the shop...'

'Mrs Trelawney is quite capable, surely? Look, Ellie, I was planning on going anyway. It would make me very happy if you came with me.'

Max didn't know why it mattered. She was a grown woman...she could do as she pleased. But although black tie dinners and awards ceremonies were a dime a dozen to him, he sensed they didn't really figure in Ellie's life. Besides, his great-aunt had loved Ellie, cared for her. It would be fitting thanks if he took her under his wing a little.

In fact he was being very altruistic.

'I appreciate the thought...'

'I'm not doing this to be kind,' he reassured her. 'My motives are completely selfish.'

'I really wasn't planning on going.'

'If we are going to be setting up a literary festival then this is the best thing you can do. I'll introduce you to some of the best publicists in the business. And who knows, Ellie? We might even have fun while we're there.'

CHAPTER FIVE

Ellie didn't actually remember agreeing to *any* of this.

Not to going to the awards ceremony and certainly not to spending two nights in London with someone she barely knew.

She'd spent far too long allowing her wishes to be overridden, doing things she didn't want to in order to placate someone else: three years indulging her mother's grief, three years trying to turn herself into the perfect wife for Simon. Both had been impossible tasks.

She'd sworn she'd never allow herself to be pushed out of her comfort zone. Not ever again.

So why was she now sitting in the passenger seat of Max Loveday's hire car, watching the miles disappear as London grew ever closer?

The thing was, she couldn't deny a certain fizz in her veins, a delicious anticipation. It was mixed with fear and dread, yes, but it was anticipation nonetheless.

After three years of living very much within her comfort zone she was ready to be stretched, just a little. And if she must be stretched then a champagne reception seemed like a reasonable place to start. It wasn't as if she was going to *win* the award. All she had to do was smile and applaud the winner.

And start to make contacts for the festival. That was a

little more daunting. But Max must know the right people. He could take care of that, surely?

'Penny for them?'

'I'm sorry?'

'For your thoughts. You've been pretty quiet the whole journey. I can hear the wheels turning.'

Ellie sank back in the admittedly plush seat and stared out at the countryside. The harsh beauty of the Cornish moors had given way first to rolling hills and now to pastoral scenes fit for a movie. Sheep grazed in fields dotted by small lines of trees; copses dominated the skyline in the distance. At any moment she expected to pass through idyllic villages full of thatched cottages and maypoles.

Ellie bit her lip. It was odd, this new companionship. She'd spent more time in the last few days with Max Loveday than she had with any other person in the entire last three years—other than Demelza Loveday, of course. That must be why, despite his complete and utter lack of suitability, she found herself wanting to confide in him.

Besides, a little voice whispered, he had confided in *her.* She'd seen a crack in his façade—and she'd liked what she'd seen. Someone who wasn't *quite* so certain of his place in the world. Someone with questions. He was ruthless, sure, and ready to sacrifice his father if need be—not for personal gain, but because he genuinely believed it would be for the best. That took a lot of strength.

'This is the first time I've left Trengarth in three years.'

He darted a look over at her. 'Seriously?'

Ellie nodded.

Max let out a low whistle. 'What are you? Twenty-five? Trengarth is pretty, but that's kinda young to be burying yourself away.'

'I didn't even realise that was what I was doing. I

feel…' She hesitated, searching for the right word, not wanting to reveal too much. '*Safe* there.'

'You haven't even visited your mom?'

There was a particular ache that squeezed Ellie's chest whenever she thought about her mother: a toxic mixture of hurt and regret and a deep sense of loss.

'She's so busy, and she and my stepfather travel a great deal. Not to Cornwall, though,' she couldn't help adding, wincing at the acidity in her voice. 'But it's good to get away. Even for a couple of days. When we drove out of the village I felt as if I was leaving a cage—a little scared, but free.'

Whoa! That was far too revealing. She peeped over at Max, but his face was smoothly bland.

'Sometimes we need the perspective we get just by being in a new place.'

'I think maybe this festival is what I need. Perhaps I have got a little…' She paused, searching for the right word. 'Comfortable. After all, I host signings and launches, book clubs and children's activities. It's just a case of combining them all.'

'You'll be great.'

Would she? It was so long since she'd struck out, dared to dream of anything but safety, a bolthole of her own.

That was what Simon had taken from her. Not just her confidence and her self-esteem but also her time. Three years with him. Three years recovering from him. Time she could never get back.

Maybe all this was a sign. Max, the bequest, the award nomination. A big neon sign, telling her she needed to stop being afraid. That she had to go out there and live.

'Once I thought I'd live in London. That I'd have a flat, go to plays in the evenings, wander around exhibitions at lunchtime. Sometimes I feel like I skipped a stage in my life. Headed right for settling down and forgot to have the fun bit first.'

Ellie risked a look over at Max.

His face was bleak. 'You and me both.'

The traffic thickened as they got closer to London, the green fields giving way to buildings and warehouses.

'Why?'

She started, the one-word question rousing her from her thoughts. 'Why what?'

'Why did you hide away?'

His words hit her with an almost physical force, winding her so that for one never-ending moment she was breathless. *Why?* Because she had allowed herself to be used and manipulated for so long that she hadn't known who she was any more. But how could she say those words out loud even to herself—let alone to the confident, successful man beside her?

He might understand a little how she had been trapped by her mother's need and grief, forced to grow up too soon, to make sure that bills were paid and food was on the table and that somehow the half of her family that was left survived. Yes, he would understand that.

But would he understand her later weakness—or despise her for it? Heaven knew she despised herself. Max Loveday had made it quite clear that he thought love was a lie, an emotional trap. What would he think of a lonely girl so desperate for affection and for someone to take care of her that she'd fallen prey to a controlling relationship, allowed her soul to be stripped bare until she had no idea who she was, what she wanted?

How could he understand it when she didn't understand it herself? It was her shame, her burden.

'I don't want to talk about Trengarth. I haven't been to London for ages. What shall we do there?'

He shot her an amused smile. 'Work, go to a party… the usual.'

She seized on the statement, glad of the change of topic. 'You've been in Cornwall for four days and in that time you've spent half the day on paperwork and the rest of the day and evening working. You make noises about sailing and surfing, but you haven't left the house long enough to do either.'

Irritation scratched through his voice. 'This isn't a holiday, Ellie.'

'No,' she said sweetly. 'It *is* the weekend, though. And as you have somehow talked me into a few days away I, for one, am planning to do some sightseeing. I'll take photos for you, shall I?'

'Okay.'

'Okay to photos?'

He sighed. 'No. Okay to the rest of the weekend off. You're right. I'm nearly halfway through this trip and I haven't stopped. We should have fun in London. Let's be tourists. For today at least.'

We? A warmth stole over her. Ellie had spent so long keeping people at arm's length that although she had plenty of cordial acquaintances she wasn't at the top of very many people's 'going out' lists.

But Max Loveday wanted to go out and have fun. With her.

'Be tourists?' she echoed. 'Like the Houses of Parliament and Buckingham Palace?'

'Like all the big sights. No work and no cares this afternoon or this evening, Heck. I might even take tomorrow off too, before we have to dress up for this award nonsense. But for today we forget about bequests and festivals and DL Media. We're just two people out and about. Just two people in the city. What do you think?'

What did she think? He wanted to spend time with her, he wanted to know what her opinion was, he wanted just to hang out. With her. To have a day of carefree, irresponsible, forget-your-worries fun.

When had Ellie *ever* had a day like that? Goodness, she was pathetic. Max was right. Didn't she deserve a day out of time?

Before she forgot how to let go at all.

'I think we should do it. Where do you want to go?' She pulled her phone out, ready to search the internet.

'Let's not plan. Let's just go for it and see where we end up.'

Ellie took in a deep breath, damping down the knot of worry forming in her stomach. She could do this. She didn't need to plan everything. Spontaneous. Fun. Those adjectives *could* describe her.

They had once described the little girl running barefoot through the sand at Trengarth, living completely and utterly in the moment. She was still in there somewhere. Wasn't she?

'Perfect. We'll see where we end up. Absolutely.'

Max seemed to take the hotel completely in his stride, but although Ellie wanted to look like the kind of girl who stayed in sumptuous five-star hotels every day of her life she was aware she was failing miserably, gaping at everything from the uniformed doorman to the gilt-edged baroque decorations.

'I don't think this is within my budget,' she whispered to Max as the doorman took her case, not betraying with so much as a flicker of his eyebrow that her old tattered holdall was easily the cheapest item in the entire hotel.

She'd known they were going to stay somewhere nice, had justified the extravagance as a business expense, but this? This was the difference between high street chocolate and hand-made truffles.

It wasn't just nice, and *luxurious* didn't come close. It was the *haute couture* of the hotel world. And Ellie was very much a high street girl.

She cast a surreptitious look around, trying to find some clue as to the tariff. But there was nothing. *If you have to ask the price you can't afford it...* Wasn't that what they said?

What if you were terrified to ask the price? That meant you absolutely couldn't afford so much as a sandwich in the lavishly decorated bar.

It wasn't as if she spent much, but one night in this hotel might severely deplete her carefully hoarded savings. Her nails bit into her palms as she fought for breath. She didn't have to stay. She could go and find a more affordable room right now.

Only the doorman had shepherded them into the lift and the doors were beginning to close. Would it be too late when he opened the door to her room? It might be okay… If she bought sandwiches from a shop down the road and didn't go anywhere near the mini-bar…

And there was always her emergency credit card. Her breath hitched. She should be glad that an emergency had been downgraded from an escape plan to paying for a luxury hotel room.

'Relax, this is on DL Media,' Max whispered back.

How had he done that? Read her mood so effortlessly?

Relief warred with panic. She *always* paid her way. Money had been just one of the ways Simon had liked to control her. One of the ways she had allowed him to control her.

'Don't be silly. Of course I'll pay my own bill.'

Max leaned in closer and his eyes held hers for a long

moment before hers fell under his scrutiny. But that was no better, because now she was staring intently at the grey cotton of his T-shirt where it moulded to his chest.

It was fair to say, Ellie had conceded in the sleepless depths of the night before, that Max Loveday was a reasonably attractive male. He was young, fit, intelligent, and he had that certain air of unconscious arrogance. Infuriating and yet with a certain charm.

But had she *really* noticed? Had she taken the time before now to appreciate the toned strength of him, the long muscled legs, today casually clad in worn jeans, the flat stomach and broad chest? Of course they had never been in quite such close proximity before. She hadn't allowed him within real touching distance.

They weren't touching now, but there were mere millimetres between their bodies. His breath was cool on her cheek and his outdoorsy scent of salt air and pine was enfolding her as every inch of her began to sense every inch of him. An ache began to pulse low in the very centre of her.

He leaned in a millimetre further. 'DL Media pays for the hotel. You get dinner tonight. Deal?'

A compromise. Sensible, fair; no games, no coercion. The ache intensified, spreading upwards, downwards, everywhere. Her pulse speeded up. She wanted to lean in, to allow herself to feel him, touch him.

'Deal.' Ellie could hardly form the word. Her throat was dry. There was no air in this lift, no air at all.

At which point had she begun to notice him? Learned the way his hair curled despite its short cut trying to subdue it into businesslike submission? Learned the line of his jaw and the way his mouth curled sometimes in impatience, sometimes in disdain. sometimes in humour? Learned the gleam in the light brown eyes and the way they could focus on a person as if seeing right into their core?

How had she learned him by heart when she had been trying so hard not to see him at all?

Ellie took a step back, perspiration beading her forehead as the temperature in the suddenly too small lift rocketed. Could he tell? Could he tell that she was horrifyingly, intensely burning up with unwanted attraction? Not that it had that much to do with him *per se*. It had everything to do with three years of celibacy, emotional as well as physical.

She wasn't superficial enough to fall for a lazy smile and an air of entitlement. Oh, no. She had been blinded by charm once. She was just ready to move on, that was all. And he was a temporary fixture in her life. Safe. A two-week stop-gap. That was why he was the perfect person to hack through the forest and reawaken those long-dormant feelings.

Only he didn't feel quite so safe now.

'This way please, sir…madam.'

Thank goodness. The lift doors were open and there was her escape. A hotel room came with a bathroom, which meant one thing: a long and very cold shower. And forget all those good intentions regarding the mini-bar, Ellie needed a large glass of wine and chocolate and she didn't much care which came first.

And then she would give herself a very stern talking-to indeed.

Max stood back to let Ellie precede him out of the lift and she resisted the urge—barely—to press herself against the opposite side of the door and keep as much space between them as possible. He fell in behind her and she stiffened, all too aware of his step matching hers.

Cold shower, wine, chocolate, stern words.

Or maybe stern words, wine, cold shower, chocolate.

And a plan. A plan to start dating. There were single men in Trengarth. Sam was interested, she was almost sure of that, and there were more eligible bachelors. She would find them. She would track them down and she would have coffee and conversation just like any girl of twenty-five ought to.

Maybe even a stroll on a beach, if she was feeling daring.

'Madam, sir…this way, please.' The doorman opened a door and stood aside, an expectant look on his face.

Only it was one door.

One. Door.

Ellie stopped still.

'Madam?' There was a puzzled note in the smooth tones. 'The Presidential Suite…'

Ellie tried to speak. 'I…' Nope, that was more of a squeak. She coughed. 'Suite?' Still a squeak, but a discernible one.

There was a smothered sound from behind her and she narrowed her eyes. If Max Loveday was laughing at her then he was in for a very painful sobering up.

'Yes, madam, our very best suite. As requested.'

Ellie swivelled and fixed the openly grinning Max with her best gimlet glare. 'Suite?'

'My very efficient PA. She must have assumed…' He trailed off, but didn't seem in the least bit repentant. 'Chill, honey. I'm sure that the suite is plenty big enough, and if not I'll find you a broom cupboard somewhere.'

'I'm afraid the hotel is fully booked, sir.' The doorman didn't sound in the least bit sorry. 'If you would like to follow me?'

Stay in the corridor and sulk? Retrieve her bag from the doorman and head out into London to find a new hotel within her budget? Or walk into the suite like an aristocrat headed for the guillotine?

The tumbril it was.

On the one hand it was pretty demoralising to see just how much Ellie Scott *didn't* want to share a hotel suite with him. It wasn't that Max had expected or particularly wanted to share a room with her, but he hadn't faced the prospect with all the icy despair of one prepared to Meet Her Doom.

Plus, he wasn't *that* terrible a prospect. All his own hair, heir to one of the biggest family businesses in the world, reasonably fit and able to string a few sentences together. In some quarters he was quite the catch. But Ellie's ill-hidden horror burst any ego bubble with a resounding bang.

Although it *was* amusing to watch her torn between her obvious dismay at his proximity and her even more obvious open-mouthed appreciation of the lavishly appointed suite.

Goodness knew what Lydia, his PA, was thinking. She usually booked him into business hotels. More than comfortable, certainly, equipped with twenty-four-hour gyms, generous desk space and the kind of comprehensive room service menu that a man heading from meeting to meeting required. A world away from *this* boutique luxury.

This suite took comfort to a whole new level. It didn't say *business*, instead it screamed *honeymoon*—or *dirty weekend*. From the huge bath, more than big enough for two, to the fine linen sheets on the massive bed the suite was all about staying in.

Luckily for Ellie's blood pressure, it also came with a second bedroom. The bed there was a mere superking-size, and the bathroom came with a walk in shower and a normal-sized bath—but the large sitting and dining area separated the two, and Ellie had claimed the smaller of the two rooms in a way that had made it very clear that trespassers were most definitely not allowed.

And in the hour since they had first entered the suite she had clammed up in a way that showed just how discombobulated she was. Even now, walking down the wide bustling street, she was pale and silent. And it didn't matter, it shouldn't matter, but Max had quite liked the way she had opened up earlier.

The way *he* had opened up.

It had almost been as if they were friends. And it was only with the resounding sound of her silence that he'd realised just how few of those he had. Buddies? Sure. Lovers? Absolutely. Colleagues, teammates, old school and college alumni, relatives, people he'd grown up with—his life was filled with people.

But how many of them were real *friends*? He hadn't discussed his parents' bitter divorce, his doubts about his father's helming of the company with anyone. Not with a single soul.

And yet he'd unburdened himself to this slim, serious English girl.

If she froze him out now then he would be back to where he had started. Dealing with feelings that were seared into his soul, struggling to keep them under control.

Besides, it would be a long two days if she was going to make monosyllabic seem chatty.

Which tactic? Normally he would try and make her laugh. Keep up a flow of light-hearted jokes until she smiled. It was the way he had always dealt with frowns and stony silences.

And if that didn't work then he would walk away without a backward glance. After all, life was too short for emotional manipulation, wasn't it?

But somehow he didn't think that she was trying to manipulate him—nor that a quip would work here. And he was honour-bound to stay. It might be time to dig out honesty…

'I didn't plan to share a suite with you. I hope you know that?'

Ellie stopped abruptly, ignoring the muttered curses of the tourists and business folk who had to skirt around her. 'I *don't* know that. I don't know you well enough.'

'I hope you know me well enough to acknowledge that I would never be sleazy enough to go for the "accidentally booked one room" trick. I don't use tricks, Ellie. If I wanted you to share my bed I'd tell you—and you would have every opportunity to turn me down with no hard feelings.'

She looked hard at him, as if she were trying to learn his every flaw, as if she were burrowing deep into the heart of him. He tried not to squirm—what would she find there? A hollowness? A shallowness?

'Okay.' She started walking again.

'Okay?' *That was all?*

'I'm sorry I doubted you.' Her voice quietened and she looked straight ahead. He got the feeling she was avoiding his eye. 'My…my ex was all about tricks. It's all I know. I don't—' Her voice broke and his hands curled into fists at the hitch in her voice. 'I don't trust what's real. I don't trust myself to see it.'

'Well…' Maybe it was time to bring in light-hearted Max. He sensed she was already telling him more than she was comfortable with. He didn't want the distance to be permanent. After all, they were together for the next forty-eight hours. It might as well be fun.

It went no further than that.

'The joke would be on me if I *was* pulling a sleazy trick. The room between our bedrooms is the size of an average hotel foyer. I think we can both sleep safely tonight.'

'Your virtue was always safe with me,' she said, but she still didn't look at him, and Max noted a flash of red high on her cheekbones.Embarrassment—or something more primal?

The hotel was centrally located, right in the heart of London. Max had travelled to the UK on business many times and was familiar with the hotels, high-end clubs and restaurants of the buzzing city—but he had never wandered aimlessly through the wide city streets, never used the Tube or hopped on a bus. It was freeing. Being part of the city, not observing it through a cab window.

They had wandered south, moving towards the river as if led by a dousing stick, and were now on a wide open street. St James's Park opened out on one side, a city oasis of green and trees in stark contrast to the golden silhouette of Big Ben dominating the skyline in front of them.

'Looks like you got your wish.' Ellie seemed to have recovered her equilibrium. 'We're in tourist central. Shall I buy you a policeman's helmet or a red phone box pencil sharpener?'

'I think I want a Big Ben keychain,' he decided. 'And possibly a shirt that says "You came to London but all you bought me was this lousy T-shirt".'

'As long as you wear it tomorrow night. So what now? We could go into Westminster Abbey? Visit the park? I think I'm allowed in the Houses of Parliament, but I might have needed to arrange it with my MP first.'

'That would be cool. I'd like to watch all your politicians yell at each other. Are you allowed to bring popcorn?'

'Nope, only jellied eels.'

'Only *what*?' She had to be kidding, right?

'They're a London delicacy. All the English love them. We just keep it hidden so the rest of the world doesn't steal our national dish. We usually wash them down with some whelks and a pint of stout.'

'Very funny.'

She laughed. 'It's true. I bet I can find you a place that sells them—if you're man enough to try them.'

'I'll take the slur on my masculinity, thanks.' He shuddered at just the thought of the slimy fish.

'Coward. Right...what would tourists do? The palace is that way.' She pointed to the park. 'And we could take your photo with one of the guards at Horse Guards. That's always popular.'

'If only I was eight... Will we get invited to have tea with the Queen?'

'Now that you've dissed the national dish it's very unlikely. You don't graduate to cucumber sandwiches until you've mastered the jellied eels.'

'Just an unworthy Yank? Another dream shattered.'

Ellie ignored him. 'So, what will it be? Trafalgar Square? Covent Garden? Or we could see a show?'

'You know, I'm pretty much enjoying just walking. Is that okay?'

Surprise flashed across her face. 'Of course.'

Their route continued riverwards to a busy intersection. Cars were such an integral part of all US cities that Max never noticed their noisy intrusion, but they seemed wrong in this ancient city, beeping and revving in front of the old riverside palaces. The road bisected the great houses from the riverfront, with pedestrians crowded onto the grey pavements.

Ellie stopped on the tip of the pavement and directed an enquiring look across the bridge. 'Shall we cross over?'

Max raised an eyebrow. 'To the dark side?'

'It *is* south of the river, but I think we'll be safe.'

'I'll hold you personally responsible for my safety.'

If Max had truly been a tourist, and if he'd had his camera, then he would have stopped halfway across the bridge and, ignoring the mutters of the tourist hordes, photographed the iconic clock tower. But all he had was his phone.

'Come here.' He pulled it out of his pocket and wrapped an arm around Ellie. He felt her stiffen. 'Obligatory Big Ben selfie,' he explained. 'Smile!'

She relaxed, just an iota, but it was enough for her to lean a little further in, for him to notice that there was softness under that slenderness, that her hair smelt of sunshine and the colours were even more diverse close up: coffee and cinnamon, toffee and treacle, shot through with gold and honey.

It took every ounce of self-control he owned not to tighten his arm around her slim shoulders, not to pull her in a little closer, to test just how well they'd fit. Every ounce not to spin her round, not to tilt that pointed chin and claim her mouth. He ached to know how she would taste, to know how she would feel pressed against him.

'Smile!'

Was that his voice? So strained? So unnaturally hearty? But Ellie didn't seem to notice, pulling an exaggerated pout as he pressed the button on the camera.

'One more for luck.' Really he wasn't quite ready to let her go. Not just yet.

CHAPTER SIX

'I've got it!'

It was a little exhausting being a tour guide, especially in a city you didn't know that well. Ellie had grown up just thirty miles away from the capital, but her family seldom ventured into the big, bad city.

And when her friends had begun to travel in alone for gigs and shopping, and to find the kind of excitement missing from their little market town, Ellie had been stuck at home, unable to leave her grieving mother.

She still didn't know how her mother had been able just to shut down. To leave her daughter to make every decision, to take responsibility at such a young age for cooking and cleaning and hiding the fact that Ellie was basically raising herself from their neighbours and her teachers.

But Ellie had had no choice. If they had found out then what would have happened? What if she'd been put into care, the remains of her family shattered?

She had never allowed herself to resent her lonely teen years—at least not until she'd been unceremoniously swept aside when Bill had entered her mother's life. But now, as they wandered towards the South Bank, she couldn't help noticing the gangs of teenage girls dressed to the max, a little too loud, a little too consciously unselfconscious. Young, vibrant, free.

What would she have been if she had ever had the chance to find out who she was? If she hadn't been the dutiful daughter, the besotted young girlfriend too scared to open her mouth for fear of showing her lack of worldliness? And then later the terrified fiancée, softly spoken, anticipatory, as nervous as a doe in hunting season.

But today was her chance. Carefree, no agenda, no expectations—and did it matter if they did get lost?

'Got what?'

'Tourist activity number one.'

Ellie tucked a hand through Max's arm. It should have been a natural gesture. Friendly. He didn't know that she rarely touched another human being. That the protective cloud she kept swirled around her was physical as well as emotional.

Carefree Ellie wouldn't mind tugging Max down the steps off Westminster Bridge.

Carefree Ellie might be thinking of how it had felt when he'd pulled her in for that selfie. How strong he'd felt. How safe.

Might want him to touch her some more.

Max didn't resist as she pulled him down the steps. It was nice that he made no attempt to take control, to assert himself as the dominant force.

'Okay, don't keep me in suspense.' Max laughed as they came to a stop. 'Where are we headed?'

Ellie put her hands on her hips and shook her head. 'You've got eyes, haven't you? Use them.'

He looked around slowly. London's South Bank was as busy as always, crammed with tourists snapping pictures, kids on skateboards heading towards the famous skate park, people strolling on their way to Tate Modern, to the Globe, to the Royal Festival Hall. Others had stopped to browse at one of the many kiosks selling a myriad of snacks. Behind them a queue snaked out of the open doors of the London Aquarium.

The atmosphere was heated with expectation, with excitement, and yet it was inclusive and friendly, completely different from the fevered, crowded rush of Covent Garden or Oxford Street, more welcoming than the moneyed exclusivity of Knightsbridge.

I could like it here, Ellie realised with a sense of shock. It couldn't be more different from her seaside sanctuary, but there was a warm friendliness and acceptance that pulled at her.

'Um…' Max's eyes were narrowed in thought. 'Are we going to get a boat?'

'No. At least not yet. That might be fun tomorrow, though.'

'Go see some penguins?'

'Oh, I *love* penguins. We should definitely do that. But, no. I gave you a clue when I said to use your eyes.'

Ellie shifted from foot to foot, impatient with his slowness. How could he not see? The dammed thing had to be over one hundred metres high. It wasn't exactly inconspicuous!

She stared at him suspiciously. Was that a smile crinkling the caramel eyes?

'Isn't the Globe along here? Got a hankering for some Shakespeare?'

Every single suggestion sounded perfect, but she shook her head. 'Last guess.'

'Or…? What's the forfeit?' His smile widened. 'There has to be a forfeit or there's no fun…'

Ellie could feel her heart speeding up. A forfeit. Thoughts of kisses sprang unbidden into her mind, thoughts of a winner's claim. Could she suggest it? *Dare* she?

She could see it so clearly… Standing on tiptoe and pulling that dark head down to hers. That moment that felt as if it would last for ever when two mouths hovered, so close and yet not touching, and the *knowing*. The delicious anticipation of knowing that at any second they would meet.

Her stomach dipped. It had been so, *so* long since she had had a first kiss.

'Ellie?'

The teasing note in his voice flustered her, as if he had read her thoughts. Her cheeks flamed red-hot and she took a step back, all the daring seeping out of her.

'The loser has to buy the winner a souvenir that sums up the day. But it can't cost more than a fiver,' she added. 'That makes it more of a challenge.'

He just looked at her levelly, that same smile lurking in his eyes. 'You never did play dare as a kid, did you, Ellie? Okay, challenge accepted.'

'So? It's not penguins, at least not yet, it's not Shakespeare, and it's not a boat-ride. What's your final answer?'

He grinned wickedly. Damn him, he had been playing her.

'It's a good thing I'm not scared of heights, now… isn't it, honey?'

It soon became obvious that Max Loveday wasn't used to playing the ordinary tourist. Not that surprising, considering his background. From what he had let slip, his holidays were usually spent either in luxurious condos in the Bahamas or in the family home on Cape Cod. His was a life of private jets and town cars, VIP passes and prestige, and Ellie suspected that queueing hadn't played a huge role in his formative years.

It showed. He couldn't keep still, jiggling from foot to foot like an impatient child.

'How long is this going to take?' He craned his neck to look at the queue. 'Why is it so slow?'

'Because each pod only takes a certain amount of people.' Ellie smiled at an excited small girl standing in front of them, holding her mother's hand tightly. 'Be patient.'

'I could have hired out a whole pod just for us. Priority boarding, no standing in line, no sharing. Did you see that you can even have a champagne pod?'

Ellie shook her head at him, although it was hard to keep her mouth from smiling at his wistful tone. 'Yes, but that's not what tourists *do*. Tourists queue. Patiently. Take a selfie of yourself in the queue, and if you're good we'll play I Spy.'

He groaned at the pun and a flutter of happiness lifted her. It was a silly little joke but she had thought of it, shared it. With Simon she had been too busy trying to be informed and appreciative to find the courage to joke around.

She was only twenty-five. It wasn't too late. She looked down the queue: excited families, groups of friends chattering loudly, orderly tour groups patiently waiting. And couples. Everywhere. Arms slung around waists, around shoulders, leaning in, leaning on, whispering, kissing, together.

An ache pulsed in her chest. She had been so glad to get away from Simon, so relieved to be on her own, that the very thought of togetherness had repulsed her. But they had never been 'together' in that way. Not even in the beginning. Simon would never have queued, never have whispered affectionately in her ear, never sneaked a kiss or pulled her in for a longer and very public display of affection.

What must it be like? To be so wrapped up in somebody who was so wrapped up in you? Ellie stole a look at Max. He was leaning against the metal barrier, staring up at the iconic wheel. What would it be like to be wrapped up in Max Loveday?

All those first kisses, all those long walks with no idea about their destination, all those awkward first dates, all those long meals not even noticing the restaurant emptying around them—how many of those simple, necessary, life-affirming things had she been cheated of? How many had she allowed herself to be cheated of?

Maybe she'd licked her wounds in Cornwall long enough.

Ellie didn't say much as they waited—and waited—to board a pod. There was a thoughtful expression on her face that Max was reluctant to disturb, but she perked up when they were finally guided into the slowly moving pod—along with what seemed like hundreds of small uniformed children and two harassed-looking adults.

'I was definitely really bad in a past life,' he whispered to her as the kids crowded in, each of them yelling at what must be several decibels louder than legal limits.

Ellie raised her eyebrows. 'Just in a past life?'

'Believe me, a few student pranks and some adolescent attitude were not bad enough sins for *this* kind of cruel and unusual punishment.'

'They're having fun, though.' Her lips curved into a smile as she watched the children explore every inch of the pod.

'Yes,' he conceded as he steered her towards a corner. '*Noisy* fun. I vote we stand our ground here.'

'There's plenty of room.' But she put both hands on

the window and looked out. 'It's pretty slow, isn't it? I hardly feel like I'm moving.'

'Disappointed? I didn't peg you as a speed queen.'

She just smiled, and they stood in silence for a long moment as the wheel continued its stately turn, lifting them high above the city. The children quietened a merciful amount as their teachers started pointing out places of interest, and filled in the questionnaires they had all been issued with in great concentration.

The pod itself was spacious, its curved glass rising up overhead, providing panoramic three-hundred-and-sixty-degree views.

'I'm glad it's not see-through under our feet. I'm not sure I want to see the ground falling away.' Ellie shuddered.

'This was *your* idea,' he reminded her as he looked out at the incredible view. 'It's funny, you think of London as an old city, but there's so many skyscrapers. It's completely different to other European capitals, like Paris or Rome. Did you know there's see-through glass on the floor of the Eiffel Tower? Do you think you would be able to stand on that?'

'Possibly…I've never been to Paris, or to Rome.' Her voice was wistful and she continued to stare out at the skyline, her finger tracing it against the glass.

Max opened his mouth to make a flippant promise, but something in her eyes stopped him. If he ever made Ellie Scott a promise he'd need to keep it. And this was one he wasn't sure he could.

A day and a half of fun? An evening of black tie glamour? A joint project? None of them was a heavy or binding commitment. Not together or separately. So why did they feel so important? As if they meant more…as if they could mean everything… There was no way he could or *should* saddle himself with any other responsibilities towards this woman. He'd be back home in a week, and Trengarth nothing but a memory. And that was how it should be.

He had more than enough on his shoulders, thank you very much.

He kept his tone light, teasing, adding much needed distance with his flippancy, 'At the advanced old age of twenty-five you should get booking.'

She didn't respond to the lightness. 'I bet you've been everywhere. Business class and top hotels.'

He grinned at her. 'Totally unlike the hovel we're staying in tonight? DL Media have offices all over the globe. I've been to most.'

She turned then, looked at him with curiosity. 'So you only travel on business? What about for fun? For culture?'

There was a shocked undertone in her voice. It put him on edge, made him feel wanting in some way. As if he'd failed some test. 'I'll have you know there's a lot of culture in your average regional boardroom. And there's nothing as cultural as a red-eye flight and dinner at a five-star restaurant. What?'

She had started to say something and then stopped, as if she'd thought better of it.

She shook her head.

He eyed her narrowly. 'Go on.'

'It's just...' She hesitated again, biting down on her lip, her eyes not meeting his.

'Just...?' he prompted, resisting the urge to fold his arms and stare her down.

'It sounds a little lonely. I mean, you travel all over the world, and I don't really leave Trengarth, but in some ways we're both a little...' She paused, the big dark eyes fluttering up to meet his. 'A little trapped.'

Max couldn't hold back an incredulous laugh. *Trapped?* He was heir to one of the biggest companies in the world. He'd visited most of the major cities in the world. His life was golden—at least it had been.

'Honey, we are *nothing* alike. You choose to hide yourself away in your pretty little seaside village and let your life be lived through the books that you read. *My* life is about responsibilities you'll never understand. Family and employees and a heritage I need to be worthy of.'

She glared at him. 'I understand about family and I understand about responsibility. Scale isn't everything, Max. And if this is the first day you have really allowed yourself to get out of the business district and into the heart of a city then, yes, you are as trapped as I am. You may have set foot in Rome and Paris, but did you *see* them?'

Of course he had seen them! Through glass, mainly. Not like today, obviously, but there wasn't always time, and it wasn't *necessary.* His justifications sounded hollow, even as he thought them.

'The highlights, yes. But I was there to *work*, Ellie.'

'I see.' She turned away and stared out of the window. 'When *I* travel, finally, I want to see it all. Not just the bits the guidebooks show me. I want to walk through the alleyways and eat in the neighbourhood restaurants. I want to find the beating heart of the city and lose myself in it.'

'Then why haven't you?'

It took a while for her to respond, and when she did her voice was low, as if she were reluctant to admit the truth out loud.

'I was afraid. Afraid I'd be disappointed, afraid I'd get it wrong, afraid it wouldn't live up to my expectations. When you know how it feels to watch your dreams shatter it can be hard to trust in your dreams again.'

'What are your dreams now, Ellie?' His voice lowered as he moved closer to her, the pod all but disappeared, the children forgotten. There was just her and the hopelessness in her voice.

'Once they were the usual, I suppose. University, then a good job, and to fall in love and have children. Lots of children...' Her voice softened. 'I always wished I was part of a big family, and after we lost Dad and Phil I felt even more alone. That's why I loved books, I think. They were the only way I could escape, travel, try new things. I wanted to be Hermione or Lyra or Anne Shirley. Lonely children who forged their own path. Now...? I don't know, Max. I haven't dared dream in such a long time.'

'I've never thought about escape...' He hesitated. That was true, but was it the whole truth? 'I'm under pressure, sure, to be a Loveday is a pretty big responsibility. But it's a privilege too.'

'Do you still feel that way?'

He shook his head slowly. 'You're right. Now I just feel trapped,' he admitted, realising the truth of the words as he said them out loud. 'My dad wants my approval, my mom wants me onside, and the business needs me to do something clever—soon. It's like everything I grew up thinking I knew was a lie.'

'How so?'

He tried to make sense of his jumbled thoughts. 'We were picture-perfect, you know? Gorgeous house, plenty of money but not showy, members of the right clubs, giving to the right causes...and Grandfather in the centre of it, the benevolent tyrant. I thought he could do no wrong.'

He blew out a breath, some of the weight on his chest lightening as he finally spoke the heretical thoughts aloud.

'But underneath it all Dad was always resentful. I

think Grandfather kept him on a tight leash. *And* my mother. In public they were this affectionate couple, but now he's met Mandy I can't help wondering…' His voice trailed off.

'If any of it was real?'

Damn, she was perceptive. 'Oh, he had affairs. I always knew that. All the weekends Dad was working, the extravagant gifts he'd bring back. The hushed rows and then the insistence on putting on a good face in public. But underneath it all I was sure they really loved each other. Now it's all corroded—Mom is so bitter all she can think of is punishing him, no matter that it could bankrupt the company.'

Ellie drew in a deep breath, her eyes searching his face. 'That bad?'

'It's possible,' he admitted. 'And if lawyers get involved it could be a hundred times worse. That's why Dad wants me to negotiate with her. Meanwhile she wants me to promise not to ever engage with Dad's new girlfriend.' He could feel his mouth twist into the kind of cynical smile he'd never worn before this year. 'I guess I've always had to be the sensible one, the adult. I just never resented it before now.'

Her hand fluttered up and for one moment he thought she was going to touch his face. His chest tightened with anticipation, only for disappointment to flood through his veins as she lowered it again, tucking it behind her with a self-conscious gesture.

He leaned in, one arm on the glass beside her, his eyes fixed on hers. Not touching her, not even invading her space—not really—although the temptation to move that little bit further in was pushing at him…the need to move his hands from the glass to her shoulderblades. To allow them to slide down her narrow back. To feel her shiver under his touch, reining in the urge to rush, making them both wait.

But he couldn't.

Her eyes had widened, her breathing shallow and he didn't know if it was attraction or fear—he'd bet that *she* didn't really know either. There were times when he could swear that she was attracted to him: the way she smiled, ran a hand through her hair, peeped from under her lashes. Even in the line for the London Eye he had caught her looking at him with a speculation that had made his blood heat.

But the next moment she would shut off totally. She was as skittish as an unbroken colt. Part of him needed to know why, wanted to help her, protect her. But he had known her for what...? A few days? Who was he to walk into her life and arrogantly assume he could put it right?

He rocked back on his feet, casually letting his arm fall back, giving her the space she needed. He smiled at her, slow and sweet and as unthreatening as an ice cream sundae.

'Ellie Scott, I do believe we are breaking the rules.'

She was still frozen in place. 'We are?'

'We said we were going to have fun and, believe me, talking about my family is anything but. So, I am going to ask one of those nice teachers for one of their quizzes, and I am going to see if I can beat you and every single one of these ten-year-olds.'

'You don't know what the quiz is actually on.' The colour had come back into her cheeks and her shoulders had relaxed.

'I don't care. Honey, in my family we play to win. Monopoly, Clue, Mario Kart, Singstar—whatever it is, we do whatever it takes to win. And if that means bribing a ten-year-old for the answers, then watch me go.'

* * *

What would have happened if she'd smiled at him instead of standing there like a faun frozen in place by the White Witch? Would he have moved in closer? Would he have touched her? Kissed her?

What must he think? Whether he was just being friendly or was attracted to her he must think her gauche at best, ridiculous at worst.

Not that you would know, because within two minutes he had charmed two quiz sheets out of the bemused teachers and proceeded to barter, beg and bribe answers from the excited group of children, high-fiving them all when they finally exited the pod, the kids to go into the attached museum, Ellie and Max to begin a late-afternoon stroll along the side of the Thames.

'What now? Penguins?' he asked.

She looked at the queue, still snaking around the block, and pulled a face. 'It's a bit late. I don't think we'd get to the front before it shuts. Raincheck?'

'Look.' He stopped beside a poster. 'You can have afternoon tea with them. How cool! Do you think we have to eat raw fish too? I mean, I like sushi as much as the next guy, but I'm not sure I could manage a whole fish, bones and all.'

'Maybe the penguins like scones.' Her eyes flicked over the dates. 'The next one isn't till next month…the twenty-second.'

'Diary it in.' He flashed a grin at her. 'Penguins, sushi, and scones for two.'

'I wouldn't miss it for the world!'

'You still owe me a souvenir,' he reminded her. 'In fact two. I aced that quiz.'

'You cheated at that quiz.'

'The destination is all that matters. How you get there is irrelevant.' He began to stroll along, quite unrepentant.

'Do you really believe that?' Lots of people did, obviously. But she'd expected more of him.

He slid her a sidelong grin. 'Sure I do. Don't worry about who you kick on the way up, 'cause you have no intention of ever coming back down again. Survival of the fittest. Family mottoes, all of them. I bet Great-Aunt Demelza grew up cross-stitching them into samplers so we could hang them on our bedroom walls.'

'Oh, ha-ha.' But she didn't mind the teasing.

A glow spread through her as she watched him from the corner of her eye. Sauntering along, dark hair ever so slightly ruffled, the morning's stubble on his chin. Just another American tourist enjoying the London summer evening.

But not every tourist attracted admiring glances from the groups of girls they passed, and not everyone exuded such happy vibes. Which was a little bizarre, because when they'd first met she hadn't pegged him as the relaxed type. Arrogant? Sure. Rude? Most definitely. It was funny to think that if someone had told her just a few days ago that she would be spending time away with him, that he would make her laugh, make her heart beat faster, she would have laughed—and prescribed a course of wholesome children's books and some early nights.

And yet here she was.

And here *he* was.

She couldn't stop looking at him, fixating on the way the late-afternoon sun glinted on his bare tanned arms, highlighting every play of muscle. How it lingered on his strong, capable hands. Her eyes followed the sun's playful light as it danced over his wrists and along his fingers. What would it be like to hold them? To slide her finger over one knuckle? Could she? Would she dare? All she had to do was reach out.

She swung her hand a little closer in a pathetic experiment, snatching it back in a panic before allowing it to swing again. A jolt shot through her as her knuckles grazed his. It was all she could do not to cling on and never, ever let go.

'Ellie.'

He stopped and turned to face her. There was a simmering heat in his eyes…a heat that mirrored the liquid fire slipping through her veins, setting every nerve alight. Nerves that had spent so long dormant sprang to fiery life.

'If you want to hold my hand, honey, then all you have to do is take it.'

She gaped, trying to formulate some response, to deny it. But she was mute.

'But, Ellie…?'

There was a roughness to his voice, as if he was trying very hard to stay measured, to sound calm. She held his gaze despite the weakness in her knees, the tremors shivering through her. Despite the fear that she was making a mistake, the urge to retreat that was almost as strong as the urge to surge forward.

'Yes?'

'If you do then I *will* kiss you. Maybe not here, in front of all these people, and maybe not as we walk, but some time, at some point, I will kiss you. And you…' his eyes dropped to her mouth in an almost physical caress '…you'll kiss me back. Are you ready for that, Ellie?'

It wasn't the heat. Not in the end. And it wasn't the rough edge to his voice that spoke of want and passion. It wasn't his words and the arrogant assumption implicit in them. It was the tone. It was the look in his eyes. A look that said he needed her. That if she turned away he would accept it—and regret it.

And she? Would she regret it too? Just as she was beginning to regret the years she had spent hidden away, as safe as a nun in her convent and as chaste—not through vocation but through fear.

Ellie lifted her chin. She was done hiding and she was done living her life in the shadows. She was going to live. She was going to risk.

Slowly, hating the giveaway trembling of her fingers, she extended her arm and slipped her hand into his. His fingers closed around her, one at a time, softly, as if he knew not to spook her. His hand was warm, comforting, strong—and just the sense of skin against skin sent sparks dancing throughout her body. A line connected her fingertips to the pit of her stomach.

'Shall we?'

Max took a step forward and Ellie watched her arm move with him, feeling the tug on her body to fall into step behind him. And as if in a dream she followed, her stride matching his, their bodies working together. Fitting together.

She didn't know where they were headed, and right now she didn't much care. As long as her hand was in his they could walk for ever while she remembered what it felt like to yearn, to want to touch.

It felt good.

CHAPTER SEVEN

He still hadn't kissed her.

What kind of man promised a girl that he would kiss her and didn't deliver? He hadn't even come tantalisingly close. Not so much as an intimate smile all evening.

Not in their stroll along the South Bank, even though their hands had been entwined the whole time. Not as they'd perused the secondhand book stalls, nor as they'd bought milkshakes from one of the many vendors. Not over a glass of wine in a quaintly half-timbered pub, nor over dinner in a tiny Italian restaurant where the pasta had tasted the way Ellie had always imagined real Italian food would.

She'd closed her eyes and listened to the shouting from the kitchen, breathed in the mingled smells of tomato, basil and wine, and had almost imagined that she was in Rome at last.

And now they were returning to the hotel, retracing their steps along the riverside path, lit up and vibrant with the evening crowd. They were holding hands once again and he still hadn't made one single move towards her.

If she burst with anticipation it would be more than a little messy—and it would totally serve him right.

He shouldn't make promises he wasn't prepared to follow through.

'Are you tired? We could get a cab? Or,' he added a little doubtfully, 'as we're being tourists we could try buses. But I have to warn you they confuse the hell out of me.'

'Do they really confuse you or have you just never been on one?'

She was pretty sure it was the latter. He might be dressed down, but he was designer all the way at heart. She simply couldn't imagine him on a bus.

He grinned. 'Both.'

'I'm fine walking. I ate so much pasta I could do with the exercise.' *Very, very cool, Ellie.* That was definitely not in the 'Things to Say on a First Date' guide.

Not that this was. A first *or* a date. Obviously.

'I don't know what you're thinking, but I can tell there's a lot of wheels turning in that head of yours. Anything you want to share?'

How could he sound so relaxed? So amused?

Because this wasn't a first date. Holding hands with someone you'd known for a less than a week and only occasionally liked was probably completely normal to him.

'No.' She wasn't lying. She didn't want to share a single thought about dates or kisses with him. 'I'm not really thinking about anything. Just that it's nice to be out and about.'

'What shall we do tomorrow? The car is coming to pick us up at six and you'll probably need a good hour and a half to get ready...'

Ellie was about to interrupt. To tell him she only needed half an hour. A quick shower, brush her hair, slick on some mascara and lipstick and decide between her not that little black dress or her slightly longer black dress, put on her black almost-heels. It was hardly the routine of a diva.

Although she *could* visit the hotel spa and get her nails

done. It would probably wipe out her entire savings, but a little bit of pampering would be nice.

Ellie watched a group of girls totter past, only just balancing on their high strappy shoes. They were like a flock of exotic birds as they trilled and giggled in tiny, sheer summer dresses in emerald and cobalt blue, silver and sunshine-yellow.

Young, vibrant and alive.

She looked down. Skinny grey jeans. Again. High-top trainers. Again. Another short-sleeved tunic, black this time. Her hair was still twisted in the loose knot she had put it into that morning; her face was make-up free. The brightest colour in her wardrobe was a deep purple. She had switched the taupes and beiges that Simon had approved of for another colourless uniform. Another way to blend in.

The knowledge that she had chosen her own uniform didn't make it feel any better. Or any less constraining.

'Actually…' She spoke quickly before she changed her mind. 'I'll need longer than that. I might need the whole afternoon.'

Max's mouth quirked. 'Of course. *Just* the whole afternoon?'

Guilt pulled at her. 'I know we were supposed to be having fun. I'll be around in the morning to do something.'

'No, it's fine.' He pulled a face. 'I always planned to be in the office tomorrow anyway. I can't really play hooky on a Monday, and there's still so much to do in Trengarth even if I employ someone to empty the house, I might not get back to London this trip. Take as long as you need.'

He didn't tell her that she didn't need the afternoon, didn't waste time on fake compliments or try and talk her out of it. He respected her decision. That was great.

Or, more honestly, it was a little disappointing. But that was okay. She'd prove to Max Loveday that she could scrub up as well as any of his high-maintenance, trust fund, well-bred, moneyed usual dates.

And she'd prove to herself that it wasn't too late to take a chance.

He still hadn't kissed her. He knew that she wanted him to. Hell, she'd given him her hand, hadn't she? Had stared at him with those Bambi eyes and slipped those slender fingers through his, trembling as if she were abseiling over a cliff and he was her lifeline. It was a little terrifying.

It was intoxicating.

And he wanted to kiss her.

Wanted to so much he was almost trembling with it too. *Almost.*

And that was partly why he was holding back. This was a short trip and anything—anyone—he got entangled with had to be on a strictly short-term basis. Right now, what with all the crazy in his life, that was fine by him.

Besides, this was exactly what he didn't need long-term. This kind of messy emotion. Sure it felt right *now*, but what about next week? Next year? With an ocean between them and completely separate lives? It would be insanity.

Once he'd kissed Ellie would he remember that? Or would he be drawn in too far? Into something he didn't have the time or the head space to handle?

That was only partly it, though. Because it was all very well thinking about the future, but when all was said and done it would only be one kiss. But over the last two hours he'd sensed that it would be so much more to Ellie. Skittish, wide-eyed, and more vulnerable than she knew. It would be so easy to hurt her without even trying, and he didn't want to be that guy.

He shouldn't have offered…should have known better. But the words were said now. He couldn't take them back.

And honestly…? He wasn't sure he would if he could.

But he hadn't kissed her. Not yet.

Their walk was over in the blink of an eye. He must have found his way back to the hotel by luck rather than judgement, because all he'd been aware of was the feel of her hand in his. The knowledge that at any second he could pull her closer and she wouldn't stop him.

How could he not?

How *could* he?

Suddenly the shared suite didn't seem quite so funny, and the sitting-room separating their rooms seemed far too small. He wanted locks, corridors, possibly a couple of floors between them.

The hotel lobby was brightly lit, with the crystals in the chandeliers dancing rainbows, casting light onto the ornate gilt walls. Ellie seemed to have shaken off her earlier nervousness and walked confidently over to the reception desk, where a perfectly groomed woman sat. Heads together, voices low, they shared a long conversation before Ellie swivelled and walked back over to him.

'All set.' She had a mysterious expression on her face, like a child on Christmas Eve, ripe with secrets. 'Ready?'

'Absolutely.' *Not.*

Her didn't take her hand, stayed a safe distance away as they took the lift up to their floor, as they walked the few short metres to their suite. He stood gallantly back, allowing her into the sitting-room before him. But his promise was hanging in the air between them. It was in every questioning glance, every rise of her chest, every nervous flutter of her hands.

'Nightcap?' He shouldn't have made the suggestion, should simply say goodnight and get out of there. But his common sense had been overridden by his need to extend the evening even by just a few minutes.

Ellie was standing in the middle of the sitting-room, her slim, casually clad figure incongruous amongst the deep purples and gold luxury of the opulent suite. She looked as fresh as a wildflower set amidst hothouse blooms.

'No, thank you.' She turned slowly. 'I don't think I fully took this in earlier. It's very...'

'Gold?' he offered.

Her mouth tilted. 'It is that. It's all very imposing, isn't it? I'm not sure it's exactly homely, though. I can't imagine myself sprawling out on that sofa, for instance.'

Max took a deep breath. Ellie. *Sprawled. Sofa.*

His mind was full of images. Tousled hair, swollen lips, languid eyes, creamy skin...

'I would like to see that.' His voice was low, a rough rasp.

Time stopped. Her eyes flickered to his and stayed there. Neither of them able to look away as his words reverberated around the room.

It was no use. What was it they said about good intentions? And if his feet were already set on the path to hell then he might as well enjoy the journey.

'Max?'

He didn't know if she had said his name or just mouthed it, but it was too late. He was past the point of thought. Of common sense.

It took him just two strides to stand before her.

The blood was rushing through his veins, boiling hot, and his pulse was beating louder, harder than it had ever beat before. There was a deep ache in his chest that could only be assuaged by one thing. By her.

He stepped closer and waited, a bare millimetre between them. He needed her to make the final move, to show that she was in on this. Whatever 'this' was. Whatever 'in' meant.

'Ellie?' Not a command, not even a question. More a query.

Her eyes were huge, dark, desire mingling with doubt. He could overcome that doubt, kiss it out of her. But he waited. Waited for her to come to him. This had to be her decision.

His hands tingled, desperate to touch her, but he kept them at his sides.

She swallowed, a convulsive movement. Then she stepped forward.

They stood there for one second. It was an eternity. He could feel the full softness of her breasts against his chest, her legs just brushing his, her hands soft on his shoulders. Her face was tilted up towards his.

Max didn't know who made the next move. Whether or not she stood on tiptoe just as he bent forward. But their lips met, found each other as if of their own volition. And he was lost.

Lost in her scent, in her taste. Lost in the grip of her hands on his shoulders. Lost in the curve of her waist, the slenderness of her back as his arms encircled her to pull her closer.

He hadn't meant this. He had meant a soft kiss, a teasing kiss, a flirtatious kiss. But this…? This was hot and greedy and needy and all-encompassing.

He pulled her in closer, crushing her body against his, needing to feel her moulded to him. And she pressed closer yet, wrapped herself round him as if a millimetre gap was too much. And it was.

His hands moved up her back, learning her curves as

they went, until finally they were buried in the glorious weight of her silky hair. It was everything he had hoped for: fine, soft, wound around his hands.

All promises of not going too fast disappeared. He needed to see her clad in nothing but that hair...needed to explore every inch of her, touch every inch. And Ellie was with him every step, her soft hands burning a trail as they slid beneath his T-shirt, roaming across his back, across his chest, and then slowly, tantalisingly, but so very surely, moving lower, across his abdomen, and then lower still.

Max sucked in a deep breath as she reached his belt. Her hands were trembling but sure as she unbuckled his belt, moving her fingers to the first button on his jeans.

He caught her busy hands in his. 'Slow down, honey. We have all night.'

He allowed his voice to linger suggestively on the last two words and heard her gasp as his hands slid over hers, then moved slowly, oh, so slowly, his fingers caressing the soft skin of her wrists, her delicate inner elbow and up to her shoulders. He held her loosely for one moment, his lips travelling down, across her pointed chin, down her neck to feast briefly on her throat.

She was utterly still, her head thrown back to allow him access, the only sign of life her rapidly beating pulse, its overheated beat marching in step with the rapid thump of his heart. And then he moved, scooping her up in his arms, his mouth back on hers, needing, demanding, wanting as he carried her across the room and through the door. Her arms were wrapped around his neck, holding on tight, holding *him* tight.

There was no letting go. There was no going back. There was only this. Darkness, touch, moans and need. Only them. Clothes were pulled off with no care for little things like buttons. Impatient, greedy hands pushed barriers aside. Until there were no barriers left…

She should have been thinking, *What have I done?*

Instead all she could think was, *Can we do that again?*

Ellie had never had a morning after the night before. She had never done a walk of shame in last night's dress, with smeared make-up, shoes in hand, tiptoeing out through the door in the grey dawn light. Never woken up next to someone alive with the possibility of a new beginning.

She'd dated Simon for several months before they'd first slept together, and by then she'd been so besotted and so terrified of disappointing him that she had been unable to think or dream about anything but him. Her first thought on waking then hadn't been excitement or happiness but worry—the familiar gnaw of panic. Had she passed muster? Had her youth and inexperience been too obvious? Had she disgusted him?

She couldn't remember enjoying it. It had all been about *him*.

Now she could see that was exactly what Simon had wanted. Could see how he had fed on her toxic mixture of inexperience, loneliness and need. Had encouraged it until she had been exactly what he'd wanted her to be: compliant, dependent and afraid.

So waking up alone, sated, in a strange bed, naked and with every muscle aching in a curiously pleasant way was far too much of a novelty for a previously engaged woman of twenty-five. But there it was.

Alone. Ellie wasn't sure whether relief or indignation was at the forefront of her mind when she rolled over to pat nothing but cold sheets.

Relief that she didn't have to worry about her hair, her

breath, the etiquette—should she go in for a kiss or sit up primly and pretend that she *hadn't* nibbled her way over his entire body in lieu of dessert?

Or indignation that she was waking up alone with just a note to remind her that she hadn't dreamt the previous night? *A note!*

There it was on the bedside table, crisp and white like in a scene from a film.

Dear Ellie
You looked so peaceful I didn't like to wake you. I should never have agreed to go in to the office—they called a meeting for nine a.m.

Hope your day is a lot more fun than mine. I'll pick you up at six. Enjoy.
Max
PS Room Service is on DL Media, so go wild. One of us should.

Hmm… She read it through again. It wasn't a love letter—there were no declarations of undying devotion—but neither was it a 'Dear John'. It was something in between.

Which was about right, she supposed.

Ellie rolled over and stretched, enjoying the sheer space of the enormous bed. She could lie lengthways, diagonally, horizontally and still sprawl out in comfort. In fact, now she was thinking about it, she had covered pretty much every inch of the bed last night.

Heat returned to her cheeks as images flashed through her mind, her nerves tingling in sensory recognition. She sat up and looked at the rumpled pillows, the dishevelled sheets. At the clothing still distributed across the room.

Her jeans, her tunic. Oh, goodness! Was that her comfortable yet eminently sensible bra?

She covered her face with her hands. Her first ever night of red-hot seduction and she had been wearing underwear as alluring as a nice cup of tea and a custard cream.

At least she hadn't been wearing it for too long. And Max hadn't seemed to have had any complaints. Not judging by the intake of breath when he'd pulled her tunic over her head, and not judging by the heat in his eyes when he had looked at her as if she were the most desirable thing he had ever seen.

Had that been *her*? Prim Ellie Scott? So wanton, so demanding, so knowing? And now that she had allowed that side of her to surface could she lock herself away again? Slide back into her hermit ways and keep this side of herself hidden?

The thing was, she didn't want to explore it with just anyone.

Ellie slumped back onto the bed, the twist of desire in her stomach knotting into dread.

'It's a crush,' she said aloud, emphasising every word slowly and clearly. 'You can't fall in love with someone after a week. Not because they quite fancy you and make you laugh. You are *not* going to become besotted with someone you barely know. Not again.'

It was as if cold water had been thrown over her. All the fire, all the sparks at her nerve-endings extinguished by reality. Ellie shivered, pulling the quilt back over her body, wanting to be warm, to be comforted. To be hidden away.

I won't let the memory of Simon spoil this, she told herself fiercely, blinking hard, refusing to let the threatening tears fall. *I am older, I am most definitely wiser, and I am not the naïve little girl I was back then. I know what this is and I can handle it. He'll be flying back home in just over a week. Enjoy it.*

She pulled the quilt tighter still, letting its warmth permeate her goosebumped body. This was supposed to be fun, not a trip down Memories I Would Much Rather Forget Lane.

She had plans today. Big, scary and long overdue plans. What was she going to do? Hide in this bed until six or get up, get dressed and follow through? She had allowed Simon to control the last three years of her life just as much as he had controlled the three years they had spent together. She might have plucked up the courage to leave and start afresh, but she hadn't moved on... not really.

And now Max. Offering her the opportunity to explore a new side of herself. A more adventurous side. To be the Ellie she'd always intended to be before her life had been so brutally derailed.

She could take the opportunity he was offering—or she could pack up and go home. Hide away with her books for the rest of her life.

Ellie sat up again and pushed the quilt away. She was going to get up, she was going to order the most decadent breakfast on the room service menu, and she was going to follow every single part of her tentative plan.

And today was the very last day she was going to allow Simon to cast a shadow over her life. He wasn't going to taint a single second of her future. She was finally going to be free.

Meetings, meetings, meetings... Normally Max's head would be spinning with the day he had spent. The London office was the most important after their New York headquarters, and on Max's last visit eighteen months ago it had been a vibrant place full of enthusiasm and talent. Now it was full of fear, with people clinging on to their jobs determinedly or leaving, like rats jumping from a ship before they were pushed.

His father hadn't even been over, having sent in management consultants instead to shake things up. They had certainly managed that—the MD Max had worked so successfully with was long gone and in his place a board full of yes-men with no ideas of their own.

It had put the present state of DL Media into stark perspective. Max might have no appetite for a family rift, but he didn't have much choice. There was far too much at stake: jobs, the company's reputation. His grandfather's legacy.

It should be weighing on his mind, his mood should be murkier than a classic London peasouper, and yet all he had wanted all day was to stride out of that infernal boardroom, find Ellie and take her right back to bed. And stay there. The awards ceremony be damned.

He curled his hands into loose fists and took in a deep, shuddering breath. He could have made his excuses and gone. But he had stayed. Because when the chips were down he was a Loveday. Old school. Bred in his grandfather's image. So he had stayed, listened, learned and reassured.

He had ordered his dinner suit to be brought to the building, the car to pick him up straight from there. Had put the business first and his own desires second.

Like a Loveday should.

But it all felt so hollow. No thrill of business. Just the sense of another day wasted. Thank goodness for tonight.

Only Ellie wasn't waiting in the foyer. The car had

pulled up outside the hotel and for ten minutes Max waited, his phone in his hand, sending email after email to his long-suffering PA. She had been expecting a quiet week or two. Well, this was going to put paid to any plans she might have had of stepping up her flirtation with Eduardo in Accounts.

Another minute, another email.

Max checked the time. Ellie was fifteen minutes late.

Had she got his note? Had he not been clear? Had she taken offence and hightailed it back to Cornwall? He'd meant to call. He *should* have called.

But for once in his glib life he had been unsure what to say. *Thank you*? *That was incredible*? *All I can think about is touching you*?

He bit back a laugh. Absolutely pathetic. But he still couldn't think of anything better.

He checked his watch again, aware of the chauffeur's eyes on him, the engine idling. He could call.

Or he could go and get her. A gentleman always did. What would his grandfather say if he could see him sitting in a car waiting for her to come to him? He would be horrified.

It only took him a couple of minutes to walk up to their suite, but Max's heart was hammering as if he had climbed to the top of a skyscraper. He was convinced that he would open the door and be confronted by an empty suite. That he had blown it.

He had never worried before. Never waited, never chased. The second it got demanding or difficult he was out of there. He knew all too well where tears, tantrums and demands led. Had grown up with their devastation.

The door handle was slippery in his hand, reluctant to turn, but finally he had swung the door open and he strode into the opulent sitting-room.

'Ellie?'

'I'm in here.' There was nervousness to her voice, a hint of panic. 'Sorry… It all took a little longer than I thought. High-maintenance really is a full-time job. Are we late?'

Max didn't know just how deep a breath he was holding until he heard her voice. The relief hit him with an almost physical force.

'No, my grandfather told me to always pick a time half an hour in advance. It's never steered me wrong yet.'

'Then I've been panicking for nothing?' Her voice had switched from nervous to indignant. 'Honestly, Max, that was mean.'

He was going to reply. He was. But then she appeared at the door and he couldn't say anything at all. All he could do was stare. He was aware in some dim corner of his mind that his mouth was hanging open, and with some effort he snapped it shut.

And then he stared some more.

Gone was the elusively pretty girl. Here instead was a stunningly beautiful woman.

'Ellie? Wow. You look…' It wasn't the smoothest line, but it was all he could manage. Then, 'You cut your hair.'

That shimmering mass was gone. In its place was an edgy bob, cut in sharp layers. It framed her face, emphasising her eyes, her chin, her defined cheekbones.

'Yes.' Her hand reached up to touch the ends, tentative, as if she couldn't quite believe it. 'I thought it was time.'

'You look incredible.' His voice was hoarse and he couldn't stop staring.

From the tips of her newly styled hair and her heavily kohled eyes to the scarlet dress, bare at her shoulders, tight-fitting down her torso, then flaring out to mid-thigh, this was a new, dangerous, deeply desirable Ellie.

'Is it too much?' The expectant expression on her face had been replaced with panic. 'Am I overdressed? Have I gone a bit over the top? I can change.'

Yes. She was. Simultaneously over and underdressed. Overdressed because he wanted to tear that dress off her right now. And underdressed because he wasn't sure he wanted his colleagues to see quite so much of her creamy skin. He knew just what long, perfect legs she had. He just didn't want anyone else to appreciate them. Maybe she had a shawl? And some leggings?

He shook his head. What was happening to him? He was thinking like a Neanderthal. His last ex had spent most of the spring in tightfitting yoga pants and a crop top and he had never once cared.

'Max?'

He held out his hand. 'No, don't change a thing. You are absolutely perfect.'

CHAPTER EIGHT

ELLIE HAD ALWAYS thought that she hated small talk.

Standing at Simon's side, her role had been to agree with him. It had been the easiest and the safest thing to do. He wouldn't retreat into one of his terrifying sulks if she didn't say anything wrong.

Of course she couldn't be too mute—then he would accuse of her being dull, of not trying hard enough. No, it had been easier to agree with him at all times.

Tonight was as different from a night out with Simon as a glass of vintage champagne was from cheap lemonade.

Max had made no attempt to keep her near him. But his eyes sought her out as she moved from group to group, catching her gaze with an intimate smile that heated her through. And he'd made sure she was introduced to his companions, supplied with a drink. If she found herself alone even for a second then he was there, as if by magic, ready to introduce her to another key contact.

He would whisk her away, off into a corner, every now and then. She usually had to slip into the cloakroom afterwards and reapply her lipstick. Every time she did she would stop and look at the girl in the mirror. The girl with the emphasised eyes, the choppy hair. The girl in the red dress.

She couldn't hide. Not like this. Her dress was so

bright, the cut exposing far more of her arms and legs than she ever usually showed, her hair left her face and her shoulders bare, and her make-up was dramatic.

She was so used to hiding behind her hair she felt exposed without it. But she also felt free, reinvented. It had been long for so many years: one length for her ballet dancing youth, uncut in her teens because her father had loved it so, and her mother would have been devastated if it was cut.

And Simon had liked long hair on women.

She had thought about changing it, in the three years she had spent in Trengarth, but had clung on to the security blanket it offered.

There was no blanket now.

This girl had to mingle, to talk.

And people wanted to talk to *her*, to know her, to discuss her shop, the tentative festival plans. They were interested in her thoughts, in her perspective.

It was a heady experience. For so long she had listened to the voices in her head telling her she was too young, too inexperienced, that she was hampered by her lack of a degree, unable to follow her dreams—and yet at some point in the last three years she had accumulated huge amounts of industry knowledge.

She was on the front line. She knew what people wanted to read, how they wanted to purchase it, what made them angry, excited—and what left them cold. Her best book club meetings were always those where the participants were polarised. And here she was, surrounded by people who spoke her language, people who knew the prefix to most ISBN numbers, got excited by new covers and new releases. People who openly admitted to sniffing the crisp new pages of a paperback book. She was in her element.

And Max allowed her the freedom to fly.

He didn't look as if he were having quite so good a time. Oh, sure, to the casual observer he probably looked as if he was enjoying himself, standing in a group, his stance relaxed, a smile on his face. But there was a tension in his shoulders, a crinkle around his eyes that gave Ellie an inkling that he was hiding his true feelings.

Not surprisingly, here in a room full of industry professionals, rumours about DL Media were running rife. And there was no escape for him in the endlessly moving, speculating, keen-eyed crowd. He wouldn't even be able to relax over dinner. There were no formal tables nor a sit-down meal. Instead endless trays of canapés circulated. It was like dinner in miniature: teeny tarts, quiches, curls of lettuce hiding a quail's egg in their leaves, delicate slivers of cheese and quince.

Normally the very word 'circulate' would bring Ellie out in a cold sweat, but tonight she was managing it effortlessly…despite the pinch of her new and alarmingly high shoes. She had a glass of wine in one hand, something delicious swiped off a passing tray in the other, and interesting conversation.

It beat The Three Herrings pub quiz. Well, apart from the night she had helped win it. That had been pretty spectacular.

'So, DL Media are sponsoring your festival?'

Ellie had to pinch herself as she remembered that she was talking to an agent: a real, live literary agent whose clients included several of her favourite authors.

He tilted his head to one side, his eyes sharp. 'Does that mean you'll only be working with their writers?'

'No!' It wasn't the first time she had heard this. News obviously spread through the publishing world at the same speed with which it rushed through Trengarth—

and with the same accuracy. 'The sponsorship comes from Demelza Loveday's personal estate. Max is festival director, but as a family member, not a representative of DL Media.'

'A good thing, if half the rumours I've heard are true.' The agent's eyes were still fastened on her questioningly. 'Is it true their book publishing division is being sold off?'

'I heard they were going digital only.' Another person had joined the group, her face avid with the desire for information.

'Either way, I would be *very* concerned about placing a client with them,' said the agent.

'All rumours of DL Media's demise are very much exaggerated.'

Max's drawl broke into the conversation, much to Ellie's relief.

'It is possible to be both cutting edge *and* traditional, you know. Ellie, I believe the awards are about to start, and they want nominees to be near the front. Just in case your name gets called. Excuse us, please…duty calls. Here's my card. Call me. I am more than happy to continue this conversation with you later.'

His voice was calm, with that slightly arrogant edge, but the hand that held Ellie's arm was gripping tightly.

'Vultures,' he muttered.

'They're just trying to pry.'

'They're not *trying*. They're doing a fine job.' He shook his head. 'Just a hint of this kind of instability and the whole company could crumble faster than a sandcastle at low tide. You heard Tom Edgar then. If he isn't going to consider our bids then we could lose out on new authors, or on re-signing profitable ones. He has a lot of clout.'

'So what are you going to do?'

'Right now? Smile, deny, and make sure you have a great evening. Tomorrow…? Tomorrow I make some serious plans. Right, no more looking so downcast. This isn't my night. It's yours. We need to be ready to toast your success as Independent Bookseller of the Year.'

She laughed, the embarrassed heat flooding her cheeks. 'Shush, this is England. We don't boast. We shuffle in a self-deprecating way and mutter that every other competitor is far more deserving and we didn't expect to win anyway.'

'Ah, but you're with an ignorant Yank, and *we* shout our successes loud and proud.'

'I haven't actually won,' she pointed out.

'Yet.' He was looking more relaxed, the lines of strain around his mouth evening out. 'I for one am ready to cheer very loudly indeed.'

'Shh!' But she was smiling. 'It's about to start.'

It was a very long ceremony. It seemed as if there was no aspect of the book trade, from industry blogs to conferences, supply chains to sales reps, that wasn't being honoured. Ellie shifted from aching foot to aching foot, wishing she had actually tried walking in her shoes before buying them.

'You're on.'

Max's breath skimmed over her ear as he whispered, the warmth penetrating her skin, and the desire to lean back warred with the nerves jumping in her stomach like a basket of naughty kittens.

'I wish we hadn't come,' she murmured, and he chuckled, low and deep, a hand at her back. To reassure her or to keep her there? Not that she could run away in these shoes…

Best Chain Bookstore, Best Bookshop Manager, Best

Event Organiser… On and on the awards went, and the pain in her feet competed with the increasing nausea gnawing away at her.

'Ellie Scott!'

The sound of her name echoed around the room as applause and a couple of cheers greeted it. She stood rooted to the spot in disbelief and embarrassment as, true to his word, Max whooped.

'Me?'

'Go on.' He gave her a gentle push. 'They're waiting for you.'

Ellie hadn't lied when she'd said she didn't expect to win—she worked alone, in a small shop miles away from the capital. Who *knew* her? Of course a quirky city independent would win, she hadn't even bothered to prepare a speech.

The sound of Max's continuing whoops rang in her ears as she stumbled in her unaccustomed heels to the podium. The glare of the lights, the people—so many people—all staring at her, smiling at her. Waiting for her.

Waiting for her to speak.

She was alone under the spotlight of their gaze. Once, long ago, she had enjoyed drama lessons, even taken part in school plays. Now she could barely recognise that girl who had soaked up the audience's attention, but there must be some residual atom of her left, because her shoulders straightened, her voice strengthened.

'When I opened a bookshop people said I was crazy…' A ripple of amusement passed through the crowd and, emboldened by their response, she carried on. 'They thought I should open a coffee shop and have a few books dotted around. Well, I do have a temperamental coffee machine. But it's not the main attraction. The books are.'

She paused, trying to formulate her thoughts.

'It's not easy, and if I had a pound for every time someone has told me the book trade is dead my cash flow would be incredible. I can't compete with the internet giants. I can't stop people browsing and buying the eBook later. But I can—I can and I *do*—offer a tailored service. I can make book-buying fun, informative and easy. I can *recommend.* Of course I have to diversify, and not just with coffee. I run book groups for all ages, knitting groups, craft groups. I go into local schools and playgroups and to WI meetings. I open seven days a week and I stay open late.'

She looked out over the anonymous sea of people and swallowed, panic beginning to twist her chest. Who was *she* to think that she could tell one single person in this room how to sell books? Who did she think she was?

She was twenty-five, and she had run her own business for three years. She wasn't rich, but the shop was in the black and they had chosen *her* to win this award. That was who she was.

'Next year I'll diversify even further, when I curate the first Trengarth Literary Festival. But at the heart of all this diversification is one very simple mission. To get the great stories around out there, into people's hands. That's what they want. Great stories. You keep producing them and I'll keep selling them. Thank you.'

'That was pretty amazing.' Max sat back in the taxi. Amazing for Ellie, a battle for him. But he wasn't going to ruin her triumph by telling her so.

'I know!'

Ellie was glowing, the streetlamps spotlighting her in gold as the car drove them through the well-lit streets. Her hair shone, her dress glittered, but the most luminous thing of all was her smile, stretched wide across her face.

'I spoke to so many lovely people and they were so kind. Loads of them want to be part of the literary festival. I have so many business cards I don't know where to start. I thought the first year would be a really small affair, but it really looks like we might attract some big names.'

'And thanks to Great-Aunt Demelza you can actually *pay* your participants,' he reminded her. 'From what I hear that's by no means usual...especially for start-up festivals. Many of them rely on goodwill alone. A pay cheque will definitely pull people in. But I wasn't talking about the festival. I was talking about *you*. About your speech.'

'Oh...' She flushed, her cheeks coming close to matching the vibrant colour of her dress. 'That wasn't a speech. It was...'

'A call to arms?'

'No! A few panicked words, that's all.'

He inched a little closer on the seat so their legs were touching, his knee firmly pressed against hers like a high school boy on a first date, sharing a booth. 'You inspired me.'

'Really?'

'Oh, yes. In fact you have been inspiring me all evening.'

'Inspiring you to concentrate on the books side of the business?'

He slid his hand up her leg. Her stockings were a flimsy barrier. How much further was the hotel?

'Amongst other things.'

Her eyebrows rose as she leaned a little closer, her body heating him wherever they touched.

'We *do* have a day of missed fun to make up for. You spent it in meetings and, although some women might find spas and boutiques relaxing, I was terrified the whole time. We could both do with some relaxing.'

'Is that so? And did you have anything in particular in mind?'

Ellie put her hand over his, the pressure moulding his fingers around her leg. 'I'm sure we can work together to think of something.'

Her hand was warm, her fingers wound through his. Was this really the same girl who had jumped like a skittish kitten whenever he touched her? Had the dress and radical haircut given her a new confidence? Or had she been there all the time? Hidden behind the layers and the no-nonsense demeanour?

If only there was more time to explore her, to explore *them*.

'It's our last night in London. We should make it memorable.'

It did no harm to remind her—to remind himself—that this trip was finite. That although he would be returning to Cornwall with her in the morning his holiday was nearly at an end.

'Real life again tomorrow.' She sounded wistful. 'I didn't even want to come here and I've had such an amazing time. I'm not quite ready for it to end—and we didn't get to see the penguins.'

Was she talking about not wanting the trip to end—or not wanting to stop spending time with Max himself? His hand stilled under hers.

'The penguins aren't going anywhere. We could see them in the morning.'

'No, I need a reason to make sure I come back. Besides, now I know I can have scones with them I won't settle for anything less.'

'Of course you'll come back. *We'll* come back.'

We? Where had *that* come from? Max didn't usually like to make plans too far in advance. Previous relationships had begun to fracture when he had refused to commit to a wedding or a family party several months in advance.

Here he was making promises for an unspecified future date.

And it didn't make him want to run.

It was because they had barely begun. He might not be the king of long-term relationships, but neither was he a one-night stand kind of guy. He liked a relationship to run its course.

That was why he was feeling odd about knowing he would have to leave in the next few days. She would be unfinished business, that was all.

'Max?'

She was sitting there, her hand still in his, as lost in her own thoughts as he was in his.

'Yeah?'

'Thank you.'

'Honey, you don't have to thank me for anything.'

'No, I *do.*' She paused, pulling her hand away from his and shifting in her seat so that she was looking directly at him. 'I didn't want to admit it, especially not to myself, but I *was* hiding in Trengarth. I'm twenty-five and the highlight of my week is the pub quiz at The Three Herrings. And I only turn up to that once every few months.'

His body tensed. 'Why were you hiding?'

She didn't answer for a moment, her hands twisting in her lap. 'I didn't trust myself.' Her voice was low, as if she were in the confessional. 'I made a couple of bad choices. I think it made me afraid to try again. After Dad and Phil died Mum clung to me. I let that be my excuse for putting off university, for not starting my own life. But I think I was just too scared. Losing them was like losing a part of myself, losing my identity, and I just couldn't pick myself up again.'

He couldn't imagine it…having your life ripped apart before it had fully begun. 'You were very young.'

Her mouth turned up in a sad approximation of a smile. 'I suppose. But at home I had to be the adult and I allowed it. I allowed Mum to rely on me…allowed her neediness to define me. So when she met Bill and didn't need me any more it was like…like…'

'Like you'd lost everything?'

'Yes. It was exactly like that. And then there was Simon. I was so vulnerable, so lonely when I met him. I guess he sensed that. I thought he was my knight in shining armour. He was ten years older than me and so sure of himself. I was blinded by him, by what he wanted from me I didn't have to figure myself out.'

She had barely mentioned her past, and her fiancé had been no more than a name, but Max's jaw clenched at the sorrow and hurt in her voice. It hadn't been just a relationship gone wrong. She had been badly wounded and her scars evidently still ran deep.

His hands curled into fists. How could anyone hurt her? Strip away her confidence?

'I was so proud of myself for getting away. I thought it was enough…thought that I was finally living the life I wanted. I live in a place I love, doing something I feel passionately about. And those are *good* choices. They *do* make me happy. But as a human being I am still a complete mess. I don't have many friends, and I don't leave my comfort zone. Not ever. I didn't dare dream of anything else, anything more. Especially not romance. Especially not love.'

Her voice broke a little on the last word.

Max was frozen. What was she saying? Was she saying that she was falling in love with him?

Surely not? Not after a week?

Sure, last night had been utterly incredible, but that wasn't love. Was it? It was passion. It was mutual understanding. It was compatibility. And, yes, he liked the way her smile lit up her whole face, turned mere prettiness into true beauty. He liked the way she was so cool and poised on the outside and yet fire and heat inside. He liked the way she stood up for what she believed in, even when it scared her to stand up and be counted.

But that wasn't love either, was it?

Love was messy and painful and loud and selfish. Love meant to hell with the rest of the world. Love meant operating on your terms, your way, no matter who got hurt. And when it went wrong you were left defenceless, revenge your only weapon.

He couldn't risk that. Couldn't be that vulnerable. There were other ways, better ways. It might sound cold: a timetable, a wish list and a criteria. But it was the key. The key to a quiet, successful life.

Although the truth was he had never met anyone who'd tempted him to more than a nice time. Anyone who'd made him want to make plans months in advance. Never met any woman he couldn't walk away from the moment things got difficult or messy.

Did that mean he was no better than his dad?

Maybe he was just a coward.

The silence had stretched wafer-thin. He needed to say something. He had no idea what to say.

'And how do you feel now?'

He held his breath. Would she make some kind of declaration? It was fine if she did. He knew it wasn't real. It would be the adrenaline from the evening, hormones still racing around after last night. If she had really been single, hadn't so much as dated in the last three years, then no wonder she was turned upside down by the attraction raging between them. It had discombobulated *him* after all.

He just needed to handle the situation with tact, with gentle skill.

Ellie leaned back in her seat. Her hands stilled. 'I feel ready to start living again. I am completely buzzed about the festival, about the work that lies ahead. And I'm not going to hide away any more. I'm going to go out there, start living, start dating again. Last night…yesterday… the whole week…' She trailed off. 'It's made me think. Think about who I want to be, *what* I want to be. And a lot of that is down to you. So, thank you.'

'You're welcome.'

Not a declaration. Not a grand passion. She wasn't in love with him. She was already thinking ahead. Thinking past him.

Which was great.

Wasn't it?

So why did he feel…well, *deflated*? Like a hot air balloon failing to lift off into the sky?

'No, I mean it. Last night was amazing. I didn't know I could feel like that, act like that. I'd never…'

She laughed. A low sound that penetrated deep into his bones, into his blood.

'I didn't think I would ever feel that free, that wanted. You showed me how it could be…how it *should* be.'

'It wasn't just me.' Max was uncomfortable cast in the role of Professor Higgins, and Ellie was certainly no Eliza Doolittle, ready for him to pluck, mould and shape. 'I think you were ready. I just provided the opportunity. Your hair, that dress…that's all you.'

The car had pulled up in front of the hotel. This was it. He would lead her back up to their suite and hopefully unzip that tight-fitting bodice, learn her body just a little bit more. Then tomorrow they would return to Cornwall and say their goodbyes. No hard feelings. Just warm memories. He would be free to sort out all the problems with DL Media and his parents; she would be free to start her new and more exciting life. A life he had helped her to kick start.

How very altruistic of him.

He couldn't have planned it better.

And he might feel a little hollow inside *now*, but give him a week and Cornwall, London and Ellie Scott would all be distant memories. His life was complicated enough without adding long-distance relationships to it.

Besides, she didn't even want a relationship. Not with him. And that was absolutely fine.

Had she said something wrong?

Max's hand was around her waist, his fingers absent-mindedly caressing the silky material of her dress, every touch sending sparks fizzing along her nerve-endings. The shock of winning, the champagne, the buzz of the whole evening and the last twenty minutes in such close proximity to Max had combined to create a perfect maelstrom of excitement—and she knew just the perfect way to work it out.

She tapped her foot, willing the lift on. As far as Ellie was concerned they couldn't get back to the privacy of their room soon enough.

But Max was distant, mentally if not physically, and had been for most of the journey. Was he thinking about work? Planning his next step? The room tonight had twittered with gossip over DL Media's crisis. It had to be weighing on him.

She'd miss him. It had only been a week, but he had made such an impact on her life, crashing into it like a meteorite and shaking up everything she'd thought she knew, thought she wanted, thought she was. He'd challenged her, excited her, pushed her.

It was only natural that she would miss him. But his life was far, far away…a whole ocean away. And she hadn't even started to live hers yet.

It was time she did.

His arm remained around her waist as they walked the few short steps from the lift to the suite door, stayed there as he unlocked it and ushered her in.

The velvet cushions, gilt trimmings, opulent colours and brocade hangings hit her again with their over-the-top luxury. Ellie had somehow grown fond of their ridiculous suite. She had been reborn there. In less than forty-eight hours had made some huge changes. She just hoped that back in her own home she could keep the clarity and confidence she had gained here.

'Congratulations again. I thought we should celebrate.'

Max steered her over to the glass table. A complicated arrangement of lilies, roses and orchids dominated its surface, flanked by a bottle of vintage champagne chilling in an ice bucket, a lavish box of chocolates and a small purple tub.

'Champagne?'

Max followed her gaze. 'This is the hotel's Romance Package,' he murmured, his mouth close to her ear, his breath warm on her neck. 'Champagne, chocolate and massage oil.'

His eyes caught hers, full of meaning. Wherever he had been he was back. Back with clear intent.

He reached out and plucked the tub from the table. 'Sensual Jasmine with deep chocolate and sandalwood undertones. Feeling tense, Ellie?'

The promise in his voice shot straight through her.

Ellie shivered. 'A little.' It wasn't a lie.

'That's good. We can do something about that.'

Ellie swallowed, her eyes fixed on the small purple tub as he casually twisted it round and round in those oh, so capable fingers. 'We can?'

'Oh, yes. But you may want to disrobe first. I believe these oils can get rather…' His smile was pure wicked intent. 'Messy.'

'Messy?' Had she just squeaked?

'Oh, yeah. If you do it right, that is.'

She'd bet a year's takings that Max Loveday would do it right.

She stood there dry-mouthed as he picked up the bottle of champagne, deftly turning the wire and easing out the cork with practised ease.

'Well?' He poured champagne into one of the two flutes waiting by the bottle. 'What are you waiting for?'

Did he mean…? 'You want me to take my dress off?'

'Honey, I want you to take *everything* off. I have plans involving this…' He held up the champagne bottle. 'This…' He held up the massage oil. 'And your naked body. So come on: strip.'

Her breathing shallow, Ellie reached for the zip at the side of her dress. Her hands were clumsy, struggling to find the fastener, to draw it down the closely fitting bodice. Finally, *finally*, she pulled it down and let the dress fall away, standing in front of him in just her underwear.

At least it wasn't sensible this time. Tiny, silky wisps of black and red exposed far more than they concealed. It had taken all her resolve to put them on earlier, but hearing his sharp intake of breath, watching his eyes darken, filled her with a sensual power she had never felt before.

He might be issuing the demands, but she was the one in command.

She looked him clearly in the eye, didn't flinch or look away. 'Your turn. You said yourself things could get messy.'

Appreciation filled his face. 'You're playing with fire,' he warned as his hands moved to his tie. 'Be careful you don't get burned.'

'Oh, I'm counting on it.'

Ellie turned and walked into the master bedroom, head high, step confident even in those heels. She didn't need to turn around to see if he was following her. She knew he would be right behind her.

CHAPTER NINE

WHAT WAS THAT NOISE? An insistent buzz, as if an angry mosquito was trying to wake them up. An extremely loud, extremely angry mosquito.

Ellie reluctantly opened her eyes but it made no difference. The room was still dark. She put out her hand and encountered flesh; firm, warm flesh. Mmm… She ran her fingers appreciatively over Max's chest, learning him by heart once again.

Buzzzzz…

The mosquito had returned. Only it was no insect. Judging by the furiously flashing lights and the way it was dancing all over the bedside cabinet it was Ellie's phone making the racket.

Who on earth…?

Was it the shop?

Her heart began to speed up, skittering as frantically as her continuously buzzing phone as she pulled herself up, hands slipping on the rumpled sheets.

The buzzing stopped for one never-ending second, only to start up again almost immediately.

'What's that?' Max turned over, his voice thick with sleep.

'My phone. I don't know. It must be a wrong number.'

Please let it be a wrong number. Terrifying images

ran through her mind in Technicolor glory: fire; flood, theft. All three…

Finally she got one trembling hand to the phone and pulled it over, pulling out the charging cable as she did so. Turning it over, she stared in disbelief at the name flashing up on the screen.

Mum.

What on earth…? She accepted the call with fingers too clumsy in their haste. 'Mum? Is everything all right?'

There was a pause, and then Ellie heard it. It was like being catapulted back in time. A painful, breathtaking blow as the years rolled back to the moment a policeman had knocked on the door and their lives had been irrevocably altered. That low keening, like an animal in severe distress.

She had hoped never to hear that noise again.

'Mum?'

'Ellie? Ellie? Oh, thank goodness, darling. It's Bill.' The words were garbled, breathless, but discernible.

Not now...please not now.

But even as her mind framed the words she pushed the thought away, shame swamping her. How could she be so selfish when catastrophe had torpedoed her mother's happiness once again?

And what *of* Bill? Big, blustering Bill? She barely knew him, not really, but he had supported her mother, loved her, given her a new life, a new beginning.

And if it was easier for her mother to cope without Ellie, the spitting image of her dad and so similar to her brother, a constant reminder of all that Marissa Scott had lost, then how could Ellie really blame her? Didn't she herself shy away from anything that reminded her of what she only now appreciated had been an extraordinarily perfect childhood?

'Mum, what's happened? Is he...?' She couldn't bring herself to utter the last word.

'He's had a heart attack. He's in Theatre now.'

Oh, thank God...thank God. 'Where are you? In Spain?'

She looked up, but Max was already firing up his laptop, phone at the ready. His poor PA was probably on hand to take his instructions. Relief shot through her. She knew instinctively that this time she wouldn't have to do it all alone. That he would sort out a flight, at least; probably cars, hotels...

'No, we're in Oakwood. Bill's daughter had a baby, so we came back for a visit.'

They were back in England, in close proximity to London. But they hadn't told her, hadn't suggested a trip to Cornwall, asked to see her. It wasn't the time for selfishness but Ellie couldn't help the sore thud of disappointment. Couldn't stop her mouth working as she swallowed back the huge, painful lump.

Knowing and understanding her mother's need for distance didn't stop it hurting.

But she had called now. She was in pain and she needed her daughter.

'I'm on my way. Give me a couple of hours. Do you need anything? Food? Clothes?'

'No, no. I'm okay. But, Ellie? *Hurry*, darling.'

Her face was pale and set, but there was strength in the pointed chin, in the dark, deeply shadowed eyes. A feeling of indomitability. Max had the sense Ellie had been here before, travelling through the night to support her mother.

'What about our things? Your hire car? You don't need to come with me.' They were the first words she had said since the town car had pulled up outside the hotel and they had exited the ornate lobby to find themselves in the strange, other-worldly pre-dawn of London.

Not quiet, London could never be completely still, but emptier, greyer, ghostlier. The chauffeur drove them at practised speed through the city streets, soon hitting suburbs as foreign and anonymous as every city's outskirts. Warehouses and concrete gave way to residential streets and then to fields and motorways.

'It's fine. Lydia will take care of it all.' He had already fired off several emails to his PA, and even though it was late night back in Hartford she had replied, was seamlessly sorting everything out. 'Our clothes will be packed up and sent back to Cornwall, and the car is getting picked up by the hire company.'

She nodded, but her attention was only half on him as she stared out of the window at the rapidly passing countryside. She was back in her usual grey. The scarlet dress was still lying on the floor of the sitting-room, a bright red puddle of silk. Make-up free, her hair pushed back behind her ears, the only hint that the evening had happened was the faint scent of jasmine on her skin; on his skin.

He shut his eyes, images of her passing through his mind like scenes from a film. Her body, long, slender, slick with oil, as his hands moved firmly over silken skin.

'What about work? DL needs you.' Her voice was toneless.

He opened his eyes, the last remnants of the night before fading away. *Not the time or place,* he scolded himself. 'It's fine. Let's see what your mother needs and I can worry about DL later. The hospital will have WiFi, won't it?'

She nodded. 'I guess. It's a long time since I've been there. Not since Dad and Phil...' Her voice trailed off.

'Your mom's back in your old home town?'

No wonder she looked so haunted.

'For fourteen years I thought it was the most perfect place in the world.' Her voice was wistful. 'I danced. Did you know that?'

'No, but I should have guessed.' Of course she had danced. That long, toned slenderness was a dancer's legacy.

'I danced, played in the orchestra and was a member of the drama society. Phil played rugby and swam. We were like a family from an advertisement, with the golden Labrador to match.'

She turned towards him, her chin propped in her hand, her eyes far away.

'At weekends we'd all bike out for picnics in the countryside and then we'd pile on the sofa for family film and pizza night. I guess Mum and Dad must have argued, and I know Phil and I did, but when I look back it's like it's painted in soft gold. Always summer, always laughter. And then it all went wrong...' Her voice trailed off.

'The car accident.'

She nodded. 'Mum blamed herself. Dad had been travelling and was jetlagged, but she hated driving on ice so she persuaded him to pick Phil up from a swim meet. It was a drunk driver. The police said there was nothing Dad could have done. But Mum always thought if he hadn't been so tired...' She blinked, and there was a shimmering behind the long lashes.

Max's chest ached with the need to make it all right. But how could he? How could anybody?

'It must have been terrible.'

'I think that's why Mum had a breakdown. So she

didn't have to face the guilt. But I had to face it all: insurance, funeral-arranging, keeping the house going. I gave up dance, drama, friends, my dreams. There was school, there was Mum and there were books—the only escape from how grey my life had become.'

'But you got away.'

A new town, a new life. The loneliness of that life was beginning to make a twisted kind of sense to him. Could he say the same for his own choices?

Ellie nodded. 'It took a while. When I finished school I was supposed to go to university, but I couldn't see how she would cope without me and I was too proud to ask for help. Then Mum met Bill at her support group and suddenly she didn't need me any more. Worse, it was as if she couldn't bear to see me…like I made her feel guilty. She went from not being able to cope without me to not wanting to be near me. I lost everything all over again.'

Max didn't know what to say. Was there anything he *could* say? Anything that could wipe away over ten years of loneliness and grief?

He reached out instead, took her cold, still hand in his.

Ellie clung on, glad of the tactile comfort. His hands were warm, anchoring her to the here and now.

'What did you do then? Is that when you got engaged?'

The chill enveloping her deepened. *Engaged.* It was such happy word. It conjured up roses and diamonds and champagne. She hadn't experienced any of those things. Just an ornate ring that had belonged to Simon's grandmother: an ugly Victorian emerald that she had never dared tell him she disliked.

Simon was her secret shame, her weakness. She had never been able to tell anyone the whole story before. But there was a strength in Max's touch, in his voice, that made her want to lean in, to rest her burden on his broad shoulders. Just for a while.

She took a deep breath. She had said so much already...would a little more hurt? 'I hadn't seen much of my friends out of school, but it was still a shock when they went to university. So I got a job at the solicitors where my father had worked, just to get out of the house. Everyone there was a lot older, and I knew, of course, that they had only employed me to be kind.'

'Simon...'

She waited for the usual thump in her chest, the twist of dread to strike her as she said his name. But there was nothing. It was just a word, an old ghost with no way to harm her. Not if she didn't allow it.

Ellie carried on, her voice stronger. 'Simon was the only person there who didn't talk to me like I was a child. After the first couple of weeks I had a huge crush on him.' She shook her head, a bitter taste coating her mouth at the memory of her naïve younger self. 'He knew, of course. Enjoyed it and encouraged it, I think.'

She fell silent for a moment, the memory hitting her hard. Her mother's happiness—one she couldn't share. The resentment she hadn't been able to bring herself to acknowledge because it was so petty and mean; resentment that she had given up her childhood and future for her mother and now *she* was the one being left behind. And the coldness of her isolation. The dawning knowledge that her mother not only no longer needed her but somehow no longer wanted her.

Ellie shivered and Max put an arm around her, pulling her in close, holding her against his warm strength.

She turned into his comforting embrace, her arms slipping around him, allowing herself the luxury of leaning on him, *into* him, just this once. She inhaled deep, that smell of pine and salt, of sea and fresh air that clung to him even after two days in London.

'Looking back now, I can see that I was just desperate to feel loved, cared for. Simon sensed it, I think… my indecision, my loneliness…and he made his move.'

Her mouth twisted.

'He was very clever. One moment he would flatter me, make me feel like the most desirable woman alive. The next he would tease me, treat me like a silly schoolgirl. He'd stand me up and then turn up to whisk me away on an impossibly romantic date. I never knew where I stood. As he intended.'

She swallowed.

'And right from the start I tried to be what he wanted. To wear my hair the way he liked, dress in a way he approved of. He never actually said anything—but he would get this *look*, you know? This terribly disappointed look. Sometimes he would stop speaking to me altogether, not contact me if I really displeased him, and I would never know why. I'd have to figure it out. I used to sit alone in the empty house and cry, stare at my phone willing him to text me. When he finally spoke to me I'd be so relieved I would promise myself I would never upset him again. I learned what was expected of me, what would make him smile in approval. My food, my clothes, the books I read, the films I watched—all guided by him. I thought I was in love. That he protected me, cared for me.'

Max's whole body was rigid, and when she peeped over she saw a muscle beating in his cheek. His fingers gripped hers tightly, almost painful in their intensity.

'When Mum told me she was moving to Spain with Bill, selling the house, Simon came to the rescue; my knight in shining armour. He asked why didn't I move in, and I couldn't think of a single reason not to.'

She laced her fingers through Max's.

'It all happened so slowly. First he suggested I give up my job so that I could study. But then he found a hundred reasons for me to delay starting a course and I agreed. Because, you see, I thought he was protecting me.'

She swallowed again.

'I don't know when it dawned on me that I didn't have a single thing to call my own. Not for a long time. I forgot that it wasn't normal to be terrified in case you said the wrong thing, in case the house wasn't neat enough, the dishes tidied away, the bed made perfectly, my hair and clothes perfect. I didn't realise for a long time that I could barely breathe, that I was terrified of his displeasure, that just one frown could crush me.

'Because the worst thing of all,' her voice was low now, as she admitted the part that shamed her most. 'The worst thing of all is that when he smiled, when I got it right, I was elated. So that's what I strived for. I looked right, said the right things. When he was happy I was happy. I thought I was so very happy.'

She blinked, almost shocked to feel the wetness on her eyelashes.

'I don't know when I first realised that living in fear wasn't normal. Never relaxing, always worrying, never knowing what would set him off. He told me time and time again how worthless I was, how lucky I was to have him, and after a while I believed him.'

Because how could a girl with nothing be worth anything? Even her own mother had discarded her like an unwanted toy.

'When he wanted to he could be the sweetest, most tender person in the world. And I craved it. I thought it must be my fault that he was angry so often. He told me it was my fault.'

Max swallowed, his voice thick as he spoke. 'So what happened?'

'It wasn't one argument or one incident. It just crept up on me that I was desperately unhappy, and that every time someone mentioned the wedding I felt as if I was being bricked up alive. And as I got more and more scared he got more and more controlling. He wanted to know where I was every hour, would be angry if he phoned home and I didn't answer. He went through my receipts, looking for goodness knows what. One day I realised that I was afraid. I think it was the first time I'd allowed myself to think like that. But once I had it was as if a door had opened and I couldn't shut it again. So I just left. Jumped on a train to Cornwall. For six months I looked over my shoulder all the time, dreading seeing him there—and yet hoping he loved me enough to track me down. To find me.'

It was out. Every last sordid detail.

Would Max judge her? He couldn't judge her any more than she'd judged herself.

Ellie turned apprehensive eyes to him, dreading the judgement she expected to see in his face. His hands tightened on hers as he looked down at her, his mouth set, his eyes hard. But not with anger directed at her, no. Compassion softened the grim lines of his face.

'Look at you now, Ellie. Just look what you've become. You didn't let the jerk stop you. Delay you, maybe, but not stop you. You're strong, independent, successful, compassionate. You should be so proud of yourself.'

Proud? Not ashamed? Strong? Not weak? Was that really, truly what he saw?

Ellie didn't move for one long moment but then she fell against him with a gulp, tears spilling down her face, her chest heaving with the sobs she had held back for far too long.

Slipping an arm around her, Max pulled her in close, let her lean on him, let his shirt absorb her tears, his shoulders absorb her pain. He held her close, rubbed her back and kissed the top of her head as the car continued to drive through the gloom and Ellie cried it all out.

Her head ached, her throat ached, her eyes ached. In fact there wasn't a part of her that didn't hurt in one way or another. Not in the languorous way she had ached yesterday morning, with that sated, sensual feeling, but a much more painful sensation, as if she had been ripped apart and clumsily glued back together, cracks and dents and all.

Max's hand was still on hers, tethering her to the here and now, keeping her grounded. When had she ever cried like that before? She didn't think she ever had. At first she had been too numb and then? Then she had had to keep it together. One of them had to.

'Are you angry with her?' Max's voice stirred the silence.

'Sorry?'

'Your mother.' He shook his head. 'I mean, I'm pretty furious with *my* mother, for being so greedy and stubborn, and I am absolutely filled with rage against my dad for—well, for pretty much everything. But none of it is about me. I could walk away tomorrow, I guess, and leave them to it. Heck, maybe I should. Difference is I'm an adult. But you? You were just a kid. She made you be the grown-up, and then when you needed her she wasn't there.'

Ellie opened her mouth, ready to defend her mother—and herself. But the words wouldn't come. 'I...'

'It's okay, you know. You're allowed to be angry. It doesn't make you bad. It just makes you human.'

Anger? Was that what she felt? That tightening in her chest, the way her fingernails bit into her palms whenever she got a breezy, brief email from her mother?

Brief, breezy. The bare minimum of contact.

And when Ellie had fled, needing somewhere to hide out and recover, her mother hadn't been there for her. Hadn't wanted her. Hadn't known or cared that her daughter was trapped in a vicious relationship. What kind of woman left her eighteen-year-old daughter alone with a much older man she hardly knew?

'I *am* angry. So angry.' The words were almost a whisper. 'That she left me to deal with it all. That she made me be the grown-up when I wasn't ready. That she let me give up university for her. That she just left me…' Her voice was rising in volume and intensity and she stopped, shocked by the shaking fury in it.

His hand tightened on hers. 'How did you feel then?'

Ellie tried never to think about that particular time, that last betrayal. No wonder, when dragging it all up cut deeply all over again. 'Lost,' she admitted. 'I think, I wonder if she hadn't gone just then, if things might have been different. If I might have gone to university, not got engaged.'

She stopped.

'But I was an adult by then,' she said instead. 'I made my choices just as she made hers. I can't blame her. I can't blame anyone but myself.'

'No, you were still a child. You have nothing to regret, Ellie. Nothing at all.'

Neither of them spoke then, but Max continued to hold her hand, his thumb caressing the back of her hand with sure movements as the car took them through increasingly familiar countryside, finally entering the outskirts of the town where Ellie had been born.

She was finding it increasingly hard to get her breath, and her stomach was clenching as they entered the hospital car park.

'Hey.' Max gave her a reassuring smile. 'It's fine. You're not alone. Not this time.'

Ellie tried to smile back but she couldn't make her muscles obey. Right now she wasn't alone—but next week he would be gone, and she would be back to square one. On her own.

Somehow Max Loveday had slipped through all her defences and shown her just what a sham her life was. Safe? Sure. Protected? Absolutely. Hardworking and honest? Maybe. But true? No. Hiding away, not having fun, trusting no one… That wasn't true to the legacy of love and happiness her father and brother had left her, that Demelza Loveday had bequeathed to her.

Max or no Max, Ellie had to find a way to start living again.

If she could only work out where to start.

CHAPTER TEN

THE CORRIDORS WERE the same off-white, the floor the same hard-wearing highly polished tiles, the smell the same: antiseptic crossed with boiled vegetables. She might be fourteen again, hurrying down the corridor, following in her mother's frantic footsteps.

But this time Max's hand was on her arm: a quiet, tacit support. Five days ago she hadn't been able to wait to see the back of Max Loveday. Today she was grateful he was here at all.

It was as if her godmother was still looking out for her, even after her death.

'Here we are. Ward Six.'

Max would have walked straight in, but Ellie came to an abrupt halt.

'I just need a moment.'

'Sure. Take as long as you need.' He was wearing jeans with the tuxedo shirt from the night before: an incongruous mix that he somehow managed to carry off. Maybe the early-morning stubble and ruffled hair helped. Or maybe it was his innate confidence.

Or it could be the surroundings. These corridors must have seen people turn up in everything from pyjamas to ballgowns. Last time she had pulled on grey tracksuit bottoms and an old football shirt of her brother's. She could see it as if it were yesterday, feel the smooth nylon of the shirt, hear the slopping of the flip-flops she had grabbed, forgetting about the snow outside.

Ellie inhaled, a long, slow breath, filling her chest with air, with oxygen, with courage. And then she pushed open the door and walked into the ward's waiting room.

Again memories assailed her. Could they be the same industrial padded chairs? The same leaflets on the notice-board? The same water-cooler with no cups anywhere to be seen? The same tired potted plant?

Only the people were different.

She half recognised Bill's family from the pitifully few occasions when they had met; his daughter, a few years older than Ellie, now cradling a baby. His brother, as tall and thickset as Bill, his sister, red-eyed and staring into space.

And pacing up and down like a caged wild animal, just as she had the last time, was her mother. A little older, her skin far more tanned, her hair blonder, a little plumper, but still recognisably, indisputably Marissa Scott.

She turned as Ellie pushed the door open and Ellie stood still for a moment, wary, as if they were strangers. She had to speak, to break the silence.

'Hi, Mum.'

It wasn't enough, and yet it was all she had. But as her mother broke into a trot and ran across the room to enfold her in her arms Ellie realised that maybe, just maybe, it was enough after all.

'What a day.' Max sat back in the uncomfortable cafeteria chair and looked down at the plate of pale fried food in front of him. He poked suspiciously at the peas, soggy and a nasty yellowish green. 'Do you think there is actually *any* nutritional value in this?'

'Not an iota.' Ellie had wisely eschewed the fish and chips and gone for a salad. 'Hospital food is like school food: something to be endured.'

Max tried not to think too longingly of the food at his expensive private school. 'We should have gone out.'

'Maybe I should have insisted you leave earlier. You didn't have to stay all day. Did you get any work done?'

'Some,' Max admitted.

He knew Ellie had had an agonising day, waiting with her overwrought mother for Bill to come out of surgery, and that his day couldn't compare—but it had been no walk in the park. He had spent the day delving deeply into DL Media's accounts and his excavations hadn't uncovered any gold. All he had found was a big pit that was getting deeper by the day.

'There are some difficult decisions to make when I get back.'

His last four words seemed to hang in the air.

'I do appreciate you taking so much time out of your schedule for me. I know you were hoping to spend more time in London.' Ellie's head was bent and she was poking unenthusiastically at her salad.

'Ellie, it's nothing. And it's not as if I'm not in contact with the London office every day.' For once Max didn't want to talk about work—or dwell on how little time he had left in the UK. 'How's Bill?'

'Out of surgery. And the doctors seem pleased.'

'And your mother?'

'Surprisingly okay.' Her cheeks flushed. 'Well enough to ask who you are.'

He raised an eyebrow. 'What did you tell her?'

Her eyes lowered. 'That we work together.'

'Okay.'

He speared a soggy chip and then laid his fork down.

He wasn't hungry after all. He looked around. The room was half full: a few patients well enough to get up and walk about, harassed-looking staff shovelling food in as quickly and efficiently as engines refuelling. And friends and relatives, many with shell-shocked faces.

He really didn't want to spend much more time here, and neither should Ellie. Her eyes were deeply shadowed, her face white with tiredness.

'What do you want to do? Are you planning to stay with your mother for a few days?'

He was surprised at how much he wanted her to say no. If she didn't return to Trengarth with him today would he see her again this trip?

Or at all.

She shook her head and unexpected relief flooded through him.

'Part of me feels like I should, but there's nowhere for me to stay and Bill's family are looking after Mum. If there was any suggestion he was still in danger of course I would... No, I need to get back to the shop. There's no reason for me to hang around. Thanks for bringing me. Max.' Her eyes met his. 'For everything.'

'Any time.' He meant it too. There had been no thought in the early morning of walking away, of putting her into a car and returning to his own world. 'Do you want to find a hotel for the night or get straight off? I could get us a car in an hour, although we wouldn't get back to Cornwall until the early morning.'

She chewed her lip, her eyes flickering as she thought. 'Is it bad that I just want to go home?'

'Not at all. It's been a long day. I'll get one ordered. We can sleep in the car if we need to. Although...' He looked at his untouched plate and then at hers. 'We may want to stop for some real food first.'

'That sounds good. I'll go and sit with Mum for a bit longer.'

'I'll fetch you when the car gets here.'

She didn't move straight away. She just sat, looking as if there was something she wanted to say. Max waited, but she didn't speak, just gave him a tremulous smile as she pushed her chair back and walked slowly out of the cafeteria.

The car rolled smoothly through the night-dark moor. Clouds blocked the stars, and as Max stared out of the window all he could see was his own reflection. Unsmiling, contemplative. Angry.

Max Loveday wasn't a violent man. His battles were in the boardroom, in sales figures and profits. But tonight his blood ran hot. All he could think about was asking the driver to turn back to Oakwood, so that he could find Ellie's ex and make him wish he had never set eyes on her.

And he'd ask her mother just exactly what she had been thinking when she had allowed her teenage daughter to become the adult. When she had left that daughter alone with nowhere to turn except to an emotionally abusive and controlling man.

Only Ellie didn't want or need him to fight her battles, even though all he wanted was to ride into the lists for her, to pull on a helmet and grab a sword and rush into battle for her honour.

And to teach that scoundrel a lesson.

His lips tightened. He hadn't felt this out of control, this primal, in years. His instincts were screaming at him to protect, to avenge.

This was exactly what he wanted to avoid. This kind of messy, hot-headed emotion, pulling and pushing him away from his goals, from his plans. Love—violent, needy love—was to blame for it all. Grieving love, causing Ellie's mother's breakdown. Twisted love, creating a hellish trap for Ellie.

His hands curled into fists. It wasn't love affecting his judgement right now. It was lust and liking, respect and admiration. But it was still dangerous.

Thank goodness he would be on his way home in just a few days.

Just a few days...

It wasn't long enough.

It was far too long. A dangerously long time.

He glanced over at Ellie. She was curled up on the seat next to him, sleeping as the car wound its way through the tiny lanes that would take them back to Trengarth. Visibly yawning as they'd finished their excellent pub dinner, Ellie hadn't taken long to fall asleep once they'd returned to the car. Max wasn't surprised; she'd exorcised all her ghosts in one day. There was bound to be a price, both physically and mentally. Better she sleep it off.

What about him? Would he be able to exorcise his own ghosts?

Max shifted in his seat, wishing he could get comfortable. He supposed the question was did he even want to? After all, hadn't they kept him safe? But he had to admit his careful planning, his definition of a suitable partner, didn't fill him with the same quiet satisfaction it had used to.

He sighed, changing position once again. The whole point of getting a driver to take them all the way back to Trengarth had been so they could rest, but Max was unable to switch off. He envied the slow, even sound of Ellie's breath.

It would have been better for him to have driven himself, forced to concentrate on the road ahead rather than sit here in the dark with the same thoughts running through his mind over and over on a loop.

'Where now, sir?'

The driver was turning down the coastal road that led directly to the village.

'Should I drop the lady off first?'

They were back.

London, the suite, playing at tourists—it was all over. He should see Ellie home and that would be an end to it, *should* be an end to it. Only she was so tired. And so alone.

'No.' Max made a sudden decision. Ellie would be tired, emotionally wrung out when she came to. She might need him. And after all he had bedrooms to spare. 'Both of us to The Round House, please.'

It was less than five minutes before the car pulled in through the gates and came to a smooth stop on the circular driveway. The outside light came on as they passed it, and the orange glow cast an otherworldly light over the still slumbering Ellie.

Max eyed her. She was thin, sure, and couldn't weigh too much. How easy would it be to get her out of the car and upstairs without waking her?

Not that easy.

But she looked so peaceful he didn't want to disturb her.

He opened the car door as quietly as he could, hoping to give her just a few seconds more, but she stirred as the door clicked open.

'Where are we?' Her voice was groggy.

Max glanced over. Her hair was mussed, her eyes still half shut.

'At The Round House. It's so late I thought we could both stay here tonight. I can make up a bed for you, if you prefer.'

'No need. I don't mind sharing.' She yawned: an impossibly long sound. 'I should walk home. It's not far, but I don't think I'd make it. I'd probably fall asleep by the side of the road and have to trust that the local rabbits and sparrows would cover me with leaves.'

'Very picturesque, but if you could make do with sheets and a mattress it might be easier.'

'Okay, if you insist.' She yawned again and allowed him to help her out of the car, leaning against him as she staggered upright.

'Come on, Sleeping Beauty, let's go in.'

Max had only stayed a few nights in The Round House, occupied it for less than a week, and yet somehow it felt like coming home.

Walking in, dropping his wallet and keys in the glass bowl on the hallway table, kicking his shoes off by the hat stand: they all felt like actions honed by years of automatic practice. And the house welcomed him back. A sigh seemed to ripple through it, one of contentment. All was right in its world.

He didn't have this sense of rightness in his own apartment. All glass and chrome and space, city views, personal gym, residents' pool on site, it was the perfect bachelor pad. But when he was there he didn't fall asleep listening to the waves crashing on the beach below. His apartment was luxurious, convenient, easy—but it didn't have family history steeped into every cornice. Sure, he could move some of the old family possessions, the pictures, the barometer, over to Hartford. But they wouldn't belong there.

They belonged here.

'Do you need anything?'

The question was automatic but he wasn't sure he could help if she did. The kitchen had been bare when he'd arrived, and he'd stocked it with little more than coffee, milk and some nachos.

Luckily Ellie shook her head. 'Just bed.'

'I'm in the guest suite.' He started to lead the way up the wide staircase. 'It didn't feel right, moving into my great-aunt's rooms.'

'That's understandable. Besides, I can't see you as a rose wallpaper kind of guy.'

'It *is* very floral,' he agreed. 'But I'm secure enough in my masculinity to cope with pink roses.'

She raised her eyebrows. '*There's* a claim.'

Max slid his arm around her waist, his steps matching hers as they trod wearily up the stairs. Yet some of that weariness fell away as he touched her.

'I don't make claims. I make statements.'

Ellie had reached the landing half a step ahead. She turned to him, stepping into his embrace, her own arms encircling his waist, warm hands burrowing underneath his T-shirt. His skin tingled where she touched: a million tiny explosions as his nerve-endings reacted to the skin-on-skin contact.

'I may need you to verify that statement.'

She looked up at him, her face serious except for that dimple tugging at the corner of her mouth. He bent his head, needing to taste the little dip in her skin. He felt her shiver against him as his tongue dipped out and sampled her.

'I'm at your service.' He kissed the dimple again, inhaling her sweet, drowsy scent as he did so. 'How exactly would you like me to verify it?' He kissed his way down her jawline, pausing at her neck. 'Any requests?'

Her hands clenched at his waist. 'Anything.'

'Anything?' He slid his hands up under her top, over her ribs to the soft fullness above.

Ellie gasped. 'Anything. Just don't stop.'

'Oh, I won't, honey. Not until you ask me to.'

He walked her backwards towards the bedroom door, his hands continuing to move upwards millimetre by millimetre.

'It's only three in the morning. We've got the rest of the night.'

He couldn't, *wouldn't* think beyond that. Not now. Not when his hands were caressing her, his lips tasting her. When the scent of her was all around him.

There were decisions to be made, places to go and a world to conquer. But it could wait until the morning.

The sun would be up in just a couple of hours, but they still had tonight and Max was going to make the most of every single second.

The sun was shining in through the half-opened curtains, casting a warm golden glow onto the bed. Ellie sighed and pulled at the sheet as she turned into the gentle heat, gloriously aware that at that very second everything was all right with the world.

Except... Except was she waking up alone again? Like some Greek nymph fated never to see her lover in the light of day?

Ellie pulled herself upright and tried to work out the time. There was no clock in the room, and her phone was dead, but judging by the brightness of the sun it had to be late morning if not afternoon.

She should really get up. Check on her shop. Head back to reality. Only she was so comfortable. Reality could wait just a little longer.

'Morning, sleepyhead. Or should that be afternoon?'

Max was lounging against the door, holding something that Ellie devoutly hoped was a cup of coffee.

'I thought you were going to sleep the day away.'

'How long have you been up?' She held her hand out for the coffee and inhaled greedily, wrapping her hands around the hot mug. 'I missed you.' She allowed her hand to fall invitingly to the empty space by her side, the sheet to slip a little lower.

'No rest for the wicked. Duty called.'

He wasn't meeting her eye, and he didn't sit by her or even slide his gaze appreciatively over her body.

The message was clear. Playtime was over. Well, she had known the deal from the start. Any disappointment was simply her due payment for the unexpected fun. Back to reality with the proverbial bump.

No wonder it stung a little.

'My solicitor wants to look at the share papers in detail. He doesn't trust the scan I sent him, so it looks like I might be heading back earlier than I expected. Don't worry about the festival, though. I've asked our marketing guys to give you a hand, and my PA can do whatever you need her to do. I've emailed you all the details.'

Max sounded offhand: more like the business partner she had been expecting him to be than the understanding companion of the last few days.

'Very efficient,' Ellie said drily. 'You *have* been busy. In that case I'd better get off. I don't want to hold you up. When are you flying out?'

That was good. Her voice was level, with no outward sign that she felt as if she'd been kicked in the stomach.

Of course she'd known this wasn't for ever…hadn't been expecting more than a few more days. Only she had been looking forward to those few more days. Looking forward to discovering more about him, discovering more about herself, about who she could be with a little support and an absence of fear.

Well, she would have to carry on that discovery alone.

'Tomorrow. I've a car booked for ten tomorrow morning.'

His eyes caught hers then, and there was a hint of an apology in the caramel depths, along with something else. A barrier. He was moving on, moving away. Oh, so politely, but oh, so steadily.

Ellie knew that she should try and get up, but she was suddenly and overwhelmingly self-conscious. Her clothes were heaped on a chair at the other side of the room and she couldn't, absolutely *couldn't* get up and walk across there stark naked. Maybe she could have if the other Max had been here. The Max who couldn't keep his eyes off her. The Max who made her feel infinitely precious and yet incredibly strong, like a rare stone ready to be polished into something unique.

But this Max was a stranger, and she didn't want him to see her in all her vulnerability.

'Thanks for the coffee but, really, don't let me keep you. We both have heaps to do. Maybe I'll see you before you leave. Come down to the shop if you have a chance. I'll find you a book for the plane.'

She could be polite and businesslike too.

'Thanks, that would be good.' Max stepped back towards the door. 'Not that I'll have a chance to read for pleasure. I'll be...'

'Busy,' she finished for him. 'Back to all work and no play, Max?'

He flushed, a hint of red high on the tanned cheekbones. 'Yes.'

Shame shot through her at his quiet acceptance. 'I'm sorry. I know you have to go. I know how difficult things are.' She smiled. 'I guess I've got used to you being around.'

The colour had left his cheeks and he smiled back, the familiar warmth creeping back into his eyes. 'I've got used to *being* around. I'll miss it here.'

And me? she wanted to ask. *Will you miss me?* But her mouth wouldn't form the words; she wasn't entirely sure what she wanted the answer to be.

He was watching her now with his old intentness, the expression that made her simultaneously want to pull the sheet right up to her chin and let it fall all the way down.

'I guess I *could* take a few hours off today. I never did get round to taking a boat out. Do you have to get back to the shop, Ellie?'

Yes. No. Things were confusing enough already. Maybe she would be better off saying her goodbyes now and putting some much needed distance between them. But what could a few more hours hurt? The end line was firmly drawn in the sand. The countdown to the final hour had begun.

'They're not expecting me back till this evening. Mrs T has the shop well in hand, I'm sure.'

'Good.' He pushed away from the doorway and advanced on her, intent clear and hot in his eyes. 'In a couple of hours we should get a picnic, and then I'll show you that the sea is for more than watching. Ready to try something new, Ellie?'

He *was* talking about sailing, wasn't he? Shivers ran hot down her body.

'In a couple of hours?'

The sheet fell a little more and this time he noticed, his eyes scorching gold as they traced their way down her body.

'A couple of hours,' he agreed. 'I haven't said good morning to you properly yet, or good afternoon. In fact I may need to work my way right through to good evening…'

'Well,' she said, as primly as it was possible to be when lying barely covered by a sheet, her body trembling with anticipation, 'we wouldn't want to forget our manners, now, would we?'

'Absolutely not.' He was by her side, his eyes fixed on hers as he began to slowly unbutton his shirt. 'Manners are very important. Want me to show you?'

She nodded, her gaze skimming the defined hardness of his chest, moving lower down to where he was just beginning to unfasten his jeans.

'Yes. Yes, please, Max. Show me everything.'

CHAPTER ELEVEN

'ARE YOU SURE you've got everything?'

Ellie hadn't intended to come and see Max off. She hadn't intended to stay with him all last night, or to wake up in his arms this morning. She had intended a civilised kiss on the cheek before turning away, as if she didn't much care whether he stayed or went.

And yet here she was. She hated goodbyes as a matter of course, but this one was proving particularly unbearable. The problem with never dating, never having had a casual relationship in her life, was that she had no idea how to act now their time was coming to an end.

Should she hug him? Kiss his cheek? Kiss him properly? Shake his hand? High-five him? All of the above? Grab him and never let him go?

That wasn't in their unwritten agreement.

Max picked up his small holdall, hefting the weight experimentally. 'I think so. I didn't actually buy much while I was here, and I packed light anyway.'

'You nearly bought a boat.'

'But I wasn't planning to check that in as hand luggage. Even first class might have had something to say about that.'

'They probably wouldn't have been best pleased.' Ellie rummaged in her bag and pulled out a gold-embossed paper bag. 'Have you got room for this? I owe you a souvenir, remember?'

He eyed the bag nervously. 'It's not a trick snake, is it?'

'No.' She bit her lip, keeping back her smile with some difficulty. 'Open it when you get home.'

'That bad, huh?'

'You have no idea.'

She handed him another bag: one of the striped paper bags she used at the shop.

'Here. I know you're planning to work solidly for the next twenty-four hours, but just in case your eyes tire of spreadsheets...'

He opened the bag and slid the hardback book out. '*Tales of Cornwall*? It's lovely. Thanks, Ellie.'

'I figured you should know a little about your ancestral folk.'

He was flicking through it, pausing at some of the full-colour illustrations. 'It's a very thoughtful gift.' He looked at her, his brow crinkled. 'I don't have anything for you. I'm sorry.'

'That's okay. I wasn't expecting anything.' She swallowed, her throat unexpectedly full. 'Just promise me you won't sell the house to anyone who doesn't love it.'

'I'd keep it if I could, but you said it yourself, Ellie. The village doesn't need any more absentee owners, jetting in for two weeks in the summer. I'll make sure I only sell it to a family who want to live here all year round.'

'A book-loving family?'

'Of course. What about you, Ellie? Are you going to be okay?'

His face was serious and the concern in his voice made her hands clench a little. It wasn't that she didn't appreciate it; it was nice that someone cared even a little. But she didn't want that kind of concern from Max.

Her preference would be for the scorching looks that turned her knees to melting chocolate—made her whole body liquefy. But she'd even take his scornful mistrust. That at least had treated her as an equal, not like something fragile.

'Yes. I have your PA's email, and I promise to call DL's London office if I need advice or help.'

'That's not what I meant. Are you sure this is what you want?'

Ellie's heart thumped painfully. What did he mean? Was he offering to stay? For her to go with him? For some kind of tomorrow beyond these two weeks? Her palms felt clammy as her pulse began to race. What would she say? What *did* she want?

'Am I sure about what?'

'This…' He swept his arm dismissively in an arc, pushing away Trengarth, the sea, the view. 'It's pretty, Ellie. But is it enough? One shop? One festival? You were amazing at the weekend: passionate, knowledgeable, brilliant. You told me you dreamt once of a life in London, in publishing. Are you really content to settle for *this*?'

It was the hint of contempt in his voice as he said 'this' that really hit her. Was that what he thought? Of her? Of Trengarth? Of everything she valued? That they weren't big enough? Not important enough?

'It's okay, Max. You can head back to your important job in the big city without worrying about me. I *am* happy and *I am fine*.'

The last three words came out slightly more vehemently than she'd meant them to and Max took a step back, his eyes widened in surprise.

'Whoa, what does *that* mean?'

'It means you don't have to add me to the list of things that Max Loveday has to sort out. I like my life, Max.

I like my shop. I love my village. We don't all need to be at the very top. We don't all need to save the world.'

Confusion warred with anger in his eyes. 'I'm not trying to save the world.'

'No?'

She put her hands on her hips and glared at him. She wanted him to look as if he might miss her, darn it. To look as if not holding her, kissing her, touching her might actually cause him some discomfort. As if he wanted to pull her into bed—not tell her everything that was wrong with her life, according to the gospel of Max Loveday.

'No.'

Good intentions be damned. She was going to have to say something.

'When you came here you accused me of being some kind of con artist. Now you tell me I'm wasting my life. Things aren't that black and white, Max. Life is richer and more complicated than your narrow definition of success. Look at your dad and his girlfriend. Have you considered that maybe, just maybe, they really are in love?'

His mouth tightened. 'I don't doubt that they *believe* that.'

'How will you know if you don't give them a chance? You carry responsibility for your parents, for the whole of DL, for your grandfather's dreams. What about you, Max? What do *you* want?'

'You know what I want.'

Yes, she did. And she wasn't anywhere on that list.

'For DL Media to work like clockwork, your parents to behave, and to find your perfect wife at the perfect time? I have news for you, Max. Life isn't that simple. Life is emotional and messy and demanding, and you can't hide behind spreadsheets for ever. When you find her, this right woman at the right time to make the perfect life with, she's going to have her own chips and flaws. Her own desires and needs.'

'I know that.' His face was white under the tan, his eyes hard.

'*Do* you?'

Ellie stepped forward and put her hand on his arm, relieved when he didn't try and shake her off.

'You have helped me so much this last week. Helped me confront the past, helped me move on. I feel free, reborn. But it's down to me now. It's always been down to me. To move on or to lock myself away. *My* choice. Just like your parents can make their own choices. And you. *You* can choose too, you know.'

'I have chosen, Ellie. I choose to honour my commitments. I choose to live and dream big, to keep pushing. There's nothing wrong with that.'

'I thought I was the one who was too scared to reach out.' She looked at him, *really* at him, trying to see through to the closely guarded heart of him. 'But you're just as bad. I hope you find what you're looking for, Max. I hope it's worth it.'

He covered her hand with his and squeezed, the rigid look fading from his face. 'It will be. Same to you. Dream big, Ellie.'

'I'll try.'

His hand was warm, comforting over hers. She might not need him but the uncomfortable truth was that she did *want* him. Her bed was going to feel larger than it had used to, her walks on the beach a little more solitary. But that was fine. She had the festival to plan. A social life to start.

She stood on her tiptoes and kissed his lightly stubbled cheek, breathing him in one last time. 'You'd better get going. Safe flight, Max.'

'See you around, honey.'

'Yes.' She paused, then stepped closer, tiptoeing up towards him again. This time she touched her lips to his...a brief caress. 'Bye.'

And she turned and walked away, ignoring the whisper in her heart telling her to turn round and ask him to stay.

What could she offer him here in Cornwall? Only herself. And that would never be enough.

When had Max's office become so confining? Oh, he still had views over downtown Hartford, still had room to pace, a huge desk, a comfortable yet imposing chair. But somehow his horizons felt strangely limiting.

Even though he could walk out now, if he wanted to. Could organise a meeting in Sydney or Paris or Prague and be on a plane within hours.

Be in London within hours.

Max picked up the snow globe that now stood right next to his laptop dock: a penguin balanced on an iceberg encased in a glass bauble. He hadn't known what to expect when Ellie had given him the paper bag but it certainly hadn't been this. Delicate, intricate, mesmerising.

Like its giver.

He shook it, watching the tiny flakes fall on to the miniature black and white bird, turning the arctic scene into a fairytale. It *had* been a fairytale. For just a few days. But he was back in reality now.

Back in reality and ridiculously restless.

He wasn't sleeping well, straining to hear the waves crashing on a shore thousands of miles away; rolling over to put on arm around a body that wasn't there.

He'd always liked sleeping alone before. Liked the rumble of the city.

A knock on the door pulled him back to his surroundings, and he managed to return the snow globe to its place and refocus his attention on the document he was reading before his PA entered the room. His pulse quickened. Had Ellie been in touch? He'd asked Lydia to tell him if she heard from Ellie, but there had been nothing at all in over three weeks.

Was she well? Was she safe? She was probably busy with the shop, with her committees. Busy going to the pub with her friends…with that blond surfer who hadn't been able to keep his eyes off her. As long as it *was* just his eyes.

He made an effort to unclench his jaw. 'Yes?'

'You asked me to let you know when your father was back in his office. He arrived back ten minutes ago.'

'Thanks, Lydia.'

His father had been elusive ever since Max's return to Hartford. Once Max had verified that Great-Aunt Demelza's shares were valid he had done his best to track his father down so he could tell him of the change in ownership in person. It had proved impossible. In the end he had had to notify him by email.

His father hadn't replied.

Max leaned back in his chair and stared at the snow globe. *This was it.* Everything he wanted was within his grasp. He should feel elated, and yet the best word he could find to describe his feelings was hollow.

Empty.

He glanced over at the snow globe again. He swore the penguin was trying to tell him something.

It was a short walk to his father's office, which occupied the other top floor corner suite. Max's great-grandfather had settled in Hartford in the early nineteen-twenties to provide printing services to the city's insurance industry, but had soon branched out into book publishing and journalism. It was Max's grandfather who had taken the company into TV, film, and expanded out of the US.

But although they now had offices around the globe—publishing headquarters in New York, digital in Silicon Valley and Los Angeles—the heart of the operation remained in Connecticut. Where it had all begun.

The door to his father's office was closed but Max didn't knock, simply twisting the handle and walking in. To his surprise his father wasn't at his desk; he was standing at the window, looking out over the river beyond, his shoulders slumped. Would he concede defeat before the battle began?

Max hoped so. It might be necessary, but he had no stomach for this fight.

'Hi, Dad.'

'Max.' The shoulders straightened, and his expression as he turned around was one of familiar paternal affability. 'Good vacation? Where did you go? Cornwall?'

As if he didn't already know.

'I wasn't on holiday. I was in London and sorting out Great-Aunt Demelza's estate. Did you know she lived in the house your grandfather was born in? She left it to me. It's pretty special.'

'Are you going to sell it?'

That was his father. Not a trace of sentimentality.

Max closed his eyes briefly and saw the round white house perched high above the harbour, the golden wood of the polished floorboards, that spectacular view. 'No. I'm thinking of keeping it.'

Ellie's words floated through his head. *'The village needs young families not more second home owners.'* It might be a selfish decision but it was the right one. For now, at least.

'It wasn't all that she left me, Dad.'

His father's jaw tightened. 'Apparently not. The papers…they're legitimate?'

'Seems so. You realise what that means?'

'That we're equal partners. Well, you *are* my son, although it seems a bit premature for you to have so much control. You're still just a boy.'

Max breathed in, willing himself not to rise to the bait. 'We need to talk, Dad. Want to take a walk?'

Hartford, like many cities, had a gritty side, and many affluent families, like Max's own, preferred to live outside the city in large estates by the river, or in one of the quaint and historic small Connecticut towns.

But since he had moved into one of the many luxury apartment blocks catering for young professionals Max had grown fond of the old city, especially enjoying the riverside paths and parks which were vibrant public spaces, perfect for walking, running and cycling. He steered his father towards the river, glad to be outside—even if the temperature *was* hitting the high eighties.

He was even more glad that, unlike his father, he had taken advantage of the company's Dress-down Friday policy and was comfortable in dark khakis and a short-sleeved white shirt.

The park was full of people: families picnicking, personal trainers putting their clients through their moves, couples lying in the sun. Steven Loveday looked around at the buzzing space in obvious surprise. He probably never walked in the city, Max realised. He would be driven in to the office, to the theatre, to the high-end restaurants he frequented, but otherwise he spent his life on his estate or at his club.

'This is all rather nice.' He followed Max down the steep steps and onto the path. 'I had no idea this was here.'

'I guess you wouldn't have.' Max wanted this talk, had sought it out, but now it was time he was finding it hard to find the right words. 'I spoke to Mom.'

A smile spread across his father's face and he clapped Max on the shoulder. 'That's my boy. Has she seen sense?'

'I spoke to Mom and I told her exactly what I am about to tell you.' Max kept his voice level. 'It's not my place to arbitrate your divorce. That's between you guys. Personally, I think you need to go and talk to her face to face. She deserves that courtesy, at least.'

Steven Loveday stood still, incongruous in his handmade suit amongst the rollerbladers, joggers and families. 'Right...' he said slowly.

'She won't come after the company.' Max took a deep breath. *Here goes.* 'As long as I'm in charge.'

His father looked at him blankly. 'What?'

'Dad, our profits are down. We're losing some of our most valuable staff. Rumours are flying through the industry that we're on the brink of collapse. The publishers tell me that agents aren't entertaining our bids. We're losing ground.'

His father waved a hand, dismissing the litany of disasters. 'That was bound to happen after your grandfather died. We knew there would be some instability.'

'It's been over a year.'

'We have a strategy.'

'*No.* No, Dad, there isn't a strategy. I don't know what we're doing, the board doesn't know, and none of our senior directors have any direction. You're on a spending spree and I spend my whole time firefighting. It's not a strategy. It's a disaster.'

'Come on, Max, things are a little tight...'

'I own fifty per cent outright.' There was no point

rehashing the same old arguments. 'You own twenty-five per cent, with an interest in the other twenty-five. Your share is yours. You can do what you like with it. But I want you to sign the other share over to me now. Not when you retire. If you do then Mom will leave the company alone. The rest of the settlement is up to you two—but you owe her, and I think you know it.'

His father's eyes narrowed. 'And if I won't?'

'Then I'll go to the board and force a vote. I'm pretty confident that they'll back me.'

His father started walking slowly along the path. The colour had left his face and he looked every minute of his fifty-eight years. Guilt punched through Max but he ignored it. It was time Steven Loveday faced the consequences of his actions.

'Dad, you are about to have another baby. A chance to do it all over again.' Max didn't add *to do it right*, but the unsaid words hung uncomfortably in the air. 'You say you love Mandy. I hope you do. I hope for all our sakes that this time it's real. Spend time with her… with the baby.'

'Take early retirement? That would be convenient.' His father's words were laced with scorn.

'Or take an executive role. Dad, honestly, are you enjoying it? Running DL Media? Does it buzz through your brains? Is it the first thing you think of when you wake up, before you sleep?'

'Well…I…'

'Or do you miss the afternoons golfing, the long lunches? It's okay if you do, Dad. I'm just saying that running DL is all-consuming. And I don't think that's what you want.'

'And you do? You want to be like your grandfather? Work first and the rest of the world be damned?'

Max looked away, across the river. 'It's all I know. All I want.'

At least it had been. But it hadn't been work occupying his mind as he lay in bed fruitlessly chasing sleep over the last few weeks.

It had been a small terraced building on a steep road and the dark-eyed, toffee-haired girl who occupied it.

She hadn't been born and brought up in his world. She didn't know the rules.

She had no interest in timetables.

But when he imagined his future she was all that he could see.

'I don't see that I have much choice. You've won, Max. I hope it's all you want it to be.'

His father turned and walked away, leaving Max alone by the river.

He should be elated. The company was his. He had won.

But he had no one to tell, no one to celebrate with. He was all alone, and the only person he wanted to share his news with was on the other side of the Atlantic.

Maybe she should get a dog. Something to walk on the beach with, something to talk to. Uncritical adoration.

Ellie breathed in and turned slowly. The briny air filled her lungs and her eyes drank in the deep blue of a summer ocean. The roaring of the waves filled her ears. Trengarth on an idyllic summer's day.

It was perfect, and yet somehow it didn't fill her with the usual peace. Discomfort was gnawing away at her and she couldn't assuage it. Not with work—the shop seemed to run itself these days. Not with the festival—thanks to the brilliant volunteers making sure not a single task remained to be done. And now not even a walk on the beach helped.

Max was right. Watching wasn't enough. But she had been on the sidelines for so long. How could she step out onto the crest of a wave?

She stepped back onto the road, for once not turning back to admire the view.

'Hi, Ellie, are you walking back? I'm going that way.' Sam was breathing hard as he caught up with her.

'You are?' Ellie looked at Sam in surprise. 'Don't you live in the old town?'

'Yeah, but I have some business on the hill.' He looked vaguely uncomfortable.

She had seen a great deal of Sam recently. He'd been walking on the beach at the same time as she had several evenings recently and always joined her. Twice he had been at The Boat House when she'd popped in for her regular Friday lunch and he'd asked her to sit with him. He was on the organising committee, on her pub quiz team. He had popped in to the shop several times, to buy presents or ask for recommendations.

They'd laughed about how they must stop bumping into each other all the time. And here they were. Again.

Ellie's stomach swooped and it was all she could do to keep walking and talking normally. She'd suspected that he liked her before. But now she was sure. He *liked* her liked her.

Her hands felt too big, her legs too long, her laugh too grating. She was hyper-aware of her every word and gesture. They all seemed clumsy and fake. *Breathe,* she told herself crossly. *Max* liked *you liked you and that didn't worry you.*

And Sam was great. A catch. He had an interesting job, he was funny, community-minded. He was handsome enough, if you liked fit, blue-eyed, blond-haired surfer guys.

Did she?

Or was she a little too fixated on dark-haired, caramel-eyed Americans?

Unobtainable dark-haired Americans.

She was supposed to be moving on.

'Sorry, what was that?' Sam had been speaking and she hadn't even heard him.

'The festival,' he repeated. 'It's going well.'

'It seems to be,' she agreed cautiously. 'Obviously it's early days yet, and we have a long way to go, but DL's London office have been really helpful. I think we're guaranteed some big names through them anyway, so that should put us on the map.'

Her phone beeped at this opportune moment and, thankful for the interruption, she smiled at Sam apologetically. 'I should get this. Go on without me. Honestly.'

He looked as if he might protest, but she turned away, pulling her phone out of her pocket as she did so. At some point she was going to have to let him know she wasn't interested.

Because she *wasn't* interested. Although how she wished she was. Darn Max Loveday. He was supposed to be the cure, not the poison.

The number on her phone was a London one, which wasn't unusual these days. She had never spent so much time on the phone, mainly to agents or publishers, trying to secure the names she wanted whilst considering the ones they were pushing at her. It was a real game of nerves, and to her surprise she got a buzz out of the negotiations.

'Hello?'

'Ellie? It's Andy Taylor here, Head of Retail Marketing at DL Media. We met at the industry awards the other week.'

'Hi, Andy. Is this about the festival? Because all my paperwork is back at the shop.' She dimly remembered him, but he wasn't one of her usual contacts.

'Festival? No, no. Actually, Ellie, I was calling you on the off-chance that you might be interested in a job. We have an opening here at DL Media and I think you might be the perfect candidate.'

Ellie stood in the street, time slowing down, until all she could hear was the slow thumping of her heart. Even the cry of the gulls, the chatter of children outside the ice cream shop faded away. That irritating, interfering man. Did Max have to try and sort out *everything*?

'Did Max put you up to this?'

'Max? You mean Max Loveday?' Andy Taylor laughed. 'Oh, no. He doesn't interfere at all with local staff, or any hiring below director level. No, it's your experience we're interested in.'

'My experience?'

Stop repeating things, Ellie or he'll change his mind.

'It's a retail marketing role. Obviously you run a really successful shop in a remote area, and I think that means you'd be able to bring a really valuable perspective to the role.'

He did? Ellie's heart and lungs seemed to expand, filling her chest with almost unbearable pressure. Her hard work had been noticed, appreciated.

'I know you live in Cornwall, and your shop is there, and this would be a really big change. But although this is a London-based post there would be some flexibility about working at home: maybe one or two days a week, depending on schedules. If that was what you wanted.

Would you be free to come in next week and have a chat about it?'

Ellie looked around at the dear, familiar village. The harbour curved in front of her. Just up the road was her own shop, her sanctuary. Her safety net. Could she leave it? Move on?

She swallowed, trying to get moisture back into her dry mouth, her stomach twisting.

But she had felt at home on the South Bank hadn't she? Had wondered what it would be like to be one of that confident sea of people at home in the city. Here was her opportunity to find out—and if it didn't work out she could always come back to the shop.

Besides, she might not even get the job. It was an interview...that was all.

'Next week is fine. The twenty-first? Yes, I'll see you then.'

See: she didn't need Max Loveday to move on. She didn't need him and one day soon she would stop wanting him too.

CHAPTER TWELVE

IT MADE ABSOLUTELY no sense to come all the way to London for just one day. Ellie had travelled up the night before her interview to make sure she was rested, on time and not too travel stained, although it was hard to look at her small, practical, budget hotel room and not yearn, just a little, for the opulence of the hotel suite she had occupied on her last London trip.

And as she had made the journey she might as well stay another day. Do some more sightseeing while she mulled over her next move. So here she was. With time on her hands. A tourist once again.

A tourist with a purpose. She was going to walk around central London and work out whether she could live here or not, even on a part-time basis.

The interview had gone well. *Really* well. More of an informal chat than a terrifying interrogation. She had found herself enjoying the experience and had to admit that the job, being a liaison between small independent shops and the publishers, sounded fascinating.

From the interviewers' enthusiasm and attention to detail Ellie was pretty sure they were going to offer her the role. She was also pretty sure that she would take it, with the proviso that she worked at least one day a week in Cornwall. Apparently plenty of people let out rooms on a weekday-only basis, and with two five-hour commutes in her week she would have plenty of time to catch up on paperwork.

Of course she would be insanely busy. She would have to appoint a shop manager, but she'd still do the accounts and work weekends, plus there was the festival. But she was young, healthy and oh, so single.

Ellie picked up her bag. That was it. She was on the verge of a new, exciting, dream-fulfilling experience and she would not mope around pathetically, thinking about holding hands on the South Bank. She was going to leave this perfectly adequate hotel room and she was going to have some fun whether she felt like it or not.

It was a warm, humid day, the sun hidden by low white cloud. Ellie hesitated outside the hotel's modest entrance, unsure which way to turn. Parks, palaces, museums, shops, exhibitions, theatres—the whole city was open to her.

It was almost paralysing, all this choice. She hadn't felt this way before, when she'd been here with Max. Then having no plan, no destination, had been exciting...an adventure. How was she going to travel and see all the places she had always dreamed of if she couldn't even walk down the street in her own capital city without panicking?

Ellie lifted her chin. Of course she could do it.

She set off almost blindly, walking through the bustling city streets. Four weeks since he had left. More than twice as long as she had actually known him. It made absolutely no sense that she missed him so badly. That it felt as if something fundamental was missing...some part of her like her liver or her lungs. Or her heart.

It made no sense that she instinctively looked for his ironic smile when committee meetings were particularly dull, that she missed his hand in hers on the beach. That she reached for him in her sleep.

He was the first person she wanted to tell when her mother called with updates on Bill's health. The person she wanted to share the amazing book she had just read with. The person she wanted to be sitting opposite her, coffee in hand, book open, reading in companionable silence.

It made no sense at all. But there it was.

Ellie had reached her destination. One huge shop, five storeys high, filled with books, books, nothing but books. It was a mecca for the bookworm, a source of inspiration for a fellow bookshop owner. She should be filled with anticipation, with the tingle in her fingers and the tightening of excitement in her stomach that exploring a new bookshop gave her.

Nothing. Not even a twinge.

Two hours later she emerged.

Five floors and she hadn't felt breathless once. Not a single display had moved her. She hadn't bought one book. Even the expensive piece of cake in the café had tasted of nothing.

It was no good. She was on the verge of an exciting new life and it was if she were dead inside. She needed to recapture some of that heady excitement from her last trip here. Maybe she should head back to the South Bank and see how much she enjoyed hanging out there in the daytime and on her own. See whether she really wanted to live half her life in the anonymity of the city.

Ellie couldn't walk at her usual rate. It was too hot and the tourists were out in force, stopping in front of her, ambling along and taking selfies at every landmark, no matter how insignificant. But it didn't take her long to reach Westminster Bridge. Last time she had walked over the bridge she had been holding Max's hand, with the promise of his kiss hanging over her like a velvet cloak; rich, decadent and all-encompassing.

In front of her the London Eye dominated the skyline. Ellie stopped in the middle of the bridge, her hands on the railings as she looked down at the wide swell of the Thames. So she missed him? That much was clear. The real question was, what was she going to do about it?

Slowly she retraced their steps, across the bridge and down the steps. The queue for the London Eye was already long and she scanned it eagerly. Hoping to see what? Their shadows? A faint wisp of Ellie and Max, still laughing in the queue?

No. No more mooning around looking for the ghosts of lovers past. She pulled her gaze away and marched on, only to be confronted by another queue. The queue for the London Aquarium. The missing piece from their last trip.

If she went in she would go alone. That had never been the deal. She should just walk on by, carry on with her plans. But her feet were heavy, her legs reluctant to move. Ellie stood still, tourists weaving around her, racked with indecision. Maybe she *should* go in. Her last and final act of being pathetic before she pulled herself together and thought about whether she wanted this job or not and where she wanted her life to go.

Just a few small decisions to make.

And then she saw it. A poster advertising tea with the penguins. *Today.* 'Diary it in,' he had said. Of course it had been a joke...a meaningless comment.

But still. It was a sign. She wasn't sure exactly what the sign meant, but no matter. A sign was a sign.

The queue to get in was ridiculous.

If Max had been there, there was no way he'd have

queued. He'd have paid top-dollar for a priority pass and probably been conveyed in on a chariot pulled by walruses. It must be nice to be rich.

Still, she was near the front at last. It was only a quarter to twelve, and she might as well enjoy the whole experience as she was there. Obviously there were several aquariums, zoos and animal sanctuaries a lot closer to home, but that wasn't the point. At all.

No, the point was that she was proving a point. She was taking a positive step. Taking control of her own destiny one very slow step at a time.

Finally she was at the front of the queue. Ellie's heart began to hammer.

'Oh, I'm sorry.' The girl behind the desk didn't look that sorry. She looked busy and tired and fraught. 'The tea with the penguins is all booked out. Do you want a normal ticket?'

Ellie stared. She had blown it. She couldn't even make a melodramatic gesture without messing it up.

'Miss?'

Ellie sighed and held out her bank card. She was here after all. 'Just one adult ticket, please.'

It didn't get easier once she was inside. The entrance was crowded with buggies, harassed families and small children slipping out of their parents' grasps to run amok. And everyone moved so *slowly*! You'd think they'd paid a fortune to look at each and every exhibit, to read all the noticeboards and interpretations, to watch the sharks feeding.

Actually, *that* was quite cool. But, no, she wasn't here to look at sharks.

Finally, *finally,* she managed to sidle past a large group, dodge a particularly active toddler and navigate her way through a group of texting teens. And there she was. At the entrance to the penguin room.

It was like entering an ice palace. White walls, white ceilings and low blue lighting. Windows on one side separated the black and white flightless birds from the spellbound watchers, giving them space to swim and play in peace. She felt a moment's pang for them, confined to this artificial room, unable to explore the wider seas, but at least they were safe from orcas and other predators.

For one long moment Ellie forgot why she was there, swept up in the icy atmosphere and the sheer wonder of the penguins, so graceful in the water, so comical on land. But she soon remembered her purpose and looked around. The room was busy, apart from a cordoned-off area by one of the viewing windows where several tables and chairs were set up. Cake stands and tea sets were neatly arranged on the tables.

Ellie inhaled, long and deep. There was no way he would have remembered that throw-away comment—and even if he had there was no reason for him to be here. But a quick look wouldn't hurt. Would it?

Of course he wasn't there.

Her chest tightened. Should she be disappointed? Heartbroken? Relieved?

Ellie watched a penguin dive into the water, its body hurtling at speed towards the pool floor before executing a neat turn and zooming back up to the surface. The truth was that she was none of the above.

She was determined.

She had queued for nearly an hour on a hot, humid day, and fought her way through the crowds. Not because she had expected to see Max; it wasn't even that she'd *hoped* to see him, amazing as it would have been if he was actually here. No, she had come here to work out what she wanted. It wasn't the most heroic quest of all times, sure. She hadn't fought a Minotaur or anything. But she had tested herself, tested her commitment, and now she knew.

Knew that there was no point leaving her happiness in the hands of fate, or hoping that coincidence would send Max back her way. If she wanted a life with Max Loveday she was going to have to go after it. Show him that she was no damsel in distress but an equal—and a far better match than some well-bred society girl who might know all the right people but would bore him to death within six months.

Really, she was going to be the one who saved him.

So that meant she needed to book her first flight abroad on her own. It wasn't going to be Paris or Rome. She was heading to the States.

Max leaned back in his chair and watched Ellie. His first incredulous happiness at seeing that she was actually here hadn't faded, but it was joined by amusement now as he watched her. Her jaw was set and she looked grimly determined.

He hoped that boded well for him. She might be planning his disembowelment.

'Excuse me.' He walked over to her, stopping behind her as if he were just another visitor, trying to find a spot to view the penguins. 'Are you meeting someone for afternoon tea? I have a table for two, right over here.'

'Max!' She whirled round, her hands against his chest, whether to ward him off or check he was real he didn't know. 'What are you doing here?'

'Afternoon tea, remember? Only they don't serve sushi. Apparently it would be a little insensitive in an aquarium. You can see their point…'

'Yes.' She bit her lip, her face an adorable mixture of confusion and joy. 'But it wasn't a real date. It was a joke.'

'Yet here you are.'

'I was in London anyway, so I thought...you know... while I was here I might as well come and...'

'See if I was here?'

'No.' Her cheeks were turning an interesting shade of red. 'I wanted to see the penguins.'

'And?'

'And what?'

He lowered his voice. 'Are they everything you hoped they would be?'

Her eyes were serious as they scanned his face. 'I'm not sure yet. I hope so. What about you? Are they living up to expectations?'

Max stared down at her, at the pointed chin, the delicate cheekbones, the candid brown eyes. 'Oh, yes...' Was that him? So hoarse? 'Everything I dreamed of.'

Her eyes fell, but not before he saw the spark of hope in them. 'You're sure?'

He took one of her hands in his. 'I've never been surer.'

At one level Max was aware that they were blocking a window, that people were moving past them, trying to look over their heads. That other conversations were taking place, children were crying, asking questions, pushing past him. But it was as if there was a bubble enclosing Ellie and him. They were in the room and yet apart from it. In an alternative universe of two.

He watched her inhale before she looked back up at him.

'What about your parents and DL?'

'Don't let it overwhelm you, but you are looking at the new CEO of DL Media. My father has decided to take an executive board position.'

She raised her elegantly arched brows. 'Decided?'

'That's the official line. As for the divorce: I'm out of it. My only request is that they behave themselves when they have to be in the same room.' He paused. 'At my wedding, for instance.'

Her lips parted. 'Your wedding?'

He held her hand just a little bit tighter. 'There's nothing worse than feuding exes at a wedding. Apart from midlife-crisis-suffering uncles hitting on the bridesmaids, that is. Don't you think?'

'I haven't really thought about it. Are you planning ahead, or have you brought your timetable forward?'

'I got rid of the whole damn timetable. Turns out you can plan for everything but love, Ellie.'

'Love?'

Was that a crack in her voice? He couldn't wait any longer. He'd spent the last eight hours practising elegant speeches but they had gone straight out of his head.

'I can be based in the London office most of the time. Obviously I'd need to go to Hartford regularly, travel a lot, but the UK would be my main home. I'd buy a place in London but spend weekends at The Round House, work from there whenever I could. Get that boat, walk on the beach, win the pub quiz. If you want to, that is?'

'Do I want to win the pub quiz?' Her voice was teasing but her eyes told a different story, shining with happiness. 'I already did. Twice.'

'But not on *my* team. And that's where I want you, Ellie. On my team—and I'll be on yours. For ever. I know it's fast, and I know I didn't make the best first impression, and I know you want time to work out who you are, and I respect that—'

He came to a halt as she put a cool finger to his lips. 'Max Loveday, stop babbling and tell me what you want.'

'I want to marry you, Ellie. Preferably right away. But I'll wait. We can take it as slow as you like.'

'That's a shame.' She stepped a little closer, one hand still in his, her other hand moving from his mouth to cup his cheek. 'Because I don't want to take it slow at all. I want to do it all, Max. Marriage, travel, babies, work. I want it all.'

'You do?'

She nodded solemnly. 'Although you might have to put up with me at more than just the weekends. I might be working in London during the week as well. Does that ruin your carefully thought out plans?'

'I'm learning to be adaptable. London? Really?' His mouth curved into a tender smile. 'Just when I thought you couldn't surprise me more.'

She narrowed her eyes. 'I was interviewed for a job at DL Media today. That didn't have anything to do with *you*, did it?'

'Not a thing. But I'll write you a reference. Although I'm not sure fiancés are acceptable referees, even if they *do* own the company.'

'Fiancé?'

She folded her arms. His cheek still tingled where she had touched it.

'I don't remember you asking. Not properly.'

He reached into his pocket. 'I don't have a ring,' he warned her. 'I want it to be perfect and exactly what you want.' He pulled out a box and dropped down on to one knee.

'Max! Get up!'

'What's that man doing, Mummy?'

Max was horrifyingly aware that the penguins were no longer the main attraction. The room was full of people and they were all looking, smiling and staring at him.

Oh, no—phones were out and pointed in their direction. She'd better say yes.

He took her hand, and as soon as he touched her he was back in the bubble. Let them watch and film.

'Ellie Scott, I love you and I want to give you the world. Will you marry me?'

He held up the box.

'I thought you said you didn't have a ring?' Her voice trembled as she took it from him.

'Open it.'

She slowly lifted the lid. 'It's a snow globe.'

'I had it made specially. Look inside, Ellie, what can you see?'

'Oh, the Eiffel Tower! And is that the Coliseum? And the Sydney Opera House? Does it snow in Sydney?'

'I'll take you to all those places and a hundred besides. We'll walk through the streets and eat in little neighbourhood restaurants and get to the heart of everywhere we go. If we go together. Will you, Ellie?'

'Yes, Max. Of course I will. I'll go anywhere as long as you are with me.'

He got up and cupped her face in his hands. 'Are you sure, Ellie?'

'I'm completely sure. I love you, Max Loveday. All my life I've been too scared to reach out for what I want, but not any more. You've shown me that I can do anything I want to. And what I really want is to spend the rest of my life with you.'

* * * * *

How could ten years fall away in minutes?

How could a decade be forgotten with the touch of his hand? How could formerly hazy memories of long, passionate nights be suddenly more real to her than the people surrounding them as Gavin took her in his arms?

"A lot has changed in ten years." His warm breath brushed her cheek and she shivered.

Sex, she told herself. That's what this was about. She'd always responded to whatever pheromones Gavin put out. That hadn't changed.

Still, if he was getting ideas that their chance meeting at the cabin could lead to anything more, she needed to set him straight. Sure, they'd gotten along fine, shared an amazing kiss. But that was a kiss goodbye, not the start of something new.

Gavin's hand at the small of her back pressed her closer. She could have resisted. But for one moment she gave herself permission to simply enjoy the feel of him.

Stop this, Jenny. Stop it before you do something incredibly stupid, said the voice in her head.

Should she listen to it?

* * *

Proposals & Promises

Putting a ring on it is only the beginning!

How could ten years fall away in minutes?

How could a decade be forgotten with the touch of his hand? How could [illegible] easy memories of long [illegible] [illegible] [illegible] than the people surrounding them as Gavin [illegible] [illegible]

'[illegible] has changed in ten years?' [illegible] [illegible] her cheek and the [illegible]

[illegible] herself. That's what this was about. [illegible] [illegible] [illegible] Gavin [illegible] [illegible] been changed.

[illegible] [illegible] [illegible] [illegible] [illegible] [illegible] [illegible] [illegible] [illegible] [illegible] [illegible]

[illegible] [illegible] [illegible] [illegible] [illegible] [illegible]

[illegible] [illegible] [illegible]

Should she [illegible]

A REUNION AND A RING

BY
GINA WILKINS

MILLS & BOON

Published in Great Britain 2015
by Mills & Boon, an imprint of Harlequin (UK) Limited,
Eton House, 18-24 Paradise Road, Richmond, Surrey, TW9 1SR

ISBN: 978-0-263-25159-3

23-0815

Harlequin (UK) Limited's policy is to use papers that are natural, renewable and recyclable products and made from wood grown in sustainable forests. The logging and manufacturing processes conform to the legal environmental regulations of the country of origin.

Printed and bound in Spain
by CPI, Barcelona

Author of more than a hundred titles for Mills & Boon, native Arkansan **Gina Wilkins** was introduced early to romance novels by her avid-reader mother. Gina loves sharing her own stories with readers who enjoy books celebrating families and romance. She is inspired daily by her husband of over thirty years, their two daughters and their son, their librarian son-in-law who fits perfectly into this fiction-loving family, and an adorable grandson who already loves books.

As always, for my own perfect match—
my husband, John. He proves every day that real-life heroes are the ones who are always quietly there for their family and friends, whether to lend a hug, a cheer or a hammer and duct tape. Forever my inspiration.

Chapter One

The headlights sliced through the darkness ahead, glittering off the torrents of rain pounding the windshield of the small car. The wind blew so hard that it took some effort to keep the car on the road. Fingers white-knuckled on the wheel, Jenny Baer leaned forward slightly against her seat belt in an attempt to better see the winding road. The weather had turned nasty earlier than she'd expected when she'd started this almost-three-hour drive.

She'd intended to leave work just after lunch on this Friday, which would have put her here midafternoon, before the rain set in. Instead, she'd been held up with one crisis after another, until it had been after six when she'd finally gotten away. She hadn't even had a chance to change out of her work clothes. She'd thought of waiting until morning to head out, but she'd been afraid she'd only be detained again, maybe until too late to even consider the rare, three-day vacation she was allowing herself.

Her grandmother would say "I told you so" in that sanctimonious tone she often slipped into. Gran had insisted it was foolish for Jenny to take off on her own and stay alone for a long weekend in a secluded mountain cabin. But then, Gran was always trying to tell her only grandchild how to live her life. Though Jenny believed the advice was generally well-intended, she had to remind her grandmother repeatedly that she was thirty-one years old, held a master's degree and was the sole owner of a successful clothing-and-accessories boutique.

Gran would be even less supportive of this private retreat if she knew the reason Jenny had decided impulsively to take it. If she'd told her grandmother that prominent attorney Thad Simonson had proposed marriage, Gran would already be arranging an engagement party, maybe interviewing wedding planners. She wouldn't understand why Jenny had asked for time to think about her answer, though Thad had seemed to consider the request entirely reasonable. After all, he'd said, Jenny's practicality and judiciousness were two of the many qualities he most admired about her. She had accepted the comment as a compliment, as she knew he'd intended—though maybe he'd been just a bit too prosaic about it?

Thad was out of state for a couple weeks on one of his frequent business trips, so Jenny had taken the opportunity to get away for a few days herself. She needed time to think about the ramifications of accepting his proposal without the distractions of constantly ringing phones and never-ending meetings with employees, customers, contractors and sales reps.

Lightning flashed in the distance through the curtains of rain, silhouetting the surrounding hills against the angry sky. The full force of the early-June storm was still a few miles away, but getting closer. What had she been thinking heading into the backwoods with this looming? She was the least impulsive person she knew—at least, that was the way she'd lived for the past decade or so—and yet, here she was, inching through a downpour in the middle of nowhere, heading for a cabin in the Arkansas Ozarks with no housekeeping staff, no room service, none of the amenities she preferred for her infrequent escapes. All with less than forty-eight hours of planning, another anomaly for her.

Considering everything, it was a wonder the cabin had even been available on such short notice, but the too-cheery rental agent had assured her it was ready to rent. Jenny had assumed the weather forecasts had scared off other prospective vacationers, but she'd planned to stay inside to think and work in blessed isolation, so the prospect of a rainy weekend hadn't deterred her. This storm, on the other hand, threatened to be more than she'd bargained for.

She turned onto a steeply rising gravel lane pitted with deep, rapidly filling puddles. The car skidded to the right as she made the turn, hydroplaning on the water beginning to creep over the road. She gasped and tightened her grip on the wheel, letting out her breath slowly when the tires regained traction, digging into the gravel and forcing their way uphill.

She gave a little moan of relief when the cabin appeared in front of her as a darker shape in the headlights. No lights burned in the windows, and there seemed to be no security lights outside. It was hard to tell if the place had changed much since she'd last been here, almost eleven years ago. Lizzie, the rather ditzy rental agent, had explained that there was a carport behind the cabin, but since there was no covered walkway from there to the back door, Jenny parked as close as she could get to the front porch.

Her luggage was in the trunk, but the purse, computer case and overnight bag in the front passenger seat held everything she needed until morning. Arms full, she jumped out of the car and made a mad scramble toward the covered porch. She cursed beneath her breath as she fumbled the key into the lock. Just from that brief dash, her dark hair was soaked, the layers hanging limply around her face and sticking to her cheek. Her once-crisp, white designer blouse was now sodden and transparent, and her gray linen pants were wet to the skin. Mud splattered her expensive sandals and she'd twisted her ankle on the slippery steps. This was what she got, she chided herself, for coming to a place with no eager doorman to assist her.

"I told you so," Gran's imaginary voice whispered in her ear, making her scowl as she shoved through the door.

The interior of the cabin was stuffy and dark, lit only by the almost-constant flashes of lightning through the windows. In the strobe-like illumination, she could see that she had entered a spacious open room with a kitchen and dining area at the far end, and a big stone fireplace on the wall to her right. It was all exactly as she remembered.

She hadn't anticipated the feelings that almost overwhelmed her when she walked in, stealing the breath from her lungs and leaving a dull ache in her chest. She'd told herself she'd sought out this cabin only because it was the first place that had popped into her mind when she'd looked for a peaceful hideaway for the serious deliberations facing her. She'd reassured herself she was drawn here because she'd recalled the natural beauty, the soothing backdrop of birdsongs and mountain breezes. The long Labor Day weekend she'd spent here with her college boyfriend's family had been one of the most pleasant holidays of her life. It had seemed a lucky omen when she'd made a couple of internet searches and phone calls and discovered, to her surprise, that not only was the cabin still on the market for vacation rentals, it was also available this very week.

She'd thought she could enjoy the setting without dwelling on the copious tears she'd shed by the end of that year, after a bitterly painful breakup. She'd thought she had long since dealt with that youthful heartbreak so she could remember the good times and forget the bad, the way any mature adult looked back at the foibles of youth. Maybe she'd even thought this would be a fitting way to put a final closure to her one previous serious relationship before committing completely to a new, permanent union.

Perhaps she shouldn't have been quite so impetuous in booking this cabin. Maybe some old memories should remain locked away, without such tangible reminders.

Shaking her head in exasperation with herself, she set her bags at her feet and fumbled for a wall switch. She hoped the light would banish those old images back into the shadows of the past where they belonged. Nothing happened when she flipped the lever. Great. The storm had knocked out the power. She stood just inside the room, debating whether she should get back in the car and make a break for civilization, preferably someplace new and memory-free. As if in answer, a hard gust of wind rattled the windows, followed by a crash of thunder that sounded like the closest one yet. Okay, maybe she'd stay inside for a while. She tugged her phone out of her pocket, using the screen for light. A very weak signal, she noted in resignation, but the time was displayed on the screen. Almost 10:00 p.m.

She might as well peel out of these wet clothes and try to get a little sleep. Suddenly exhausted, she kicked off her muddy shoes and carried her overnight bag toward the open doorway on the left side of the room. Tomorrow morning, after the tempest had passed, she would decide what to do if the power wasn't restored. She'd anticipated that by the end of this retreat she would have a pile of paperwork completed, crucial decisions made, the rest of her life neatly planned out. Had she been hopelessly naive?

She had her blouse unbuttoned by the time she reached the doorway. She couldn't wait to be out of these wet things and into her comfy satin nightshirt. She hoped the mattress was decent. Not that it mattered much. She was tired enough to sleep on a bag of rocks.

The bedroom was tiny, taken up almost entirely by the bed. Just as that fact registered, she stumbled hard over something on the floor. Her overnight bag fell from her hand and landed squarely on one bare foot. Pain shot all the way up her leg, making her yelp and hop. Her phone hit the floor, screen down, plunging the room into total darkness. She fell onto the bed.

"What the hell?" The sleepy, startled male voice

erupted from the darkness as hands closed around Jenny's arms.

Instinctively, she reached out, and her palms landed on a very warm bare chest sprinkled with wiry hair. She choked out a cry and shoved herself backward. She'd have fallen off the bed if the man hadn't been holding on to her.

"Let go of me!" she ordered sharply, barely suppressed panic making her throat tight. "What are you doing here? I'm calling the police."

"Lady, I *am* the police. And you're breaking and entering."

She struggled to her feet. Holding on to her with one hand, the man sat up on the bed and reached across with his other hand to fumble around on the nightstand. Cold fluorescent light beamed in a small circle from an emergency lantern he'd set beside the bed, making her squint to adjust her vision. Seeing the man who still gripped her arm did not exactly inspire confidence.

His shaggy hair, dark blond with lighter streaks, tumbled around a hard-jawed face stubbled with a couple days' growth of dark beard. She couldn't discern the color of his narrowed eyes, but she could see that his mouth was a hard slash bracketed by lines that probably deepened into long dimples when—or if—he smiled. His bare shoulders were tanned and linebacker broad. Dark hair scattered across his hard chest and narrowed to the thin sheet pooled at his waist. A large white bandage covered his right shoulder, but the evidence of injury made him look no more vulnerable. Overall, she got the immediate first impression of coiled strength, simmering temper and almost overwhelming masculinity.

It took another moment to realize that she knew him. Or had once known him. Quite well actually. Had his fingers not been biting into her arm, she might have thought her weary, memory-flooded mind was playing tricks on her.

"Gavin?"

Surely fate's sense of humor wasn't this twisted!

He blinked up at her and she wondered for a moment if he even recognized her in the shadows. Though he didn't release her, his fingers relaxed their grip. "Jen?"

Of all the improbable possibilities she could have imagined for the start of this poorly planned vacation, falling into bed with Gavin Locke wouldn't have even been on her list. She stared mutely at him, unable to think of a thing to say. Her heart pounded in her chest, her throat suddenly so tight she couldn't draw air in, much less force words out. Once again memories filled her mind in a rush of images so vivid that she could almost feel his hands sweeping over her bare skin, could almost taste his lips on hers, could almost hear his low, hoarse groans of arousal and satisfaction.

Even as her face warmed and her pulse raced in reaction to those arousing flashbacks, she struggled to tamp them down again. She'd simply been caught off guard, she told herself irritably. It was only natural that unexpectedly finding Gavin in bed, half-naked, would remind her of all the times she'd seen him that way before. Just because she'd long since moved on didn't mean she'd forgotten her reckless, youthful love affair. Just as remembering didn't mean she hadn't put it all safely behind her.

"What are you doing here?" he demanded. "How did you get in?"

His words roused her into a response, though she wished her voice emerged a little steadier. "I came in through the front door. What are *you* doing here? Did you break in?"

"Did I… No, I didn't break in! I used my key."

Following his sweeping gesture, she glanced toward the nightstand. Beside the plastic lantern sat a couple of medication bottles, a holstered handgun and a metal ring holding several keys. She swallowed, unable for the moment to look away from the weapon.

"Look, Jenny, I'm running on too little sleep, and I'm fairly pissed that someone got all the way into my bed without me hearing a thing, so maybe you could start explaining. Why are you here?" His voice was a growl underlain with steel. It was deeper than she remembered, but his cranky tone was familiar enough. She'd heard it often during the last few weeks of their ill-fated college romance.

She lifted her chin, refusing to be cowed by his mood. "I rented the cabin from Lizzie, the agent at the leasing company. I paid in advance for the weekend, and I have the paperwork to prove it in the other room."

His fingers loosened even more in apparent surprise, and she took the opportunity to snatch her arm away and move a step back from the bed.

He seemed to process her explanation slowly. Perhaps his mind was fuzzy from whatever was in those prescription bottles. "Lizzie rented the cabin to you?"

She nodded. "She said there was a cancelation and that it was available."

"Lizzie is a…"

A clap of thunder drowned out his words. Probably for the best. When the noise subsided a bit, Gavin shook his head, tossed off the sheet and swung his bare legs over the side of the bed. He wore nothing but a pair of boxer shorts. Though she'd seen him in less, that had been a long time ago, and seeing him like this now was not helping to ease the awkwardness of this encounter.

She became suddenly aware that she was standing in front of him with her wet blouse hanging open, revealing the lacy bra beneath. She reached up hastily to tug the shirt closed, fumbling with buttons. Her foot throbbed, she didn't know where her phone had landed and her hair still dripped around her face. In her wildest imagination, she couldn't have predicted her retreat starting out like this.

Seemingly unconcerned with his own state of undress, Gavin stood just at the edge of the lantern's reach. Lightning flashed through the nearby window, revealing, then shadowing, his hard face and strong torso. As inappropriate as it was, considering the circumstances, she still felt a hard tug of feminine response somewhere deep inside her. The years had been very good to Gavin Locke.

She cleared her throat. "If you want to see my paperwork…"

"Come on, Jenny, you know I believe you. Besides, I've dealt with Lizzie enough recently to know that your story is completely plausible."

The wind howled louder outside, so Jenny had to speak up to ask, "Are you saying she rented you the cabin for tonight, too?"

"She didn't have to rent it to me. I own this cabin now."

"Oh, crap." When had he bought it? Why? She had a vague memory of it belonging to an old friend of his family's, but she'd never imagined Gavin would now be the owner.

"You can say that again." He shook his head in disgust. "I told Lizzie not to rent the place this week, that I needed it myself. I should have known she'd get it mixed up. She's new at the job and she's incompetent."

"I..." A gust of wind blew so hard she could feel the cabin being buffeted by it. Something hit the roof above them and she cringed, glancing up instinctively. She couldn't help thinking again of the tall trees surrounding the place. She suspected a branch had just fallen on the roof, and she hoped it wouldn't be followed by the whole tree.

Gavin looked up, too, and then staggered, as if doing so had made him dizzy. He put out a hand to steady himself and nearly knocked the lantern off the nightstand. Without thinking, Jenny moved to steady him, her hands closing over his shoulders. He flinched away from her grip on his bandaged shoulder, and it was obvious that she'd hurt him. Even as she snatched her arms back, she realized that his skin had seemed unnaturally warm.

Frowning, she reached out again, this time laying her palm tentatively against his cheek. She tried to keep her touch relatively impersonal, merely that of a concerned nurse. "You have a fever."

He brushed her off. "I was sleeping. I'm probably just warm from that."

"No, it's definitely a low-grade fever. Is your shoulder wound infected?"

"I'm taking antibiotics," he muttered.

"Since when?"

"Since this morning. Saw my doc before I drove up

from Little Rock. He said it's not too bad and the meds will clear it up soon."

She stepped back. "Have you taken anything for the fever?"

"I'm fine."

"I've got some aspirin in my bag. Maybe you should lie back down while I try to find it. If I could borrow the lantern?"

One hand at the back of his neck, he stared at her. "You broke in here to take my temperature and give me aspirin? Are you sure my mother didn't send you?"

Oddly enough, the mention of his mother made her relax a bit. She had always liked his mother. "I didn't break in. And I'm leaving immediately. I apologize for the misunderstanding. Do you want the aspirin before I go or not?"

Looking steadier, he scooped up a pair of jeans from the floor and stepped into them. She noticed only then that she'd tripped over a pair of his shoes. He must have pretty much stripped and fallen into bed earlier. If he'd taken a pain pill beforehand, that could explain why he'd slept so heavily he hadn't heard her entrance over the noisy weather.

He swung an arm in the direction of the single window in the little bedroom. The glass rattled in the frame from the force of the wind blowing outside, and a veritable fireworks exhibit played across the slice of sky visible from where she stood. Thunder had become a constant grouchy roar, as if the night itself was grudgingly surrendering to the storm.

"You aren't going back out in that. The way that rain's coming down, I wouldn't be surprised if the road is flooded. And the full force of the storm hasn't even hit yet. We're in for worse before it passes."

She thought of the water already creeping over the road when she'd approached the cabin. That frightening moment when she'd hydroplaned. She swallowed. "I'll be fine," she said, wishing she sounded a bit more confident.

She bent to retrieve her dropped phone just as Gavin took a step toward her. "Don't be foolish. The storm is too…"

The collision knocked her flat on her behind and nearly caused Gavin to sprawl on top of her. Somehow he steadied himself, though it involved flailing that made him grunt in pain from his injured shoulder.

Sitting sprawled at his feet, she shook her head. Could this ridiculous evening get any worse? Or was she tempting capricious fate to even ask?

Gavin was beginning to wonder just what was in those pills he'd taken before he'd turned in. Was he hallucinating? Or had a gorgeous, wet woman with a smoking body revealed by an open blouse really fallen out of the storm and into his bed? A woman right out of the memories he thought he'd locked away long ago, though they'd escaped a few times to haunt his most erotic dreams. Was he dreaming again now?

No. The way she sat on the floor glaring up at him told him this was no fantasy. The dream-Jenny had been much more approachable.

Muttering an apology, he reached down to haul her to her feet with his good arm. He released her as soon as he was sure she was steady on her feet.

"It wasn't your fault," his uninvited guest conceded.

"I was picking up my phone. I dropped it when I stumbled over your shoes."

Which made it still his fault, in a way, but he wasn't going to get into a circular argument with her. "Are you expecting anyone else to arrive tonight?"

Was he unintentionally intruding on what she'd planned to be a romantic, rustic retreat? He told himself the possibility annoyed him only because he didn't want to have to deal with yet another intruder. What other reason could there be after all these years?

"No. I was going to hide out here alone for a few days to get some work done without interruptions."

He was still having trouble clearing his thoughts. He couldn't begin to understand why Jenny had come to this particular place to work. What the hell was he supposed to do with her now?

An unwelcome recollection from the last time they'd been together here slammed into his mind in response to what should have been a rhetorical question. He could almost see himself and Jenny, naked and entwined, lying on a pile of their clothes in a secluded, shaded clearing. Laughing and aroused, they'd made good use of the stolen hour. His blood still heated in response to the distant echoes of their gasps and moans.

Shoving the memories fiercely to the back of his mind, he half turned away from her. The storm assaulting the windows made it obvious she wasn't leaving immediately. He released a heavy sigh. "Maybe you remember there's another bedroom at the back of the cabin, behind the kitchen. You can crash there tonight, and we'll get this all figured out in the morning."

"Spend the night here? With you?"

Pain radiated from his shoulder, and his head was

starting to pound. He hadn't had a full night's sleep in a couple days. Patience was not his strong suit at the best of times, but he'd lost any semblance of it tonight.

"I didn't suggest sleeping in the same bed," he snapped. "The other room has a lock on the door. Use it, if you're so damned afraid of me. Hell, take my weapon and sleep with it under your pillow, if it makes you feel better."

She sighed and shook her head. "I'm not afraid of you, Gavin."

"Great. I'm not afraid of you, either."

A soft laugh escaped her, sounding as if it had been startled out of her. "You're in pain," she said. "I'll get the aspirin."

"I had a pain pill before I went to sleep. Probably shouldn't take aspirin on top of it."

"Oh. You're right. How long has it been?"

"Couple hours, maybe. I can take one every four hours, but I don't usually need them that often."

"What did you do to your shoulder?"

"Long story." And one he had no intention of getting into at the moment. "There's another emergency lantern in the kitchen. I'll help you find it. I'm thirsty, anyway."

"Thank you."

He saw her glance up nervously when something else hit the roof, and he wondered if she was anxious about the storm. He remembered that she'd never been a fan of storms. Yet, she'd been prepared to go back out in it? He shook his head.

Carefully pulling on a loose shirt, he picked up the lantern and moved past her toward the doorway. He heard her pick up her bag and hurry after him, trying to stay close to the light. He retrieved the second fluorescent lantern from the kitchen counter, pushed the power button, then turned to offer it to his visitor. She accepted with barely concealed eagerness.

He could see her more clearly in the double lantern light. She'd been very pretty just out of her teens, but the intervening decade had only added to her attraction.

Her dark hair, which she'd once worn long and straight, now waved in layers around her oval face. He remembered how it had once felt to have his hands buried in its soft depths.

Her chocolate-brown eyes studied him warily from beneath long, dark lashes. There had been a time when she'd gazed at him with open adulation.

She was still slender, though perhaps a bit curvier than before. He'd once known every inch of her body as well as his own, and he noted the slight differences now. He tried to stay objective, but he was only human. And she looked damned good.

Her expensive-looking clothes were somewhat worse for wear after her jog through the rain. He wasn't one to notice brands, but even he recognized the logo on the overnight bag she carried. Apparently she had achieved the success she had always aspired to.

He hadn't kept up with her—quite deliberately—but his mother had mentioned a few months ago that she'd seen Jenny's photo in the society section of the local newspaper. She'd watched his face a bit too closely as she'd commented casually that Jenny had been photographed at some sort of community service awards dinner for Little Rock's young professionals. She'd added that Jenny was reported to be dating a member of one of central Arkansas's most prominent and long-established families. He'd answered somewhat curtly that he read the sports pages, not the society gossip, and that he had no particular interest in who his long-ago college girlfriend was now dating. He wasn't sure he'd succeeded in convincing his mother that Jenny never even crossed his mind these days.

So what had really made this country-club princess choose to vacation at his rustic fishing cabin? As unlikely a coincidence as it was, he had no doubt that she was as dismayed to have found him here as he was that she'd shown up so unexpectedly. The genuine shock on her face had been unmistakable.

He reached into a cabinet and drew out a glass. "Are you thirsty? I doubt there's anything cold in the fridge, but I can offer tap water. Or I think we've got some herbal tea bags. It's a gas stove, so I can heat water for you, if you want."

Despite the circumstances, he was trying to be a reasonably gracious host, though he wasn't the sociable type at the best of times. After all, it wasn't Jenny's fault the agency he'd hired to rent out the cabin had recently employed a total airhead. He'd have more than a few pointed words for someone there tomorrow.

Hal Woodman, an old friend of his father's, had built this cabin on the Buffalo River as a fishing retreat and rental property when Gavin was just a kid. Hal had let Gavin's parents use it frequently for family vacations. A few years later, Gavin's dad bought the cabin from his then-ailing friend. Gavin and his sister inherited the place when their father died a couple years ago. His sister lived out of state now with her military husband, so Gavin had bought her portion. To defray the costs, he rented it out when he wasn't using it—which was more often than he liked because of his work schedule.

The cabin was close enough to hiking trails, float trip outfitters and a couple of tourist-friendly towns that it rarely sat empty for long. Yet, had anyone suggested that Jenny Baer would be one of his weekend renters, he would have labeled that person delusional.

Jenny shivered a little, and he realized her clothes were still damp. Hell, she'd likely sue both him and the leasing agency if she got sick. "Go put on some dry clothes. I'll heat some water. The bathroom's through that door."

Jenny hesitated only a moment, then tightened her grip on the lantern and turned toward the bathroom. Grumbling beneath his breath, he filled the teakettle and reached for the tin of herbal teas his health-conscious mom had insisted he bring with him. She was still annoyed with him for taking off to heal in private rather than letting her nurse him back to health from his injury, which would have driven him crazy. He disliked being fussed over, even by the mother he adored.

Jenny wasn't gone long. When she returned, she wore slim-fitting dark knit pants with a loose coral top that looked somewhat more comfortable than her previous outfit. She'd towel-dried her hair and her feet were still bare, but other than that, she could have been dressed to host a casual summer party. Had she really packed this way for a cabin weekend alone? He had to admit she looked great, but out of place here. No surprise.

He set a steaming mug of tea on the booth-style oak table. A bench rested against the wall, and four bow-back chairs were arranged at the ends and opposite side of the table, providing comfortable seating for six adults. He brought friends occasionally for poker-and-fishing weekends, and the family still tried to gather here once a year or so, but usually he came alone when he needed a little downtime to recharge his emotional batteries.

Setting the lantern on the table, Jenny slid into a chair and picked up the tea mug, cradling it between her hands as she gazed up at him. "I'm really sorry about this mix-up. And that I woke you so abruptly when I'm sure you need sleep."

He started to shrug his right shoulder out of habit, then stopped himself at the first twinge of protest. "Not your fault," he said again. "How long were you planning to stay?"

She looked into her mug, hiding her expression. "I paid for three nights, which would let me stay until Monday afternoon if I'd wanted."

"By yourself." That still seemed odd to him. Was she still seeing Mr. Social Register? Or had there been a breakup? He couldn't help thinking back to the weeks following his breakup with Jenny. He'd dropped out of college and holed up here alone for a couple of weeks, until his parents had shown up and practically dragged him back into the real world. He'd entered the police academy as soon as he could get in after that, putting both the pain and the woman who'd caused it out of his mind and out of his heart. Or at least that's what he'd told himself all these years since.

Still, just because he'd retreated here after a split didn't mean Jenny's reasons for being here were in any way the same.

No particular emotion showed on her face when she spoke, still without looking up at him. "I've gotten behind on some business and personal paperwork and I thought it would be nice to have a little time to myself in peaceful surroundings to tackle it all. I needed a chance to concentrate without constant interruptions, and it's usually hard to find that back at home."

Leaning against the counter, he raised his water glass and murmured into it, "I know that feeling."

She glanced at him from beneath her lashes. "You're getting away from everyone, too?"

"In a way. I, um, had surgery on my shoulder last week and I'd rather hide out and heal alone rather than be hovered over by my mom."

Her full lips curved then into a faint smile. "From what I remember about you, that doesn't surprise me at all."

He didn't want to discuss memories, good or otherwise.

"So you drove straight here from Little Rock?"

"Yes. It wasn't storming when I left. I had hoped it would hit later, or maybe skip this area completely."

She looked up when thunder boomed again, louder and closer. "Thor's really angry tonight," she murmured with a wry, somewhat nervous-looking smile.

A chuckle escaped him. "The myth or the superhero?"

"The myth, of course." She gave a husky little laugh that echoed straight from those memories he was trying so hard to hold back. "And the superhero. I've seen all the movies, even though my, um, friend calls them cheesy. Don't get me wrong, I enjoy more intellectually challenging films for the most part, but I..."

She stopped herself with a grimace. "I'm sorry, I'm babbling. This whole situation is just so...awkward."

"Yeah." He set his glass beside the sink, his attention lingering reluctantly on her mention of a "friend."

Something about the way she'd said the word made him wonder…

He motioned abruptly toward his bedroom. "I'm going back to bed. Make yourself at home. We'll sort it all out in the morning. You'll be getting a refund, of course, for anything you've paid up front."

Lightning zapped so close to the cabin he could almost smell the ozone. The near-deafening clap of thunder was almost simultaneous. He saw Jenny flinch, her hands visibly unsteady around the mug. Wind-driven rain hammered the windows, and he thought he heard some hail mixed in. The full force of the storm had definitely arrived.

"Do you know if we're under a tornado warning?"

He shook his head. "My phone would sound an alarm if we were. It's only a severe thunderstorm warning."

"You'll let me know if it turns into anything more?"

"Of course."

He took another step toward the bedroom just as another barrage of hail hit the roof and windows. Hearing a sound from Jenny, he looked over his shoulder. She sat at the table holding her mug, her face pale in the circle of lantern light. She made no move toward her own bedroom. "Are you okay?"

She glanced his way. "I hope this hail doesn't damage my car."

His truck was under cover in the carport, but he wasn't about to offer to go out and swap places with her. He figured she had insurance. "Maybe the hail won't last long."

"I hope you're right," she said, her voice almost drowned out by thunder. The storm was so loud now it seemed to echo inside his aching head.

Raising his left hand to his temple, he said, "Let me know if you need anything."

"Thanks. I'm okay for now."

Nodding, he turned and headed grimly for the bedroom, thinking he'd better lie down before he embarrassed himself by falling down. He'd been assured the wound infection was not serious and should heal quickly with a five-day course of antibiotics, but combined with everything else, it was kicking his butt tonight. He could only blame that for his inability to think clearly about the woman now sitting at his table.

He'd been far too rattled ever since she'd tumbled out of the storm, out of the past and into his bed.

Jenny watched Gavin walk away. His thin shirt emphasized the breadth and muscularity of his shoulders and arms. His well-worn jeans encased a tight butt. At thirty-one, he'd put on a few pounds since she'd seen him last, but those pounds were all muscle. She saw no evidence of his injury from the back, which only enhanced the impression of strength and power. She waited only until his bedroom door closed sharply behind him before she sagged in her chair and hid her face in her hands.

She had always wondered how she would feel if she saw Gavin again. She'd hoped she would have enough warning to brace herself. As it was, it had taken every ounce of control she could muster to hide her shock and dismay at finding him here.

Gavin had certainly shown no particular emotion, other than the initial, understandable confusion when he'd first recognized her. Since then, he'd given no evidence that he viewed her as anything more than an annoying intrusion. Remembering how angry he'd been when she'd broken up with him, she supposed that shouldn't surprise her.

She felt suddenly alone in her little circle of lantern light. A crash of wind and thunder made her jerk, almost spilling the dregs of her tea. She swallowed, squared her shoulders and stood to carry the cup to the sink.

Retrieving her bag and the lantern, she moved into the back bedroom, which was even smaller than the one in which she'd found Gavin. A full-over-full bunk bed was pushed against the wall, leaving little walking room. She'd forgotten about the bunk bed. Just over ten years ago, on that pleasant Locke family getaway, she and Gavin's sister had slept in this room. His very traditional parents had taken the bedroom and Gavin got the sleeper sofa.

Which hadn't prevented her and Gavin from sneaking off a few times to be alone, she recalled with a hard swallow. They'd found one particularly inviting clearing in the woods, carpeted with soft moss, serenaded by the sound of lazily running water.

The unsettling memory was so clear she could almost hear that water now. She took a step forward into the room and started when her bare foot landed in a puddle of cold water. Lifting the lantern, she discovered a steady stream of rain pouring in onto the top bunk. Another, smaller leak dripped onto the floor where she'd just stepped.

She raised the light higher, looking up at the ceiling. Another surge of hail pounded the windows and more water gushed through the leak above the bed. Obviously, shingles had been loosened or blown off. She rushed back into the kitchen, set her bag on the table and began to rummage quickly in the cupboards for containers in which to catch the leaks. Maybe she could save the wood flooring if she intervened quickly. She tried to be quiet, but pans clattered despite her efforts. She pulled out the largest pots she found, then tried to juggle them with a couple of dish towels and the lantern. This no-electricity thing could get old very fast.

The other bedroom door flew open. "What are you doing out here?" Gavin sounded both sleepy and irritated.

"I'm sorry I disturbed you again," she replied over her shoulder. "The roof in this bedroom is leaking in two places. I'm trying to catch the water before it does any damage."

"Well, hell."

Moments later, he knelt beside her with another towel, though she'd already mopped up most of the standing water. His now-bare shoulder brushed her arm as they reached out together, and she felt a jolt of electricity shoot through her. Just static, she assured herself, scooting an inch away. She stuck a pot beneath the leak and heard the rhythmic strike of drops against metal.

"Should we try to move the bed away from the leak?"

"Nowhere to move it to." He picked up the other pot and set it on the top bed. Now the water splashed in stereo, thumping against the pots like miniature drumbeats. "There are waterproof covers on both mattresses. I'll strip the beds and try to dry everything tomorrow."

He turned toward her, his partially shadowed face inscrutable. "Obviously you can't stay in here. That dripping would drive you nuts."

"True."

He let out a sigh and motioned toward the doorway. "Looks like you're sleeping in my bed tonight."

Her heart gave a hard thump simultaneously with the loud clap of thunder that accompanied his words.

Chapter Two

Jenny woke with a start Saturday morning at the sound of a closing door. Disoriented, she blinked her eyes open, only then remembering that she'd spent a restless night on the sleeper sofa in the cabin's living room. Gavin had offered the use of his bed, but she'd refused. She wouldn't displace an injured man from his bed because of a mix-up that was no fault of his own. Not to mention that the thought of crawling into sheets still warm from his body had been disconcerting enough to make her toes curl.

Though the fold-out mattress was comfortable enough, she hadn't slept well, and the noisy storm had been only part of the reason. She'd lain awake for a long time trying to come to grips with the reality that after all these years her ex-boyfriend lay only a few feet away. Old memories—some bittersweet, some wrenching—

had whirled through her head, leaving her too tense to relax. It had simply never crossed her mind that she might run into Gavin at the cabin she'd only visited before with him. Some might say there was a complicated Freudian explanation behind her decision to come here to consider another man's proposal, but that was ridiculous. It had been the peace and quiet that had drawn her here, certainly not nostalgia.

Gavin stood in front of her when she turned her head toward the front door. Dressed in a gray T-shirt, jeans and boots, he was damp and mud-splattered. He pushed a hand through his wet hair, which was so long it touched the back collar of his shirt, indicating he'd missed a couple of cuts. He still hadn't shaved, adding to his roguish bad-boy appearance. Her pulse jumped into a faster rhythm at the sight of him. If she'd had any doubt that she still found Gavin strongly attractive, that question was answered definitively now.

"Sorry I woke you," he said.

Self-conscious, she swung her feet to the floor and pushed herself upright, trying to smooth her tousled hair. It bothered her to think he'd walked right past her as she'd slept, leaving her feeling uncomfortably vulnerable. That was a little hard to deal with this morning.

Light filtered in through the windows. She could hear rain still falling on the roof, though the height of the storm had passed. She saw no lights burning inside, so she assumed the power was still out. "What time is it?"

"A little after eight."

Later than she usually slept, but she hardly felt well-rested. "What's it like out there?"

His response was blunt. "A mess. Lots of limbs on

the ground. There's a big tree over the road a few yards from the house, totally blocking the drive, and I'm sure there's flooding beyond that. You're lucky you got here when you did last night. You won't be leaving for a while yet. No way to get down the hill in your car."

Not promising. She moistened her dry lips before asking, "Is my car damaged?"

"A few hail dings. You were fortunate. A good-size limb fell only a couple feet away from your hood."

While she was relieved her car hadn't sustained damage, she wasn't sure *fortunate* was the right word to describe her current situation. "How long do you think it will take for them to clear the tree from the road?"

"Them?"

"The county? Highway department? Whoever does that sort of thing."

"Highway department doesn't take care of rural gravel roads. And the tree's on private property, so the county isn't going to deal with it. I'm sure they have their hands full elsewhere. From what I saw on my phone news feed, there was quite a bit of damage around this part of the state last night."

"Oh." She swallowed, feeling suddenly a bit panicky at the thought of being trapped here with Gavin for much longer. It wasn't that she feared for her safety—but she couldn't say the same for her peace of mind. "So, what are we going to do?"

"I've got a chain saw in the back of my truck. I was planning to do some light trimming and clearing this weekend, anyway, assuming my shoulder cooperated. I'll tackle the tree when the rain stops, but it's going to take a while with only the one sixteen-inch saw. As for the flooding, you'll just have to wait for that to recede.

There's too much water over the road for you to risk driving through it, even if you could figure out a way to get around the tree. You'd be swept into the river before you made it across."

Unsurprised that he hadn't planned to let his injury stop him from the work he'd wanted to do, she twisted her fingers in front of her. "How long do you think it will take for the flooding to recede?"

He glanced upward, silently indicating the still-falling rain. "This county remains under a flash flood alert. It's going to take a few hours for all the water to drain off once the rain stops."

"Have you heard from home? Was there storm damage in the Little Rock area?"

He shook his head. "The worst of the storms were confined to this part of the state."

She was relieved that her family and her business had escaped the brunt of the storms she'd so foolishly driven into, but she wasn't looking forward to spending several hours alone here with Gavin and their shared memories. "Surely I can get out somehow. Is there a back road, maybe?"

"Look, Jenny, I'm no more pleased about this than you are, but you might as well face facts. You'd be risking your life to try to make it down that hill now."

She sighed and pushed her hair out of her face, silently conceding his point. At least he wasn't pretending to be delighted to have her here. If there was one thing she remembered about Gavin Locke, it was that he had always been bluntly, sometimes painfully, honest.

"You had planned to stay for three nights, anyway," he reminded her. "It's not as if you have anyplace else you need to be today."

"True. But I had expected to be here alone."

"I'll try to stay out of your way."

"That's not what I meant. I'm the one who's intruding."

He made a dismissive gesture, though he didn't assure her that it was no bother to have her here. They both knew better.

"At least let me cook breakfast," she said, deciding to attempt to act as dispassionate as he was about the situation. "I brought a few nonperishable groceries with me. The bags are out in my car. I was going to try to find a market for some fresh food if I decided to stay the full three days, but I…"

"I have food," he broke in curtly. "The kitchen's stocked. Help yourself to anything you find in the cabinets or pantry. I doubt there's anything salvageable in the fridge. I'm not hungry, but I'd take coffee if you want to make it while I wash up. There's a French press in the cabinet by the stove."

"Are you still running a fever?" She resisted an impulse to step forward and touch his face. He hadn't seemed to like that last night. It was probably best to keep the touching to a minimum, anyway, while they were stranded here together.

"I'm fine."

She wasn't sure she believed him entirely, but figured it would be a waste of time to argue. Or even to point out that a man with an injured shoulder probably shouldn't be out in the rain clearing storm debris.

He disappeared into his bedroom. After folding away the sleeper sofa and neatly stacking the sheets and pillows, Jenny rummaged in the kitchen. She filled the kettle with water and when it boiled she made the coffee, then two bowls of instant oatmeal she found in the pantry. A few bananas were turning brown on the counter, so she sliced a couple on top of the oatmeal and set the steaming bowls and mugs on the table. She'd just taken her seat when Gavin joined her again. He hadn't changed, but he'd tried to clean the mud splatters on his clothes, leaving damp, streaked spots behind. She had to glance quickly down at her oatmeal to hide any hint of the feminine appreciation that flooded unbidden through her again. She was really going to have to put a stop to this, she thought irritably.

"I said I'm not hungry." He dropped into his chair and studied the oatmeal with a scowl, proving himself to be just as grouchy as she was feeling. Was it possible he was dealing with some of the same unwelcome emotions she was trying to suppress?

She shrugged and answered with outward nonchalance. "Don't eat it, if you don't want it. I'll have yours for seconds. But it's there if you think you need to fuel up before doing any work outside today."

After a moment, he heaved a gusty sigh and picked up his spoon. "Fine."

She smothered a smile by stuffing a spoonful of oatmeal and bananas into her mouth. After washing it down with a sip of the passable coffee, she tried to ease the tension between them with small talk. "When did you buy the cabin?"

"My dad bought it nearly seven years ago. When he died five years later, I ended up with it."

She replied with genuine sympathy. "I'm sorry. I didn't know about your dad. He was a good man."

Gavin nodded. "He was."

"How's your mother?"

"She's well, thanks. Yours?"

"Still working as a nurse in a hospital in Little Rock." Her mother had liked Gavin, and had been openly disappointed when Jenny broke up with him.

"And your grandmother? Still living?"

Her grandmother, on the other hand, had not approved of Gavin, and the antipathy had been reciprocal. Jenny could still hear the faint edge of resentment in his voice, though the question had been civil enough. She focused on her breakfast when she said, "Still feisty as ever."

He responded to that understatement with a grunt.

Maybe that subject was a bit too touchy still. She changed it quickly. "How's Holly?"

"Married to an air force pilot. They've got two boys, Noah and Henry, six and four. They're living in Illinois at the moment. Scott Air Force Base."

An only child herself, Jenny had always been somewhat envious of the warm relationship Gavin had with his older sister. They'd gotten along amazingly well for siblings. During the time Jenny had spent with them, there had always been friends of Gavin's and Holly's around, usually engaged in good-natured but fierce competitions—basketball or softball or flag football, or spirited board games indoors. The memory of all that fun and laughter made her throat tighten as she studied the unsmiling, hard-looking man across the table. It had taken a lot worse than a college breakup to leave those dark shadows within his navy eyes.

"How do you like being an uncle?"

She was pleased to see a shadow of his old grin flit across his firm lips. "The boys tend to think of me as an automatic treat dispenser. Tug at my jeans and candy magically emerges from my pocket. Holly says it's a good thing I don't see them often or she'd have to put a stop to it. As it is, she turns a blind eye. She knows I won't overdo it. And I always get them to work up a sweat to burn off the extra sugar."

An image of him roughhousing with two cute little boys distracted her for several moments. As prickly as he could sometimes be with adults, Gavin had always liked kids, and the feeling had been mutual. She would bet he was the kind of uncle who would roll in the dirt with his nephews, let them climb all over him, sticky fingers and all.

Thad would be more likely to teach his nephews, if he had any, to play chess. Which would also be quite cute, she assured herself quickly, feeling a vague, totally unjustified ripple of guilt course through her, as if she'd been disloyal.

Gavin changed the subject. "What are you doing these days?"

"I own a fashion and accessories boutique in Little Rock."

"What's it called?"

"Complements."

He nodded. "I've heard of the place. Someone I dated briefly shopped there a lot."

"That's good to hear. That she liked my store, I mean."

He chuckled drily. "She complained about the high prices, but she still shopped there enough to max out her credit cards."

"We carry high-end merchandise," Jenny replied without apology. "Designer items that can't be found in the local department stores."

"Yes, well, it's been a year or so since I've seen her, but I'm sure she's still a loyal customer."

Judging from his dispassionate tone, she doubted he'd been particularly invested in the relationship. If the woman was a regular patron at Complements, it was entirely possible Jenny knew her, but she had no intention of asking him. It was none of her business who Gavin had dated since she'd last seen him. Nor if he was dating anyone seriously now. Just as she saw no reason to discuss Thad with him.

He pushed away his empty bowl and picked up his coffee cup. "So you accomplished your lifelong goal. You own your own successful business. I assume you obtained an MBA, as well? That was always the plan, wasn't it?"

She felt her chin rise in instinctive irritation, and she lowered it deliberately, keeping her expression composed. "Yes. I'm planning to open a second store in the next few months. I love my work."

Which was absolutely true—and another reason she was having trouble deciding whether to accept Thad's proposal, she thought somberly. Marrying Thad would change her life significantly. Though he'd always expressed his respect and admiration for her business achievements, he'd been quite candid about what he was looking for in a life partner. Supporting his political aspirations was high on his list of attributes in a mate. To keep up with the demands of that undertaking, she'd either have to sell her business eventually or at the very least turn over most of the daily operations to employees. After spending so much time tenaciously building her clientele and reputation, it was hard to contemplate putting Complements in the hands of anyone else.

None of which she was going to discuss with Gavin, of course. She sipped her rapidly cooling coffee, then set the cup on the table. "So, you did what you wanted, as well. You became a police officer."

She hadn't forgotten that he'd once wanted that career more than he'd wanted her. She wouldn't lie to herself that there wasn't still a little sting to the memories, but she hoped she'd hidden any remaining bitterness.

He nodded. "Went back and earned a degree in criminal justice, too. I took night classes and online courses when I was off-duty. Made my dad somewhat happier, anyway."

Both Gavin's parents had been educators. Neither had been pleased when he'd decided at an early age that he wanted to be a police officer. Their objection hadn't been the social status or modest pay scale of police—which had been the bluntly stated basis of her grandmother's disdain for the job—but rather the danger and unsavory situations in which their son would spend many of his working hours. They'd made no secret that they'd hoped he would change his mind while he obtained his college degree.

Jenny had met him in a sophomore sociology class. The attraction had been immediate and powerful. After they'd started dating, she'd added her arguments to his parents', trying to convince him to channel his interest in criminal justice into a less dangerous profession. At first, he'd seemed to concur and begun to study for the law school entrance exam, to put away bad guys as a prosecutor rather than an officer. Truthfully, she'd been aware of his underlying lack of enthusiasm for that career path, but in her youthful optimism, she'd been sure he would learn to like it.

On the very rare occasions when she had looked back at their eighteen-month-long relationship through the viewpoint of a more mature adult, she'd realized it was probably his feelings of being pressured into a career he didn't want that had made him turn sullen and difficult. He must have felt as if his own desires were always being disparaged and discouraged. He'd quarreled more and more often with his parents, and with her. He'd accused her of being so obsessed with her own ambitions, of trying so hard to please her grandmother, that she was willing to sacrifice their relationship to achieve her aims.

Maybe her lofty goals didn't include being married to an ordinary cop, he'd snarled. Maybe the reason she kept urging him to go to law school had been more for her own ambitions than for his. During the ensuing years, she'd wondered uncomfortably if there had been some grain of truth in his allegations. She'd always assured herself that, like his parents, she had worried more about the risk and uncertainty of a police officer's work rather than any lack of social status. She had witnessed her own mother's grief after being widowed at a young age by a charming, daredevil firefighter, who'd been as reckless off-duty as on the job and had died in a drag-racing accident. Having struggled with that gaping loss herself, Jenny hadn't been able to deal with the thought of losing the man she loved in the line of dangerous duty. The image still made her blood chill.

She'd been unable to convince Gavin exactly how upsetting that possibility had been to her. They'd had one last, fierce quarrel in which they'd both said very hurtful things, and that had been the end of their romance. The emotions had been too raw, the anger too hot, to allow them an amicable parting. A week later, she'd been shocked to learn that Gavin had left the university, only three semesters short of graduation. She assumed he'd entered the police academy soon afterward, though she'd never heard from him again. She had thrown herself into her studies, shedding her tears in private and burying the pain as deeply as possible, rarely to be acknowledged since.

Maybe Gavin's thoughts, too, had drifted back to their painful breakup, because before she could reply, he shoved his chair back abruptly from the table. "I'm going to start on that tree. Thanks for the breakfast."

"You should take care with that shoulder."

He merely gave her a look and walked out, leaving her shaking her head in exasperation. While Gavin had changed in many noticeable ways since she'd last seen him, it was obvious that he was still as stubborn as ever.

The rain had dwindled to little more than a cool mist while he'd been inside. Gavin tossed damp hair out of his face and lifted the chain saw from the back of his truck with his good arm. Pulling the starter was going to be a challenge, but he'd manage. The sooner he cleared that tree out of the way, the sooner he or Jenny or both of them could get away from here. And the sooner there would be an end to those uncomfortable catch-up conversations.

Why the hell had he felt the need to tell her he'd gotten his degree? He'd heard himself blurting it out almost before he'd realized it. That damned degree didn't make him any more worthy, as far as he was concerned. Jenny could have a dozen advanced degrees and own a

Fortune 500 company, and he would still take pride in the uniform he donned every working day.

He remembered vividly the way Jenny's grandmother's lip had curled when he'd mentioned his intention to enter the police academy after finishing college. Lena Patterson had made it quite clear that she had higher aspirations for her granddaughter than to align herself with a "low-level civil servant." Having known by then that Jenny's father's death had left them grief-stricken and financially burdened, Gavin had decided that Lena Patterson was a pompous, bitter woman. She had channeled her personal disappointments into her bright, beautiful and motivated granddaughter, pushing Jenny toward higher education and a socially and economically advantageous marriage.

The old woman had done a damned good job of programming her granddaughter from a very early age. He'd seen the way Jenny lit up in response to Lena's sparsely doled praise. That had been hard for him to compete with at twenty-one. He doubted he could do so even now, if he were inclined to try.

He set the chain saw beside the other tools he'd already gathered around the fallen tree and stepped back to analyze the project. The oak was big. The uptilted root ball came almost to his shoulder. A tangle of leafy branches covered the driveway in a dense barrier. Even with two good arms, this tree would require hours to remove.

His phone buzzed in his pocket and he removed one bulky work glove to draw it out, sighing when he saw his mother's number.

"I'm fine, Mom," he said without giving her a chance to say anything.

She laughed softly, unperturbed by his sardonic tone.

"I'm glad to hear it. It sounds as if your area got hit hard by last night's storms."

"Lost a couple of trees, a bunch of limbs. Couple leaks in the back bedroom I'm going to have to patch. Other than that, no real damage done."

"I heard there was flooding up that way."

"There's flooding down the road, but just a few wet patches up here on the hill." His dad had always said that the river would have to be at hundred-year flood stages to creep up to the cabin.

"Can you get out?"

"Not yet, but the water should go down fairly quickly once the rain finally stops." He hoped the road would be dry enough for safe travel by the end of the day, though the heavy cloud cover did not look promising. He wouldn't be surprised to be drenched again at any minute.

"How's your shoulder? Is the infection better?"

"Better. No fever today."

"I'm glad to hear it. Now, please use common sense and try not to overdo it with the storm cleanup. I know better than to try to make you promise not to tackle any of it today."

"I won't overdo it."

"I worry about you being up there all alone when you haven't been out of the hospital for a whole week yet. I know you don't like being hovered over, but I wish you'd stayed a bit closer to home for at least a few more days."

"Gavin, do you have an extra pair of work gloves I can use?" Jenny called from behind him before he could reassure his mom again. "I'd be glad to help you clear this… Oh. I'm sorry." Spotting the phone in his hand, she grimaced in apology.

He should have known his too-perceptive mother wouldn't miss a beat. "Gavin? Someone is there with you? Is it anyone I know?"

There was no way he was telling her at the moment about his ex-girlfriend's presence. His mom had liked Jenny back in the day, even though she'd reacted in true overprotective mama-bear mode when Jenny broke up with him. She'd insisted that Jenny had broken her son's heart. Gavin wouldn't have phrased it quite that way. Then again, he couldn't really argue it, either.

"I have to take care of some things around here before the rain starts again," he said into the phone, ignoring her questions. "I'll call you later, okay?"

He heard her sigh, but his mother surrendered to the inevitable. No doubt she'd grill him good later, face-to-face. "Fine. Just…take care of yourself, will you?"

"Bye, Mom."

He disconnected the call and shoved the phone back into his pocket before turning to Jenny, studying her through the clear plastic protective glasses. She'd changed into a T-shirt and jeans. She'd pulled her hair into a loose ponytail. Beads of fine mist already glittered within the dark strands. Trendy, neon-green running shoes not at all suited to muddy manual labor encased her feet.

She held up her perfectly manicured hands. "I'm sorry, I didn't realize you were on the phone. I'm looking for an extra pair of work gloves so I can help you."

"I can handle this."

"It will go faster if I pitch in."

He wasn't so sure about that. She could prove to be more of a distraction than a help. But he could think of no way to decline the offer without coming across as a jerk. If he tried too obviously to avoid her, she might even think he'd never quite gotten over her.

He cocked his chin toward the back of the house. "Extra work gloves and safety glasses are behind the seat in my truck. It isn't locked."

He figured she'd tire out quickly and head back inside. Until then, he would keep her too busy to reminisce.

He had the chain saw running by the time she returned wearing the too-large, leather-and-canvas gloves and an oversize pair of plastic safety goggles. He'd deliberately waited until she was out of sight to fire up the saw so she wouldn't see him wince and curse when he pulled the starter cord. He had no intention of showing her how much discomfort he was in—not actual pain, but that would probably set in before the day ended. Didn't matter. He wanted this road cleared as quickly as possible.

Because the saw was so noisy, he communicated with shouts and hand motions, instructing her to stay at a safe distance while he cut, after which she could drag the smaller pieces off the road and into the ditch. Considering her formidable resolve, he supposed he shouldn't have been surprised that Jenny threw herself into the job. It was dirty and sweaty work, but she pushed on gamely until her ponytail straggled against her damp neck, her clothes were muddy and her shirt had a small tear at the hem, perhaps from catching on a sharp branch. And still he had to force himself to concentrate on the potentially hazardous job at hand when his eyes wanted to turn in her direction instead. Even tousled and grubby—or perhaps especially so—something about her made his thoughts wander into dangerous and forbidden directions and brought back memories that heated his blood and hardened his groin.

Didn't mean anything, he assured himself. He was a reasonably healthy male in the middle of a dry spell, so it was only natural for him to react to an attractive, temptingly tousled woman.

After two hours, she looked as though her energy was fading fast. He felt as though he'd been kicked in the shoulder by an angry horse. Turning off the saw, he set it on the ground and swiped at his sweat-beaded forehead with the back of his left hand. He'd removed several of the large limbs, but a few more needed to come off before he could even attempt to move the tree off the road. It was taking longer than he wanted to cut through the hard wood. He only hoped he had enough gas and oil on hand to finish the job.

He still needed to figure out a way to pull the tree out of the roadway, but maybe he could think more clearly after taking something for pain. He knew better than to swallow prescription pills and then run a power saw, so he'd settle for over-the-counter remedies. He glanced at Jenny. "You need a break."

Even muddy, wet and wilted, she could skewer him with a lifted eyebrow. "*I* need a break?"

"We need a break," he conceded grudgingly.

She nodded in satisfaction. "I just want to move this last branch."

She took hold of a leafy limb the size of a small tree and gave a tug. It didn't budge. Gavin stood beside her, grabbing the branch with his left hand. Their gloved hands almost touched. He had only to shift his weight a little to be pressed against her from behind. She glanced up at him over her shoulder and their eyes locked. Hers dilated a bit; his probably did, too.

He told himself again that some reactions were purely biological. And then quickly slid his hand down a couple inches from hers, ostensibly to get a better grip. "On three."

With his count, Jenny pulled so enthusiastically he nearly fell backward when the branch shot forward. He put one foot back to steady himself, and reached out automatically with his right hand to get a better grip. A grunt of pain escaped him before he could swallow it. He hoped Jenny hadn't heard, but he should have known better. She didn't say anything, but he saw the sympathy on her face when he glanced at her.

He turned away. The one thing he had never wanted from Jenny Baer was pity. "Let's go inside."

Gavin insisted Jenny take the bathroom first to get cleaned up while he put on the kettle for tea. He was still making an effort to be a thoughtful host, she thought. Smiling a little, she closed herself in the bathroom, then glanced into the mirror. Her smile faded immediately. She reached hastily for a washcloth and a bar of soap.

When she rejoined Gavin in the kitchen, she spotted a bottle of over-the-counter pain relievers by the sink that hadn't been there earlier. His shoulder had to be giving him fits, but he hadn't complained once and she didn't think he wanted her to ask.

"Thank you," she said, accepting the mug he offered her. The tea was still too hot to drink, so she carried it to the table and took a seat to wait for it to cool a bit.

"I checked the weather on my phone. Rain's moving

this way again, but maybe this round will pass through quickly."

"I hope so."

Gavin moved toward the bathroom, carrying his mug with him. "I'm going to wash up. Make yourself at home."

She waited until he was out of sight before she let out a sigh and allowed her shoulders to sag. Spending time with Gavin was both easier than she might have expected and harder than it should have been. She'd come here to make decisions about her future and instead had been slapped in the face by her past. Wasn't that ironic?

Needing a distraction, she reached for her phone. The signal was weak, but there was no one in particular she wanted to call. She'd texted her mother and Thad to let them know she'd arrived safely. She hadn't mentioned that she wasn't alone in the cabin. That had been a bit too complicated to explain to them by text or a quick, static-filled call.

When Thad traveled, he called every evening at 6:00 p.m., so reliably that she could set her clock by his ring. It was an arrangement they'd worked out together as a way of managing their equally hectic schedules, making sure they didn't miss connections. "Their thing," Thad called it teasingly. He'd phoned at that time yesterday, just as she was trying to get away for the drive here. He hadn't hidden his concern about her solitary vacation, but he'd added that he hoped she had a relaxing few days and returned ready to make plans for their promising future together.

She'd always appreciated that Thad respected her choices, though sometimes she wondered fleetingly if it was mostly because his own life was so busy that he hardly had time to think about her issues. Still, he went out of his way to find time for their calls, proving he was willing to make compromises in their potential marriage, which was certainly important to her. After all, she and Gavin had broken up partially because neither had been willing to compromise their disparate goals and dreams. Wasn't that only further evidence that a relationship based on logic and respect was more reliable than one based on passion and emotion?

She refused to answer. She'd been stubbornly resisting the unhappy memories her surprise reunion with Gavin had stirred up, and she certainly wasn't going to sit here brooding about the past now. She focused more fiercely on her phone. The signal was strong enough to allow her to access her email. There weren't many to deal with. Amber, her assistant, was taking care of the business for now. She read her text messages and saw a note from her long-time good friend, Stephanie "Stevie" McLane, checking to make sure she'd survived the storms. She typed a confirmation and received an immediate response.

Bored yet?

Jenny smiled wryly. Hardly, she typed.

Thought you'd have your fill of rustic isolation by now.

Not as isolated as I expected, she returned.

Meaning?

After hesitating for a few moments, Jenny drew a breath and replied, Gavin Locke is here.

No way!

That was pretty much how she'd expected Stevie to react. She could clearly imagine her friend's blue eyes rounded with shock. Stevie had been her staunchest supporter after the split with Gavin, though Jenny had always wondered if her friend secretly considered the breakup a mistake.

Her phone beeped to announce another text. Did you know he'd be there?

Of course not.

Details, girl.

Will call later. She wanted to make that call only when she was certain Gavin wouldn't overhear.

What about Thad?

Jenny frowned as her fingers tapped the screen. What about him?

Does he know?

Jenny moistened her lips before entering her answer. Nothing to know. Not like I planned it.

She bit her lip as she read Stevie's answering text. How does Gavin look?

He looks… Jenny gave it a moment's thought before typing good.

Still single?

Far as I know. Call you soon, okay?

You'd better.

"If you're trying to make a call, you'll get better service outside." Gavin nodded toward her phone as he ambled back into the room. "I usually sit on the porch swing for clearer reception."

Jenny set her phone aside. "Thanks, but I was just texting with Stevie. Do you remember her?"

"Of course. She was your best friend in college."

"Still is."

"Did she marry that guy she was dating? The drummer?"

Funny. Jenny had almost forgotten the drummer. She suspected Stevie had, too. "No. They broke up not long after… No."

For some reason, she was reluctant to even refer to her breakup with Gavin.

"She's still in Little Rock?"

"Yes. She's dating another musician," she confided with a faint smile. "A bass player this time."

When it came to romance, Stevie was nothing if not an optimist. Yet Jenny had been increasingly aware that Stevie hadn't said much about Jenny's deepening relationship with Thad. She wasn't sure why. She'd have thought Stevie would agree that Thad appeared to be Jenny's ideal Mr. Right. He was handsome, wealthy, successful, socially secure. A junior partner in his family-connected, long-established law firm, Thad was already being courted by political-party bigwigs. He was considering a run for state representative in three years, and had already made a few trips to Washington to meet with some big shots there. Everyone they knew—their families, their friends, their associates—seemed to consider them the perfect couple.

Yet, oddly enough, rather than being as enthusiastic as Jenny might have expected, Stevie had been somewhat restrained in her encouragement for the match. Was Stevie too wrapped up in her own romance, or did she have some doubts about Thad that she wasn't sharing? Did she question whether Jenny would ever truly be happy in a partnership based on considerations other than what Stevie would consider epic romance?

Sure, Thad was a confirmed workaholic who sometimes became so immersed in his ongoing projects and future goals that he tended to forget about everyone and everything else, but then Jenny had always been type A herself. She didn't need a man's constant attention. She genuinely liked Thad and she enjoyed his company when they found time to be together. She was sure they'd get along quite nicely as they built a satisfying future together. Why shouldn't that be enough?

Realizing impatiently that she'd allowed her thoughts to wander again, she glanced at her watch. "Should we eat something before we go back out? Are you hungry?"

Gavin shook his head. "That next round of rain's not going to hold off much longer. I'll try to get some more clearing done while I can."

She stood and moved toward the cupboards. "I spotted packages of peanut-butter crackers in here. At least eat some of those to protect your stomach from the meds." She opened a door and motioned toward a top shelf, just above her head. "It was always your favorite snack."

He moved behind her to reach the carton. The action

brought them very close together. All he'd have had to do was lower his arm to wrap it around her shoulders. She'd have moved aside, but the counter was in the way. Any move she made would only brush her against him. Instead, she froze in place, almost holding her breath until he stepped back, the carton in his hand.

"You remember my fondness for these, do you?"

Able to breathe again now that there was a bit more distance between them, she laughed softly, grateful it came out relatively steady. "How could I forget? You stashed them in your car, in your backpack, in your dorm room, in my dorm room. Your friends used to joke that you should buy stock in a cracker company. I'm just a little surprised you haven't gotten tired of them by now."

His mouth quirked into a faint smile as he shrugged. "I don't eat them as much as I used to, but they're still a pretty good snack."

She watched him rip into a cellophane packet, her smile feeling more natural as an amusing memory occurred to her. "Remember when your sister's little white poodle tore into a whole carton while we were outside watching July Fourth fireworks at your parents' house? We came back inside to find paper and cellophane and crumbs everywhere and the poor dog had peanut butter smeared all over her face. Holly got hysterical thinking her pet was going to die, but fortunately the dog got more in her fur than her belly."

Gavin chuckled wryly. "Mom insisted on rushing the dog to an emergency animal clinic, just in case. We were going to have homemade ice cream after watching the fireworks, but it had all melted by the time the crisis was over. You know, that dog lived to be fifteen. Just died a couple years ago."

"What was its name again? I can't remember."

Gavin made a face. "BiBi. I can't forget because it ran off from Mom's house one day when she was dog-sitting while Holly was out of town, just before Christmas. Mom called me in tears. I had to drive slowly around her neighborhood in my cruiser, calling the stupid name from my open window. 'Here, BiBi. C'mere, BiBi.' I felt like an idiot. It was sleeting. Took me an hour to find the half-frozen mutt, and then it had the nerve to pee on me when I picked it up."

She couldn't help laughing. He'd have hated every minute of that episode—but for his mother and sister, he'd have done it with only token grumbles. "That is too funny."

"Glad you think so," he muttered, though his lips twitched.

For a moment, she was swept back again to the early days of their romance, which had been filled with laughter. Her smile faded as she returned abruptly to the present. Leaning casually against the counter, Gavin gazed down at her, his eyes gleaming in the shadowy light. She felt the hairs on her arms rise, as if the air between them charged suddenly with static. She really needed to stop those mental flashbacks before they got entirely out of control.

Did Gavin sense the change, as well? His eyes narrowed, and even the hint of amusement vanished, leaving his face carved again into hard, inscrutable lines.

He grabbed a couple more packets of crackers and turned away. "I'm going back out. Rest awhile, if you want. I can handle things out there."

She released a long, unsteady breath when the front door closed behind him. Wow, that had turned quickly. She'd just been reminded all too vividly of how quickly the laughter in their youthful relationship had dissolved into tears. She was annoyed to realize the memories could still sting, even after all these years, even after she'd long since assured herself she was over it.

She was tempted to stay safely inside while he continued the cleanup. Because that made her feel cowardly, she lifted her chin and refused to give in to the impulse. She reached for her borrowed work gloves and headed for the door. The sooner the road was cleared, the sooner this blast from the past would be over.

Chapter Three

Almost an hour later, most of the branches were off the tree trunk and dragged to the side of the road. Jenny felt her muscles protesting the hard labor, and she suspected she would be sore tomorrow. She kept a close watch on Gavin, noting his face grew tighter as their work progressed. He was obviously favoring his right arm, certainly making an effort not to exacerbate the injury, but she could tell he was hurting and that he was overdoing it regardless. Yet, he'd tried to assure her he could handle this on his own. Right.

They were both panting after dragging and shoving yet another limb into the now-full ditch. Jenny wasn't sure if the moisture on her face was due more to perspiration or the mist that was beginning to fall more heavily now, making the ground slick beneath her sneakers. She slid on a patch of leaves, did a little flailing dance, then planted her heels firmly in the dirt to anchor herself. Gavin applauded, his sawdust-covered gloves thudding dully together. She smiled and bobbed a careful bow in his direction. His long slash of dimples appeared briefly, then vanished when he turned back to the tree.

"Now what?" she asked, motioning toward the huge trunk still completely blocking the narrow gravel road.

"Now that the trunk is light enough not to yank the bumper off my truck—I hope—I'm going to try to hook a chain to it and pull it out of the way, at least enough for us to get around it. Once I can drive past it, I'll go down and check the flooding at the foot of the hill. As long as the rain holds off a while longer, maybe we…"

The sky opened. It was the only way to describe the way rain dumped suddenly onto them, as if someone had turned on a showerhead full blast above them. Gavin snatched up the chain saw and followed Jenny's mad dash to the covered porch, but both of them were soaked by the time they ducked under the overhang.

"Are you *kidding* me?" She shoved her sodden bangs out of her eyes, shaking her head in dismay. "Could this weather get any crazier?"

Gavin ran a hand through his wet, shaggy hair, spraying raindrops around his feet. "It's spring in Arkansas. Crazy weather is pretty much expected this time of year. They've been predicting these storms for a couple weeks now."

"I know," she admitted with a sigh. "I just hoped the worst forecasts would be wrong. They often are, you know."

He leaned back against the wall of the cabin, gazing out at the downpour without answering. An occasional windblown gust of rain blew in at them, but they were already so wet it didn't seem to matter. Actually, the wet breeze felt rather good after the sweaty work. She settled into a damp rocker and watched a rivulet of water slide down a porch post.

His gaze focused intently on the falling rain, Gavin spoke quietly. "You're not getting much of your paperwork done today. Didn't you say that's why you came?"

She shrugged. Once again, she had a perfect opening to tell Gavin exactly why she'd needed some time to herself, but once again, she decided to let the opportunity pass. She told herself it would just be too awkward to discuss Thad with Gavin, especially considering she hadn't even given Thad an answer to his proposal yet. "I'll find some time later, once I get off this hill."

"You make a habit of taking off on your own like this to work?"

That made her laugh, though without much humor. "This is the first weekend I've not spent at my office in longer than I can remember. And I very rarely have time just to myself. This trip was an aberration in almost every way—and wouldn't you know, it would turn out to be a disaster."

"Sorry you were disappointed."

Realizing she might have sounded a bit ungracious, she shrugged. "You had no control over the weather. And the booking mix-up wasn't your fault, either. Just all-around bad luck."

Because that didn't sound much better, she added, "I mean, it's very nice seeing you again, it's just..."

"Jenny." His tone was dry, and she figured he must find her sudden discomfiture amusing. "It's okay. You didn't hurt my tender feelings. And it's nice to see you again, too. Sort of."

Because she understood exactly what he meant by that, she gave him a quick, wry smile. "Yeah. Sort of."

He didn't return the smile. "Always figured we'd run into each other again someday, both still living in the area and all. I'm kind of surprised it took so long. Guess we hang in different circles these days."

She was determined to act as nonchalant as he appeared to be. "It's funny that we reconnected here, three hours from where we live."

"Not so strange, I guess, since I own the cabin and you were looking for a secluded place. Maybe the fact that you remembered it so well is a little odd."

"I hadn't thought about it in years," she assured him quickly. "My assistant unintentionally reminded me of it when I jokingly said that I needed to crawl into a cave or something for a few days to think and get organized and she said maybe I should find a nice, secluded mountain cabin. This place popped into my head and I did an impulsive internet search and...well, here we are."

"Here we are."

She twisted her fingers in her lap. "It's nice that we can be..." *Friends* didn't seem to be quite the right word. She quickly substituted, "Civil."

"Why wouldn't we be civil? We dated as kids. We went our own ways. It's been—what, a decade or so? Life's gone on, for both of us."

It had been ten years and two months since they broke up. Not that there was any reason to get that specific, but she couldn't help wondering if he, too, remembered the exact date. Still, as he said, they'd been very young. A lot had happened since for her, and certainly for him, too. She was in a relationship, and for all she knew, he could be, too. Neither had been pining for the other all these years. There was no reason at all they couldn't be…well, friendly. She couldn't see them hanging out as buddies. Not because of any difference in social status, but because she suspected there would always be undercurrents between them that made their interactions too potentially volatile.

As if to reinforce that thought, Gavin pushed away from the wall with a bit more force than necessary. "I'll be right back."

Jenny was torn between enjoying the sound of the rainfall on the porch roof and being impatient for the rain to end so they could get back to clearing the road. She glanced behind her. Gavin had left the door ajar, probably to allow fresh air into the stuffy rooms. It was quiet inside the dim cabin. She didn't hear him moving around at all.

Curious, she stood and walked inside, leaving her muddy shoes on the doorstep beside his boots. She had just moved farther into the room when she heard a heavy thud and a heated curse from Gavin's bedroom.

Tentatively, she headed that way. "Gavin? Are you all right?"

His bedroom door was open. Shirtless, he stood in front of the dresser mirror, an open first aid kit in front of him, the bandage on his shoulder hanging crookedly. A plastic bottle of isopropyl alcohol lay on the wood floor beside his feet; fortunately, the lid was still on so it hadn't spilled.

"Do you want some help changing that bandage?" she asked, deliberately offhanded. "I'm sure it's a little hard to do with your left hand."

"I've managed before. Just knocked the bottle off the

dresser with my elbow. I usually change the bandage in the bathroom, but the light's somewhat better in here."

"I didn't say you couldn't do it yourself. I said I'm here to give you a hand, if you'd like. If you'd rather handle it yourself, fine."

After only a momentary hesitation, he nodded. "It would be faster if you help. Uh, thanks."

Because she knew what it probably cost him to accept assistance from her—from anyone, really, being such a fiercely independent sort—she wasn't bothered by his somewhat less than gracious acceptance. "Maybe you should sit down so I can reach it better. Does it need to be cleaned? Should I bring a washcloth?"

"It's not dirty. The bandage was wet and uncomfortable, so I thought I should swap it for a dry one."

"Makes sense." She reached for the half-removed bandage and eased it away from his injury. With an effort she kept her expression impassive when she saw the jagged, six-inch row of close-set stitches that marched across his shoulder. The skin around the threads was puckered, but the redness didn't seem to be spreading and his shoulder wasn't hot to her touch, so the meds must be working.

"Are you supposed to put antibiotic ointment on the stitches?"

Sitting on the end of the bed, he nodded toward a tube on the dresser. "Just a little. Only reason I wear the bandage is to keep my shirt from rubbing the stitches."

Using a square of gauze, she dabbed ointment lightly over the wound. Their heads were so close she felt his warm breath on her cheek.

Did he lift weights these days? When she'd known him before, he'd been slender and athletic, but the muscles in his arms and chest hadn't been quite as well-defined. He was definitely a man in peak condition despite the injury. And if her fingers lingered for a moment on a taut bicep—well, that could be attributed to incidental contact while she prepared the area for the new bandage.

The shadowed room was silent except for the soft splash of rain on the windows. She was all too aware of the rumpled bed, the masculine clutter of clothes and toiletries, the mounting warmth in the air. She felt a need to fill the quiet, though she would try not to slip into nervous prattling. "You said you had surgery on your shoulder? Did you tear a ligament or something?"

"Something like that."

The very blandness of his nonreply made her hands go still. In a flash, she was taken back to her childhood, watching her mom patch up the latest injury her dad had acquired in one of his reckless stunts, either on the job or off. Just as it had when she was an anxious child, her stomach knotted painfully.

"You weren't, um, shot, were you?" she asked, voicing the worst nightmare that had haunted her when Gavin announced his determination to don a badge.

"I wasn't shot."

And that was all he was going to tell her. He couldn't have made it clearer if he'd said it outright.

Taking the less-than-subtle hint, she bit her lip and finished applying the bandage without speaking again. She smoothed tape over the clean gauze, taking her time to make sure the edges were well sealed. Her hand still resting on his shoulder, she glanced at his face to make sure she wasn't hurting him, only to find him looking gravely back at her. For a fleeting moment, she saw in his eyes a hint of the Gavin she'd once known—younger, more open, less hardened by his job and experiences.

Her breath caught hard in her throat as more memories crashed through her mind in a kaleidoscope of broken images. Hungry kisses. Heated caresses. Nights of passion more overwhelming than anything she'd experienced before. Or since, for that matter. Which was totally understandable, right? Wasn't it supposed to be that way when a woman's thoughts drifted back to her first love?

The shadows seemed to deepen in the room around them, enclosing them in a cozy corner of soft light spilling in through the single window. Her gaze lowered slowly, pausing on his mouth. His lips looked so stern and firm, yet she remembered them as warm and eager. If she allowed herself, she suspected she could still recall their taste. It was probably—definitely—best if she kept that memory locked away along with all the others.

His voice was rough when he broke the silence. "That should do it."

"What? Oh." Realizing he referred to the bandage, she dropped her hand and stepped quickly back. "Yes, that should hold."

"Jenny…"

A heavy pounding on the front door made them both start and turn in that direction. Jenny heard someone shouting, a muffled male voice calling Gavin's name. They hadn't locked the front door. She heard it open, heard the voice more clearly. "Gavin? Hey, buddy, you in here? You okay?"

"Rob." Shaking his head, Gavin pushed himself to his feet and called out, "I'm here. Hang on."

Snatching up a dry T-shirt, he moved toward the bedroom door without looking back at Jenny. She followed quickly. It occurred to her that if someone had made it up the road to the cabin, that meant she could now drive down. It was probably only because she was so tired that she wasn't more excited by that realization.

Rob Lopez peered around the cabin door, squinting into the shadows as he called out again. "Hey, Gav? Are you— Oh, there you are."

Pulling the T-shirt over his head, Gavin moved to greet his friend. He was surprised to see him there. His pals had a standing invitation to join him whenever he was using the cabin, but usually they called before showing up. "Hey, Rob. What are you doing here? How'd you get past the flood and the downed tree?"

Rob opened the door all the way, shaking water out of his curly dark hair like a wet labradoodle as he stood just outside on the porch. "I won't come in—my boots are too muddy. We drove up in J.T.'s off-road rig. Nearly floated it at the bottom of the hill. You have two trees uprooted, by the way. There's another a quarter mile down the road. I left the other guys working down there, and I hiked up to let you know we're here—in the rain, I might add, though it's almost stopped now, at least for a little while. You're going to owe me for this one."

"Other guys?"

"Yeah. J.T. and— Oh. Hello." Rob was looking over Gavin's shoulder and it wasn't hard to guess what, or rather who, had brought the look of surprised speculation to his face.

Belatedly realizing that donning his shirt as he'd entered Rob's field of vision might have given him the wrong idea about what he and Jenny had been doing in the bedroom, Gavin cleared his throat. “Rob Lopez, this is Jenny Baer. Jenny and I knew each other back in college. Long story, but Lizzie at the leasing office screwed up and rented the cabin to Jenny for the weekend. Jenny didn’t expect to find me here when she arrived in the middle of the storm last night.”

Rob’s eyebrows lifted. “Well, that’s awkward. Is that your car out front, Jenny?”

“Yes.” If she was at all uncomfortable, it didn’t show in her polite expression when she moved fully into the room. “I arrived just ahead of the worst part of the storm. Gavin allowed me to sleep on his couch last night and I’ve been trying to help him clear the drive today.”

Rob glanced from her to Gavin and back. “He put you on the couch? What’s wrong with the back bedroom?”

“Roof’s leaking,” Gavin grumbled. “Lost a few shingles in the storms last night. I was going to work on that after I got the trees out of the road. Power’s out, too.”

Rob nodded. “We can help with the roof. Looks like you’ve made good progress on the near tree. Won’t take long to haul it out of the way, assuming the next wave of rain holds off long enough.”

Feeling increasingly disoriented, Gavin pushed his left hand through his hair. “You want to tell me what y’all are doing here?”

With a shrug, his friend answered lightly, “Impulsive road trip. We heard about the storm damage in this area. There wasn’t any destruction to deal with in our part of the state, so we figured you could use an extra hand—or six—with cleanup here. You being short a hand of your own and all. We didn't know you already had a very nice pair of hands up here helping out."

Rob winked at Jenny as he spoke. The way she smiled in response made it clear that the woman who'd been so notably composed during the past few hours was not immune to Rob's notorious charm. Gavin felt his brows drawing into a scowl, and he deliberately smoothed his expression. It wasn't his business if Jenny fell for Rob's overused lines.

He moved abruptly toward the door. "I left my boots and gloves on the porch. Jenny, now that the guys are here to help, there's no need for you to come back out. You can just rest in here for now."

Reaching up to tidy her ponytail, she crossed the room behind him. "Actually, I'd just as soon help rather than sit in here in the dark. My tablet and phone are getting low on power, so I can't really work, anyway."

He had no good argument. He certainly couldn't tell her he found her presence too distracting while he tried to work.

"Whatever you want to do." Without looking back at her again, he all but pushed past Rob to step out onto the porch and reach for his boots.

"Easy, bro," Rob murmured with a low chuckle. "A guy might think something—or somebody—has got you all hot and bothered."

Gavin shot his friend a look that made Rob back off quickly with both hands raised and a devilish twinkle in his dark eyes.

Rob watched as Jenny perched on the edge of a porch chair to lace on her bedraggled, once-bright sneakers. "Hate to tell you this, but I think those shoes might be goners," he said. "Doubt they'll ever be clean again."

She wrinkled her nose. "I've pretty much figured that out already. I didn't think to bring work boots with me."

"I told you it wasn't necessary for you to slog through the mud with me this morning," Gavin felt compelled to point out. "But I'll pay for the shoes, anyway, when I refund your rental money. None of this was your fault."

Pulling the second lace tight, she stood and reached for the muddy gloves she'd worn earlier. "Of course you won't pay for my shoes. Don't be silly."

Something about her tone made him scowl again. Had she just brushed him off? He glared after her as she walked down the steps with Rob, but she didn't glance back. With a grumble, he snatched up the chain saw and followed.

"Big tree," Rob commented unnecessarily as they approached the fallen oak. "You got a lot of it cut up this morning."

"I figure I can drag the rest of it out of the way with my truck. There's a heavy chain and a few more tools locked in the utility shed behind the cabin."

Rob nodded. "Might be better to hook it up to J.T.'s heavier rig. They should have the other tree out of the road pretty quick. It's not nearly as big as this one. They were dredging out the ditches at that low spot with shovels, too, to help the water run off faster."

"Maybe I should take that branch off while we wait." Gavin motioned toward the one he meant. "If the trunk rolls when we try to move it, that one could dig in and give us problems."

"Agreed. But why don't you let me cut it? That shoulder's got to be giving you fits by now."

Actually, the pain was a heck of a lot worse than that, but he didn't want to admit it. Especially in front of Jenny. "Fine, you cut the limb while I get the chain. It's too bulky to carry, but I can bring it around in the back of my truck. Jenny…"

"I'll help Rob." Donning her safety glasses, she moved into position to grab hold of the branch after it was cut. As he turned to head around the side of the cabin, Gavin could already hear Rob chatting with Jenny as if they were old friends. But then, Rob had never met an attractive woman he didn't like. An impressive percentage of them liked him in return.

He wouldn't have thought Rob was Jenny's type. An EMT Gavin had met in the line of duty a few years ago, Rob was hardly in the same league with the guy his mother said Jenny had dated—and was possibly still seeing. But whatever.

Feeling increasingly grumpy and blaming it on the weather, his discomfort and his weariness, he shoved his hand into his pocket to retrieve the key to the utility shed. All in all, the best thing he could do now was to focus on the tasks at hand. He'd deal with his unexpected visitors—all of them—as best he could during the process.

It didn't take Rob long to cut through the branch Gavin had pointed out. Jenny realized only then how much Gavin had been held back by his injured shoulder. Remembering the stitches that had marched across his taut skin, she bit her lip. He must be terribly uncomfortable, to say the least, though he would fall over face-first before he would admit it. Even as a young man, he'd hated acknowledging when he was sick or hurting. She'd once teased him of being afraid testosterone would leak out of his ears if he confessed to any weakness. She could still remember the way he'd grinned, kissed her and murmured, "You're my only weakness, Jen."

Breaking into the painful memory, Rob planted his foot on the tree trunk and snapped off a smaller branch with his hands. He tossed it in the ditch on top of the others. "Sounds like a pretty harrowing night. You're lucky you made it here safely through the storm."

"I was foolish to be out in it. I didn't pay close enough attention to the weather reports."

He eyed her over another fallen branch he'd just picked up. "Were you planning to do some fishing while you were here?"

She laughed softly at the image of herself handling a squirming fish. "No. It was just supposed to be a private work retreat."

Didn't other people feel the need occasionally to get away, to find a quiet place alone to think and plan and evaluate? True, it wasn't something she had done before, but it had made sense to her when the idea had occurred to her. Gavin had had a similar plan; he'd holed up here to rest and heal in peaceful privacy. The weekend hadn't worked out as either had expected obviously.

Casting a lingering look around at the sodden landscape, Rob said, "Couldn't ask for a more peaceful place for a hideaway, normally. Gavin's been really generous letting me come up here when I needed to get away and if the place wasn't already rented out. I've spent quite a few pleasant hours sitting on that porch in the dark, drinking a cold beer and listening to the frogs and crickets."

"That was my plan," she said with a wistful smile. She hated beer, but she mentally substituted a cup of tea and was sorry she would miss the experience. "Of course, it wouldn't have worked out even if it hadn't been for the storm. Once I'd discovered Gavin was using his cabin and it had been leased to me by mistake, I'd have left immediately and found another place to stay for the weekend."

"I doubt he minded sharing for one night," Rob murmured just as Gavin parked his truck nearby and climbed out with a slam of his door.

Gavin reached into the back of the truck and started to lift a chain, but he dropped it almost immediately. The metal links clanked against the truck bed, not quite drowning out his muttered curse. Apparently he'd unthinkingly used his right arm and the heavy chain had hurt his shoulder. Instinctively, she moved toward him to help, but Rob cleared his throat softly, stopping her midstride. Without looking their way, Gavin switched arms, grabbed the chain with his left hand and hauled it out of the truck, dropping it at their feet. Hefting another branch, Rob acted as though he'd noticed nothing.

Hearing the roar of a motor, Jenny looked around to see a heavy-duty rig powering up the muddy hill. With an extra set of oversize wheels on the back, an extended cab and a row of floodlights across the top, the truck looked made for hauling, towing and chewing up rough terrain. It stopped just short of the downed tree, and two thirtysomething men climbed out. The driver was well over six feet tall, black, broad-shouldered and male-model handsome, the passenger shorter, ginger-haired and built like a linebacker. Gavin definitely hung out with the athletic crowd, but then he always had. As a matter of fact, he'd been hanging out with the redhead for quite a long time, she realized.

Avery Harper glanced curiously in her direction as he and his companion approached. He stopped suddenly in his tracks. "Jenny? Jenny Baer?"

She pushed a wet strand of hair out of her face. "Hello, Avery. It's nice to see you again."

Green eyes wide with shock, Avery looked from her to Gavin and back again. "Wow. Are you two…? I mean… Wow."

"Jenny didn't know I was here when she drove up last night." Gavin sounded weary, as if he had already grown tired of explaining. She could understand. How many more times were they going to have to recount, both together and separately, how they'd ended up spending a night together in his cabin? He finished giving the quick summary of last night's events to his friends, introduced J. T. Dennett to Jenny, then barely gave them time to exchange hellos before launching into his plan for clearing the drive.

Feeling somewhat in the way, she moved back as the four men attached a chain to the fallen tree and then connected it to the tow hitch on J.T.'s truck. She noticed that Gavin's friends did most of the heavy work, nudging him out of the way to keep him from overusing his injured arm. They weren't particularly subtle about it, but were so casually jovial that he took no offense.

"Better stand back," Avery advised, moving to Jenny's side when J.T. climbed behind the wheel of the truck. "Just in case."

Together they moved a few feet backward while Gavin and Rob stepped off to the other side to call out directions to J.T.

"So, you didn't know Gav was here," Avery commented a little too blandly.

"No," she said firmly. "Not a clue. And he had no warning that I'd rented the place."

"Huh. I have to admit, I was surprised to see you here, but his explanation made sense, even if it was a crazy coincidence."

"Well, I'm glad you found it believable," she said drily.

His nod had a slightly mocking edge. "More believable than if he'd announced the two of you had gotten back together," he murmured.

Her relationship with Avery had been rather acerbic while she'd dated Gavin. He probably liked her even less since the breakup. But that was okay. She didn't have to try to make Gavin's friends like her anymore, though she was getting along well enough with Rob.

Still, it was only polite to try to make conversation. "So, Avery, are you still on the force with Gavin?"

Avery had actually entered the academy a year earlier than Gavin, and Jenny had blamed him for having so much influence over Gavin. At the end, Gavin had snapped at her that he knew his own mind, made his own choices and wasn't just following his friend's lead. He'd actually set law enforcement as a career goal even before Avery, he'd informed her defensively.

Avery nodded in response to her question. "Different division, but yeah, still a cop. Made sergeant a few months back. And I got married last fall. My wife's a dispatcher for the department. She's on duty today."

She tried to inject a measure of genuine warmth into her smile. "Congratulations on both your promotion and your marriage."

Not notably disarmed, Avery nodded again. "Thanks. Gavin's still catching up after he quit for more than a year, but he'll be promoted soon himself. Wouldn't be surprised if he eventually makes captain before I do."

"Um, he quit?" she asked casually.

"Yeah, when he… Oh, he hasn't mentioned it to you."

"We haven't talked much since I've been here. Last night we were dealing with the storm and the leaks, and today we've been trying to clear the drive, so there hasn't been a lot of catching up."

She wondered why he'd quit, what he'd done instead, why he'd gone back—all questions she had no business asking. It was obvious Avery had clammed up now and would be revealing no further tidbits about his friend's current life.

After unhooking the chain from the now-out-of-the-way tree, the men stood around the trunk arguing the best way to cut it for firewood. They all agreed they should tackle the leaking roof first.

"I've got some extra shingles in the utility shed," Gavin said.

Jenny felt a fat raindrop splash against her cheek. Swiping at her face, she turned to Gavin. "Now that the road's clear, maybe I should leave before the bottom falls out again."

All four men spoke at one time, and all with some variation of "no."

"You haven't seen how much water is over the road down there," J.T. explained, motioning with one hand. "To be honest, it was pretty stupid for me to drive through it, even in my rig. That lightweight little car of yours would never make it."

Deflated, she sighed. "So how long do you think it will take for me to be able to get out?"

J.T. glanced at Gavin. Both shrugged.

Avery scowled up at the dripping sky. "It would help if this damned rain would stop. Now that we've cleared out the ditches down there, the water should go down pretty quick once they stop refilling with rain. Even then we're talking about a couple hours before the road would be completely safe."

Rob nodded and winked comically at Jenny. "I'd rather you wait until it's safe. It's my day off. As pretty as you are, I'm still not in the mood to administer CPR today."

"Rob's a compulsive flirt, but you should know he's an EMT," Avery said so quietly to Jenny that she wasn't sure anyone else could hear. "Just another lowly civil servant who doesn't move in your social circles. I doubt you'd be interested in him."

A little gasp of indignation escaped her. Had Avery just blatantly accused her of being a snob?

Before she could retort, Gavin surged forward, planting himself in front of his friend with a glare of warning. "Jenny is my guest here," he said in a low but unyielding voice. "I expect her to be treated courteously. Is that clear, Avery?"

Avery had the grace to look a little sheepish as he muttered, "Sorry, Jenny."

Biting her lower lip, she nodded to acknowledge the halfhearted apology. The inexplicable acrimony between her and Avery had come between Gavin and his pal on several occasions back in college. She certainly wouldn't want to cause a rift between them now. As unfair as the remark had been, she couldn't entirely blame Avery. He was just watching out for his friend.

"Hey, Avery, help me carry this cooler and stuff," J.T. shouted from his truck, seemingly unaware of the tension between the trio. "We might as well dig into the sandwiches and beer we brought until the rain stops again."

Avery turned and walked away without looking back. Clearing his throat, Rob followed quickly.

"I'm sorry, Jen," Gavin said quietly. "I'll talk to Avery."

She shook her head. "No, that's not necessary. He has a right to his opinions of me. Even though they're wrong."

She didn't expect to have to deal with Avery much longer, anyway. And she was perfectly capable of defending herself, if she had to. He'd simply caught her off guard this time.

"You know, I have driven in bad conditions before," she said, turning to face Gavin fully. "If I'm very careful, and make sure to stay on the highest ground at the foot of the hill, maybe I could get around the flooded area. The road's paved after that, so…"

She was startled when Gavin took hold of her arm. Feeling the tingle where damp palm met damp skin, she swallowed. "Um…"

He gave a light tug. "Come over here a minute."

She allowed him to lead her off to the side of the property, a few yards to one side of the woods-lined drive. He motioned toward the river below them, at the bottom of a steep, muddy, rock-and-root-tangled incline. She remembered that the stairs down to the river lay at the back of the property. Only a few feet from the bottom of that staircase, a path led to the clearing in the woods where they'd sneaked away for a couple of sweet, private hours together the last time they'd been here.

She gazed down now with a sinking feeling in her

stomach and an old, dull ache in her heart. The sight below wasn't encouraging. Swollen by the storm, the river rushed and tumbled, carrying branches and other storm debris on its churning surface. "Maybe if I hurry, before the rain really starts falling again…"

"Sorry, Jen. That road's always dangerous when it's flooded. Dad and I talked about trying to get better drainage downhill, but the county hasn't been in any hurry to address the problem. If I thought I could drive that little car of yours safely through the flood zone, I'd have the guys follow me down and I'd do it for you. But even as long as I've been coming up here, I wouldn't risk your car or my life just to get you out a couple hours quicker."

A few more raindrops trickled down her face and she glanced toward the cabin. "Then I guess we should go inside before we get soaked again."

He released her arm, but didn't immediately move away from her. Instead, he raised his hand to wipe her cheek with his thumb, his gaze locked with hers. "So," he asked in a low, deep voice, "are you more anxious to run away from Avery or from me?"

She jerked away from his touch, then wished immediately that she'd been a little more discreet about it. "I'm not running away from either of you. I just… need to get out of this rain."

With that, she turned and moved briskly toward the cabin, resisting an impulse to run.

"Jenny…"

Pretending not to hear him, she walked a little faster.

It seemed her grandmother had been right about this trip to the cabin being a bad idea. But then, her grandmother claimed to be right about a lot of things. Gran had always said Gavin would break Jenny's heart. And now Gran claimed Thad and Jenny were the perfect match. She'd been right about the former. Maybe she was right about everything.

Jenny sat on the couch with a book she'd dug out of her bag, pretending to read in the glow of the fluorescent lantern next to her. She found the book dull as dishwater, but it was trendy among the social circles she and Thad moved in. It had been brought up during a dinner party last week, and she was the only woman there who couldn't intelligently discuss the book's theme. Thad had brushed off her chagrin later, telling her everyone should understand that her business kept her too busy for much reading time, but she'd made a mental note to try to stay more current. After all, there would be many more such gatherings in her future with Thad as he cultivated important connections among potential donors and supporters.

Being a political wife was a full-time job in itself, she'd murmured then with a nervous sigh. Thad hadn't disagreed, but he'd squeezed her hand and told her he had no doubt she would be as successful in a political partnership as she had been in everything else she'd tackled.

Not that everything she'd ever attempted had been a success, she mused, glancing up from the book to study Gavin across the cabin through her lashes.

She ran a fingertip absently along the page she was trying to read and chewed lightly on her lower lip. One of the reasons she'd needed this time to consider Thad's proposal was because she was so keenly aware of all the repercussions of accepting. How important it would be not to fail if she decided to take on the challenge. She wouldn't be simply formalizing a relationship, adjusting to day-to-day life with a partner who shared her bed and her breakfast table. Marrying Thad would change everything in the life she had worked very hard to achieve. And while she could certainly see the rewards, she was also aware of what she would be giving up. Her self-assigned task this weekend had been to weigh those pros and cons and decide once and for all which path was best for her, even though she'd been fairly confident her answer would be yes.

She closed the book. She would read it. Eventually. It was just too hard to concentrate with insufficient light and the distracting noise coming from the other side of the room. Frankly, she was more interested in the men's conversation.

Gavin and his friends sat around the table with beers and cards, playing poker while they waited for the rain to stop again. They had invited her to join them, but she'd declined. Aware that she was in the room, the men probably toned down the language a bit in their lively conversation. She'd smiled to herself when she heard a couple of quick substitutions for off-color adjectives. It didn't take her long to deduce that J.T. was also in law enforcement, though he was a state trooper rather than a city cop like Gavin and Avery. Their anecdotes, like their language, were probably toned down for her benefit, but still she winced a few times at the reminders of the unpleasant situations the three officers and the emergency medical technician found themselves in on a regular basis. She couldn't help thinking that this was a very different type of discussion than the ones

Thad and his friends engaged in. She wasn't judging, she assured herself, just noticing.

In addition to their work, they'd chatted about rowdy gatherings for barbecues and touch football games at various homes and parks, and about an upcoming charity baseball game between cops and firefighters that would apparently involve lots of beer and trash talk. They'd mentioned a patrolman who'd been hurt in a car crash during a high-speed pursuit, but was apparently recovering well. She bit her lip at the reminder that this cheerful, gregarious group willingly put their lives on the line every day in the course of their jobs. It was a brief glimpse of Gavin's life now—perhaps of the life she'd have shared with him had they stayed together. Lively, communal, but always with that underlying edge of worry.

She set the book aside and wandered to the window. The rain had almost stopped, though the gray sky looked more like dusk than midafternoon. She turned from the window to find Gavin watching her from the table.

"Do you need anything?" he asked. "Want me to put the kettle on?"

"Thanks, but I can do it." She forced a smile as she moved toward the stove. "I was just wondering how the road is looking down there."

J.T. looked up from the phone in his hand. "I just checked the weather radar. Looks like the rain's finally cleared. The flooding should start receding fairly quickly now. State and county police have been busy working wrecks all day, but it seems to be getting better out there."

"Considering everything, it's amazing we all have

the weekend off," Rob commented. "Can't even remember the last time that happened."

"So you decided to waste your day off cleaning up my property?" Gavin shook his head in skepticism.

Jenny saw his friends exchange quick glances, but Rob replied with a lazy chuckle and a shrug. "We owe you a few favors. Remember when you drove an hour and a half to help me out after that drunk ran a stop sign and hit my car in Brinkley? It wasn't raining, but it was cold. Below-freezing cold. We nearly froze our, uh, body parts off before we arranged to have my car towed and unloaded my things from it. All while you were facing the graveyard shift that night."

Gavin shifted uncomfortably in his chair. "That's not…"

"You sat up with me at the hospital for three nights straight when my dad was sick last year," J.T. joined in to add. "Brought me coffee and sandwiches, made calls for me, anything I needed. Mom was able to go home and get some rest because she knew you were keeping me company."

"Guys…"

Speaking over Gavin's embarrassed protest, Avery said flatly, "Truth is, we all owe you more than a few favors. Least we can do is to help you out here to keep you from doing any more damage to that shoulder."

Jenny wondered if most of that exchange had been for her benefit. Just what had Avery said to Rob and J.T. while she and Gavin had lingered for a few moments outside earlier? Had he told them that she and Gavin had once dated, that he believed she'd broken up with Gavin because she hadn't thought him good enough for her? Surely they didn't feel they needed to defend Gavin's character to her?

She gave Avery a narrowed look, but he merely gazed blandly back at her. Rob and J.T. weren't looking at her, but were smiling at Gavin. They seemed to enjoy their friend's discomfiture, as if good-natured ribbing was very much a part of their typical interactions.

Gavin tossed his cards on the table and scraped his chair against the floor as he pushed back. "Can't really focus on poker right now. I'm going to check those leaks in the bedroom again, make sure they aren't getting any worse."

"We can help with that, too," J.T. assured him. "Won't take long to nail down those shingles. That is, unless Avery tries to help. Boy's useless with a hammer," he added, making Avery grumble and the others laugh.

Biting her lip, Jenny filled the kettle. It was truly nice of Gavin's friends to have driven up to help him. Obviously they'd been worried about him up here, supposedly alone after a damaging storm, at risk for reinjuring himself with the repairs they knew he'd feel compelled to tackle. Perhaps they'd thought to cheer him up with their surprise visit, unaware that he had a visitor, even if an uninvited one. Very thoughtful and supportive of them, and yet...she could never have imagined she'd end up stranded here all day with Gavin and his buddies.

How much more bizarre could this weekend get? She wasn't having a bad time exactly, but it was just all so... awkward. And she still had to figure out a way to try to explain it all to her mother, her grandmother and Thad. They were certain to ask how her solitary weekend had gone, and she wouldn't lie to them.

"You want me to look at that wound for you?" Rob asked Gavin, who was pacing the living room and stretching his arm.

"No, that's okay. Jenny helped me change the bandage when it got wet earlier. It's fine."

She felt all eyes turn to her again, though she kept her attention focused on the selection of teas in the cupboard. She reached for the chamomile, deciding she needed its soothing benefits.

Avery stood, shifting his weight restlessly. "Did you lock the utility shed, Gav? The rain's done for now, I think. I can start hauling the ladder and extra shingles to the back porch so they'll be ready for us to use."

"I can help you with it."

"Rest your arm awhile. No need to overdo it."

"Avery's right," Rob agreed. "You've likely overused it already today. We're here now. Let us help."

"Look, I appreciate the offers, but…"

"C'mon, Gav, it's not every day you get offered free labor," J.T. chimed in with a laugh. "Most folks have to pay for repairs on their rental properties. All *you* had to do was get shot."

The box she'd just taken from the cupboard fell from Jenny's suddenly limp fingers, scattering tea bags over the countertop. The kettle whistled, but it took her a moment to remove it from the burner and turn off the gas. She felt as if she were trying to move through molasses as J.T.'s words reverberated in her mind.

Shot. Gavin had been shot? He'd lied to her?

She hadn't realized until that moment that after all these years, he still had the power to hurt her.

Chapter Four

J.T. seemed to sense immediately that he'd said something wrong. Maybe he picked up on the sudden tension radiating in waves through the room following his joking remark.

"I wasn't shot." Jenny sensed that Gavin directed the words to her, though he spoke to his friend.

Rob nodded. "Technically, that's true."

"Semantics," Avery pronounced with a wave of one hand. "I'd say being hit by shrapnel from a ricochet counts as being shot."

Gavin jerked his chin toward the back door in a less-than-subtle hint. "The utility shed is unlocked. The ladder's on the left and the spare bundle of shingles is on the shelf to the right."

"I'll help you carry the stuff, Avery," Rob offered, springing to his feet.

J.T. ambled toward the door behind them. "Might as well go out and take a look. We should be able to get started on the roof now that the rain's stopped."

"I'll be out in a couple minutes," Gavin said as his friends moved noisily outside.

Gavin waited only until the door had closed behind them before speaking to Jenny in a firm tone. "I wasn't shot."

She dunked her tea bag very deliberately into a mug of steaming water, her gaze focused fiercely on the task. "That's what you keep saying."

"I didn't lie to you, Jen."

He still read her all too easily. She moistened her lips. "Someone shot at you."

"I was responding to a domestic disturbance call. A guy high on meth was shooting wildly in a courtyard. I ducked behind an open door of a panel truck, he fired a few shots in my direction and some sharp pieces of metal from the truck embedded themselves in my shoulder. The wounds weren't life-threatening, but I had to have a minor surgical repair and I developed a mild infection afterward. Once the stitches come out in a few days, I'll do some physical therapy to loosen up the shoulder, and then I'll be back on the job. End of story."

She tossed the tea bag in the trash can. "Until the next time someone shoots at you."

"He wasn't shooting at me. Just firing in all directions. Like I said, he was high as a kite."

"Was anyone else hit?"

"No. The whole incident only lasted a few minutes. His weapon jammed and he was taken into custody. He's being held now for mental evals before standing trial."

She suppressed a shudder as she all too clearly envisioned the harrowing scene he'd described. "I guess I missed the news coverage."

How would she have reacted, she wondered, if she'd heard Gavin's name in a report of an officer shooting? It was one thing to hear about it when she could see him standing in front of her, looking relatively healthy and strong. But would she have panicked at not knowing how he was, even after all those years of not seeing him? Would she have hoped for the best and let it go, or would she have felt compelled to find out for certain that he would be okay?

He shrugged his good shoulder. "It happened the same day as that big warehouse fire downtown. The next morning there was that six-car wreck that shut down the river bridge and backed up rush-hour traffic for a couple hours. An addict with a gun in a high-crime neighborhood didn't make the lead coverage. Since I didn't actually take a bullet, the department downplayed the reports at my request."

"Just another day at the office," she murmured through a tight throat.

"Hardly. Despite what you see on TV, it's a very rare occasion when I have to draw my weapon, much less fire it. I was just standing in the wrong place at the wrong time that day. The only reason I didn't explain earlier was because I knew even after all these years, you'd turn it into an I-told-you-so."

She met his eyes fully then. "That was a rotten thing to say."

"Well?" he challenged, his brows drawn into a scowl. "Isn't that exactly what you're thinking? That you predicted ten years ago I'd probably get shot on the job?"

She hadn't predicted it exactly. But she had feared it with every fiber of her being. She saw no reason to point out that those fears had even more justification now. By how much had that shrapnel-scattering bullet missed burrowing into his chest? A few inches? Less? Would it have made the front page if the bullet had slammed into him rather than the truck door?

"You were willing to accept the danger."

"But you weren't."

Staring blindly into her tea, she heard a vague echo of her widowed mother's heartbroken sobs whispering in the back of her mind. Remembered her own grief at the untimely loss of her father. She had never wanted to risk that devastating loss again for herself. "Do we really want to have this discussion again?"

After a moment, he muttered, "No. Hell, no."

He moved toward the back door. "I'll go help the guys with the shingles. No need for you to come out this time. Enjoy your tea."

She had no intention of going back out unless her assistance was specifically requested. She very much needed some time alone, to regain her emotional equilibrium and steel herself against any further painful reminders of the past.

"Here, Gav, let me get that," Rob said as he reached for the good-size fallen limb Gavin had just picked up. "I'll haul it over to the burn pile for you."

"I've got it."

"It's a little heavy. Maybe I should…"

"I said, I've got it."

Rob held up both hands in response to Gavin's snap

and backed off deliberately. "Yeah, okay. It's cool. I'll just go get that one over there."

Gavin let out a gusty sigh and pushed a hand through his hair. Water was still everywhere, gathered in puddles, dripping from raised surfaces, running down every incline. The ground was a slick coat of mud over the rocky surface, making them have to plant their feet carefully. They hadn't yet started on the roof, but they'd been cleaning up debris. He'd been relieved that the damage was limited and easily repairable. It could have been much worse. Which didn't explain his lousy mood.

Avery stood nearby when Gavin turned from throwing the limb on the pile. Hands on his hips, he scowled at Gavin. "Damn it, you're letting her mess with your head again, aren't you?"

"I don't know what you're talking about."

"Right."

"She's not messing with my head."

"Then why'd you almost rip into Rob just because he offered to help you carry a branch?"

"Long day," Gavin muttered, a little embarrassed. "I'm tired. Shoulder's sore. And I'm hoping we don't find too much damage up on that roof."

Avery shook his head. "Yeah, that's a lot of excuses. And I'm not buying any of them."

"Okay, it's a little…weird that Jenny's here." He stumbled over the adjective, but he couldn't come up with a better one. "I wasn't prepared to see her, especially under these circumstances. It's not like I still have feelings for her or anything," he felt compelled to add. "It's just weird."

"Just don't forget how bad she—well, she and her

family—messed you up last time," Avery warned in a growl. "I'd sure hate to see that happen again."

"Not likely. Jenny's champing at the bit to get off this hill, and chances are I won't run into her again for another decade, if that."

"I notice you didn't say you're in a hurry to get rid of her."

Avery was concerned about him, Gavin reminded himself. And while the words annoyed him, he supposed the intention should count for something. "Why the hell do you think I've spent all morning trying to get that tree out of the drive?"

"Good," Avery said with a firm nod. "Because I doubt she's really changed all that much. Probably still a snob."

"Jenny wasn't a snob," Gavin said without stopping to consider. Her grandmother, on the other hand, was, though there was no need to get into that now. "We just had different goals in life. Being a cop's wife wasn't one of hers, for a lot of reasons."

His friend gave him a narrow-eyed scrutiny, as if trying to decide if he'd defended Jenny a bit too fervently. Gavin was relieved when J.T. called for his attention then. "Hey, Gav, I'm going up on the roof now. I forgot to ask where you keep the roofing nails."

"They're in a box on the shelf above the shingles," he called back.

"Didn't see them."

"I can't find them, either, Gav," Rob agreed from the open door of the utility shed.

"Hang on." With a glance at Avery's still-frowning face, Gavin moved away somewhat too eagerly.

He didn't want to talk about Jenny just then, neither

past, present nor future. Maybe because he was still trying to figure out his own convoluted feelings about all three. Maybe because he was starting to realize that after all these years he still wanted her. That he'd never really stopped wanting her.

Because the hammering from the roof was giving her a headache, Jenny moved out to the front porch. She wasn't sure what the guys were doing exactly, but it required lots of banging and a few shouts and a couple of trips in and out of the back bedroom, so she just got out of the way.

A cool, damp breeze brushed her face and toyed with the strands of hair on her cheek. The clouds were lifting, letting glimpses of sunlight glint among the rain-heavy leaves of surrounding trees. Emerging from their shelters, birds were starting to chirp again and a couple of squirrels played tag across the wet ground. If she ignored the sounds of the men in the backyard and on the roof, she could hear the river rushing past below the cabin.

This, she thought, was the scene she had envisioned when she'd booked the cabin. She'd pictured herself sitting on this porch rocker, perhaps watching a gentle rain fall around her—no stress, no interruptions, no reason at all to be "on" for anyone else's benefit. Away from her daily routines and obligations, she'd be able to reimagine her future, to see herself in a new reality. Once she returned to real life, rested and refreshed, she would be very busy planning a wedding, attending social and political functions, getting more acquainted with Thad's family and associates, business, personal and political. After the wedding, she and Thad would travel quite a bit, and when they were in town there would be functions nearly every evening.

She'd always wanted to travel, to see all the places she'd only read about. But she'd been so focused on establishing her business and planning for the second store, and others down the road, so careful with her budget, that she hadn't traveled nearly as much as she would have liked. All of that would change if—when—she married Thad. They would travel in style. Thad had even commented that she could take her mom and grandmother to some of the places they enjoyed exploring through television documentaries. Both women had worked so hard for so long, had seen so many of their dreams fall apart, it would mean a great deal to her to give them a few treats now.

It would be a good life. Comfortable. Secure. She would be able to use the skills she had developed in business and marketing, though perhaps not in the ways she'd expected. She'd be pushing Thad's objectives more than her own—though as he'd predicted, she would surely make them her goals, as well. She could still make her mark, just in different venues than she'd planned.

Thad promised to be a loyal and considerate partner. Their children would have all the advantages of a comfortable social position, he'd always said—the best education, exposure to the arts, chances to see other parts of the world. They would be raised with an awareness of the obligations of privilege, and with knowledge of the inner workings of government. Just as Thad himself had been raised, and look how well he'd turned out, he'd added with a charmingly self-deprecating chuckle.

Not once in the seven months she had dated him had

Jenny had to bandage Thad's injuries or pace the floor worrying about whether he would be shot on his job. Thad wasn't even a criminal lawyer. Unlike her firefighter father, whose favored off-duty pursuits were as risky—if not more dangerous—than his work, corporate attorney Thad could generally be found on the golf course when he wasn't helping some business VIP wade through legal paperwork. The odds were fairly good that Thad's daughter, if he should have one, would not be left fatherless at a young, particularly vulnerable age.

Maybe she'd finalized her decision, after all. With all the points she'd just enumerated, she would be foolish not to accept Thad's proposal. There were cons, of course, as there were to any decision, but the pros certainly outweighed them. There was no good reason at all for her not to marry Thad.

"Hey."

With a start, she turned to find Gavin watching her from the open doorway to the cabin. She had no idea how long he'd stood there. She'd been too lost in her thoughts to hear the door open. She cleared her throat. "Hey, yourself."

"We got the leaks fixed, I think."

She hadn't even noticed the hammering had stopped. "That's good. I hope there wasn't much damage."

"I don't think so, but I'll have someone out to check it before I rent the place again."

"Good idea."

"Look, I'm, uh, sorry about earlier. If I sounded..."

She shook her head quickly and cut in. "It's fine. Really."

His expression rather grim, he nodded. "The guys brought a big box of chocolate-chip cookies that J.T.'s wife made. They look really good. We thought you might like one."

"Thank you, but I'm not hungry."

"We're going down to check the road in a little while, after we take a short coffee break."

She sat up a bit straighter. "You think I'll be able to leave soon?"

"Maybe another hour or so, just to be sure."

She glanced at her watch. It was already four o'clock. It wouldn't yet be fully dark by five, so it should be safe for her to leave.

"You'll still have a long drive ahead of you back to Little Rock," he warned. "It will be late when you get back home."

"I could always stop somewhere along the way if I get tired. I'll be fine."

"You're in quite a hurry to get away, huh?" he said after a moment.

She shrugged, her eyes trained on her car in the driveway. "It seems best, considering everything. You've been a very gracious host and I appreciate it. But if I can get out safely today, I think I should go."

He didn't try to make another argument for her to stay. He would probably be relieved when she was gone, though she couldn't read any emotions in his expression.

"Go have your cookies and enjoy your company," she said. "I'll just sit out here and read awhile longer."

He hesitated only a moment, then nodded. "Let me know if you need anything."

"Thanks. I will."

He moved back into the cabin and closed the door quietly.

For the next fifteen minutes, she tried to read, but the

book still didn't hold her attention. Was she ever going to finish it? Did she really want to waste any more of her time with it? For all she knew, everyone's attention had already moved to another trendy title she would be expected to discuss.

She heard hearty male laughter coming from inside the cabin and she felt suddenly lonely. Maybe she'd go inside for a little while, after all.

"Hey, Jenny," Rob called out, looking up from his chair at the table when she walked in. He shook his shaggy dark hair out of his dark eyes and winked at her. "Come help me. I'm getting stomped over here."

She had assumed they were playing poker again, but she saw now that some sort of board game lay in front of them. Approaching them curiously, she laughed in surprise. "Scrabble? Really?"

"J.T.'s obsessed with the game," Rob answered with a gusty sigh. "He has to stay in practice because he and his wife bet household chores when they play each other."

"Hey, last time she beat me I had to cook dinner every night for two weeks," J.T. insisted with a laugh. "Well, every night I was home, anyway. I figure if I pick up some new words from you guys, I'll have an advantage next time I play her."

Sprawled in his chair, Gavin looked up from his rack of tiles. "I keep board games here for guests. J.T. dug this one out to play while we finish our coffee and cookies."

"Just don't tell anyone you caught us playing Scrabble and eating cookies instead of high-stakes poker with booze and cigars," Rob entreated comically.

"Your secret is safe with me." She was aware that Avery's laughter had faded when she'd entered the room, and he seemed to be making a point of not looking at her, but she wouldn't let him put her on the defensive again.

She circled round to stand behind Rob and look over the board and his rack. Some of the words on the grid made her raise an eyebrow. Her grandmother would certainly disapprove of a few. This explained some of the raucous laughter she'd heard.

With an exaggerated clearing of her throat, she reached out and rearranged a couple of Rob's tiles on his rack. He frowned at the board a moment, then laughed and slapped all of his tiles down in a triple-score play. "Boo-yah!" he crowed. "Top that, losers."

"Oh, that's no fair," J.T. protested with a shake of his head. "Jenny gave you the word."

"I'd have come up with it on my own. Probably."

"Right." Gavin's chair creaked as he shifted his weight. Though he was smiling lazily, he rested his right arm rather gingerly across his lap, and Jenny thought she saw a shadow of pain in his eyes. He had so overdone it that day, not that he had listened to anyone who tried to dissuade him, she thought in exasperation.

"Jenny's deadly at Scrabble," he drawled. "Dad thought he was the Scrabble champ until he took her on. The two of them got into some serious competitions. Holly called it full-contact Scrabble."

There was a barely notable moment of silence before Rob and J.T. responded with smiles. Jenny moistened her lips even as Gavin suddenly frowned, as if he'd become abruptly aware of just what he'd unthinkingly revealed about their past. It would be hard to maintain now that they had simply been passing acquaintances in college. Judging by the speculation on their faces, she realized that Avery must not have enlightened the others earlier, after all. She would leave it to Gavin to decide how much he wanted to tell them later, after she'd gone her own way again.

"Your dad was a worthy opponent," she said casually. "You were always pretty good yourself, but not your sister. Holly tended to make up words as she went."

"Yeah. Holly calls herself a 'cheerful cheat' when it comes to games."

She smiled. "I remember that."

Avery's chair scraped against the floor as he stood. "Let's go check that flooding down the road. Might need to shovel more brush and leaves out of the drainage ditches so Jenny can get out of here. And I've got to head back before long myself. Lynne and I are planning to stream a movie tonight."

She bit her lower lip. Avery was making no secret that he wanted her gone. Seriously, he acted as though she were a ticking time bomb or something. She couldn't imagine why she still roused such hostility in him after all these years.

The men were gone longer than she'd expected. After half an hour, she was beginning to worry that something had gone wrong. She sat on the porch for a while, then went inside and busied herself wiping the kitchen counters and cleaning the mud-tracked floor with a mop she found in the pantry. She preferred cleaning to sitting and waiting.

She had just put away the mop when she was startled by a burst of noise. Lights came on in the kitchen and the refrigerator began to hum, cooling the contents that would mostly have to be discarded. A ceiling fan in the living area began to spin lazily. Country music flowed from speakers she hadn't noticed before. Apparently Gavin's taste in music hadn't changed. Her heart clenched when she recognized the tune and the artist. But it wasn't "their" song, she realized after a moment, and thank goodness for that. It had been a long time after she and Gavin had broken up before she'd been able to listen to country music again, for fear that she might hear Diamond Rio's "Beautiful Mess," the song they'd both loved and which they'd always sung along to whenever it came on the radio in his truck.

She'd never been the type to have a little too much wine on a melancholy night, put on an old song and wallow in bittersweet memories. She started across the room with the intent to find the music player and silence it now. She liked this song just fine, though the sentiment about wanting a chance to spend one more day with a loved one made her a bit uncomfortable.

The front door opened before she'd taken more than a couple of steps. Looking as though he'd pretty much rolled in mud, Gavin entered alone.

She'd have thought the sight of him would have grown more familiar, that the impact of seeing him would have lessened. Yet, still her heart gave a hard thump when his eyes met and held hers across the room. She cleared her throat. "The power just came on," she said unnecessarily.

Gavin strode across the room and flipped a switch at the entertainment center. The music was abruptly silenced. Had he, too, been carried back to a more innocent time by the sound of a familiar voice? Or did he just want the music off?

"Where are the other guys?" she asked, her voice sounding loud in the sudden silence.

"They left. Avery wanted to get home, so I thanked them for their help and sent them on their way. All of them said for me to tell you goodbye and that they enjoyed meeting you today."

She doubted that Avery had sent quite those words, but she let it go. "How's the flooding?"

"It's going down fast," he assured her. "We dredged out the ditches again and pulled out some debris that was acting as a little dam. I'd give it another fifteen, twenty minutes, maybe, and then the road should be passable if you're careful."

A check of the time told her that in just over an hour, Thad would call. She'd like to be on the road by then. She could always pull over somewhere and take the call. She'd just rather not be here at the time.

Gavin pushed a hand through his hair. "I'm filthy. I'm going to try to scrape off some of this mud."

"Okay. I'll be carrying my things out to my car."

"Need any help with that?"

"No, thanks. I didn't bring in much last night."

He nodded, then disappeared into the back room. Moments later, she heard the shower running. She swallowed hard, deliberately cleared her mind of any unbidden images and started gathering her possessions.

His hair was still wet when he emerged again, but he wore a clean T-shirt and jeans and looked as though the shower had revived some of his energy.

"You didn't need help with the bandage?" she asked, glancing toward his covered shoulder.

He shook his head. "I managed. Thanks."

Lacing her hands, she glanced around the now cheerily lit room, trying to think of anything else to say. Coming up blank, she gave him a strained smile. "I guess I should try to make it out, then. Unless there's anything else I can do for you before I go?"

As she'd expected, he declined the offer. "No, it's all good."

She nodded. "Then I should go before it starts getting dark."

"I'll follow you down the hill in my truck, make sure you get across okay. I need to put my truck away for the night, anyway."

She'd be wasting her breath to tell him it wasn't necessary to see her off, so she merely nodded again. She took a step toward the door, then stopped when he moved to block her way. "What?"

His gaze was so intent on her face that she almost felt as though he could see her thoughts. "Just one more question before you go."

Suddenly nervous, she smoothed the hem of her shirt. "What is it?"

"Why did you really come here this weekend?"

She moistened her lips before answering. "I told you. I had work to do."

"Yeah, that's what you told me. And it's probably true. To an extent. But there's something more you haven't told me. Something that's been nagging at you. Probably none of my business, but you can always tell me to butt out, if you want."

"What makes you think I haven't told you everything?" she challenged, not quite meeting his eyes.

"Jen." He reached out and lifted her chin with a surprisingly gentle hand, so that their eyes met fully again. "I know it's been a decade since we've seen each other, but there was a time I knew you as well as I knew myself. There's a reason other than work that you came here, isn't there?"

She sighed. Perhaps it was the bittersweet reminder of their past that loosened her tongue. "The man I've been dating proposed to me last week. I came here to decide what my answer will be."

Chapter Five

She felt Gavin's hand twitch against her face, a spasmodic jerk he'd been unable to contain. And then he dropped his arm to his side, his thoughts now closed to her. She was sure her announcement had come as a surprise to him, but she couldn't tell how he felt beyond that.

"Well, isn't that a dilemma," he said. It wasn't quite a snarl.

Her chin rose. "It isn't an easy decision. Thad's a wonderful man, but I've worked hard to build the life I have now and obviously marriage would mean big changes for me. If you still know me so well, you should understand that I need to make sure I've considered all possible ramifications before I make a lifelong commitment."

"Sorry I got in your way this weekend. But I'm sure you'll make the decision that's right for you, anyway. You always have."

He opened the door and stepped outside before she could decide if she'd just been complimented or insulted. Wishing now that she'd kept her mouth shut, she swallowed a sigh and followed him outside.

"You have all your stuff?" he asked, pausing on the porch to don his mud-caked boots.

She nodded. "I think I have everything."

"I'll drive down ahead of you and make sure it's safe before you go through."

Though she thought he was being overcautious, she nodded. "Fine."

He climbed into his truck without another word. Apparently he wasn't going to say anything else about the admission she'd made to him. But wasn't he even going to say goodbye?

After a moment, she slid into her car. If he wanted to part with nothing more than a wave at the bottom of the hill, that was okay with her. It was probably even for the best.

He drove slowly down the hill and she followed at a safe distance. The road looked different in the afternoon light than it had in the darkness and rain on the way up. Much less forbidding and narrow, though the riverside fell away a bit more sharply than she'd have liked.

At the foot of the long hill, the road was still covered with a muddy puddle, but it looked no deeper now than it had when she'd driven through last night. Water rushed in the deep ditches along the roadside, and she saw the fresh trenches cut into the mud by the men's shovels. Gavin braked at the foot of the hill, then drove slowly through the puddle. As far as she could tell, he had no trouble getting to the slightly higher ground on the other side. He pulled over as far as he could on the woods side of the road, hopped out of his truck and motioned for her to proceed. Following his example, she drove slowly, staying in the center of the road. She heard the water sloshing against the bottom of her car, but her tires held their grip. Her enforced stay was at an end.

Gavin flagged her down when she'd reached the other side. She put the car into Park as he approached. So he was going to say goodbye, after all. She should at least thank him for his hospitality before she drove away.

Leaving the motor running, she opened her door and climbed out. "That was definitely interesting," she said with a wry smile.

"A little too interesting. If that puddle had been an inch or two deeper, I'd have insisted you turn around and drive back up the hill."

She was glad it hadn't come to that. "Well, it's been…"

She almost said "interesting" again, but decided she was getting a little repetitive. She couldn't actually think of an appropriate adjective, so she allowed her voice to fade into a wry smile.

"Yeah. It's been." He, too, left it at that. "Drive carefully."

"Thanks, I will."

"Again, sorry about the mix-up this weekend. I'll make sure that refund goes through immediately. I assume it can just be credited back to your card?"

"Yes, that would be fine, thank you."

"I'll have someone other than Lizzie take care of it, so it's done right."

She cleared her throat. "So…"

He met her eyes, though she still couldn't tell what he was thinking or feeling. "So…"

"Goodbye, Gavin. Be careful with that shoulder, okay?" *And on the job*, she wanted to add. *Please don't get shot.*

"I'll take care," he replied without smiling.

She nodded and started to turn back to her car.

"Jenny…" His hand fell on her arm, detaining her before she could slide behind the wheel.

She glanced up at him. "Yes?"

She was too startled to move when he lowered his head and covered her mouth with his. Or at least that was what she told herself. She wasn't sure if she reached up to push him away or steady herself, but her fingers curled into his shirt.

His lips were as firm as they looked and so very warm. The kiss was brief, but it rocked her to her toes. Her heart pounded against her chest. She suddenly understood every old cliché about fireworks and trumpets.

During the past years, she had spent a great deal of effort trying not to remember explosive kisses and mind-blowing lovemaking with Gavin. On the rare occasion when erotic memories slipped through the cracks, she'd written them off as exaggerated by time, perhaps made more spectacular through the eager lens of youth and innocence. She'd convinced herself that no mere embrace could be that powerful now that she was a more experienced adult. No mere press of lips could turn her into a mindless mass of quivering nerves.

It seemed she'd been wrong. She couldn't for the life of her figure out why her eyes suddenly burned as if with long-held-back tears.

Oddly enough, Gavin was smiling a little when he lifted his head.

"Sorry," he said, though there was no apology in

his expression. "Guess you could say that was for old times' sake."

She realized that her hand rested just over his bandaged shoulder. She drew it away as if her fingertips had been burned. Her voice was hardly recognizable to her own ears when she said, "Goodbye, Gavin."

Only when she was in her car and driving away did it occur to her that he hadn't said goodbye in return.

At least their parting had been amicable this time, disturbing as the unexpected kiss had been. Maybe there'd been a little sarcasm on his part when she'd mentioned her potential engagement, but no anger, no accusations. Perhaps her chest ached a little, but that was probably a normal reaction. Gavin had been an important part of her past. Of course there would be some nostalgia, some vague reflections of what-might-have-been.

The weekend could not have turned out more differently than she'd expected, but maybe she'd accomplished what she'd set out to do, anyway. She'd said a final goodbye to her past. While sitting on the porch in the rocker, she had reminded herself of all she had to gain by marrying Thad. All in all, a surprisingly constructive day.

So why was there such a hard lump in her throat and a knot in her stomach? And why couldn't she stop reaching up to touch her lips, as if to see if they somehow felt different to her? And why was she finding it so hard not to compare that disturbing kiss to the pleasant, affectionate embraces she'd shared with Thad?

She had to stop. Going down that path could only lead to heartache again, surely, and she'd had enough of that to last a lifetime.

* * *

The dashboard clock said 5:59 when her cell phone buzzed half an hour after she'd driven away from the cabin. Knowing Thad, she figured her car clock was off rather than him.

She pulled into the parking lot of a closed tire dealership to take the call. She had to draw a deep breath before she answered with her usual measured tone. "Hello, Thad."

"Hi, sweetheart. How's the vacation?" His voice was rich and clear, mostly free of accent because he'd been raised to speak with a neutral Midwestern cadence rather than a Southern drawl.

"Over," she replied lightly. "You were right, it seems. The weather was just too unpleasant this weekend. I'm headed home."

"Are you all right?" She heard the concern in his voice. "You sound odd."

"I'm just a little tired. The storm kept me from sleeping well last night."

She would tell him about Gavin, she promised herself. Just not over the phone.

"I'm sorry to hear that. I hope you get more rest tonight."

"Thanks. How's your trip?"

"Successful." His tone was satisfied now. An image of him popped into her mind—gym-toned and slender, clad in pressed slacks and a discreetly expensive shirt, his chestnut-brown hair combed into his usual impeccably groomed style. If he'd been working in his room—as he almost always was when he wasn't out making valuable contacts—he was wearing the horn-rimmed glasses she teased made him look like a roguish professor. His handsome face would be creased with the indulgent smile he usually wore when he spoke with her.

Picturing Thad made her feel calm. Comfortable. Much preferable to jangled nerves and trembling fingers and knotted muscles, right?

They concluded their call with his usual breezy, "Love ya, Jenny," and her habitual, rather lame response of "You, too." The routine satisfied them both, so she saw no reason to change it.

She put her phone away and started her car again. She had quite a few more miles to travel that evening. She turned up the music—classical, not country—to distract her from the emotions that seethed inside her as she left the cabin and its owner behind her.

Gavin stood on the front porch of the cabin later that evening, studying the moon-washed grounds with weary satisfaction. The rain had stopped for good finally, and the clouds had parted. Tomorrow was supposed to be dry and sunny, which would let him put in another full day's work. He needed to stack and burn the remaining storm debris, and rake the lawn immediately around the cabin. The roof was repaired now, thanks to his friends, but he had a couple places to patch on the ceiling of the back bedroom. He had linens to launder, floors to clean and a couple of broken steps down toward the river to replace.

He was sore and bone-tired from all he'd done today. Every joint protested the very thought of all he planned to tackle tomorrow. But he was glad he had so much to do, mostly because the work would keep him too busy to brood about Jenny. Jenny, who was on the verge of marrying someone else, putting her out of Gavin's life again, this time forever. Jenny, whom he'd once planned to marry himself. He'd even fantasized about proposing here at the cabin, beside the river. Maybe in their private clearing, where he'd go down on one knee and offer her his paternal grandmother's ring. The pretty little diamond-and-sapphire band had been passed down to him when his grandmother died while he was still in high school. His grandfather had wanted him to have it to one day offer his own bride.

Maybe someday he'd pass it down to his eldest nephew. It seemed unlikely he'd ever use the ring himself, even if he found another woman he wanted to marry. In his mind, that ring would always have been meant for Jenny. Jenny, who hadn't wanted him, at least not without changing him into something he could never become.

Frowning in response to having her name pop up in his mind again—he'd lost count of how many times he'd had to push it away since she'd driven off—he spun on one heel and went back inside the cabin. It was time for his antibiotic, so he downed one with a glass of water. He flexed his shoulder tentatively, satisfied that it felt slightly less stiff, though still plenty sore. It would feel even better when he had the stitches out in a couple days. He was anxious to get back on the job and put this whole misadventure behind him.

The cabin seemed unusually quiet now that he was here alone. Usually he welcomed the tranquility. Tonight, though, the silence seemed almost oppressive. He thought about turning on music to listen to while he ate a can of chili he found in the pantry, but decided to dial in the television satellite instead. For some reason, country music didn't seem like a good choice tonight.

After eating, he cleaned the kitchen and carried the trash out to the plastic bin on the back porch. He opened the animal-proof lid, then froze when he saw the muddy, ruined green sneakers atop the other refuse.

He told himself to leave them alone, to bury them beneath the kitchen waste. Instead, he found himself cradling one of the small shoes in both hands, gazing down at it with a scowl. He'd promised to replace them, so it only made sense for him to check the size.

He was not prepared for the surge of hot blood that coursed straight to his groin. It wasn't the shoe that aroused him, but the wave of memories.

"Your toes are funny."

A girlish giggle, followed by "What's funny about my toes?"

"They're so tiny. You have teeny, tiny toes."

"I know. Stubby toes. I hate them."

"No. They're perfect. Funny, but perfect."

Naked and lazy, they had sprawled on a tumbled bed, bathed in candlelight. He'd proceeded to show her just how erotic funny little toes could be. And when her laughter had dissolved into low moans of need, he'd surged up her body to pay thorough homage to the rest of her.

Brought back to the present by the screech of an owl in search of dinner, he shifted his weight, preparing for a long, uncomfortably restless night ahead.

Something told him his dreams, if he slept, would be very disturbing that night.

Jenny opened her apartment door Sunday afternoon to find her friend Stevie standing on the other side, a bottle of wine in one hand, a familiar bakery box in the other. Her artificially blond hair brushed into a riot of curls, Stevie made a striking picture with her long-lashed, sapphire-blue eyes and generous, full-lipped mouth. She was the type of woman who turned heads wherever she went, a reaction she found more amusing than disconcerting. She was gregarious, energetic, generous to a fault and fiercely loyal. Jenny had several good friends, but Stevie was as close as she'd ever had to a sister.

"Moscato. Fruit tarts." Stevie held up each in turn. "I provide the treats, you spill the beans. I want to know everything about the night you just spent with Gavin Locke."

Though she rolled her eyes, Jenny motioned her friend into her living room. "I didn't spend the night with Gavin. Well, I did, but not… You know what I mean."

Stevie laughed musically and set the goodies on the kitchen bar. "I nearly dropped my phone when I saw your text saying Gavin was there at the cabin."

They'd talked briefly by phone earlier, so Stevie knew the basic details about how the mix-up had occurred, but she'd said she wanted the play-by-play in person. Truth be told, Jenny wasn't unhappy that her friend had come by. Sure, she could be tackling some of the paperwork she'd planned to complete that weekend, but it could wait. She reached into the cabinet for wineglasses. "You know where the plates are."

As at home in Jenny's place as she was in her own, Stevie was already serving the little tarts topped with glistening fruit. They carried the plates and glasses into the living room, where they kicked off their shoes and settled onto the couch.

"Have you told your mom and grandmother yet? About Gavin, I mean," Stevie asked, diving right into the conversation.

Jenny popped a glazed blueberry into her mouth, chewed and swallowed before she admitted, "No. They had a luncheon with their Sunday school class today. I didn't want to mention Gavin on the phone, so I just told them I came home early. I figured I'd tell them the whole story when I see them." Usually she had dinner with them on Sunday nights, but since they weren't expecting her to be in town this evening, they'd made plans with friends. She was seeing them tomorrow.

"Your grandmother's going to totally lose it when she hears Gavin's name," Stevie predicted with some relish. "Especially when she hears you spent a night with him."

"Stop saying that. We spent a night in the same cabin. We didn't spend the night together."

Stevie waved a hand. "Figure of speech."

"But an important distinction nonetheless." She certainly wasn't going to mention that she'd literally fallen into bed with Gavin when she'd arrived at the cabin.

"Maybe it would be easier if you don't tell them he was there."

Jenny shrugged in resignation. "Mom's going to ask about my weekend. She worried about me being there alone, and I know she'll ask how I weathered the storm. You know how she likes to hear all about my life. I don't want to lie to her. Even though they'll probably fuss, it just seems easier to tell them what happened. It wasn't my fault or Gavin's, so I'll just make it a funny-thing-happened story." At least, she would try to keep it that light and breezy, hoping to make it sound like no big deal that she'd run into him again.

"What was it like you when first saw him again? Did he look different? Does he look a lot older? Did he get, like, fat and bald?"

"He looks pretty much like he did, just a little older. More mature. Not fat. And he still has all his hair."

"He was always hot, in a sort of rough-cut way."

"You'd probably say the same about him now."

"Nice. So, he was surprised to see you, I guess?"

"Yes, he was. And he was embarrassed by his leasing company's error." She could so clearly picture him all tousled and grumpy and sleepy when she'd barged in on him. The image made her throat close. She set the plate aside and reached hastily for her wineglass.

"And you really had no idea he owns the place now?"

Stevie already knew the answer to that question, but Jenny shook her head and replied, anyway. "Of course not. I thought it was still just a vacation cabin, maybe owned now by the leasing company I contacted. I wasn't even entirely certain it was the one I'd visited before, though the photos and directions on the internet looked familiar."

"So Gavin didn't even cross your mind when you rented the place."

"Only in passing. I remembered what a good time I had with his family there. Maybe I wondered where he was these days, how he was doing—but I certainly never expected to get stuck in the cabin with him."

Stevie scrutinized a strawberry half. "So he's still single."

"Well, he's not married."

"Has he ever been?"

Jenny ran a fingertip around the rim of her glass. "I don't know. It didn't come up."

"So I guess you told him about Thad?"

"Yes, of course. As I was leaving," she added.

"As you were leaving? Seriously? What *did* you talk about until then?"

"Mostly about the storm and the damage it did. He told me a little of what's going on with his family. His sister has two little boys now, and I could tell he's crazy about them. Then his friends showed up and there wasn't a lot of time for personal talk. Um, Avery was with them. Did I mention that?"

"No, you just said some of his friends came to help clear the road." Stevie eyed her speculatively. "How's Avery?"

"He looks pretty much the same, too. Maybe his temples are a little higher, but he's still got red hair."

"How'd he act toward you?"

"Let's just say I'm still not his favorite person. He wasn't actively hostile..." Well, with the exception of the one low dig she saw no need to mention now. "But he wasn't overly friendly, either."

"He was always kind of a jerk."

Jenny bit her lip. She hadn't forgotten an unfortunate attempt at a double date when she and Gavin, who had been a new couple at the time, had invited their friends to join them in an unsuccessful bid at matchmaking. Avery and Stevie had not hit it off, to say the least. As she recalled, they'd argued about whether Nickelback "sucked"—Stevie liked their music; Avery hated it. A petty disagreement, but it had quickly escalated until they were hardly speaking by the end of the evening.

It was after that night when Avery had turned cool toward Jenny. She'd never known whether he'd blamed her for setting him up on an unsuccessful date, if he just didn't like her or maybe if he'd thought from the start that her relationship with Gavin had been ill-fated. Nor did she know why he disliked her now. Surely he didn't believe she still had any power to hurt Gavin.

"Had to be weird sleeping in the same house with Gavin again."

"I didn't sleep much," Jenny agreed, candid with Stevie in a way she didn't feel comfortable being with most other people. "Weird is pretty much an understatement for the way it felt to be there with him."

"I guess it brought back a lot of memories."

"Yes."

Stevie nodded thoughtfully. "It would be strange for me to spend the night with one of my exes. Though it's not like my past relationships were as epic as yours with Gavin. It took you a long time to get over him. For months you couldn't even talk about him. I can't imagine what it must have been like to suddenly be alone with him again."

Jenny squirmed a little on the couch and protested, "Come on, Stevie, there's no need to be so dramatic about it. It was a college romance, not a tragic love story. Yes, I was hurt when it ended, but obviously I got over it. I've dated since. Now I'm in a serious relationship with someone else. It's not as if I've spent the past ten years pining over Gavin."

"Hmph." Without pausing to expand on the enigmatic murmur, Stevie asked, "Did you tell Gavin you and I are still friends?"

"Your name came up. He asked if you were still dating the drummer."

"Who? Oh, him." Stevie laughed and shook her head. "I'd almost forgotten about him."

"Yeah, that's pretty much what I'd figured."

"Sticks was seriously cute. But sooo dumb."

"I remember."

Setting aside her plate, Stevie drew her bare feet beneath her and nestled back into the sofa with her wineglass cradled in her hands. "So what did Thad say? About Gavin being there, I mean. I assume you feel the need to tell him, too, since you're planning to tell the family."

Slowly swirling the liquid in her own glass, Jenny cleared her throat. "I haven't told him yet. I will, of course. It just wasn't the sort of thing to mention during a phone call. I figured I'd wait until he gets home so I can assure him face-to-face that it was all a perfectly innocent mix-up."

"Do you think he'll be mad?"

She chose her answering words carefully. "He won't like it, of course, but I doubt he'll be angry. Thad understands that mistakes happen. This particular mix-up was certainly awkward and unexpected, but he knows he can trust me. He'll be civil about it."

"Civil," Stevie murmured. "Yes, Thad is certainly civil."

Jenny frowned. "You make that sound like a criticism."

"Do I? Huh." Stevie sipped her wine, then asked, "So, I'm the only one you've told about your weekend adventure?"

Though she was tempted to press her friend to explain exactly why she was acting so oddly about Thad, Jenny decided to let it go. "I haven't really talked to anyone yet, other than you. Technically, I'm still on vacation."

"You are, aren't you? Want to go see a movie or something tonight? It's been forever since I've been to a movie. We'll find one with hunky guys who take off their shirts and blow things up—no sappy love stories."

Jenny set aside her glass. "I like the sound of that."

For one thing, there would be no need for conversation during a movie. Not to mention that she occasionally enjoyed watching hunky, shirtless men blow stuff up. Thad had never quite understood that, telling her it seemed out of character for her. The films weren't to his taste, but she'd told herself she was content to share those outings with Stevie while she and Thad confined their movie dates to more cerebral offerings. Most of which she also appreciated. She particularly enjoyed the lively discussions that followed over coffee or wine. It was just that every once in a while, she liked to turn off her brain and simply be entertained for a couple hours. And why not?

They decided to have dinner before the movie. They chose a popular, inexpensive Southwestern restaurant not far from the theater. Jenny kept an eye on the time, and she excused herself from the table they had just claimed when her phone buzzed quietly. She'd warned Stevie that Thad would call at six. Splashing hot sauce onto her burrito, Stevie waved her off good-naturedly, telling her there was no need to hurry with the call.

She took the call outside. It was hot and there was no shade from the still-blazing, early-evening sun, but these calls never lasted long. "Hi, Thad."

"I was beginning to wonder if you'd answer. Is everything all right?"

"Stevie and I are at a restaurant and I wanted to move outside to take the call."

"Oh, sorry. I didn't mean to interrupt your dinner."

"It's okay. We're just having burritos before we see a movie."

Thad's cultured laugh sounded quietly in her ear. "An adventure film, I'm sure."

She smiled. "Well, of course. It *is* Stevie."

A big "dually" pickup truck with chrome pipes and pounding bass passed in the parking lot. She waited until the noise had abated before asking politely, "What are your plans for the evening?"

"Another client meeting and then a dinner with some local associates. Oh, and I believe there's a celebrity on the guest list." He named several prominent national politicians, then an actor whose name she recognized immediately, which wasn't surprising. Thad was, after all, in LA representing one of his corporate clients.

"He's a friend of one of the senators," he explained. "I don't think I've seen any of his films, but I looked him up online so I won't sound completely disconnected from popular entertainment."

"You should have asked me," she quipped. "I think I've seen all his movies."

"Of course you have." He laughed again. "Once you start attending all these events with me, I'll depend on you to keep me up-to-date. I know you'll want to continue to make time for your girls' nights with Stevie because you enjoy her company so much, so I'll shamelessly pump you for details about the action films I miss."

He was obviously taking for granted that her answer to his pending proposal would be yes. And why shouldn't he be? They were obviously a well-suited couple; even the activities they didn't share in common complemented each other. It went without saying that it might be harder to make time for these girls' nights after the wedding, but Thad was making it clear he'd never deliberately interfere with the longtime friendship.

Theirs wasn't, perhaps, an "epic love affair," to use Stevie's words. But she and Thad were comfortable together. She could make that be enough.

Two squealing adolescents streaked down the sidewalk, shoving their way past her with insincerely muttered apologies. An ambulance shrieked by on the street, the decibel level making her wince. The parking lot smelled of exhaust, warm asphalt and fried foods. She pictured Thad in his five-star hotel surrounded by quiet elegance, and then imagined herself there beside him, choosing jewelry to enhance a little black dress rather than the cool cotton top and cropped pants she wore now.

Roused from her mental drifting, she blinked when he spoke again. "I'll let you get back to Stevie. Have fun. Love ya, Jenny."

"You, too." She lowered her phone to her side, stood for a moment staring at the traffic moving in front of her, then turned abruptly to go back inside.

"I'm sorry," she said, sliding into her seat across the little plastic table from Stevie. "I'm muting my phone for the rest of our evening. Anyone who needs me can leave a voice message or send me a text."

Stevie sipped from a straw, then set the paper cup of soda aside. "How's Thad?"

Stevie used almost exactly the same tone whenever she spoke of Thad. Always polite, not quite cool but not really warm, either. Perhaps that warmth would come with time. But even if Stevie and Thad were never close, their careful courtesy was certainly better than the resentment Avery had always exhibited toward herself when she'd dated Gavin.

"Thad's fine. He's having dinner with a few names you'd know tonight." She listed the ones she remembered, including the actor, and watched Stevie nod in recognition.

"Cool. So, Thad's really working the political connections, huh?"

"He's certainly drawn in that direction."

"Does it bother him that you've never been all that interested in politics?"

"I've always been active in the community," Jenny countered quickly. "You know how many organizations I've been involved with. Not political exactly, but civic-minded. I like the idea of helping Thad make a difference with whatever talents I have to contribute."

"Mmm."

Jenny figured if Stevie bit her lip any harder, it would start to bleed. She focused on her meal and changed the subject. "How's your burrito?"

"It's good. So, Gavin's still a cop, huh? I guess it's worked out well for him."

"Gavin was at the cabin to recuperate from being shot in the shoulder," Jenny said bluntly, if not entirely accurately. "If you call that working out..."

Stevie flinched dramatically. She knew all too well the fears that had come between Jenny and Gavin all those years ago. "Oh, crap. You didn't mention that. Is he okay?"

"He's fine. I heard him tell his buddies that he was eager to get back to work."

She changed the subject abruptly, and Stevie got the message that talk of Gavin was over for the evening.

Yet Jenny couldn't help but remember the determination in Gavin's expression when he'd assured his friends he would be back in uniform the minute he was cleared for duty. And they'd all cheered him on, damn it. Had she been the only one who worried that he wouldn't be so lucky next time?

Chapter Six

"I can't imagine what it must have been like to be stranded in a mountain cabin with an ex-boyfriend." Tess Miller stared wide-eyed across the restaurant lunch table at Jenny the following Thursday, shaking her auburn head in dismay. "If that had been me with my ex, there might have been bloodshed before morning."

"Now that's a story that sounds interesting," Stevie commented with a lifted eyebrow.

Tess laughed and shook her head. "It would take a great deal of wine and longer than any of us have for a lunch break."

Tess had called earlier that morning to say she was going to be running a business errand near Complements at lunchtime and to ask if Jenny and Stevie, both of whom she had met in a yoga class, would be free to join her. Stevie worked as a freelance interior designer specializing in kitchen remodels, and she'd happened to have a couple spare hours that afternoon to meet them at a favorite restaurant in the same shopping center as Jenny's store.

"Maybe we should have another girls' night soon," Stevie suggested, scooping rice onto her chopsticks. "I haven't spent nearly enough time with my girlfriends lately. I really should spend more time doing things I want to do, rather than… Well, anyway."

Which only confirmed to Jenny that Stevie's relationship with Joe, the bass player, wasn't going all that well, though Stevie hadn't yet admitted it. Even to herself, perhaps?

Tess sighed. "I have plenty of free nights to hang out when I'm not working, considering that my experiment in online dating has been pretty much a bust so far."

Jenny grimaced. "The latest one didn't work out?"

"Let's just say he sent me some photos of himself. I have now blocked all future communications from Captain Underpants."

Stevie laughed. "Captain Underpants? Oh, I *definitely* have to hear this story."

Tess shuddered delicately. "It's going to take more than wine for that."

All three laughed.

"Did you ever find the nerve to tell your mom and grandmother who you found in the cabin, Jenny?" Stevie asked.

Groaning, Jenny nodded. "Yes. It was…uncomfortable."

She was wildly understating that exchange and Stevie probably knew it. Her grandmother had been horrified.

"Nothing happened, Gran," Jenny had assured her firmly. "Gavin was a perfect gentleman. We slept in different rooms. Considering the damage done by the storm, I'd have been in more trouble if he hadn't been there. I'd have been stranded up there alone."

Pointing a fork at Jenny over the dinner table Monday night, Gran had grumbled, "That's exactly why I said it was foolish of you to go there alone in the first place. I could understand if you'd wanted to visit a nice spa, or fly to New York to shop and see shows, or some other civilized vacation. But to make a three-hour drive by yourself to some backwoods fishing cabin made no sense to me at all."

Jenny's mom had tried to defend her. "She just wanted some quiet time to work and to think, Mother."

"She lives alone," Gran had pointed out acerbically. "All she had to do was turn off her phone and lock her door."

"I wanted to get away from the sounds of traffic and sirens for a few days. Maybe walk alongside the river and listen to birds sing. That's not really so strange, is it?" Jenny had tried not to sound defensive, but wasn't sure she'd been successful.

"Hmph. I can't help wondering if you knew that man would be there," Gran had muttered darkly. "He always had a strong hold on you. Seems like a strange coincidence that the minute your nice, ideal boyfriend is out of town, you run off to a cabin that just happens to be owned by that…that cop." She spat the word as if it were a synonym for *criminal*.

Jenny had to bite her tongue to keep herself from snapping at her grandmother, though she had spoken acerbically. "I don't appreciate your implication that I would sneak around and lie to either you or Thad. If

I had chosen to meet Gavin—or anyone else, for that matter—at the cabin, I'd have made no secret of it."

"How was Gavin?" her mother had interceded, just a hint of wistfulness in her tone. "He was such a sweet boy. And his mother was a nice lady. Did he say how she is?"

Before she could reply, her grandmother had interrupted. "For heaven's sake, Brenda, what do you care about that man's family?" Gran had demanded with a scowl. "You should be more interested in *Thad's* lovely mother. Have you heard from her since he's been out of town, Jenny? You have spoken with Thad, haven't you?"

"I talk with Thad every evening," she'd answered with every ounce of patience she'd possessed. "His parents are on a Mediterranean cruise to celebrate their fortieth anniversary."

"A Mediterranean cruise." Lena Patterson's eyes had gleamed with envy. "I'd always hoped to take a cruise with your grandfather, bless his soul. We'd have had a nice life like that, had he lived."

Gran made no secret of her lifelong sorrow that her young physician husband had died of an unforeseen, massive heart attack at the age of twenty-nine. He'd died just before he'd paid off the last of his education loans, before he'd been able to set up his practice and provide her the life of a respected doctor's wife she'd fantasized about. Gran had worked long hours to help put him through medical school, along with the loans they'd taken out, and she believed now that her efforts had gone unrewarded. She'd been left a pregnant widow with no one to support her except herself. Not at all the life she'd planned.

Still, Lena had always been a resourceful woman.

She'd served as the secretary to the president of a medical supplies company, working up to a good salary and a tidy pension there. After paying off her late husband's loans, she had invested the small life-insurance settlement from him and a modest inheritance from her own parents into rental property. For nearly forty years, while still working full-time, Gran had been a landlady. A shrewd one, at that, providing a good life for herself and her daughter. She'd sold her last property a few years ago, for enough to supplement her pension and Social Security quite comfortably. She had never remarried, which always made Jenny wonder if Gran had truly loved her husband for more than his potential earnings.

Gran had been bitterly disappointed when her daughter had also become a debt-ridden, widowed single mother after marrying beneath her, in Gran's opinion. Gran had been determined the pattern would end with her granddaughter.

Gran saw Thad as embodying everything she had wanted for herself, whereas Gavin had seemed to represent all the heartache and regret she and her daughter had suffered. Gran had insisted that she didn't want her granddaughter to marry only for money; but she'd often quoted the old adage that it was just as easy to fall in love with a rich man as a poor one.

Jenny realized suddenly that Tess and Stevie were studying her across the table with mirroring looks of concern. She blinked. "What?"

"You kind of zoned out there for a minute," Tess replied quietly.

Jenny sighed and shook her head. "I'm fine. Let's

just enjoy our lunch, okay? I have a meeting with a supplier later this afternoon, and I need to prepare for it."

Stevie started to speak, then stared over Jenny's shoulder toward the entrance door with widened blue eyes. "Oh, my gosh, is that…? Yes, I think it is. Wow."

Jenny looked up from her lunch to study her friend's face curiously. "Someone you know?"

"Someone *you* know," Stevie murmured. "And let's just say, time has been very good to him."

Jenny set down her chopsticks. The tiny hairs on her arms were suddenly standing on end. She didn't have to ask her friend for further clarification. If she were a superstitious woman, she'd wonder if she had somehow summoned Gavin with her wandering thoughts.

Jenny couldn't blame either of her friends for staring when Gavin stopped at their table. He was the type of man who elicited such a reaction. Heightened senses. Accelerated heartbeat. Visceral feminine awareness. It was the way she had responded to him the first time she'd noticed him in a college classroom. She reacted the same way now.

He was dressed in dark jeans and a short-sleeved navy pullover almost the same color as his eyes. The casual clothing emphasized his broad shoulders, strong arms and solid thighs. He hadn't cut his hair yet. It waved back from his clean-shaven face as if he'd just run his fingers through it, the lighter streaks gleaming in the dark blond depths. She doubted that he'd deliberately tried to look like a walking sexy-bad-boy poster—he'd be appalled at the very suggestion—but he did, anyway. And judging by the admiring looks from women at nearby tables, she and her friends weren't the only ones who noticed.

"Hello, Gavin," she said when he didn't immediately speak. She took some pride in hearing the evenness of her tone; she doubted that anyone who heard her could tell how rapidly her heart was racing. "Were you looking for me or is this another crazy coincidence?"

"The manager at your store told me I could find you here." He set a bag from a nearby shoe store on the table next to her plate. Her left hand rested there and he brushed her bare ring finger with his fingertips as he released the bag. Was that merely an accident?

"I figured since you were close by, I'd deliver this to you personally," he said, his voice a shade deeper than usual.

"What…?" She glanced into the bag, then shook her head when she saw the familiar shoebox. According to the label, this was an identical pair of shoes to the ones she'd ruined at the cabin, right down to the neon-green color. They were not inexpensive shoes. Even though he'd told her he would, she hadn't really expected him to replace them, especially not in person. "You didn't have to buy me new shoes."

He shrugged. "It was the least I could do after you helped me clean up the storm damage. Did the new leasing agent refund your credit card?"

"Yes, thank you. Did you fire Lizzie?"

"Wasn't my call to make, though I did file a complaint with the company. I understand she quit Monday afternoon. She didn't care for the job apparently." He turned his head to nod to her companions. "Ladies."

Remembering her manners, she said quickly, "Oh,

sorry. Gavin, this is my friend Tess Miller. And you remember Stevie McLane?"

"Of course he does." Stevie hopped from her chair to give Gavin a typical Southern greeting of a quick hug. "Gavin, you look great. You've hardly changed. I knew you right away."

He gazed down at her when she stepped back. "Were you this blonde in college?"

She giggled. "Why, of course I was."

Though they all knew she wasn't fooling him in the least, he merely chuckled. "Well, it works for you. You look good."

Stevie batted her lashes. "Thank you, sir."

Jenny remembered that Gavin and Stevie had flirted teasingly in college—all in good fun, neither of them taking it seriously. She'd never felt even a twinge of jealousy toward them then. She told herself it didn't bother her now that he was smiling down at her friend, looking relaxed as he hadn't been with her.

Tess was eyeing Gavin with a slight frown. "I think we've met before. Aren't you the officer who responded to a break-in at my office a couple of months ago? Prince Construction Company?"

"Yes, I thought you looked familiar. Your boss's office was ransacked, but nothing taken that you could see, right?"

She nodded. "We finally decided it was someone looking for quick cash. And since we don't keep cash at the office, they were out of luck."

"It's nice to see you again under more pleasant circumstances."

"You, too, Officer Locke."

"Call me Gavin."

"This is quite a coincidence. That you've met before, I mean," Stevie said, looking from Gavin to Tess.

Gavin's eyes turned to Jenny as he murmured, "There've been quite a few of those lately."

Stevie made a sound as if she'd suddenly had a brilliant idea. Because she'd seen so many of Stevie's brilliant ideas go terribly wrong, Jenny tensed as Stevie tugged at Gavin's arm and burst into excited speech.

"My boyfriend's band is playing on the deck at Benoit's Pier Saturday night. Very informal, and it's an over-twenty-one-only crowd, so we don't have to deal with teens and frat boys. It's a twenty-dollar cover charge to pay the band and to keep out the troublemakers. There's going to be a donation box to raise money for the victims of the spring storms that have hit Arkansas this year, but it's a no-pressure fund-raiser. You could even bring one or two of your buddies if they'd like to come hear some great music and meet new people. Or, um, bring a girlfriend if you have one."

Jenny had to stop herself from openly grimacing. It seemed she'd been right to worry. What was Stevie thinking?

Gavin smiled at Stevie as if her wording had amused him. "No girlfriend at the moment."

"All the more reason for you to come, then." She patted his arm lightly. "Lots of hot single women will be there. Tess, here, for example."

Tess choked on a sip of tea. "Stevie!"

Stevie gave her a blandly sweet smile. "Just saying."

She gazed back up at Gavin. "Well? Are you interested?"

He shrugged the shoulder Jenny knew to be uninjured while she held her breath waiting for his reply. He would say no, wouldn't he? Surely he would say no.

"Maybe," he said instead, making her fingers curl tightly in her lap. She wasn't sure who she most wanted to strangle, him or Stevie. Gavin glanced her way before asking, "Are you all going to be there?"

"Yes, we are," Stevie answered cheerily. "Tess and Jen have already promised they'd be there to keep me company while my boyfriend is playing. My friends always keep their promises."

Jenny glanced at her friend and resisted the urge to shove the napkin in her mouth.

"So, we'll see you Saturday?" Stevie prodded Gavin.

"Sure. Why not?" He winked at Jenny and her heart clenched. "See you."

He turned and strode out of the restaurant in a rolling gait that was undeniably sexy. Jenny was well aware that she was only one of many appreciative women studying his very fine backside as he left. Damn it.

Dragging her eyes away, she whirled on Stevie, who was settling back into her seat with an exaggeratedly innocent expression. "What the hell was that?"

"What?"

"Why did you invite Gavin for Saturday night?"

"Just an impulse. Why not invite him? Maybe he'll bring some cute cop friends."

Jenny asked pointedly, "Aren't you going to be there with Joe? You know, your current boyfriend?"

Stevie waved a hand. "I am. But Tess, here, is looking. And I have other single friends who'll thank me for inviting Gavin. Sandy, for example. You know she has a thing for men in uniform."

"Sandy has a thing for men. Period." She could only

imagine how Sandy would react to seeing Gavin among the usual crowd. Like a hungry hawk spotting a particularly tasty prey, most likely. The image made her stomach tighten, but only because she'd hate to see any of her male acquaintances caught up in Sandy's avaricious talons, she assured herself.

Stevie giggled. "True. But there's still Tess. You thought Gavin was good-looking, right, Tess?"

"I have eyes," Tess said drily. "But I also have a rule against dating friends' exes. That never works out well for the friendship."

This was Jenny's cue to assure Tess that she had no objections at all if Tess and Gavin were to hook up at the party. But she toyed with the remains of her lunch and said nothing.

"Besides," Tess said speculatively, "it seemed to me as though Gavin is still interested in Jenny. You saw the way he looked at her, right?"

Jenny reached hastily for her water glass and took a deep sip before saying, "You're wrong about that. He's aware that I'm seeing someone else. But even if I weren't, trust me, Gavin is no more interested in getting involved with me again than I am with him. That ship sailed—and sank—a long time ago."

"So you'd be fine with him dating Tess, or anyone else he might meet at the party?"

Shooting Stevie an irritated look, Jenny muttered, "Of course."

She pushed her plate away then. "I really should get back to the store. I have a ton of things to do today."

Stevie reached out quickly to touch her hand. "Sorry, Jen. Don't rush off. I'm just teasing you."

"Yes, I know. It's just a busy day for me."

Her teasing amusement gone now, Stevie looked anxious. "You didn't really mind that I invited Gavin, did you? You said the two of you got along fine at the cabin, so I figured it was okay to invite him and maybe some of his friends. For the band and the fund-raiser's sake, of course."

"No," Jenny lied evenly. "Of course I don't mind. It just surprised me, that's all."

Maybe she'd come up with a reasonable excuse so she wouldn't have to attend. It wasn't her type of gathering, anyway. She was only going because Stevie had wheedled a promise out of her, saying she needed someone to talk to while Joe was playing. Since Thad was out of town, anyway, it wasn't as if Jenny had anything better to do. Now if only there were some honorable way to get out of that promise…

"You did tell Gavin that you're seriously involved with Thad, didn't you, Jenny?" Tess asked curiously. "I mean, the way he looked at you, I'm not sure he understands you're fully off the market. And he bought you shoes."

Snatching up her purse and the shopping bag, Jenny stood. "I really do have to go. I'll pay at the register on my way out. I'll talk to you both later, okay?"

Her friends probably watched her hasty departure with open mouths of surprise. They would certainly be unable to resist speculating about why she'd felt the need to bolt. But she had a sudden, almost desperate need to find someplace quiet where she could just be alone to think.

She was well aware of the irony that it was the same aspiration that had gotten her into this mess in the first place.

* * *

After mentally debating for a couple of days about whether he would attend, and then going back and forth on whether to ask one or more of his friends to come along, Gavin showed up at the Saturday-night event alone. Even as he'd made the drive to the venue, he'd almost turned around a couple of times and headed back home, asking himself why he was doing this. He wasn't a party guy, and he wouldn't know anyone here other than Stevie and Tess…and Jenny, of course. His suspicion that spending more time with Jenny was his primary motivation for going almost made him change his mind again.

He'd thought of asking Avery, but since Avery and Jenny didn't get along—not to mention the bad history between Avery and Stevie—that hadn't seemed like a great idea. So he'd come stag. He had nothing better to do that evening, anyway, as it would be another week before he was cleared for duty again. The fund-raiser seemed like a worthy cause, though he wondered if it was simply an excuse for a party. And yes, maybe he wanted to see Jenny again, if only because he'd been wryly amused by the expression on her face when Stevie invited him.

It wasn't that he expected anything to happen between them, he assured himself. After all, she was seeing another guy. She was considering getting engaged, if she hadn't already. Yet, he'd noted the lack of a ring on her finger, which could mean she hadn't yet made that leap. She certainly hadn't seemed all that sure about it when she'd broken the news to him. If she wanted to marry the other man, wouldn't she have jumped on the chance to accept his proposal? If she really loved the guy, would she need to go off by herself to "consider all possible ramifications" before giving her answer?

None of those things were any of his business, of course. If Jenny wanted a practical, socially advantageous marriage which probably had her snobby grandmother salivating in delight, then it was entirely her choice. Hell, maybe she'd even be happy in such a union. But if she really loved that Thad guy, would her skin have flushed, her eyes dilated, her heart have pounded in her throat when Gavin had impulsively kissed her? He'd looked at her closely when he'd drawn reluctantly away, and he'd seen every one of those reactions. Had her response to him been due to nothing more than surprise? Had he only imagined that the sizzling attraction between them had flared back to life the moment she'd stumbled into his bedroom? Did those old feelings still burn only in him?

Maybe he just needed to make one last attempt at finding out for certain before he closed the door on their past again, this time for good. He wasn't one to encroach on another man's claim, but the last he'd heard, Jenny hadn't given an answer yet. It wasn't a done deal until she made that pledge, right?

Maybe he'd meet the guy tonight, and see for himself that Jenny was happy. Wasn't that all he'd ever wanted for her? For himself?

The band was playing on the open-sided, covered deck of a Little Rock restaurant and club located on the bank of the Arkansas River. The sun had just set when he arrived. The big deck glowed with gold fairy lights hanging from overhead and strung in numerous potted trees. Soft floodlights were tucked discreetly into corners. A dais was set up for the band with the river view behind them, but as he paid his cover, he was informed by the hostess that the band was on a short break. Recorded music played from speakers until they took their places again.

He scanned the milling crowd for familiar faces. Surprisingly, he spotted a few, though they weren't people he knew personally. Quite a few were young movers and shakers not yet in the upper ranks but on track to get there. People who didn't blink at spending twenty bucks just to get into a club, not to mention whatever they'd stuff into the donation box or spend on drinks. As for himself, this was a fairly expensive evening.

Tables of nibbly-type food flanked the sides of the deck, and drinks were served at a cash bar by white-coated bartenders. The chatter and laughter was lively and animated, but acceptably modulated. This was not one of the clubs to which he and his associates in uniform were regularly summoned for disturbance calls.

He glanced automatically down at his clothes. He'd opted for khakis, a dark green polo shirt and brown slip-ons. He'd even had a haircut. Outwardly, he supposed he blended in fine with the other men in attendance, many of whom wore similar attire, but he still felt like the outsider for some reason. He had to admit he'd be more comfortable in a sharply pressed uniform with his sidearm at his hip.

"Hello." A busty brunette in a fluttery top and tight miniskirt approached him, making him wonder how she could walk at all in heels so high they practically put her feet at a vertical angle. She looked good, he had to give her that, but his tastes ran toward a more subtle beauty. "I'm Sandy. Are you looking for someone in particular?"

He smiled. "Hi, Sandy, I'm Gavin. And I'm trying to find Jenny Baer or Stevie McLane. Do you know them?"

She ran a hand over her hair, a gesture perhaps intended to hide her disappointment with his answer. "As a matter of fact, I do. I just saw them by the railing looking over the river. Behind that big ficus tree with the little gold lights in it?"

"I'll find them, thanks."

"Catch you later, maybe?"

He nodded. "Sure."

Threading through chatting guests, he made his way to the railing. Stevie had her back to him, but he recognized her immediately. Her bright blond curls gleamed in the yellow lights from the potted ficus. She stood next to a tall, lanky man. Despite the warmth of the evening, he wore a wrinkled, long-sleeve, black-and-green plaid shirt over a white tee, black pants turned into cuffs at the hems and scarred brown work boots. A misshapen gray porkpie hat with a plaid band and a stupid little feather sat on top of his floppy hair, and he'd finished the look with horn-rimmed glasses and sideburns that covered his jaws almost to his chin.

Gavin almost groaned. Seriously? This dated hipster poser was Stevie's latest? She might have done better to have stuck with the grunge drummer from college.

The poser shifted his weight and someone else came into view. Gavin swallowed. Here was the reason he'd cut his hair, ironed his khakis, shelled out twenty bucks and risked embarrassment to come to this gathering that was so far from his comfort zone.

Jenny looked cool and lovely in a sleeveless white scoop-necked summer dress that hugged her bust and flared out from her hips to just above her knees. Her dark hair was loose in soft layers around her pretty face and fell just to her bare shoulders. He noticed a touch of glitter on her eyelids and peach gloss on her full lips. His gaze lingered on those lips that he'd tasted so recently and which he suddenly hungered to sample again.

You are such an idiot, Locke.

Would he really even think about putting himself through it all again, even if she were willing to try? He recalled everything they'd been through, all the obstacles that had stood between them back then and hadn't really changed since, all the pain he'd endured, the ache of missing her that had tormented him for a long time after he'd walked away from her. Was there any chance in hell that anything would turn out differently if she'd be willing to dump Prince Charming to give it another shot?

And still he wanted her. Had never really stopped wanting her.

Idiot indeed.

She'd been talking to someone when he'd approached. Tess, he realized, dragging his gaze away only long enough to identify the other woman and then feeling his eyes drawn inexorably back to Jenny.

He'd tried to love other women in the years since they'd split. He'd made a concerted effort to move on, focusing on his training, his job, his friends and a procession of women as different from Jenny as possible. He'd even considered one relationship fairly serious. It had never gotten as far as an engagement, but they'd flirted with the idea, until they had decided by mutual agreement that, while they'd had fun, they weren't meant to spend a lifetime together. The night he and

Blair had called it quits, he'd sat alone in his darkened apartment until dawn, drinking and thinking not of Blair, but of Jenny. And that had been several years after he'd last seen her, leaving him to ask himself despairingly if he was destined to end up a grumpy old bachelor cop, haunted by memories of the one who'd got away.

And here she was again. Tying him in knots just like before. And no matter what happened from here, seeing her again had already put her firmly back into his… his mind, he substituted quickly, refusing to acknowledge the word that had almost formed in his thoughts.

She glanced his way, then froze momentarily. For one unguarded moment, he saw the reaction in her eyes. A flood of emotions he couldn't quite decipher, but that he couldn't mistake. And then she seemed to gather herself, hiding those feelings behind a placid expression and a polite smile. "Hello, Gavin."

He returned the greeting and moved closer to her, nodding to the others as he did so.

Pivoting fast enough to make the fancy drink in her hand slosh against the sides of the glass, Stevie smiled brightly at him. "Gavin, I'm so glad you could come. Joe, this is Gavin Locke, the friend of Jenny's I told you about. Gavin, this is Joe Couch, the bass player for Eleven Twenty-Five."

Joe switched his beer mug to his left hand so he could stick out the right toward Gavin. "Hey."

"Eleven Twenty-Five?" Gavin asked, briefly shaking the other man's hand.

"My band. We're about to start playing again." Joe eyed Gavin somewhat warily through lenses Gavin cynically suspected to be clear glass. "So Stevie says you're like a cop or something?"

"LRPD," he confirmed.

"Uh. That's cool, I guess."

Gavin got the distinct impression that Joe was not a fan of police. Probably believed all the bad stories he heard and ignored the good ones. Gavin was all too familiar with the type. He had no intention of defending the integrity of law enforcement officers to this guy, though, so he merely turned back to Jenny. He nodded toward her empty hands, then glanced at Tess, whose hands were also free. "You two aren't having anything to drink?"

"Tess and I just got here," Jenny replied lightly. "I'll probably have a glass of wine in a few."

"And I'm the driver, so I'll stick to strawberry lemonade," Tess added. "They mix a really good one here."

"Let me buy you both drinks. Strawberry lemonade for you, Tess, and still white wine for you, Jen? How about you, Stevie? Another beer, Joe?" He wasn't trying to buy favor among Jenny or her friends. Just being polite, he told himself.

He was pretty sure Joe was about to eagerly accept the offer of a free drink, even though the one he had was only half-empty and even if it was being offered by a cop. But Stevie spoke up quickly. "I'm good, thanks. And, Joe, it looks like the rest of the band is getting ready to play again. You should probably join them."

"Oh. Yeah, okay. Catch you later, Gavin."

"Sure." As the other man moved away, Gavin turned toward the line at the bar. "I'll get the drinks."

"You can't carry them all by yourself," Stevie pointed out. "Jenny, why don't you help him? Tess, I see a guy I know who you might enjoy meeting. He's still married, but separated, so he's sort of eligible, right? Jenny and Gavin can find us after they get the drinks."

Gavin wasn't sure who looked more reluctant to agree with Stevie's suggestions, Tess or Jenny. Jenny's hesitation around him certainly wasn't doing much for his ego. Yet, he still couldn't seem to back away.

He placed a hand lightly on her back to keep her close to him as they made their way to the bar. He ordered the drinks and tipped the bartender.

"Thank you," Jenny murmured when he handed her the wineglass.

He sipped his beer, then asked casually, "Where's the fiancé tonight?"

Jenny's brows creased with a frown that she quickly smoothed. She glanced quickly around, as if to make sure no one had overheard his question. "He's not officially my fiancé yet," she answered quietly. "I'm not ready to make any announcements. And he's not here this evening. He's been out of town for more than a week and won't be back until Wednesday."

So her suitor had been out of town when she'd headed for the cabin to consider the proposal. And she hadn't seen him since she'd returned, meaning Gavin's had been the last kiss on her lips.

For some reason, that gave him a sense of satisfaction.

Chapter Seven

"Hi, Jenny." The woman Gavin had met when he'd first arrived—Cindy? Sandy?—rushed toward them with an avidly curious look on her made-up face. She rushed into speech before Jenny could even respond to the greeting. "I'll be coming into your store this week. I'm going on a week-long Caribbean cruise with some of my sorority sisters from college next month and I need all new beach and party clothes. Since I've started my new workout program, all my clothes are just falling off me."

"You look wonderful, Sandy," Jenny assured the woman with cheery warmth. "And make sure you come in. If I'm not in the store, tell Amber I said to give you a ten percent discount. I'll leave a note in your account file."

Sandy's face lit up. "Really? Thanks, Jen! I'll definitely stop in."

"I'm sure you'll find exactly what you're looking for. We have a whole new line of cruise wear and accessories that should meet your needs."

"I can't wait to see it." The woman eyed Gavin again, open speculation in her expression as she looked from him, then back to Jenny. "So, where's Thad this evening?"

He noted that Jenny's smile didn't waver as she answered lightly. "He's in LA on a business trip. I'll be sure and tell him you said hello. But where are my manners? Sandy Powell, this is Gavin Locke. He went to college with Stevie and me."

"We met when I arrived," Gavin replied smoothly. He wasn't thrilled about the offhanded way Jenny had introduced him, but he let it stand. "Sandy welcomed me quite graciously."

He thought he heard just a hint of a wry note in Jenny's voice when she responded, "I'm sure she did. Don't forget to ask Amber for that discount, Sandy. And let her or me know if there's something else we can do to help you prepare for your cruise."

"I'll do that. Thanks, Jenny." Perhaps Sandy decided that the discount was more valuable than digging for more gossip fodder. With a little wave, she hurried off as quickly as her tight skirt and ridiculously high heels would allow, to join a small group of women gathered nearby.

Gavin suspected there would still be some speculation about his presence at Jenny's side while the man she'd been seeing was out of town. Though he could only guess how Jenny felt about that, he decided it didn't really bother him all that much.

Moving out of the way of other thirsty guests, Jenny

looked up at Gavin with a somber expression. She opened her mouth as if to speak, but was interrupted when Tess descended on them to pluck her lemonade out of Gavin's hand.

"Thank you," she said, her smile strained. "I'm going to try very hard to pretend this is something stronger than lemonade."

Coming up behind her, Stevie sighed heavily. "Art's not that bad, Tess. Obviously he thinks you're hot. That's a good thing, right?"

Their auburn-haired friend sighed and took another gulp of her tart drink before replying. "He asked if I have any moral objections to sleeping with a man who's still technically married. He said he wanted to get that little detail out of the way before we went any further. Doesn't like wasting time, he said. And we'd barely shaken hands!"

Jenny gave a little gasp. "Seriously? Gross."

"Right?" Tess motioned dramatically with her glass, nearly splashing her drink over the rim.

"He's just going through that awkward stage between married and single," Stevie explained with a shrug. "It's been a while since he's dated and maybe he's a little..."

"Desperate?" Gavin supplied drily.

She chuckled. "Maybe. And sure, he needs to take it down a notch."

"Or a dozen notches," Tess muttered darkly. "No more attempted fix-ups tonight, okay, Stevie? Let's just enjoy the music."

The band had taken their time setting up again, chatting with one another and with some of the people hanging around the dais, but now the first chords of a song began. Some of the guests turned expectantly to pay attention, while others carried on with their avid conversations, the evening's entertainment being merely an excuse for professional and social networking. Jenny located a table with three recently vacated chairs, and Gavin snagged another from nearby, dragging it up to join them.

The volume of the music wasn't earsplitting, but it was loud enough to make conversation more difficult now. Gavin leaned back in his chair and sipped his beer, content to listen and to watch Jenny with her friends. Stevie managed to make herself heard as she chattered away, though occasionally she remembered to try to look as though she were paying rapt attention to her boyfriend's performance.

The band was good, he supposed, though their brand of wailing alternative rock wasn't really to his taste. Give him country any day. Strait, Jackson, Brooks, some of the newer stuff by Chesney, Shelton, Florida Georgia Line. He still listened to some classic Diamond Rio occasionally, though he tended to avoid the memories their songs invoked. Jenny had loved their music back in the day. Did she still, or had her tastes become more sophisticated to suit her new status?

A few people drifted out onto the smallish dance floor, followed by a few more once that ice was broken. A slightly chubby guy with thinning hair and a winning smile paused by the table. "Hi, Tess. I thought that was you. How's that boss of yours? Still a slave driver?"

She laughed. "Hi, Glenn. And yes, Scott will never change."

"Would you like to dance? Unless your lucky friend here doesn't want to share any of the lovely ladies at his table."

Gavin chuckled.

Watching as Tess and Glenn moved to the dance floor, Stevie exhaled gustily. "That's not going anywhere. No chemistry between them at all."

"Okay, I have to ask. Why are you so hell-bent on fixing Tess up with someone?" Gavin asked with a bewildered shake of his head. "Seriously, she's great-looking and seems nice enough. I wouldn't think she'd need you to round up dates for her."

Stevie wrinkled her nose. "You'd think. But she and Glenn weren't joking about her boss. Tess works *all* the time. Even more than Jenny, and Jen's a major workaholic. Tess has been saying she's ready to get married and start a family, but she's had trouble meeting anyone with her crazy hours. Online connections just aren't working out for her so far, so I hoped maybe she could meet someone here tonight on her rare chance to mingle. Um, you said you're single, right?"

Jenny groaned, but Gavin only laughed. "Yes, I'm single, and yes, I think Tess is great, but..."

"But no chemistry with her," Stevie finished with another sigh.

He made a concerted effort not to look at Jenny. "Not that I've noticed, no."

"Oh, well, if you change your mind, I've got her number."

Jenny set her wineglass down with a thump. "Seriously, Stevie."

Gavin thought it might be time to turn the tables on Jenny's meddling friend. "So what about you and Joe Porkpie Hat? Seriously?"

Stevie had never been easily offended, and apparently that hadn't changed. She merely spread her hands.

"Yeah, I know, he's kind of a nerd, but he's a very talented musician. And he's a lot of fun when he's not trying to be the cool bass player, you know? When it's just the two of us, or a few close friends, rather than a crowd like this."

"I'll take your word for it."

A new song started, a bit slower this time.

Gavin turned to look at Jenny, who was being very quiet. "How about it, Jen? Want to dance? For old times' sake?"

She had always loved to dance. He couldn't imagine that ever changing, no matter what else might be different about her now. Yet, she hesitated, leaving him to wonder if she'd tried and failed to find an acceptable reason to decline. Was she, too, afraid of the electricity he sensed sparking between them again?

He knew she'd been hurt by their breakup, maybe almost as much as he had, though that was hard to believe. He couldn't blame her for not wanting to reopen those old wounds, any more than he did. And yet…

He stood and offered her his hand. "Just one dance?"

She placed her hand in his. "Just one," she said.

He noticed that Stevie watched with a suspiciously smug smile as they walked toward the dance floor.

How could ten long years fall away in the space of only minutes? How could a decade of change and growth be forgotten with only the touch of a man's hand, the warmth of his body next to hers? How could formerly hazy memories of long, passionate, wondrous nights be suddenly more real to her than the people surrounding them as Gavin took her in his arms on the dance floor?

Jenny closed her eyes with a touch of despair as the foolish questions flooded her mind, making her stumble a bit as he guided her into the dance. Opening her eyes and glancing up at him, she murmured an apology.

Stop this, Jenny. Stop it before you do something incredibly stupid.

"Stevie hasn't really changed a bit, has she?" Gavin spoke with his mouth close to her ear to be heard over the music. His warm breath brushed her cheek, and she almost shivered, but managed to control herself.

"Of course she has. We've all changed in ten years."

He eyed her a bit too closely, as if trying to read her expression. "Okay."

"You've changed quite a bit, too," she couldn't help pointing out. "I'm sure some of your experiences as a police officer have left their mark on you, in addition to the scar on your shoulder."

If he had other physical scars from his service, she hadn't seen them, but then she'd been hesitant to look very closely. For various reasons.

"I'm sure you're right," he agreed equably. "It gets ugly at times."

She had no doubt that was an understatement. Oddly enough, she was torn between wanting to hear more about his work and being reluctant to know the grim details. She shook her head. "The thing is, we're all different now. We've all changed."

"I'm kind of hoping that's a positive thing."

He was gazing into her eyes again, and once again her thoughts scattered. She tried desperately to keep them in line.

Sex, she told herself flatly. That was all this was about. She'd always had a somewhat primitive response to whatever pheromones Gavin put out, and apparently that was one thing that had not changed. It wasn't as if she were unique in her response to him. Even women who looked quite happy to be with their own partners couldn't help glancing Gavin's way a time or two. There was something so very virile and masculine about him that no red-blooded woman of any age or eligibility status could help but notice.

Still, if he was getting ideas that there was still something between them, that their chance meeting at the cabin could lead to anything more, she needed to set him straight. Sure, they'd gotten along fine at the cabin, worked well as partners in cleaning up after the storm, shared a few meals. Shared an amazing kiss. But that was supposed to have been a kiss of goodbye, not the start of something new. And if she'd thought of that kiss a few times—more than few times—since, well, that, too, was only natural, right?

Perhaps a crowded dance floor wasn't the ideal place to remind him that it was too late for them to try to recapture the past. It was bad enough that people who knew she was dating Thad were eyeing her curiously now, wondering about the identity of this sexy guy she was dancing with and talking with so intently. Did any of them know Thad well enough that they'd be on the phone to him soon, oh-so-casually asking if he knew what was going on? He wasn't the jealous type, she acknowledged candidly, but she doubted he'd like being the subject of gossip.

Gavin's hand moved at the small of her back, pressing very lightly inward to bring her an inch closer to him. She could have resisted; he didn't hold her that tightly. But for just that one moment of weakness, she allowed her eyelids to go heavy, gave herself permission to simply enjoy the remainder of the dance without thought of what would come after. It was unlikely that she would ever dance with Gavin again. Might as well enjoy it while she could.

The music ended with a flourish of Joe's bass guitar. Swallowing a regretful little sigh, she stepped back. "Gavin, do you think we could find someplace to talk? In private?"

Looking steadily at her, he nodded. "I think that can be arranged."

She turned toward their table. Stevie had been joined by Sandy Powell and a couple of other women Jenny didn't recognize, as well as two guys who hung around the table, flirting, laughing. But she didn't see Tess among the group. Was she still dancing with Glenn? No, there was Tess, hurrying toward them, a phone in her hand and a very familiar look on her face.

"I'm so sorry, Jenny."

"Don't tell me. His Majesty needs you again."

Tess nodded somberly. "I'm afraid so. I have to leave. Do you want me to drop you off at your place on my way or…"

"I'll drive her home," Gavin cut in, his tone encouraging no argument.

Tess looked to Jenny for guidance.

Jenny moistened her lips. The thought of being driven home by Gavin made her entire body tighten with nerves. So many emotions still simmered between them. So many words that were probably best left unsaid after all these years. Yet, as she'd just told him, they needed to talk. Alone. She supposed this was as good a time as any.

She nodded. "That will be fine. Thank you, Gavin. Do what you have to do, Tess. But it wouldn't hurt you to tell His Majesty that you deserve a night off every once in a while."

"It's not another break-in, is it?" Gavin asked with a frown, slipping into cop mode.

"No," Tess assured him. "There's been an incident at one of the job sites. My boss is out of town, and the foreman hasn't been able to reach him. So they called me."

"You're on call during your off-hours?"

Tess chuckled drily. "I'm pretty much on call 24/7. It's the downside of having made myself indispensable."

Gavin lifted an eyebrow. "Maybe you should consider looking for another job?"

"I would, but...well, I love the one I have," Tess confessed almost sheepishly.

Jenny smiled. "Not to mention that she pretty much runs the company. Her title might be office manager, but the whole place would go under without her. As Scott is the first to admit."

Flushing a little, Tess shook her head. "That's hardly true. Scott is a brilliant man. He just needs a little organizational assistance."

She hurried away a few moments later to handle whatever crisis had occurred at ten o'clock on a Saturday night.

"How much later are you expected to stay at this thing?" Gavin asked Jenny.

Looking toward the gregarious Stevie again, Jenny made an on-the-spot decision. "I'm ready to leave whenever you are."

At least she didn't live far, so the drive wouldn't take

long. And she could have her little talk with him in the privacy of her apartment.

Stevie made no argument when they took their departure of her. In fact, she looked just a bit too pleased that Gavin had offered to drive Jenny home.

Jenny was definitely going to have to talk to Stevie tomorrow. She knew her friend wasn't Thad's biggest fan, but surely she wasn't trying to deliberately sabotage the relationship by throwing Gavin in Jenny's path. Why on earth would she think an ex-boyfriend from a spectacularly failed relationship would be a better match?

She and Gavin made their way through the crowded bar area near the exit door, then stepped out into the darkened parking lot. They could still hear the muted strains of Eleven Twenty-Five playing behind them. In front of them a steady stream of traffic traversed the road that ran past the restaurant, parallel to the river. Pebbles on asphalt crunched beneath their feet as they walked to Gavin's truck. He didn't speak, and she could think of absolutely nothing to say, either.

He opened the door for her, then held out a hand to give her a boost into the tall cab. She settled into the seat, arranged her dress around her legs and fastened her seat belt. Gavin climbed behind the wheel, slanted a smile at her that made her nerves flutter again, then started the engine. Country music blasted from the speakers before he quickly turned it off. Fortunately, it had been a new song and not one that carried any old baggage with it.

She gave him the name of her apartment complex and he nodded to indicate that he was familiar with it. He didn't seem to be interested in conversing as he drove, so she settled back into the taut silence and mentally rehearsed a breezy, casual speech about how nice it had been to see him again, how she was glad they'd had a chance to put the hard feelings behind them, how she would always remember him fondly even as she went on with the hard-won life she'd been leading before they'd reconnected.

"You'll turn right at the next light," she said, mostly to ease the mounting tension.

"I know." His tone wasn't curt exactly, but there was an edge to it that made her aware she wasn't the only one dealing with discomfort during this drive. She thought wistfully of how effortlessly he'd teased with Stevie and how comfortable he'd seemed with Tess, but there was entirely too much history between her and Gavin to allow them that easy interaction.

With a couple of cars stopped ahead of him, he braked for the red light, his fingers drumming restlessly on the steering wheel. She found herself mesmerized by the movement. The light must have changed and he eased forward. Because she was studying his strong hands instead of looking out the windshield, she didn't see what happened next, but Gavin suddenly braked and pulled into the parking lot of the gas station on the corner. The station was closed for the night, but one other car was parked in the lot. She noticed someone standing outside the other vehicle—a woman, she thought, but it was hard to tell in the shadows under the yellow security lights.

She frowned toward Gavin. "Is something wrong?"

"Sit tight. I'll be right back," he promised, and slipped quickly out of the truck.

She watched as he approached the other car, his

hands out in a nonthreatening position at his sides. Squinting, she saw that the woman was bent over, one hand on the top of her car and the other hand on her stomach. Either she was quite overweight, or…

Or pregnant, she realized suddenly. Despite Gavin's instructions, she reached for her door handle and jumped out of the truck to see if there was anything she could do to help.

The woman was probably close to her own age, though it was hard to tell in the pale lighting. She leaned heavily against her car, crying, gagging and moaning while Gavin talked soothingly to her. To make things worse, Jenny could hear wails from the backseat of the car, at least two separate little voices. "What's going on?"

Gavin had the woman by the elbows now, supporting her as he summed up succinctly, "She was stopped at the light ahead of us and had some sudden sharp pains and felt dizzy. She was able to pull in here and stop the car but now she's in severe pain and nauseated. I told her I'm an off-duty cop and I'll get her help. I've already called for an ambulance."

He'd done all that in the brief minutes it had taken her to even see that someone was in trouble, Jenny realized. Still speaking in the same calming tone, he supported the woman while she was sick again beside the car, and he was apparently unfazed by the unpleasant situation.

Another shriek came from the car.

"My babies," the woman gasped, taking a staggering step that way.

"My friend is going to check on the kids right after she grabs a blanket from behind the seat of my truck,"

Gavin assured her with a glance at Jenny. “I need you to lie down until the ambulance gets here. Your kids are safe for now. They’re just frightened and upset.”

Jenny whirled toward the truck, located a plaid stadium blanket folded neatly behind the seat where Gavin had said it would be and whipped it out onto a relatively clean patch of pavement. She’d spotted a first-aid kit, too, but couldn’t imagine anything they’d need from that at the moment. Gavin was certainly prepared for anything, it seemed.

She helped him carefully lower the crying woman onto the blanket and then she opened the back driver’s side door of the woman’s car. Two children were strapped into car seats, the older a boy of maybe four, the younger no more than eighteen months, if that. Both were fighting their restraints and howling for their mother. It was late, and she was sure they were sleepy and scared. The baby—a girl—was closest to her, so she fumbled with the straps and buckles to take her out of the seat and cradle her soothingly as she hurried around to the other side of the car to comfort the little boy. The baby clung to her so tightly Jenny could hardly breathe. She patted the little back as she opened the second door to look in at the boy.

“It’s okay,” she assured him over the lessening wails of the baby in her arms. “My friend is a policeman and he’s helping your mommy. What’s your name?”

“M-Marcus,” he snuffled. “Can I get out?”

She wasn’t at all sure she could safely control two children in a parking lot this close to a street that, while mostly deserted at the moment, was often quite busy. The few cars that passed were driving too fast, and none bothered to stop to offer assistance. Unlike Gavin, most people didn't instinctively leap to help strangers on the side of the road this late at night.

"Why don't you stay in your seat just a little longer?" she suggested, bouncing the clinging baby, whose cries were down to a whimper now. "We'll get you out just as soon as we can."

The boy burst into shrieks of protest. "I want out. I want my mommy!"

The baby began to cry again, not as loud as before, but still sounding pitiful. She probably needed a diaper change, a bed and a familiar face, not necessarily in that order, and Jenny was helpless to comfort either of the unhappy siblings. Considering their mother was still crying loudly nearby, Jenny was close to bursting into tears of sympathy herself.

The sound of a rapidly approaching siren was the most beautiful music she had ever heard. Moments later, the ambulance was parked nearby and medics bustled around the woman in distress. Gavin appeared at the car door, giving Jenny an encouraging nod as he reached into the car to unbuckle the howling little boy much more easily than Jenny had freed the baby.

"Hey, buddy, I'm Gavin," he said, lifting the boy easily into his arms. "You see those guys there? They're medics and they are taking good care of your mom, okay? She's going to be fine."

Being out of the car seat was already having a positive effect on the boy's mood. He swiped at his wet, runny-nosed face with one hand as he studied Gavin's face somberly. "My name's Marcus, not Buddy. You're a p'liceman?"

"Yes, I am." Tugging a handkerchief from his pocket,

Gavin dealt with snot and tears with an efficiency that reminded Jenny that he had two young nephews.

"I got a badge," Marcus informed him. "It's at home. It's a sheriff badge. Like Woody's."

"Yeah? That's cool, Sheriff Marcus."

The boy gave a watery giggle and rested his head trustingly on Gavin's shoulder, sucking a finger and looking toward the activity by the ambulance. Alternately rocking and bouncing the baby, who'd quieted again and was starting to doze against her shoulder, Jenny looked at the strong, steady man and the frightened little boy and felt her heart turn a hard somersault. The sensation felt a lot like panic. Delayed reaction to the tense situation—or was it something else that was suddenly making her hands tremble against the little body she held?

Finally the mother was on her way to the nearest hospital, the children were handed off to anxious relatives who'd been called to the scene and Gavin's blanket was returned to him, dirty and somewhat worse for wear. He stuffed it into his toolbox to deal with later and helped Jenny into the cab again. He sighed as he started the engine, and she could tell he was tired. It had been more than half an hour since he'd jumped out of the truck.

"Just another day in the life of a police officer, even when off duty?" she asked wryly.

He gave a weary chuckle. "Yeah, I guess."

"How on earth did you realize what was going on? Before I could even see that someone was in trouble, you were already out there dealing with the situation."

Driving onto the street toward her apartment, he shrugged. "I saw her car swerving a little when she was driving ahead of us. I thought she might be a drunk driver, and I was keeping an eye out in case I needed to call it in. Then she pulled over and climbed out of her car and started puking, and I could see she was pregnant. Thought she might need some help."

She shook her head slowly in amazement. "You were so calm. I was a nervous wreck until the ambulance arrived. I thought you might have to deliver a baby right there in that parking lot."

"Wouldn't be the first time for that, either," he said with a quick grin in her direction. "But I didn't think it was that. Mike—one of the EMTs—said he thinks it's a stomach virus."

"I saw you talking with him. Another friend?"

"I've met him a time or two. He's a friend of Rob's."

It suddenly occurred to her what he'd just said. "You've really delivered a baby?"

"Just once. Back when we had that ice storm five years ago, a woman gave birth on the side of I-30 when her panicky husband hit a slick patch and got stuck in the median. I happened to be close by, so I jumped out to help. The husband and I delivered the baby, though he wasn't a whole lot of help, to be honest. They named the kid after me—well, the middle name, anyway."

"They named him Gavin?"

He laughed shortly. "They named *her* Alexandria Gavin Smallwood. They send me photos on her birthday every year. She's starting kindergarten this fall."

She smiled in delight. "That's a very sweet story."

He grunted, typically uncomfortable with her description, then turned into the drive of her apartment complex. She gave him the entry code to the gate, and her amusement faded as he keyed it in. "I doubt that all your stories about your work have such happy endings."

"No," he said, his tone grim now. "Not all of them. But I like to think everything I do in the course of my job serves the community in some way."

"I know," she almost whispered. "That was always what mattered to you most about becoming an officer. You wanted to uphold the law and serve the community. Hands-on, you said, not from the comfort of an office or a courtroom."

If it surprised him that she remembered his rationalization word for word, he didn't comment, merely nodded again as he parked in the space she indicated. "I still feel that way."

Without yet reaching for her door handle, she stared at the stairs directly in front of them that led up to her apartment. "Avery said you left the force for a while."

"That's sort of a long story," he said after a moment. "Do you want to hear it here in the truck or are you going to invite me in?"

Now she was rethinking her earlier decision. She should probably tell him what she needed to say and politely send him on his way now. When or why he'd left the force and returned was really none of her business, especially since she might never see him again, barring another surprise meeting. Inviting him up to her place, even just to talk, was certainly not the wisest course of action, considering. Some people just had that…that thing. *Chemistry*, she thought, remembering Stevie's word from earlier. It didn't mean they were meant to be together long-term, though. The same was true in reverse. Just because a connection was somewhat more serene, more understated, more cerebral, perhaps—take herself and Thad, for example—that didn't mean a couple couldn't have a long and quietly contented union. Right?

"Why don't you come in?" she said with a sigh, despite her trepidation. "We do need to talk."

Chapter Eight

Minutes later, Gavin stood inside her living room, looking around curiously. She studied her home for a moment as though through his eyes. The entire two-bedroom apartment was done in shades of cream with a select few deep-orange accents because she couldn't resist adding touches of her favorite color. Everything was arranged just so, nothing out of place, not a speck of dust on anything. Her draperies framed a beautiful view of the Little Rock skyline at night. Stevie had helped her decorate, so everything looked classic, coordinated, tasteful and more expensive than it actually was. Exactly the tone she'd wanted to convey. Because she knew Gavin so well—or had at one time—she suspected it looked a little too calculated for his taste.

Her grandmother loved the place. She'd brought several friends over to see it, just to preen a bit about her granddaughter's success. Thad approved, too, telling her she had excellent taste. He said he wanted to build a big home, and he wanted her to help him design it, decorate it, fill it with elegant dinner parties and intimate gatherings of vibrant conversationalists. Perhaps a couple of kids, maybe even a dog. As long as it wasn't the slobbery, shedding sort of dog, he'd added ruefully. He just wasn't the big, slobbery dog kind of guy.

Gavin loved big, slobbery dogs. His family had always had one or two when she'd known them.

"Nice place," Gavin said, the compliment obviously no more than a social formality.

"Thanks."

"I like the painting."

It hung over the fireplace, an explosion of orange from peach to near-red, a depiction of a sunset over a tropical beach. The colors refracted in the gathering clouds, bled into the waves, stained the sand, spilled over a single shell lying in the foreground. It was the only item in the harmonized decor Thad didn't care for. He thought the artist, a student Jenny had met at a local university gallery showing, had been too heavy-handed with the color. Jenny didn't agree. She'd visited Hawaii once for a conference about six years ago, and she'd seen a sunset exactly like this, so bold and bright and fiery that it had completely engulfed her, had taken her breath away. In that moment, she had been purely, deeply happy in a way she hadn't been since she and Gavin had…

She bit her lip, cutting off the thought.

Gavin turned away from the painting. "You asked why I quit the force for a while."

Despite all her internal lectures, she still found herself asking him to sit down, and she knew it was because she wanted to hear this. When it came to Gavin, she really was pathetic.

He looked so out of place on her delicate cream brocade wing-backed chair. Too big, too masculine, too colorful somehow for the neutral room. His words made that contrast even more jarring. "About four years ago, I got in the middle of a knife fight when I responded to a 2:00 a.m. disturbance at a sleazy club we're called to at least once most nights. One guy, young, barely out of his teens, had been stabbed in the chest and I knew from looking at him he wasn't going to make it. Others were bleeding. Someone pulled a gun and the shooting started just as we got there. I watched another kid go down. Saw one of my friends in uniform wounded so badly he spent two weeks in ICU. I watched the hysterical girlfriend of one of the punks pick up a knife and run at my friend who was down. I had to fire my weapon to stop her from shoving the knife into him."

He'd given the details in a flat, emotionless monotone that sounded memorized, as if he'd told the tale many times before. Only his eyes told the real story, and that one twisted her heart. "Did you…did you kill her?"

"No. But I was prepared to in order to save Bob's life."

Enormous relief flooded through her, strictly for Gavin's sake. She was glad he hadn't had to live with that. She swallowed hard. "Were you injured?"

"Nothing serious."

"It sounds like a chaotic scene, to say the least."

Still in that oddly detached tone, he agreed. "It was. Not the first I'd dealt with. Hasn't been the last."

"So what was different about that one?" she asked perceptively.

He spread his hands, his face bleak now. "I saw the eyes of the kid who'd been stabbed before we got there. He was so young. Scared, but resigned. As if that was exactly the way he'd expected to end up. And I found myself asking what was the damned point of it all? Sometimes it feels like we do the same thing every night and then come back and do it all again the next. We arrest the same people over and over, then watch them get out and go right back to what they were doing before. I started having nightmares about being unable to stop the girl from slashing Bob while he was lying there hurt and unable to defend himself. Mom was nagging me to find a safer job, Dad was sick, the father of the woman I was dating kept offering me more and more money to work for him handling security for his company in Hot Springs. So, I gave it a shot."

It didn't escape her that he'd let himself be influenced to quit by another woman, though he'd refused with her. Had it been because he'd been ready to try something different for himself that time? She pushed that question away, as it shouldn't matter to her at this point. Still, she couldn't resist asking, "The woman who shops at my store?"

He grimaced. "No, someone else."

So there had been several women after her. She supposed she shouldn't be surprised. Though she didn't think of him as a player, Gavin Locke was never going to be a monk.

"You didn't like security work?" she asked to distract herself.

"Hated it. Especially after Molly and I broke up and

it got too awkward to work for her dad. So I left that job and took one selling construction equipment for my uncle. When that didn't work out, I tried my hand at driving a delivery truck. Bored out of my mind. I thought about going back to school, maybe training to be an EMT, maybe some sort of medical technician. But when it came time to make a decision, I knew what the answer had to be. I'm a cop. I'm pretty sure I was born a cop. It's all I've ever wanted to be, all I know how to be. It's not always a nice job—it can be ugly and traumatic and sometimes even boring. It gets too little respect and damned little gratitude most of the time. But sometimes, someone names their kid after you. So, I told everyone who wanted me to do something else that I was sorry if it disappointed them, but this is what I had to do. And I'm never again going to try to change who I am just to keep someone else happy."

Gavin knew who he was. What he wanted. Where he belonged. As much as it pained her to admit it, she both admired and rather envied his certainty.

If she'd had even the most tentative thought that perhaps he'd be ready now to move on to something less hazardous, that his latest on-the-job injury would discourage him from staying on the force, she surrendered it then. Studying him through her lashes, she realized he might as well be wearing a uniform rather than his polo shirt and khakis. Even off-duty, he was all cop. And anyone who loved him would have to be willing to love that part of him, as well.

"So, anyway, there's my story for the past ten years," he said, spreading his hands. "You asked, and I've answered. I trained for my career, got a degree, had a few relationships that didn't work out, tried a couple other jobs I didn't care for and made a lot of good friends. All in all, I'm content with my life. I'm looking forward to being on the job again soon. When I take time off, I want it to be for vacation, not sick leave."

"So this latest, um, incident didn't shake your confidence." Making it a statement rather than a question, she nodded toward his shoulder.

"No. Maybe a few bad dreams the first night or two, but no more than to be expected, and I was prepared for it. I can handle my work and everything that comes with it. Just had to make sure before that I'd made the right choice."

As candid as he was being with her, Gavin wouldn't like being seen as vulnerable. Nor did she think of him in that way.

"It sounds like a good life," she said quietly, trying to smile. "Exactly what you always wanted."

"Maybe not exactly," he said, his eyes locked with hers. "But close."

She didn't know how to respond, other than, "I'm glad you're happy."

"And you? Are you happy, Jen?"

Shifting her weight on the sofa where she'd perched, she twisted the ring on her right hand, a nice costume piece from her shop. "I told you about my career when we were at the cabin. I love owning my own store, and I'm excited about the second store I'll be opening in Jonesboro. The work keeps me insanely busy, but I've enjoyed almost every minute of it."

"It was what *you* always wanted to do. Be a successful business owner, I mean."

"Yes, and I've accomplished that."

His eyebrows rose, and she wondered what he'd heard in her voice. "Why did that sound like past tense?"

She felt a muscle twitch in her jaw, a quickly suppressed grimace. "Not past tense," she assured him. "I'm just keeping my options open. I mean, I want to stay busy and productive and useful, whatever direction I take next. Even if I'm not personally overseeing the boutiques on a daily basis, I could start a charitable foundation or get involved in a political cause. Something important that would let me utilize my talents and training."

He eyed her with a hint of skepticism. "Since when do you care about politics?"

"I've always been involved in community activities," she reminded him a little too heatedly. "Even in college, I was a member and officer of several civic organizations."

"True. But mostly because you were already starting to make future business connections," he murmured, and she couldn't argue with him because he wasn't entirely wrong.

"I've matured," she said instead, both her tone and her posture a little stiff. "We all do eventually. It's important to me to try to make a positive difference, just as you do in your daily work."

"Are you thinking about selling your shops after you open the one in Jonesboro?" he asked bluntly.

Even hearing the possibility put into words made her throat tighten, but she answered candidly. "Maybe."

"Why? The boyfriend doesn't like sharing you with your work?"

And here was finally the subject they'd been avoiding, and yet was the primary reason they'd needed to talk. Gavin's tone was cutting enough to make her chin rise defensively.

"Thad would never tell me what to do with my career. But if I accept his proposal, I'd be traveling with him quite a bit and busy with a lot of things outside my boutique business. I'm not sure I'd have time to do justice to both endeavors, and you know how I feel about doing anything halfway."

"Thad Simonson, right? One of *those* Simonsons. Of Simonson, McKenzie and Ogilvie."

She nodded to confirm the long-established law firm that had jump-started so many political careers, from local offices to Washington, DC. The Simonson name was on a few buildings in the area, including a law school library, so it was no surprise Gavin was familiar with the family, though she didn't think she'd mentioned Thad's last name to him yet. She didn't ask how he knew. She and Thad had appeared together at several prominent local events during the past few months, so maybe a mutual acquaintance had mentioned to him that she'd been seeing Thad Simonson.

"Congratulations, Jen." His voice was indifferent now, deceptively so, judging by the way his eyes had darkened to a glittering navy. "You snagged yourself a lawyer, after all."

She swallowed a gasp that would have only rewarded his deliberate dig. When she was certain her voice would be steady, she said icily, "That doesn't deserve a response."

His nod might have been meant as an apology, but didn't come across as very penitent. "When's the wedding?"

Still stinging from his barbed comment, she glared

at him. "There's no date yet. As I said, I'm taking my time to make certain of my answer."

"How long have you been seeing him?"

"About seven months."

After a moment, he asked brusquely, "Are you in love with him?"

She moistened her lips. "Thad is a great guy. He and I have a lot in common, and we enjoy each other's company. I wouldn't even consider marrying him if I didn't have feelings for him."

It was a pathetically lame response and she was all too aware of it. Gavin's expression made it clear that he thought so, too. "That's not what I asked you."

Her chest tightened. Rather than continuing that line of questioning, she shut it down. "You wanted to know what was going on in my life. Now I've told you. I'm in a relationship with Thad. I don't think you need all the details."

"So were you thinking of him when we kissed at the cabin? Or when we danced tonight?"

The wave of sensations those reminders invoked stole the breath from her lungs and made her fingers clench despite her efforts. She cleared her throat before saying tightly, "For old times' sake, you said. That's all it was."

With a shrug, he pushed himself off the chair. "Yeah. Okay. Fine. That's all it was."

She stood, too, relieved that her shaky knees supported her. She didn't know why this conversation was quite so upsetting. It wasn't as if anything had really changed in her life because she'd run into Gavin a couple of times.

He moved toward the door, his steps long, purposeful. She hurried after him, though she wasn't certain what she wanted to say. "Gavin…"

Pausing at the unopened door, he turned to look down at her. "Goodbye, Jenny. I hope you have the life you and your grandmother have always wanted for you. That's exactly what you deserve."

She could tell he didn't mean the words as a compliment. She was sorry they were parting again with bitterness, but maybe that was just the way it was supposed to be between them. "Stay safe, Gavin," she whispered, reaching for the door to let him out.

He'd reached out at the same time. Their hands fell on the knob together, his atop hers. His warmth engulfed her. Both of them went very still. She wasn't sure which of them recovered first, but they both let go at once. Her hand tingled as if she'd just touched a live current. Did his?

"I'll get it," Gavin said, and opened the door for himself. "Bye, Jen."

She didn't have time to respond before he was outside, the door closing hard behind him.

Out of habit, she turned the dead bolt. And then she rested her head against the cool wood. Tears leaked from the corners of her eyes, traced slowly down her cheeks. She thought she'd shed the last of her tears for Gavin a long time ago. She should have known there would always be a few left when it came to him. She didn't even know why she was crying now.

Her feet felt heavy when she turned to take a couple steps away from the door. For some reason, she found herself looking toward the sunset painting, seeking… something from the warmth and colors. She wasn't sure what exactly. Not finding it there, she turned her head and her gaze fell onto a small, hammered silver box Thad had given her for Valentine's Day. It sat on her clear glass-topped coffee table, seeming to float above the white rug that lay beneath the table on the wood floor. In stark contrast to the riotous painting, the box was pretty, delicate, a little on the formal side.

She pushed a hand wearily through her hair, her mind spinning with doubts again.

Someone rapped sharply on the door, making her start and whirl toward it. Was there something more Gavin wanted to say? Hadn't he hurt her enough?

She opened the door slowly, her fingers trembling. She looked up at him with still-damp eyes she couldn't hide. "Did you forget something?"

Surging through the opening, he reached out to snag the back of her neck with one strong hand. "Yeah," he muttered. "This."

She heard the door close even as his mouth claimed hers in a hard, hungry kiss.

Every nerve ending in Jenny's body responded to the passion in Gavin's kiss. Momentarily paralyzed, she couldn't breathe, couldn't speak, couldn't move to either push him away or draw him closer. Her hands lay on his chest, her fingers curled into his shirt. She didn't remember resting them there. His were at her hips, holding her in place while his lips and tongue made sure she could think of nothing but him.

He broke the kiss very slowly, tugging lightly at her lower lip as he reluctantly released it. He lifted his head, his gaze burning into hers. She knew what he saw when he looked at her. Her hair was mussed, her cheeks still tear-streaked, her mouth damp and reddened. Her heavy-lidded eyes probably told him exactly how much turmoil he'd stirred in her.

"Gavin." His name came out on a whisper, and she wasn't sure if it was meant as reproach or plea.

His voice was a growl, rough but still somehow gentle. "You know all you have to do is push me away and I'm gone."

She did know that. One word, one small shove, and he would leave. And this time he wouldn't come back.

Her fingers tightened on his shirt. "I can't think when you kiss me. You confuse me."

His hands cupped her face. "You aren't confused, Jenny. You know what you want. What you've always wanted. And it isn't this," he added with a quick, dismissive glance around the room. "This sterile, impersonal, colorless place. I saw more of your personality when I went into your store the other day than I do in your home. And you're thinking of giving that up, selling the business you've planned and worked toward and sacrificed for, just to stand at some politician's side and smile?"

She started to draw back, vaguely offended that he'd disparaged the apartment she'd so painstakingly put together. Not to mention her potential lifestyle choice. "That's not what I'd be doing. Not—not most of the time, anyway."

"And this guy you can't say you're in love with? Does he like this place?"

"Yes, he does."

"Is he aware that the only real glimpse of you in this room is hanging over the fireplace?"

She bit her lip.

He eased her lower lip from between her teeth with his thumb. "Does he confuse you when he kisses you?"

"Don't," she whispered, aching for something she couldn't define.

He understood her quandary better than she did, it seemed. "Don't kiss you? Or don't tell you that I want to kiss you again? That I want to do a hell of a lot more than kiss you? That I've wanted you again ever since you fell into my bed at the cabin? That I realized I couldn't walk away without telling you?"

He rubbed the pad of his thumb slowly across her trembling mouth. "You made a point to tell me you aren't actually engaged yet. That he asked you days ago and you still haven't decided on an answer. Doesn't that tell you something? Even if I weren't here confusing you, should it really take that long to make up your mind if you knew it was the right choice for you?"

She sighed heavily, old wounds throbbing deep inside her. "Gavin, you and I—we tried it before. It didn't work. It was always too intense between us. I'm…I'm comfortable with Thad," she added, trying to make that sound more satisfying than it suddenly felt.

He shook his head and she thought she saw sympathy and understanding in his eyes now. "I didn't come back to ask you to choose between him and me. I just couldn't leave without asking if you're sure he's any more right for you than I was. The real you, who escaped to a cabin in the woods to think rather than staying in this dainty apartment. The you who gets excited about opening a second store, but looks serious and logical when talking about a proposal of marriage. The you who comes alive in my arms every time we kiss."

She swallowed a low moan.

Lowering his head a bit more, he looked deeply into her eyes. "Don't throw away everything you've worked for just because it seems like something you *should* do, Jenny. Something you'd be doing mostly to impress your grandmother and to give you a shortcut into that lifestyle you were always told you should want for yourself. Despite what I said in anger before I walked out, you deserve a hell of a lot more than that."

"I'm quite capable of making my own decisions about what's best for me," she assured him, though her heart had flinched with his words.

"You're one of the most capable and intelligent women I've ever known," he answered evenly. "But you were indoctrinated from an early age to equate money and social standing with happiness. We both know who's to blame for that."

"My grandmother has always wanted the best for me. She didn't want to see me end up like my mother, struggling and grieving," she reminded him, on the defensive again.

"I always thought she should let you make up your own mind about what's best for you."

She pulled away from him, freeing herself from his tempting touch. "I've always looked out for myself. Why else do you think I made myself walk away from you ten years ago when doing so was so hard I thought I'd never stop hurting inside? I knew I couldn't change you, couldn't persuade you to choose a safer career, but I knew also that I couldn't handle the fear and uncertainty that came with it. I walked away to protect myself and because it wouldn't have been fair for me to keep asking you to give up your dreams. And I've done quite well for myself since, I might add."

Pushing a hand through his hair, he nodded. "I never doubted you would. You've accomplished almost everything you said you wanted. Are you really considering walking away from it, Jen? He can give you every material thing you desire, but can he give you the joy and fulfillment your shops bring you?"

He lifted his hand again, resting it against her cheek, and she remained frozen in place as he lowered his head to brush his lips against hers, very lightly. No pressure, no insistence, but so much tenderness that she could feel a fresh wave of tears pushing at the backs of her eyes.

"I can feel you starting to tremble again," he murmured against her mouth. "I can almost hear your heart racing. It's always been that way between us, from the first time we touched. We're older, more experienced now, but the electricity between us hasn't changed, not for me at least. You're still the only woman in the world who can make my head spin just with a brush of your skin against mine."

A moan escaped her before she could stop it. Her knees turned to gelatin, and her pulse roared in her ears. No, she thought in despair. No one else had ever made her feel the way Gavin had. The way he still did. Kissing Thad was pleasant. Even occasionally arousing. But not like this. Never like this.

She melted into him.

This time her mouth was as ravenous as his, as bold in acting on that craving. Her fingers still gripped his shirt, but in demand now, tugging him closer, holding him there even though he displayed no interest in moving away. She nipped his lip as if in punishment for making her acknowledge this desire, and she reveled in his throaty moan that was more pleasure than protest. Her tongue dueled with his, equally angry, equally hungry, equally fierce.

Equal.

His hands left her hips to sweep over her, as if to explore the changes time had brought to the body he'd once known as well as his own. She was a bit curvier than she'd been as a teenager, but judging by his murmurs of appreciation and by the impressive hardening against her upper thigh, Gavin was more than satisfied.

She'd admired his broad shoulders and solid chest when she'd changed his bandage at the cabin, but she hadn't allowed herself to explore them thoroughly then. She did so now, sliding her hands beneath his shirt, spreading her palms against the hot skin and well-defined musculature. The bandage was gone now, as were the stitches. A thin smattering of chest hair tickled her fingers. His stomach muscles contracted sharply when she slowly followed that thinning line of hair downward toward the waistband of his pants.

He caught her hand. His voice was hoarse when he warned, "You're playing with fire, Jen."

"I've been cold for too long," she whispered, her own tone stark.

"Jenny." He pulled her into his arms, wrapping himself around her. She pressed even closer, soaking in his heat, her mouth joining his in a kiss that was less frantic now, more savoring, more tender. Her tongue stroked his rather than battling it. Her hands caressed him over his shirt, over the muscles that felt familiar yet new at the same time. She pushed away his shirt to provide her better access.

Focused solely on him, she hardly remembered moving from the living room to the bedroom. But she was keenly aware of every other detail. His hands beneath her dress. Hers tugging his shirt over his head and tossing it aside. His mouth on her throat, her shoulder, her breasts. Her fingers tugging at his belt, his zipper, eager to remove the garments between them.

Somehow he remembered little caresses that made her gasp and squirm in pleasure against the snowy bedclothes. And he'd learned some new tricks that caused her to arch and cry out helplessly as her toes curled into the tangled sheets. He took his time, teasing her and pushing her right to the edge before drawing back, slowing down. She heard an almost feral growl escape her. Even as she shoved him onto his back to retaliate, she was a little startled that the sound had come from her throat.

She used her teeth, nipped at his ear, his chin, his throat, his chest. Her hand slipped down between them, grasping him, stroking him until he was the one arching and groaning and the husky laugh of satisfaction was hers. She laughed again when he deftly flipped their positions. She landed among the pillows with her hair tangled wildly around her damp face. One pillow fell over her, threatening to smother her.

Gavin shoved the pillows off the bed and to the floor with one idle sweep of his hand, his gaze focused intently on her face. "Now?"

"Yes, *please*."

He chuckled and kissed her thoroughly. A condom appeared from somewhere, and he donned it swiftly, impatiently, while she held her breath in anticipation. When he returned to her, she welcomed him with open arms, lifted knees and eager lips. He gathered her to him and joined their bodies with one smooth, hard thrust, then stilled for a moment to allow them both time to process the moment.

Yes. This. I remember this. This...completeness.

Shushing the little voice in her head, she wrapped herself around Gavin and allowed herself to exist solely in the moment. No past to haunt her. No future to worry her. Only this man and this bed.

He began to move, slowly, steadily. Then, at her urging, faster, more forcefully. She realized that their hands were linked at either side of her head, fingers intertwined. They'd always held hands as they approached climax. How could it still be so familiar, so natural? Her heart pounded so hard it almost hurt; her breathing was raw and ragged. Her eyelids were heavy and she wanted to close them, but she needed more to keep them open, to look at Gavin's tautly drawn face above hers. Meeting her eyes, he flashed a smile at her—and she came with a cry that was echoed mere moments later by his groan of release.

Only then did she close her eyes.

Chapter Nine

Exhausted, she slept. She wasn't sure how much time had passed when she woke with a start, but she knew she'd been dreaming. She bit her lip as bits and pieces of the dream replayed in her conscious mind. She'd dreamed of her father. Of presents he'd bought her, giggles he'd tickled from her, hugs he'd shared with her. She'd seen her mother pacing, worrying. And she'd dreamed of the day her father hadn't come home.

She was annoyed with her own subconscious. *Seriously?* Daddy dreams, now of all times? She would have liked to think even her sleeping mind wasn't that clichéd.

Opening her eyes and turning her head on the pillow, she looked somberly at Gavin. He lay on his left side facing her, a corner of the sheet covering his hips. The rest of the sheet dangled over the side of the bed to puddle on the floor. Her bed was pretty much wrecked from their activities. She'd have to strip it down to the mattress to return it to its usual immaculate state. Not that the disarray seemed to bother Gavin. His eyes were closed, his breathing even. She wasn't sure he was deeply asleep, but he was dozing.

The only light in the room came from the little lamp still burning on her nightstand. The illumination flooded softly over him, casting intriguing shadows across his tanned skin. Because he'd thrown the pillows on the floor earlier, he cradled his head on his bent arm. His hair tumbled appealingly around his face, the lamplight bringing out the gold streaks.

Her leisurely inspection paused at his right shoulder. She swallowed. Even with the stitches gone, the scar was still red and puckered. She looked away.

Reaching hastily for the white duvet crumpled on the floor by her side of the bed, she wrapped it around her body as she rose a little shakily to her feet. She caught a glimpse of herself in the dresser mirror and nearly stumbled. Who was that woman with the tangled hair, swollen mouth and wild eyes, her nude body wrapped in a coverlet? She was hardly recognizable even to herself.

She slipped into the bathroom and took her time washing up, brushing her hair and teeth, trying to put her thoughts in order along with her appearance. She donned a white robe she kept on a hook on the door and tied the sash tightly at her waist, making sure the front of the garment was securely closed. Only then did she feel somewhat prepared to face Gavin again.

He was awake when she walked back into the bedroom with her shoulders squared and her chin lifted in a show of confidence. He sat up against the headboard, his tanned skin an attractive contrast to all the white surrounding him, the sheet draped across his lap and thighs. His eyelids were still half-closed, but she knew he studied her with full alertness behind that lazily satisfied expression. "Everything okay?"

She tightened her belt again. "You should go, Gavin. It's late."

"Throwing me out?"

"I just need to be alone for a while."

He thought about that for a moment, then nodded. Unselfconscious, he rolled out of the bed and gathered his clothes. She stood for a moment staring at her tousled bed, then turned abruptly and went into the other room. Rounding the granite bar, she reached into a white-painted cabinet for a water glass. She filled it and had thirstily emptied it by the time Gavin found her.

"Would you like a glass of water before you leave?" she asked without quite meeting his eyes.

"No, I'm good. I'd kind of hoped to stay a little longer, but I can see you need time to deal with this." Spotting a pad and pen on the bar, he scribbled something on the top sheet. "Here are my numbers. Call me when you're ready to talk."

At the moment, she hadn't the foggiest idea what she would say. She merely nodded.

He hesitated, as if there were many things he wanted to discuss. But obviously he could see that she simply wasn't up to that conversation yet. He took a step toward her and rested his hands on her shoulders as he bent his head to kiss her. He didn't immediately move away when he released her mouth, but looked at her with a serious expression.

"I want to see you again, Jenny. I think that goes

without saying. But even if you decide you don't want to take another chance on us, don't let anyone else try to change you to suit them. Trust me, I've been there. It doesn't work. It only makes you miserable."

"You should go now, Gavin," she whispered. Her eyes felt suddenly hot and she did not want to cry in front of him. She needed desperately to cling to what little self-control she had left. "We will talk. But not tonight."

"Take all the time you need," he said gruffly, taking a step backward. "I'll be waiting to hear from you."

She merely nodded. With a last brush of his hand against her face, Gavin left. Only then did she allow herself to sink into a chair and bury her face in her hands.

Everything had changed tonight. All her carefully laid plans had shattered beneath Gavin's kisses. No matter what happened with him, she knew she couldn't accept Thad's proposal now.

She couldn't tell Thad over the phone, of course. He deserved a face-to-face answer to his offer. He would be disappointed, though in all honesty she doubted he would be heartbroken. Nor would he be angry; in all the months they'd dated, they'd exchanged no more than a few cross words. In all likelihood, he would wish her the best, maybe try one more time to convince her how good they'd have been together, and then he would graciously accept her answer.

Thad had a plan that would remain intact despite her decision. It wouldn't take him long to implement it with someone equally suitable as his partner. Another attorney, perhaps, or a professor or marketing executive. He had no interest in vacuous young arm candy. He claimed to be attracted to intelligence, competence and poise. She'd been pleased that he'd set his standards so high and that he thought all those flattering adjectives applied to her.

As for herself—maybe she'd known all along it would turn out this way. Not that she would find Gavin again, of course, and certainly not that the powerful attraction that had always existed between them would draw him to her bed. But maybe when she'd taken off for the woods to consider and deliberate, she'd secretly known she would be unable to commit to Thad in the way he wanted.

As Gavin had pointed out, her joy lay in the business she'd built for herself, the plans and goals she still had for it. Maybe that should be enough for her. Maybe, like her mother and grandmother before her, she was destined to be single and self-sufficient. Maybe, unlike them, she'd been fortunate enough to come to that realization without the agony of losing someone she loved and with whom she'd planned to live out her lifetime. The dread was still there, still sharp and discouraging.

She had to admit now that she didn't love Thad enough to be happy with him. But she still feared she loved Gavin entirely too much.

She had almost forgotten she'd made plans to have breakfast with Tess late Sunday morning at a new café they'd both wanted to try out. Tess sent her a text asking if they were still on, and after a brief deliberation, Jenny agreed, hurrying to get ready in time.

After a near-sleepless night in her now memory-filled bed, she wanted to get out of the apartment for a while. Tess's serene, soothing presence could be just what she required to calm her jangled nerves. She definitely needed calming before she joined her mother and grandmother for their regular Sunday dinner later that evening.

"Well?" she asked as they sat at a little table in the cute but crowded café. The tables were arranged so close together that she was almost elbow to elbow with one of the three prim-looking elderly ladies at the nearest one. From their conversation, conducted in a volume meant to compensate for the noisy room and their own poor hearing, she determined that they were indulging in a nice brunch after early church services. She wasn't interested in eavesdropping, however, choosing instead to focus on her breakfast companion. "Did you handle the big work emergency last night?"

Tess looked up from her spinach, tomato and feta quiche with a rueful grimace. "Eventually. It took me a while to reach Scott. He'd let the battery run down on his phone and I had to make half a dozen calls to finally track him down at a client dinner. He took care of everything after that."

Tess probably would have been called on even if Scott were easily reachable, Jenny thought with a slight shake of her head.

During the year and a half she'd known Tess, she'd figured out a few things about her friend's relationship with her boss. Scott Prince was a brilliant businessman who'd built his commercial construction business into a successful and rapidly growing enterprise, but the day-to-day details were left to others, usually Tess. Twenty-nine years old, she had worked for Scott for six years. He'd been just striking out on his own when he'd hired her. She'd worked her way up till from clerical assistant to office manager. No one got to Scott except through her, and everyone who worked for him was more invested in keeping her happy than him.

Tess was fiercely loyal to her employer, but the first to call him out when he got "too full of himself," as she phrased it. If she had ever had romantic feelings toward her unmarried boss, she'd never said.

At the moment, Tess apparently wasn't thinking about her own hectic life. "So," she said, deftly turning the conversation around. "Gavin drove you home last night?"

Jenny took a quick sip of her coffee to delay answering, nearly burning her mouth because of her inattention. She set her cup down carefully. "Yes."

"He seems nice."

"He is."

"I think Stevie was trying to fix me up with him, but I could tell pretty quickly that it wouldn't work even if I were interested in pursuing him."

Jenny dug a mushroom out of her omelet with her fork. "I don't really see you with Gavin."

"Considering he's still head over heels in love with you, neither do I."

Jenny's fork clattered loudly against her plate, drawing a disapproving glance from the nearby church ladies. Ignoring them, she frowned across the table at Tess. "He's not still in love with me. Until last week, we hadn't even seen each other for ten years."

"Maybe he wasn't pining for you those whole ten years, but I think seeing you again brought his feelings for you back to the forefront," Tess mused aloud. "The way he looked at you last night…well, the hair on my arms stood on end. Talk about chemistry."

Jenny swallowed a groan in automatic reaction to her

friend's words, which so eerily echoed the way she'd always privately described her own reactions to Gavin. "I'll admit there is still an…attraction between us."

"Mmm." Tess sighed a bit wistfully. "I wouldn't mind knowing what it's like to be on the receiving end of that sort of attraction."

After swallowing another, more cautious sip of coffee, Jenny couldn't resist asking, "You never had that feeling when you saw me with Thad?"

Tess grimaced. "I, um…"

"I'm asking honestly, Tess. You won't hurt my feelings, whatever you say."

After a moment, her friend shrugged in resignation. "No. I never felt that way about you and Thad. I mean, he's a very nice man. I admire him quite a bit, and I'll probably vote for him for whatever office he eventually pursues. He seems very, um, fond of you."

"But the hairs on your arm have never stood on end around us?"

"Well, no."

Jenny nodded with a touch of regret.

Tess spoke quickly. "Look, that doesn't mean you and Thad won't be very happy. I mean, marriage should be based on more than physical attraction. You and Thad have so much in common intellectually and philosophically. You make great partners. Everyone says so."

"Everyone but you and Stevie."

Tess cleared her throat. "Stevie's an incurable romantic, and I'm maybe a little too choosy for my own good. We're probably not the best judges of anyone else's relationships."

Jenny pushed away her half-eaten egg-white omelet.

"I'm breaking it off with Thad. I'm just waiting until he gets home so I won't have to do it over the phone."

Her amber eyes going wide, Tess asked, "Because of Gavin?"

"Not in the way you mean. I'm pretty sure I wouldn't marry Thad even if I hadn't run into Gavin again. Gavin just made me realize that I'm very happy with my life as it is, and that my feelings for Thad aren't deep enough to justify what I'd be giving up for him. I mean, Thad hasn't asked me to abandon my career, but he and I both know I couldn't give it the attention it requires and still be the full-time political partner he's looking for. He's on the road more than he's in town, and he's made it clear he would want me to travel with him. As much as I enjoy my time with him, I think in the long run I'd regret giving up my own goals."

Tess nodded without surprise, proving that she'd had the same doubts about Jenny's future with Thad. "So… Gavin? Did you and he talk when he took you home last night?"

To her dismay, Jenny felt her face redden. She looked quickly down at her coffee, hoping Tess wouldn't notice. She should have known better.

"Um, Jenny?"

"I'm not breaking up with Thad because of Gavin," she muttered crossly. "That's not what this is about."

"Okay. Unlike Stevie, I won't pry into what happened last night. But you know she's going to ask."

"And I'll tell her to butt out," Jenny snapped, her frayed nerves unraveling. "Yes, Gavin and I have electricity or chemistry or whatever the hell Stevie calls it, but that's just sex. Okay, maybe it's great sex, maybe once-in-a-lifetime, mind-blowing, teeth-rattling sex, but that's not enough to build an entire future on. Because it wouldn't—it couldn't—always be that good, right? And then what would we have?"

Tess cleared her throat.

Realizing she'd spoken with a bit more passion than she'd intended, Jenny bit her lip. The three gray-haired ladies at the next table stared at her with wide eyes and open mouths. And then one of them grinned and winked at her.

Jenny covered her face with her hands. She had never been so happy to hear Tess's phone beep than she was at that moment.

Tess read the text message on her screen, then exhaled heavily. "As much as I would love to continue this fascinating conversation, I have to run. Duty calls. But, um, maybe you should calm yourself a bit before you speak to Stevie."

Jenny groaned into her hands. Perhaps having breakfast with a friend hadn't been the best idea today, after all. Clearly it would take more time than she'd expected to recover her characteristic composure that had been shattered last night. She would go home and work on that before she spoke with Stevie.

She would most definitely have to get a grip before she saw her mother and grandmother that evening, a meal she wasn't looking forward to at all.

Though Gavin had promised himself he would wait for Jenny to phone him, he kept second-guessing that decision as Sunday crawled by. Maybe he should call her, just to make sure she was okay. But he'd told her he'd give her time.

Though he hadn't heard a ring, he checked his phone

for missed calls Sunday afternoon, vaguely disappointed to see that there were none from Jenny. Was she waiting for him to call her? Had she talked to that other guy yet today?

Had last night been a one-time thing, an impulsive trip to the past, a way for Jenny to get him out of her system for good before moving on? Before making what Gavin was certain would be the biggest mistake of her life?

Surely she would break it off with Thad now. She couldn't marry some other guy after what she'd shared with him last night, could she? No one else could possibly make her feel what he did, just as the reverse was true for him. She couldn't even considering marrying someone else when all it took was a touch, a kiss, to ignite a blazing fire between them. Could she?

"Hey, Gav, break's almost over." Holding a basketball and wearing shorts and a tee, Avery approached. "You are still playing, right?"

Gavin stashed the phone in his gym bag again. He, Avery and J.T. had been playing Rob and a couple other medics in three-on-three basketball. The score was tied at two wins, and they'd agreed to play a twenty-one-point tiebreaker. "I'm coming."

"You weren't thinking of calling her, were you?" Avery asked suspiciously. He didn't bother to clarify who he'd referred to, as there was no need. Gavin hadn't told his friend about last night, but somehow Avery knew something was up.

"Let it go, Avery. Let's play basketball."

"Damn it, Gav, why are you letting her do this to you again?"

"Just give me the ball. The way you're playing this

afternoon, the medics are going to kick our butts this time."

"I'm not the one who got distracted and let the ball hit me in the jaw," Avery reminded him irritably. "One guess who you were thinking about."

Gavin scowled and rubbed his chin.

"Hey, guys, come on. Let's get this massacre over with," one of Rob's friends called out. "I've got to be home in time for dinner."

"Drop it," Gavin said when Avery started to speak again. "Just play ball."

With a gusty exhale, Avery spun on one athletic shoe and stalked toward the court with Gavin following. Gavin didn't really blame his buddy for being so pushy. Avery had been there to see what the last breakup with Jenny had done to him. Just as Gavin had been there during Avery's painful divorce from his first marriage a few years ago. He would give anything to make sure his friend wasn't hurt like that again. Avery certainly felt the same about him.

His friends wanted the best for him, he thought with a sigh. Maybe he should listen to them.

Maybe he'd call Jenny after this game.

Or maybe he'd wait and let her call him.

Damn it, Avery was right. He really was letting her mess with his head—and his heart—again. If he had a lick of sense, he'd forget he ever ran into her again. But when it came to Jenny, he'd never had a great deal of sense.

"So I told Margaret this morning after Sunday school that I don't care what her grandson's excuses are, there's no way I'd spend any more hard-earned money to bail out his sorry butt if I were her," Gran proclaimed over dinner, completing a story that had droned on endlessly through salad and now to the ham and potatoes course. "They've spoiled that boy something terrible and now the whole family's paying the price for it, especially Margaret, since she's the only one of the bunch who had enough sense to put away a little money for her latter years."

Jenny's mother shook her head in disapproval. "I feel sorry for Angie and Don. They don't deserve to be punished this way. But Angie still makes excuses for him, blaming all his problems on everyone but him. She can't accept that he's a grown man in his twenties now, and that he has to take responsibility for his own failings."

As uncomfortable as she was by the gossip, Jenny was relieved that at least they were focused on someone other than her for now.

Maybe the thought had crossed her mind too soon. Her grandmother turned to smile smugly in her direction. "I told Margaret that I hated to brag, but I was glad I haven't had to deal with that sort of disappointment from my grandchild. I said that Jenny hasn't given us a day's trouble since her little college rebellion, and even that was fairly mild and short-lived. Only natural, I suppose, for a teenager to test her wings when she's away from home, but we'd given her enough solid raising that she straightened up with only a little guidance from us."

Wincing at the indirect reference to Gavin, Jenny said peevishly, "I'm right here, Gran. Must you talk about me as if I weren't?"

"Just telling you what I said to Margaret."

"Well, you shouldn't have. She's upset about her grandson, and it seems unkind to boast about me to her. Besides, I'm hardly perfect." Nor was she a possession to be pulled out and shown off, she added silently. It wasn't the first time she'd felt that her grandmother saw her that way.

For years, she'd tried to please her exacting grandmother, who had dealt out gestures of affection like earned rewards.

Jenny's mom had been more generous with her affection, but as a hospital nurse, her hours had been very long, leaving Jenny more often in her grandmother's care. Her mom was also quieter, often overshadowed by her forceful parent, so it had been Gran who had most inspired trepidation in Jenny. Funny how those deeply ingrained patterns could carry over into adulthood, she mused as she played with the food she didn't want but was afraid to push away for fear of rousing her grandmother's suspicions.

"Margaret understands that I was only expressing my gratitude that I've been blessed with a more successful grandchild," her grandmother shot back, oblivious to the offensiveness of her comment. "At least I know I won't have to worry about my bank account being drained by irresponsible family members. Both you girls have worked hard for your livings, and once you marry Thad, I'm sure you'll make sure your mother and grandmother have what we need, won't you, sweetheart?"

It was another not-so-subtle reminder of how selfish Jenny would be if she didn't take advantage of an opportunity her grandmother had prepared her for all her life.

"I will always do everything I can to take care of you and Mom, Gran," Jenny replied carefully.

So far, her popular boutique had proven satisfactorily lucrative, and she hoped her new venture in the northeastern part of the state would be as successful. She had ideas for more stores in Conway and Fayetteville, two other Arkansas college towns with demographics that suited her line of youthful, trendy, high-end merchandise. She knew the risks of opening new businesses, but she had prepared herself as thoroughly as possible for this venture. She knew about budgeting, advertising, creating buzz on social media, targeted selection of merchandise. She'd reassured herself often that she would be able to put that training to good use as Thad's wife, but now she wondered how she could have even considered voluntarily giving up the business she loved.

She wanted to believe she'd have come to her senses eventually on her own. But if Gavin hadn't been at the cabin that weekend, would she actually have convinced herself that providing security for herself and her family outweighed her personal desires? Would she have allowed herself to be swept into a marriage with Thad that might have proven successful, but never truly fulfilling? A tiny part of her wondered…

"Jenny, is everything okay?" her mother asked quietly as they cleared the table after dessert. "You seem so distracted this evening."

"I'm sure she's missing Thad," Gran answered, complacently certain of her accuracy, as always. "Perfectly understandable, Jenny, but don't mope. It isn't becoming."

Jenny drew a deep breath and held it for a moment before replying, "I'm not moping. Just a little tired. I didn't get much sleep last night."

"You work too hard," her mother fretted. "Why don't you sit in here with your grandmother and I'll clean the kitchen?"

"I'll help you clean up, Mom," Jenny countered quickly. "It's the least I can do after you cooked this delicious meal."

"I want to watch television, anyway," Gran proclaimed. "You know I always watch my program at this time every Sunday night. Jenny's not interested in it, so she can help you."

Carrying with her the tiny glass of red wine that had been part of her nighttime routine for the past forty years or more, Gran retired to her bedroom with restrained cheek kisses for her daughter and granddaughter. She was the early-to-bed and early-to-rise type, so this was good-night. It was with some relief that Jenny watched her leave the room without any further discussion of Thad. Soon enough she would have to tell her grandmother that there would be no fancy society wedding, but she wasn't ready to deal with that tonight.

She and her mother talked of inconsequential things during the brief cleanup. Summer trends at the shop. A party her mom's hospital coworkers had thrown for a retiring administrator. Afterward, they moved out to the patio to sit in gliders, her mom with a cup of hot herbal tea, Jenny with a mug of coffee.

Her mom nodded toward Jenny's steaming mug and shook her head. "I don't know how you can drink that this late and still get any sleep."

"One cup after dinner doesn't usually affect me."

"I know. You got that from your father. He could drink strong coffee right up until bedtime and still sleep like a log for a good six or seven hours, the most he ever needed." She laughed softly at the memory, her expression suddenly looking far away.

Jenny bit her lip and ran a fingertip idly around the

rim of her mug. She and her mom never talked about Jenny's dad when her grandmother was around. Probably because Gran always had something disparaging to say about her late son-in-law.

"Honey, are you sure there's nothing wrong? You look so unhappy."

"I'm not unhappy, Mom. I'm just, well, a little distracted."

Her mom sighed. "It's Gavin, isn't it? Ever since you ran into him again, you seem troubled. Mother was livid that he came back into your life even for a brief encounter, but she's convinced herself since that you haven't given Gavin another thought. That you are totally committed to Thad. I haven't been so sure."

Jenny turned her head to look at her mother. Though she knew her grandmother couldn't possibly overhear, she spoke quietly when she said, "I'm not going to marry Thad, Mom. I'm sorry if you're disappointed, but I just can't go through with it."

If there was a momentary wistfulness, it was well hidden when her mom said flatly, "You have to make the decision that's right for you, Jenny. If you don't love Thad with all your heart, then you shouldn't marry him. It wouldn't be fair to either of you."

Jenny could imagine how her grandmother would snort in derision at such a sentimental remark. She would be sure to point out that Jenny was quite fond of Thad and vice versa, and that was a perfectly adequate foundation for a successful marriage.

"As for whether I'm disappointed, you mustn't even think that, dear," her mom added warmly. "Nothing you could do would ever disappoint me. You've been the best daughter I could ever have imagined, and I am so proud of you. I wouldn't change a thing about you. I know your father would be proud, too."

"I hope he would," Jenny murmured. "I wish I remembered him better. I was so young when he died."

"We both were. I was too young to be widowed and you too young to be left fatherless. Even in my grief, I was angry for a time that he was so reckless and irresponsible, that he died doing something so wild and foolish. I let Mother poison my mind against him for a few years, and I regret that now. I should have talked about him more to you despite her disapproval, kept him alive for you. Kevin was a good man and I loved him madly. I've never been able to feel that same way about any other man."

Staring somewhat fiercely into her cup, Jenny said, "That's so sad. That you've had to live all these years with the pain of losing him, I mean."

"Of course I wish he'd been with us longer, but despite whatever my mother says, I don't regret marrying your father, Jenny. I knew when I fell in love with him that he would never play it safe. He was a charming daredevil, what they now refer to as an adrenaline junkie, but he was also loving and kind and generous. Too generous sometimes. Money meant very little to him. But he had a heart as big as the sky, and he adored us. He even tolerated my mother. He said we should understand that her bitterness was rooted in pain and disappointment. He never failed to kiss her cheek when he parted from her, even when she batted him away. He even teased a smile out of her a few times. She cried when he died, though she tried her best to hide her tears from me, and then she just grew more bitter that another man she'd started to care for had left us too soon and in a financial bind."

That must have cemented her grandmother's hard-earned belief that it was better to marry for security than for love, Jenny thought sadly. No wonder Gran hadn't allowed herself to like Gavin, and that she promoted Thad.

"Have you told Thad yet?" her mother asked gently.

"No. I'm waiting until he gets back. Please don't tell Gran yet. I'll deal with her tantrums when it's all settled."

"Of course. I'm glad you felt comfortable talking to me."

"You've always been there for me when I needed you, Mom."

"And I always will be."

"If you need anything, anything at all, I'm doing fairly well with the store, you know. I have a little put away…"

Her mother stiffened. "Jennifer Gayle Baer, if you're implying that I wanted you to marry Thad for his money, or that I expect you to support me when I am perfectly capable of supporting myself, then I'm going to be very offended."

Smiling a little, Jenny held up a hand. "I wasn't implying anything of the sort, Mom." Though she was a little relieved to have it spelled out. "I just wanted you to know I'm here for you, too."

"I do know that. Thank you."

They glided and sipped in silence for a moment, and then her mom asked the inevitable question. "What about Gavin?"

"I don't know," Jenny admitted. "He… I have to admit there are feelings, but…"

More than anyone, perhaps, her mother understood. "But he's still a cop."

Jenny nodded somberly. "And I still don't know how to deal with that."

"Lots of jobs carry risk. He could be a pilot. Or a soldier. Or he could be a firefighter, like your dad. I always worried about the danger in his job, though sadly his off-duty hobbies were even more dangerous," she added with a little break in her voice. Speaking more firmly, she continued, "Actually, construction jobs are quite hazardous. Take it from someone who worked in ER for several years and saw some fairly nasty construction injuries. Would you be just as wary of Gavin if he were a roofer or a high-rise worker at the end of a harness? Or would you feel free to love him only if he worked in an office or a classroom, where he'd be relatively safe barring an unexpected illness or car accident or tornado or mugging?"

So many things to go wrong, Jenny thought with a little shudder. So many ways to lose someone. She knew her mother had been driving home a point, but rather than reassure her, the list only made her more afraid to give her heart completely.

"I'm scared," she whispered. "It didn't work out last time, and it almost broke my heart. What if…?"

She swallowed a huge lump in her throat.

"As I said before, you have to decide what's right for you, Jenny. Whether it's Gavin or Thad or life as a single career woman, whatever makes you happy is what you should choose. Not what pleases your grandmother or me or your friends or anyone else. Think about what it is that gives you pure joy—the way your father did for me—and go after it with your whole heart. I have no doubt that you can do anything you set your mind to. And don't worry about your grandmother. She'll throw a tantrum, but we'll deal with her together."

"Thanks, Mom."

"Any time, sweetie. I love you."

"I love you, too." And despite everything, Jenny loved her contrary, bossy, pretentious and damaged grandmother. Which only went to show, she supposed, that there was no logic to her heart. Now if only she could decide whether to listen more to her heart or her mind, her courage or her fears, when it came to Gavin.

Chapter Ten

Her tensely awaited reunion with Thad could only be described as a dark comedy of errors. Almost everything that could go wrong did.

Before he'd even left on his two-week trip, they had arranged for her to accompany him to an important fund-raiser Wednesday evening at an exclusive downtown hotel. The tickets had cost a thousand dollars each, but Thad hadn't blinked at the price. It was important, he'd said, for him to attend this particular event. All his law-firm partners would be there, and his presence was expected.

The plan had been for his plane to land early that afternoon, giving him time to go home, shower and change and pick up Jenny for a nice dinner before the gala. That schedule didn't leave a lot of time for the conversation she needed to have with him, but she was prepared to talk with him as soon as he arrived to collect her. She would be dressed to go out, but she would assure him that she would understand if he'd prefer she stay behind.

She rather hoped that would be his decision, which would be far less awkward, but she'd promised to accompany him and she would keep her word if he wanted her at his side for one final event. She knew Thad would smile and mingle and be a courteous escort regardless of his feelings about her turning down his proposal.

She hadn't heard from Gavin since she'd pretty much kicked him out of her bed. She knew he was waiting for her to call, but she wasn't quite ready for that. She told herself it was because she needed to settle things with Thad, but she suspected it was more cowardice than courtesy that held her back.

She still wondered if it wouldn't be better for both of them to leave it as it was. At least this time they would have parted with a few hours of amazing pleasure rather than angry words, with kisses instead of tears. Wouldn't that be infinitely preferable to trying again and probably failing again?

Thad called from the airport in Phoenix. His connecting flight had been delayed an hour. An hour later he called to say he'd been delayed again. Just before he was finally able to board, he gave her a quick, terse call to let her know there would be no time for dinner.

"I hate to do this, but I'll have to pick you up in a rush to make it to the fund-raiser at a decent time. I'm so sorry, Jenny."

So their talk would have to wait until later in the evening. "It's okay," she assured him. "You couldn't help the delays. I'll be ready to go as soon as you arrive."

"Thanks, sweetheart. I'll make it up to you, I promise. The attendants are telling us to turn off our phones now, so I have to disconnect. I'll see you in a few hours. Love ya, Jenny."

He disconnected before she could respond, though she didn't know what she'd have said. Why had she not noticed before how empty the words sounded from him?

She was ready an hour early, dressed in a tasteful black, knee-length dress with an unexpected pop of hot pink in glimpses of lining at the swirling hem. The dress came from her boutique, as she would be sure to tell anyone who complimented her.

Thad wore an apologetic smile when she opened her door to him. Despite his hectic hours of travel, he was impeccably groomed, as always.

"I'm so sorry to rush you this way, Jenny," he said, brushing a careful kiss close to her mouth so as not to smudge her lipstick. "You look beautiful, as you always do. Did you have dinner?"

She hadn't been able to eat a bite, but she merely nodded. "I'm fine, thanks. And again, the delays weren't your fault."

"We should go, then."

She buckled herself into the soft leather seat of his sports car while he rounded the hood after closing her door for her. Climbing behind the wheel, he shot her a smile as he started the powerful engine. "We'll have a good time tonight, I'm sure. We've gotten off to a harried start because of the inefficiency of modern air travel. I'm thinking about investing in a private jet, perhaps shared with a couple of partners. Some of my associates do that, and it's so much more convenient for them."

"I can see where it would be."

Private jets, she thought with a tiny shake of her head. She rarely even traveled first class.

He didn't speed as he drove them toward downtown, but he hovered right at the limit. "You have to admit it will be easier after we're married when we have only one home from which to operate. No more hasty pick-ups and drop-offs. Won't that be better?"

She almost bit her lip, but remembered at the last moment to guard her makeup. Instead, she looked out the window at the familiar landscape they passed. Though she sensed Thad glancing her way, probably wondering what was going on with her tonight, he seemed to understand this wasn't the time or the place to ask.

A small crowd of student-age demonstrators carrying signs and chanting circled outside the hotel entrance, blocking traffic and generally causing a disruption. Jenny saw several uniformed police officers trying to corral the group off the street, but it looked as though they were trying to herd cats. Defiant cats.

Thad pulled into the portico, where a slightly harried parking valet hurried to open the door and take the keys. Someone snapped a photo using a bright flash as Thad helped Jenny out of the car. Local press covering the event, most likely. Thad would have been instantly recognized. She could already imagine the cutline: Prominent Attorney Thad Simonson and Guest.

Shouts broke out from the street and she turned curiously, as did Thad and everyone else waiting to enter the fund-raiser. Some of the protesters had turned violent in their resistance to being restrained. Fists flew as more uniformed officers converged on the scene. One particularly large demonstrator threw a hard punch, sending an officer flying backward to land with a grunt of pain on the street only a couple feet from where Jenny stood.

Instinctively she took a step forward, thinking she recognized something about the man in the uniform, her heart skipping a beat in dread. It started again with a jolt when he climbed angrily to his feet and she realized it wasn't Gavin. Of course it wasn't. He hadn't even returned to work yet, she thought with an exasperated shake of her head.

Thad followed her gaze, then gave her a searching look. "Someone you know?"

She shook her head. "No."

An ambitious public defender Jenny had met a couple times before, and disliked considerably, glared at the melee and motioned dramatically to her companions as they waited impatiently to be admitted to the high-security event. "That'll just get the other uniforms riled up," she said with a long-suffering sigh. "They'll be breaking out the riot gear. I certainly hope they don't resort to excessive force just because a few protestors get out of hand. We've all seen how cops can behave."

Jenny spun on one heel to face the woman, incensed on behalf of the officers who were already succeeding in calming the scene, though several angry youths were being led away in restraints. "Protecting us, you mean? Getting punched in the face so that we can go into our thousand-dollar-a-plate gala without being harassed by people who are obviously unhappy about something? Helping women and children in distress, protecting property, keeping criminals off the streets?"

She realized belatedly that her disdainful comments would not be appreciated by this conservative crowd of politicos who at least gave lip service to supporting men and women in uniform.

The other woman gave a quick, strained laugh and apologized insincerely. "I guess I didn't word that very well. I certainly wasn't casting a bad light on all officers, merely expressing concern that this protest doesn't get out of hand on either side. Oh, look, the line's finally moving. We should go inside."

A little embarrassed now by her own vehemence, Jenny looked apologetically at Thad as he rested a hand on her back to accompany her inside. "I'm sorry. I didn't mean to cause a scene."

He chuckled. "Far be it from me to criticize you for taking a stand on a subject that's important to you. You've heard me get wound up over a few issues myself, right? I can't consider going into politics without being aware that I'll be called on frequently to defend my beliefs."

He was such a nice guy, she thought wistfully. A great catch, as her grandmother had insisted so often. And yet…his hand on her back didn't make her pulse race or her hands tremble. She wasn't in love with him—not in the way her mother had described loving her dad, or the way Jenny had loved Gavin all those years ago. The way she still loved him now.

Both men had strong convictions and noble causes. But only one of them held a permanent place in her heart. Now if only she could find the courage to open that wary heart to him, despite the risks of loving without reservation.

Fortunately, they weren't required to stay long at the fund-raiser. Satisfied to have made an appearance, and connections, Thad made excuses early, blaming weariness from travel and early appointments the next day. He offered to take her someplace for a late dinner after they made their escape, but Jenny politely declined. They made the drive back to her place in near silence.

No one had ever accused Thad of being oblivious. He waited only until they were inside her apartment before asking quietly, "You've made your decision, haven't you? About my proposal, I mean."

She moistened her lips. "I have."

He nodded in resignation. "You're turning me down."

"I'm sorry, but I can't marry you, Thad. I think you're a very special man, and I'm extremely flattered that you asked me, but it wouldn't be fair for me to accept when I don't truly believe it's right for either of us."

He sighed lightly. "I still think we'd have been a great couple. But I accept your decision, of course. I'm sorry it didn't work out."

"So am I," she said candidly, a hard lump in her throat.

Thad squeezed the back of his neck, then dropped his arm and straightened his shoulders. "If you don't mind my asking—who is he?"

"Who is who?" she asked cautiously, studying him through her lashes.

Smiling crookedly, he shrugged. "I was told you were with another man at a bar last weekend. I thought perhaps it was just a friend, but something I've heard in your voice when we've talked since made me wonder if there was more to it. Now I suspect I was right."

She cleared her throat before answering candidly. "I *was* with someone Saturday night. It wasn't planned exactly. I wasn't sneaking around seeing anyone behind your back or anything like that. I fully intended to tell you everything when you returned." *Well, maybe not everything.* "You remember me telling you about the guy I dated in college?"

He looked as though a lightbulb went on in his head, perhaps as he recalled her little speech before the fund-raiser. "The one who became a police officer?"

She hadn't told him much more than that when they'd exchanged a few tales of past loves over dinner and drinks one night not so long ago. Maybe one too many drinks. "Yes."

"You're seeing him again?"

"We sort of ran into each other. It's a long story, and I'll spare you the details. But Gavin isn't the main reason I have to turn down your proposal, Thad. I don't know for certain if he and I will continue to see each other. It's just, well, I've realized that it wouldn't be fair of me to marry you when I'm not able to totally commit to you. I can't walk away from my business. Sink or swim in the long run, it means too much to me. And I couldn't do justice to you if I'm not free to travel and attend all these functions with you and everything else you need from a wife and a partner in your future. I'm sorry. I hope we can still be friends," she added, because such a speech was always supposed to conclude that way.

"I hope so, too." He leaned over to brush a kiss across her lips. "Be happy, Jenny. And if you change your mind...you know where to find me."

She wouldn't change her mind, she thought as she closed her door behind him. And he knew it. She doubted it would be long before he started seeing someone else. And while it made her a little sad to think that their relationship was over, she had no other regrets about her decision.

Apparently she was more like her mother than she'd ever realized. And despite what her grandmother or anyone else might think, maybe that wasn't such a bad thing, after all.

The drive up the hill to the cabin was much nicer in pretty weather. Emerald-green leaves rustled in a slight breeze against a brilliantly blue, cloudless sky on this Saturday afternoon. A few trees showed fresh gashes from having limbs broken off in the storm winds earlier in the month. The road was still bumpy, pocked with new holes left from the floodwaters. Much tamer now than it had been when she'd seen it last, the river ran cheerily alongside the rising road. The only storm raging now was the one inside Jenny's heart as she neared the cabin.

This was probably the most reckless thing she had ever done in her life. And it frightened her to her toes. But here she was.

She parked in front of the cabin. She didn't see anyone around, but she knew Gavin was here.

She climbed slowly out of the car, her new, bright green sneakers crunching against the gravel drive as she moved toward the front door. It was a warm day, and she'd dressed accordingly in a sleeveless top and cropped pants. A bag of similarly casual clothing sat in the backseat of her car. She was prepared to stay overnight, if things went well.

She was just about to knock when a hammering sound from around back caught her attention. Following the sound, she stepped off the porch and walked around the cabin. Gavin had his back to her as he hammered at something he was building with long wooden boards.

"At least I'm not waking you up this time," she said, speaking over the noise. "But you did look very appealing all rumpled and sleepy."

He froze, then turned slowly to face her, the hammer dangling at his side. He still looked sexy as all get-out in his loose jeans and damp tee, both covered in sawdust. "Jenny?"

It was taking everything she had to keep her posture relaxed, her tone casual, her smile easy. "What are you building?"

For a moment, he looked as though he couldn't remember. "A window box," he said after a pause. "My mom thought some flowers would look nice under the kitchen window."

"She's right. It would look nice."

He shook his head, impatiently putting an end to small talk. "Jenny, why are you here?"

"I don't like having important conversations over the phone," she replied with a shrug. "I tracked down Rob to ask him where I could find you and he told me you were here doing a little maintenance in preparation for your summer renters. I thought about waiting until you were back in Little Rock, but then I decided to invite myself to join you here. I can leave, if you'd rather be alone."

He dropped the hammer and dusted off his hands without looking away from her face. "I saw your picture in the paper a couple days ago. Avery made sure to show it to me."

She knew which picture he meant. The photographer had caught her smiling up at Thad as he'd helped her out of his expensive car. Stevie had told her it was the fakest smile in the entire history of fake smiles, but most people would probably not have realized that at first glance. Had Gavin?

"Wasn't that sweet of Avery?" she asked with an equally false smile now.

"Not particularly. You looked beautiful, by the way. I'm sure your boyfriend was very proud to have you there with him."

"Thad's not my boyfriend." She'd cried herself to sleep that night, not because she'd been brokenhearted over her breakup with Thad, but because she'd been so confused about what to do about her overwhelmingly intense feelings for Gavin. That wasn't something she would admit now. Probably ever. "He and I agreed to remain friends, but we aren't seeing each other anymore."

Gavin went very still. "Is that why you're here? To tell me you aren't going to marry him, after all? Took you a few days to get around to letting me know, didn't it?"

"I needed some time to think," she admitted. "I didn't want to rush into anything without making sure I knew what I was doing. I'd already hurt one person, though I expect he'll recover soon, and I infuriated my grandmother, who might take a little longer to get over it. So I wasn't going to come to you until I was sure I wasn't being too impulsive. Until I'd had a chance to overcome my fears and decide I could handle trying again with you, if you're still interested."

"I don't understand why it scares you so much. I mean, yeah, my job carries a risk, but so does…"

"So do firefighting and race-car driving and construction work and piloting," she cut in with a wry smile. "My mom reminded me lately that there are few guarantees in life. But I'm not going to lie, Gavin. I'm still scared."

"Of ...?"

"Of you. Of everything about you," she confessed. "Of loving you and losing you, either on the job or off. Of spending the rest of my life missing you and grieving for you, the way my mom has for my dad. The way Gran did when her husband died. I'm afraid of loving you so much I lose myself, the way I almost did in college. You warned me about giving up too much for Thad, but there was always a part of myself I held back from him. I could never hold anything back with you. And that's terrifying."

He shook his head as he took a step closer. "You honestly think I don't understand that? Seeing you again in my cabin scared the crap out of me, because the minute I did I knew I still wanted you. It took me so damned long to get over you the first time. You think I wanted to go through that again? I've tried to change to please other people before, to please *you* before, and it never worked. And yet I was half-afraid that if you asked me again, I actually might try one more time, just to be with you. Even knowing it would only lead to failure again."

Another step brought him even nearer. "And do you really think I don't worry about losing someone I love to an accident or an illness or any of the other tragedies that strike good people every day? Things I see every day on my job? Loving someone is accepting that risk, Jenny. It's learning how to push the fear aside and to enjoy every day together, just in case."

She swallowed a lump in her throat, but spoke as lightly as she could manage. She knew he wouldn't want her to get too maudlin. "That's very deep."

"Yeah, well, I'm a complicated guy."

Her lips twitched, though he wasn't smiling. "You are at that."

She reached out to him, needing desperately to touch him. Kiss him. "Gavin…"

He held her off, his face so stern that for a moment her heart stopped. Had he changed his mind? Had he decided she'd hurt him too badly the last time for him to ever trust her again? Had he concluded that it would be foolish to try again after so much time had passed?

His eyes held hers. "I'm not a daredevil, Jen. I don't take unnecessary risks on the job or for fun. I can't promise nothing bad will ever happen to me, but I can assure you I'll take every reasonable precaution. You have to decide right now if you can deal with that. If you can take me exactly as I am."

"I'll take you however I can get you," she answered quietly, beginning to breathe again. "That's what I came here to tell you. That I know now that we're right for each other, just as we are."

His eyes warmed as the faintest hint of a smile curved his firm lips. "We were never wrong for each other, Jen. We were just together at the wrong time. Before each of us knew who we really were and what we wanted. We know now. I'd never stop you from going after your dreams. I'll support you in whatever you choose to do, even if it's to enter politics yourself. Hell, you're as qualified as that pretty boy in the photo. If you want to open a whole chain of boutiques, I'll back you in that, too. All I ask is that you offer the same support for my career, even if it's not what you'd planned for your life."

"Sometimes plans change," she said, blinking back

a haze of mist from her eyes. "I'm trying to learn to be more flexible. And to appreciate surprises."

He surged forward, taking her in his arms and spinning her around. Clutching his shoulders, she laughed, not caring that he was grubby and a little sweaty from his work. She was definitely learning to appreciate surprises, she thought as his mouth closed over hers.

The cabin bedroom was dark, not from lack of electricity this time, but because they hadn't bothered turning on the lights as one hour blended into the next in the big bed. Sated and exhausted, they lay tangled together on even more tangled sheets, bare skin pressed to bare skin, heart beating against heart.

"Gavin?"

"Mmm?" The sound was a sleepy, satisfied murmur in the shadows.

"As much as I love this cabin, I'm still going to want to vacation somewhere with room service and a pool occasionally. Maybe even a spa that offers facials and massages."

He chuckled lazily. "I could appreciate that sometimes myself, but I wouldn't mind you taking Stevie and Tess for an occasional pampered weekend while the guys and I gather here for poker and beer. Or Scrabble and beer, if it's up to J.T.," he added drily.

She appreciated that he still saw them having interests of their own even as they built a life together. Tomorrow they would return to Little Rock, where he would reintroduce her to his mother and she would present him to her welcoming mother and her sullen grandmother. Gran would either accept Gavin eventually or she wouldn't. Jenny couldn't let her grandmother's wishes guide her anymore.

"Jen?"

"Mmm?"

He rose on one elbow, and she could see him just clearly enough to tell that his expression was very serious now. "We're all-in this time, right? No more getting scared and running away?"

"I wouldn't have come here today if I wasn't ready to fully commit to you," she answered evenly.

"I'm in, too. And to prove it..."

He turned to rummage in the nightstand drawer, from which he drew out a small box. "I dug this out after I left your place the other night. I'm not sure why exactly, but I've been carrying it ever since. Maybe in the hope that I'd finally have the chance to give it to you. I've wanted you to have it for more than ten years now."

Sitting against the pillows with the sheet tucked beneath her arms, she blinked a little when he turned on the lamp. "What is it?"

"It belonged to my dad's mother. I inherited it when I was just a teenager. I was going to give it to you for your twenty-first birthday, but, well..."

She bit her lip. They'd broken up two weeks before that birthday.

"Anyway, it's always been yours," he said quickly, putting those bad memories to rest. "I never wanted to give it to anyone else."

Her hands shook so hard that he had to help her open the box.

The vintage ring was lovely. A simple gold band was set with a diamond flanked by two sapphires. None of the stones was particularly large, but all three were perfect. "It's beautiful," she whispered.

Gavin closed his hand over hers. "All-in?"

She had to admit she was still a little scared. She suspected she would always worry when Gavin donned his badge and weapon and went out on the streets. Every report of an injured officer would terrify her. But she'd learn to deal with that. Maybe she'd make friends with J.T.'s wife and Avery's wife and the husbands and wives of some of Gavin's other coworkers. Maybe she'd pick up a few tips from them on how to deal with the fear. The man she loved was a cop, and he wasn't going to change until or unless he was ready for something new. Because she'd fallen in love with him—twice—just as he was, she realized she didn't even want him to change.

They'd been given a second chance. As he'd advised, she was going to appreciate every minute they had together. Starting now.

"All-in," she told him, her voice entirely steady this time.

His smile flashed in the shadows.

She set the box aside and turned to wrap herself around him, one hand sliding beneath the sheet as she pressed her mouth to his throat.

"What are you doing?" he asked, making no effort at all to resist.

She smiled up at him. "I'm enjoying the moment. Do you have a problem with that?"

She could tell by the way he hardened in her hand that he had no problems at all.

With a laugh, he flipped her onto her back and towered over her. "I could get used to this new risk-taking Jenny."

"Good," she murmured, drawing his mouth down to hers. "Because I plan to be around for a very long time."

His murmur of approval was muffled in a kiss that sealed the deal.

* * * * *

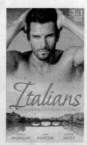